Y0-BQJ-944

GENTLY, HE BROKE OFF THEIR KISS AND STEPPED BACK.

Seguín stroked the sculptured curve of Diana's spine through her muslin gown. Her eyes flew open. She pulled away from him. Her cheeks were tinged pink, and she took several unsteady steps. Keeping her eyes averted, she sat down on the stone bench again. She traced an imaginary pattern on the flagstones of the patio with the toe of her slipper.

Without looking up she whispered, "I think you'd better leave."

"At least think about what I've said, will you?"

She nodded. He thought he detected the bright sparkle of moisture on her eyelashes. That he might have made her cry hammered at him. He couldn't be certain. Her head was lowered.

He waited as the minutes ticked by. He didn't know why. She had already told him to leave.

When he turned to go, her voice stopped him. "You were right that day at the *posada*, Seguín. I've never been kissed before." She brushed her fingers across her lips as if she couldn't believe it. "Why did you kiss me now?"

Silently, he cursed himself for the ugly things he had said to her that day. She sounded so wounded and vulnerable. She probably wouldn't believe what he was going to say.

"I kissed you because you look so lovely with the sunlight shining on your hair. Because I *wanted* to kiss you, Diana. It was as simple as that."

<u>BOOK YOUR PLACE ON OUR WEBSITE</u> AND MAKE THE <u>READING CONNECTION!</u>

We've created a customized website just for our very special readers, where you can get the inside scoop on everything that's going on with Zebra, Pinnacle and Kensington books.

When you come online, you'll have the exciting opportunity to:

- View covers of upcoming books

- Read sample chapters

- Learn about our future publishing schedule (listed by publication month *and author*)

- Find out when your favorite authors will be visiting a city near you

- Search for and order backlist books from our online catalog

- Check out author bios and background information

- Send e-mail to your favorite authors

- Meet the Kensington staff online

- Join us in weekly chats with authors, readers and other guests

- Get writing guidelines

- AND MUCH MORE!

Visit our website at
http://www.zebrabooks.com

LOVE ME ONLY

Hebby Roman

Zebra Books
Kensington Publishing Corp.
http://www.zebrabooks.com

ZEBRA BOOKS are published by

Kensington Publishing Corp.
850 Third Avenue
New York, NY 10022

Copyright © 1999 by Hebby Roman

All rights reserved. No part of this book may be reproduced in any form or by any means without the prior written consent of the Publisher, excepting brief quotes used in reviews.

If you purchased this book without a cover you should be aware that this book is stolen property. It was reported as "unsold and destroyed" to the Publisher and neither the Author nor the Publisher has received any payment for this "stripped book."

Zebra, the Z logo and Splendor Reg. U.S. Pat. & TM Off.

First Printing: May, 1999
10 9 8 7 6 5 4 3 2 1

Printed in the United States of America

For my three sons:

Jose Juan Roman
on starting his adult life

Juan Luis Roman
honor student and varsity
baseball player

and

Kevin Matthew Saller
honor student and
neophyte writer

your love and support compel me to always
write my very best story

Prologue

"One potato, two potatoes, three potatoes, four," Diana McFarland chanted, covering her friend's fists with her own.

"Five potatoes, six potatoes, seven potatoes, more," Sarah York replied, placing her fists on top of Diana's.

Their voices pitched higher, singsonging in unison, "Potatoes for breakfast, potatoes for dinner, potatoes for supper, more, more, more." Then followed a frenzy of fists offered and withheld. "My . . . mother . . . told . . . me . . . to . . . pick . . . this . . . one!"

Diana finished with one fist uncovered, and Sarah shouted, "You're it! I'll go hide."

The two girls rushed to opposite sides of the weed-strewn yard. Diana embraced a live oak tree and pressed her body against its rough bark. Trembling with excitement, she squeezed her eyes shut and started counting.

When she reached twenty, her mother's voice interrupted with, "Diana, come inside. Sarah, you'll need to go home."

Surprised by her mother's summons, she released the tree and took a few tentative steps toward the porch, her eyes still tightly closed. She didn't want to give up the game yet. It was several hours before dark. She and Sarah always played after school until dark.

She felt a light touch on her shoulder. Startled, her eyes flew open. Sarah stood beside her, her eyebrows raised in question. She must have been surprised by the unusual summons, too.

"Mother, why does Sarah have to go home?" Diana asked. "It's not near dark yet."

Elizabeth McFarland gazed at them and shook her head. Diana recognized the sadness in her mother's gray eyes, bone-weary sadness. She'd seen that look before. Suddenly, she was sad, too, and frightened.

"I guess we can tell you, Sarah. You'll find out soon enough. Your father tried to help, but it was no use." She shook her head again. Her thin frame appeared to sag. "The mine superintendent let Diana's father go. We need to pack and leave by morning."

Wailing filled the air. It took Diana several moments to realize the awful noise emanated from her own mouth. Sarah's thin arms enclosed her in a tight hug. She clung to her best friend like a drowning man to a spar of wood.

How many times had her father been "let go" from a job? Her teacher said she was a whiz at arithmetic, but she couldn't count the times. And this time was worse than all the others put together. This time, she would be forced to leave Sarah, her first and only best friend.

As she clung tightly to Sarah, a thousand wild thoughts played through her head. She would run away and take her best friend with her. They would be adopted by a band of gypsies, or join the circus. Sarah could do cartwheels by the score. Diana knew how to keep her balance on a bareback horse.

The sobs came from deep inside. Her mother's hands pulled her away from Sarah. Her best friend retreated a few steps, a look of bewildered dismay stamped on her face.

Elizabeth said, "Go home, Sarah. It'll be all right."

But Diana knew better. It would never be all right.

One

"Your father is dead."

The words reverberated through Diana's head, bouncing off the edges of her comprehension. Perhaps she had misunderstood the innkeeper, she thought, clutching at hope. After all, this was the first time she'd heard Spanish spoken.

"*¿Señor* McFarland *es muerte?*"

"*Sí, señorita.*" The innkeeper bobbed his head, his brown eyes filled with compassion. "*Lo siento.*"

Diana returned his nod, woodenly accepting his condolences. She couldn't believe it. She had to know more.

"How did he die?"

A flood of Spanish followed. She strained to understand. Piecing together the words she recognized, she felt the horrible truth emerge. Her father's room had been broken into, and he had been stabbed to death.

Her father had been murdered!

She should do something. Alert the authorities? Or had the innkeeper already done that? She didn't know. A sudden exhaustion washed over her; she didn't have the strength to question him further.

Elizabeth McFarland's voice penetrated her numb

mind, demanding, "Diana, what is it? What's the problem?"

Turning slowly, she faced her mother. How could she tell her? What words could she use to soften the blow? She wished she could feel something more, but right now all she felt was irritation—irritation because she had to translate. She had begged her mother to study Spanish before coming to México, but Elizabeth had refused, saying she was too old to learn.

Surprised at her thoughts, she wondered what was wrong with her. Her father had been murdered, and she was annoyed that her mother couldn't speak Spanish.

"Father is dead."

"No!" Her mother cried out.

Before Diana could react, her mother crumpled to the floor. Dropping to her knees, she bent over her mother and loosened her collar. The innkeeper rushed to their side, his face filled with distress. She implored him, "Water and smelling salts if you have them, please." He nodded and scurried off.

The innkeeper brought a basin of water, and she bathed her mother's temples. He thrust a small, clay jar at her. Uncorking the jar, she waved its pungent contents beneath her mother's nose. Her mother coughed and sneezed. Her eyes fluttered open, and Elizabeth levered herself into a sitting position.

Grasping her mother's arm, Diana offered support, but strong hands pushed her aside. Surprised, she stared into the eyes of a stranger. He ignored her, concentrating on helping her mother to her feet.

"Thank you, *señor,* ah, *gracias*—" She fumbled for the words.

"*De nada, señorita.* Don't exhaust yourself. I speak English."

Staring at him, she noticed his eyes were hooded and licorice-black. Instinctively, she reached for her mother and sheltered Elizabeth in her arms. Bowing her head, she patted her mother's shoulder, trying to impart a reassurance she didn't feel. They clung together, wordlessly.

The innkeeper cleared his throat and offered, "Perhaps your grief should be shared in private. *Señor* McFarland's room is sealed off, but I have the adjoining room ready."

Blindly, she followed the innkeeper, pulling her mother with her, placing one foot in front of the other. She felt as if she were moving through a dark cloud, every sense muffled and distant. Nothing seemed to matter. Her thoughts were slippery, springing up half-formed, only to slide away in confusion.

A hand touched her elbow, and her senses recoiled. She turned. It was the stranger again, thrusting his unwanted presence into her private world.

"A word, *señora y señorita*. I know this is a terrible time, as you've just learned—"

"Yes." Diana felt her lips moving.

"I knew Jamie McFarland, your father. He was a brilliant man. An *amigo* of mine." He nodded toward her mother, "*¿Señora* McFarland, *sí?* And you must be Diana."

She inclined her head.

"You see, I know who you are," he declared. "And you have my deepest sympathies. I'm shocked, too. I came today to speak with *Señor* McFarland. I did not know that . . ."

His perfect sentiments alarmed her. Who was this man? And how did he know her father? She felt the armor of her reserve slide into place. "Sir, we appreciate your condolences, but my father had many friends. Who are you?"

"Forgive me for not introducing myself. My name is Seguín Torres."

Recognizing the name, she relaxed a fraction. Her father had written them about Señor Torres. He was her father's business partner in México. It was the promise of untold riches, in partnership with this man, that had brought them here.

"*Señorita,* I wish to help"—his deep voice flowed over her—"knowing your tragic news, and remembering your father speaking with affection about his family. You are strangers to this land . . . and women. Surely, a friend could help."

Her mother slumped against her shoulder, moaning softly. Stiffening beneath her mother's weight and the burden of their grief, she replied coldly, "My mother must lie down. Your offer is kind, but I think we would like to go to our room."

"I understand. I will call again later."

"As you wish."

Stepping back, he bowed.

Climbing the stairs to her room, she couldn't stop thinking about Seguín Torres. Her father was dead, and all she could think of was Torres and his untimely appearance.

He had the look of a hawk about him—a dark fierceness, enhanced by his sable hair, worn long and clubbed in the back. His nose curved like a beak over the slash of his mouth. But it was his black, hooded eyes that haunted her, impenetrable in their wild beauty.

A shiver trickled down her spine. She shook herself. What was she thinking, mooning over a stranger when her father was dead?

After undressing Elizabeth and making her comfortable, she gave her mother a draught for her nerves and waited for sleep to come. Once Elizabeth was asleep, Diana moved quietly to the other side of the room. Removing her spectacles, she rubbed the bridge of her nose.

Exhaustion and grief sucked at her, making the simplest task an effort to perform. She fumbled for what seemed like hours with the buttons of her dress before she managed to undo them. Her corset was another struggle that took its toll, her hands shaking as if they were palsied.

Finally free of her dusty traveling clothes, she retrieved a nightgown from her battered carpetbag and slid it over her head. Her skin felt feverish, and half-formed thoughts nagged her like a sore toothache.

Climbing into the single bed across from her mother, she knew she should brush her hair, but she didn't have the strength. It hurt to think. Grief weighed on her heart like a stone.

She wanted to sleep . . . not to think or feel. As if in answer to her silent wish, the blackness of slumber engulfed her, a blackness that was both comforting and disturbing. The disturbing part was that it reminded her of Seguín Torres's eyes.

"Tell me everything," Seguín commanded, placing some coins in the innkeeper's outstretched hand.

"Sí, señor, as you wish," Señor Gutiérrez agreed, slipping the coins into his pocket. "Three nights ago, my wife awoke me. My wife, she is a light sleeper," he added as if in explanation. "She bade me listen, as there were loud noises coming from upstairs. When I heard the noises, I got out of bed and called to my eldest son, Jorge, to accompany me. The closer we got to Señor McFarland's room, the louder the noises became. My other boarders were in the hallway, distraught but afraid to intervene. I was afraid also, Señor Torres," he admitted with a small shrug. "But this is my posada. It was my duty."

"And?" he prompted, growing impatient.

"My hands were shaking, trying to get the key in the lock, when I heard a horrible scream. A moment later, we were inside. A man climbed out the window. Jorge rushed to the window, but the man jumped and ran away. I found Señor McFarland lying on the floor with a knife in his heart."

He rocked back on his heels. Jamie McFarland had been

stabbed to death because of him. He couldn't shake the burden of guilt. He was certain his stepfather was behind the murder.

"Did your son get a look at the man?"

"It was dark, and he moved fast. Jorge noticed he had a scar on his face."

A scar on his face, he mused. It wasn't much to go on. "Did you send for the authorities?"

"Sí, señor, immediately. And a doctor, but it was too late for the *Americaño."*

"What about the knife?"

"The authorities took it, *señor."*

"Of course." He patted Gutiérrez's shoulder, offering, "You did your best. No one can fault you." His show of sympathy was calculated to ease the innkeeper's mind, because the next question was crucial.

"About the room . . . you said you heard a struggle. How did the room look? Could the motive have been robbery? Was the room ransacked?"

Gutiérrez's eyebrows lifted quizzically, as if he were trying to understand the question. In that instant, Seguín knew he wasn't part of a plot. He was either innocent or a very good actor.

"The room was torn up, papers scattered and chairs overturned." He shook his head slowly. "If the man tried to rob *Señor* McFarland, he didn't succeed. I found *Señor* McFarland's watch on the bureau. A very handsome watch, too."

The murderer hadn't gotten what he came for. Jamie must have surprised him. Then their struggle alerted the innkeeper, and the murderer didn't have time to find the formula, Seguín surmised.

"Did you find anything else in the room?"

The innkeeper drew himself up, squaring his shoulders and demanding, "What do you take me for, *señor?* A common thief? I did not touch *Señor* McFarland's belongings.

After his body was removed, I sealed his room off, just as I found it. I knew his family would be arriving shortly. *Señor* McFarland was very excited when he received their message from Veracruz."

There would be an easy way to prove Gutiérrez's honesty. McFarland should have had a substantial sum with him. Unfortunately, he couldn't prove anything. The room wasn't his to search, not for the money or the formula. The room's contents belonged to his grieving family.

"What about the authorities? Did they search the room?"

"No, I wouldn't allow it. I explained that his family was coming." Gutiérrez shook his head again, observing, "It is sad, is it not? For this to happen before he could be reunited with them. I hope they can repay me for the burial," he added, gazing at Seguín with expectant eyes.

He ignored the ill-disguised hint. It *was* sad, horribly sad. Jamie had been devoted to his family, eager to tell him about them. From Jamie's descriptions, they had been easy to recognize.

Why hadn't he placed a guard on Jamie? The question tore at him. Because he believed his stepfather couldn't possibly know about the formula? But he had been complacent, thinking the secret was safe. He was responsible for his friend's death, and no amount of rationalization would take the blame away.

"*Gracias, Señor* Gutiérrez. You've been very helpful. *Por favor*, make certain the McFarlands have everything they wish. You will be handsomely paid for your efforts. Don't worry. I'll return tomorrow."

The innkeeper bowed low and murmured, "I will personally look after *Señor* McFarland's family. *Hasta la vista.*"

Seguín left the *posada*, vowing to himself he would do everything in his power to keep the McFarland women safe. He needed to place a guard at the *posada* tonight. If his stepfather had failed to obtain the formula, Seguín had no doubt he would try again.

Who could he trust? Someone in his inner circle must be working for his stepfather. The thought was chilling. Who would be willing to betray him? Or might have Jamie, innocent of the repercussions, let the secret slip to the wrong person? It was possible, but a long shot.

Now Jamie's family, the very people he felt honor-bound to protect, stood in the way of his plan. The formula belonged to them. He must keep them safe, whether he cared about them or not. He owed Jamie that much. But he wanted the formula for himself.

His thoughts turned to the women. *Señora* McFarland shouldn't prove to be an obstacle. Jamie had described his wife as a sweet woman without an ounce of business sense.

Diana, Jamie's only child, had replaced the son he never had, educated as a man. Her father had expected great things from her. Jamie had never mentioned Diana's appearance, just her intelligence. At first glance, he could understand why.

With her eyes hidden behind spectacles and her lips thinned in distress, she wasn't very appealing. She was tall for a woman, and thin as a stick. Only her hair had captured his interest.

She was blond, *una rubia*. In his society of dark-haired people, she stood out like a beacon. From the highest society matron in México to the lowest whore, they all used henna at some point in their lives, to bleach their hair. It was almost a cult of worship, the desire for golden hair.

But it was her intelligence that concerned him. He had admired her attempt at speaking his native tongue, although her accent was atrocious. And she had proven to be a natural leader, cool and collected while she took care of her distraught mother.

If he had to place a bet, he would wager she would prove to be a worthy adversary.

* * *

Diana stared sadly at the unmarked grave. Jorge, the innkeeper's son, had brought them here. Without his guidance, her father's grave would be just another pauper's anonymous resting place.

Sad as it was, it was somehow appropriate that her father had been laid to rest in a strange land far from home. He had been a wanderer, always searching for the pot of gold at the end of the rainbow. Irish and mystical to his core, Jamie McFarland had dragged his family across the southwestern United States in search of a dream.

Her father had been trained as a mining engineer, but his personality overshadowed his credentials. Arrogant in his brilliance, he lost numerous jobs in arguments with his supervisors.

When her father was booted from Virginia City, her mother had returned to Nashville to care for her ailing parents. She accompanied her mother to help. Her father headed south to a new country, México.

Jamie wrote them letters, glowing reports of México. Her mother was skeptical at first, thinking it was just another dream of her erstwhile husband. A partnership in a silver mine changed Elizabeth's mind.

She lifted her eyes. México was a glorious place. The sweep of the central basin was lovely, ringed by mountains. The altitude made the air wonderfully clear and crisp. In the background stood the twin volcanoes, Ixtaccihautl and Popocatépetl. Even in this tropical climate, their loftiness ensured they were capped by snow.

Sighing at the beauty of the landscape, she wished her father were with her to share it. Diana hadn't been blind to her father's flaws, but despite them she and he shared a special relationship. The spark in her mind that craved knowledge met an answering fire in her father. No expense or effort was spared for her education. When a school wasn't nearby, her father personally tutored her.

But he was gone forever. Life wouldn't be the same without him. She wished there was something she could do, some way to express her grief.

"I want to buy Father a marker." She gave voice to her feelings.

"What?" Her mother sniffed. "It's a waste of money. No one knows us here. No one will come to visit his grave."

"You're right, Mother, no one knows us here. He's buried in a strange land. We will probably leave him here . . . by himself. It's the least we can do."

Her mother sniffed again and blew noisily into her handkerchief. "I want to do my Christian duty by your father."

"Yes, Mother."

"All right, you have my permission. You may buy a marker, Diana. But nothing elaborate, you understand? Something simple."

"I understand."

When they returned to the hotel, Seguín Torres was waiting for them. He sprang to his feet as they entered and took her mother's hand while nodding politely to Diana. "*Señora* McFarland, could I please have a word with you? The innkeeper, *Señor* Gutiérrez, has offered us the *sala.*" He gestured toward a small room off the lobby.

Her mother appeared flustered by the request, and Diana didn't hesitate to intervene. "Mr. Torres, I cannot think what you need, but anything you have to say will be said to both of us. My mother's emotions are very fragile." She put her arm around her mother's shoulders.

"As you wish. *Señora, señorita,* if you would just step inside. I will open the shutters and let some light into the room. Please be seated."

She surveyed the inn's parlor, which was set aside for the use of its patrons. It was small and shabby. The room looked dusty and neglected. The furniture was monstrous and overstuffed and badly in need of a thorough cleaning. She could understand why Mr. Torres wanted to open a window. Even at midday, the shuttered room was dark as a tomb. Diana and her mother seated themselves on the musty, horsehair cushions of the only sofa.

Placing a chair in front of them, Seguín perched on its edge and leaned forward. "Yesterday, I told you I was a friend of *Señor* McFarland's."

Diana merely nodded, irritated that this stranger kept turning up to annoy them. Couldn't he leave them alone for a few days with their grief?

"I don't know if you're aware, but Jamie—you don't mind if I call him Jamie?"

"Certainly not, Mr. Torres," her mother replied. "After all, you say you were friends." Diana snorted at her mother's easy acceptance of this stranger's familiarity.

He must have registered her voluble skepticism because for the first time he looked directly at her. With his black gaze on her, she shivered. She tried to stare back at him, but as she did so her face grew warm. Angered by his self-assured posture, she rose to her feet.

"Mr. Torres, we're tired. We've just come from my father's grave. Could you please get to the point?"

Seguín rose also. He was a tall man. She was considered tall for a woman, but he towered over her. Forced to look up to see his face, she didn't like his intimidating attitude one bit. Toe-to-toe, they confronted one another, and she was determined not to back down.

Her mother touched her arm. "Please, Diana, sit down. Let's hear what Mr. Torres has to say. Then we can rest afterwards."

Frustrated, she threw herself onto the sofa. Her vehement movement caused a small cloud of dust. Her mother fumbled for her handkerchief and covered her nose. Diana felt idiotic, like an errant child who has upset a vase.

One glance at Seguín confirmed her feelings. A corner of his mouth quirked in wry amusement. She turned her head and stared out the window, determined not to let him unnerve her again.

His voice broke the silence, soft and cajoling, in stark counterpoint to her agitated words. "As I was trying to explain, Jamie and I were business partners. He had invented a new process for purifying silver ore. I won't bore you ladies with the details, but his formula will make silver processing more efficient and less expensive. He and I had reached an agreement—"

"You aren't boring us, Mr. Torres," Diana cut in. "But please don't patronize us, either. I know about your partnership with my father. And I'm familiar with the process. My father wrote us, explaining everything."

He regained his seat and stared at her as if she were trying his patience.

She squirmed under his gaze. Despite her vow to herself, seconds before, she was allowing him to upset her again. Who gave him the right? He was infuriating! Overbearing, arrogant, and . . .

"I wouldn't patronize *you*. Your father often spoke of your intelligence, Diana."

Involuntarily, she thrilled when he said her name. His accent made it sound lyrical. But *what* he'd said was distressing. Her father had talked about her to this stranger. Even more distressing, her father had discussed her intellect.

Self-consciously, she removed her spectacles and massaged the bridge of her nose. Realizing what she was doing, that she had been hoping he would notice her eyes, she replaced the glasses, chiding herself silently.

Not bothering to thank him for the unwanted compliment, she laced her hands in her lap and stared at a point above his shoulder. He had incredibly broad shoulders. She couldn't help but notice. A vision of sleek, bronzed muscles underneath his white shirt assaulted her. She shook herself. What was wrong with her? Had her father's death unsettled her mind?

Seguín turned to Elizabeth. "You've been very patient. I will come directly to the point. I believe Jamie's discovery to be worth a great deal of money." He cleared his throat. "Jamie was unable to find steady employment in Mexico. As his friend and business partner, I felt compelled to help. I advanced him money when he learned you would be joining him. It was a loan against the partnership."

"That was very kind of you, Mr. Torres." Her mother blotted the perspiration from her upper lip. "But if you want to discuss money, I'm afraid I haven't the head for it." She smiled at Diana and patted her arm. "You must explain to my daughter. Her father taught her about business."

Leaning back in the chair, he crossed his arms over his chest. His obsidian gaze swept her again, and she felt like an unsavory insect under his scrutiny.

"I hope we can deal together, Diana."

Beneath the straightforward statement, she detected the hint of a threat. Never one to back down from a challenge, she squared her shoulders, but kept silent, waiting for his next move.

"I'm willing to offer ten thousand *pesos,* which is the equivalent of ten thousand of your American dollars," he declared without further preamble. "Your husband borrowed one thousand dollars from me. That will leave you nine thousand dollars for the formula."

Elizabeth stiffened, but said nothing. Glancing at her mother, Diana realized she was overcome by the magnitude of his offer.

She felt uncharacteristically smug. She had always believed in her father's brilliance, even if she deplored his erratic behavior. Her mother had only focused on his flaws. It was gratifying to know her father had finally found his pot of gold. But Seguín's offer wasn't enough. Her father had been promised a partnership in the mine. Why was he reneging on his agreement and trying to buy them out?

Before she could formulate a reply, her mother gushed, "Mr. Torres, what an incredible offer! I'm flattered and overwhelmed by your—"

"Mr. Torres, what my mother was about to say is that your offer, on the face of it, seems generous," she interjected, taking control. "But the agreement you had with my father was a partnership. I believe he mentioned a ten percent interest in his letters."

Seguín's eyes glittered, filled with impatience and something else burning in their midnight depths. It was his turn to look uncomfortable.

Despite her mother's statement that Diana would speak for them, he directed his question to Elizabeth. "*Señora* McFarland, is this your wish, to ask for a partnership?"

Her mother shifted nervously and glanced at her. Diana recognized the genuine confusion in her gray eyes. She squeezed Elizabeth's hand.

"Mr. Torres, my daughter makes a good point. Why aren't you prepared to honor your agreement with my husband?"

He cleared his throat again and gazed out the window. It was obvious he didn't want to answer. Diana wondered if he would be so dishonorable as to try and swindle them out of what was rightfully theirs. It wouldn't be the first time her father had misjudged a man's character.

The silence grew. Diana counted the ticks of the grandfather clock.

Returning his gaze to them, he murmured, "With all due respect, *señora y señorita*, I thought you would want cash so you could return home."

"What if we don't? What if we want to make a new life

for ourselves in México? What if we want a partnership, not the money?" Diana countered.

Elizabeth gasped at her daughter's audacity. Elizabeth McFarland had been born and reared in the South. For a woman to engage in commerce was unthinkable, bordering on not respectable.

Diana possessed no such compunctions. Her father, concerned that she might not find a husband, had raised her to fend for herself. Silver mining wasn't what she would have chosen as a vocation—she had another plan in mind—but she hoped, as her father had, that a few years of silver profits would secure their financial future.

Seguín's obvious discomfort rose a few notches. He shifted in his chair and uncrossed his arms. Rising to his feet, he paced beneath the window.

"I apologize in advance, but I won't have women as partners. In México women are . . ." He stopped himself and shook his head, as if rethinking his argument. Turning to face them, he declared, "It's impossible. Silver mining is too dangerous for the fairer sex. I won't allow it."

Suddenly, the value of her father's formula, and the thought of financial security became secondary to Diana. Her father had raised her to question the prevailing prejudice against women. She refused to let this arrogant man denigrate her sex. Women were just as capable as men, and she was prepared to prove it.

"Was my father going to work in the mine, digging silver?" she inquired sweetly, barely able to keep the sarcasm from her voice.

"Of course not."

"Then we won't, either. I don't see the problem."

"Your father was prepared to make improvements to my mining operations. That was part of the agreement between us."

She rose to her feet. "I'm prepared to make improvements."

"I suppose you have a degree in engineering, too." He failed to keep the sarcasm from his voice.

"No, but my father taught me everything he knew. I'm prepared to honor my father's bargain. Why aren't you?"

Seguín's face was a mask of barely controlled fury. His voice vibrated with frustration. "You cannot work at the mines, *señorita*. It's dirty and dangerous work. I won't be responsible for your safety."

"I'm responsible for myself, Mr. Torres."

"Children, children," Elizabeth intervened, rising to stand between them. "This is getting us nowhere, only sowing ill feelings." Turning to Diana, she said, "I'm surprised by your position. As I said before, I don't understand business, and I want you to explain yourself to me." Turning her attention to Seguín, she apologized, "Please excuse our confusion. It's obvious we need to discuss this privately. I hope you understand, and are willing to extend your offer."

Bowing low, he agreed. "Of course, *Señora* McFarland. Please discuss my offer." Diana thought she detected a hint of triumph in his voice. He was certain her mother would persuade her.

Furious, she started to argue again, but her mother forestalled her, begging her to wait until they'd talked. Respecting her mother's wishes, she subsided.

"I'll give the innkeeper my address, and the name and address of my attorney as well," he offered. His gaze fell on Diana. She understood the implicit challenge. The mention of an attorney was another ploy to frighten her into giving way. But she could hire an attorney, too.

"Thank you for your patience." Elizabeth thrust out her hand, and he took it, bowing again.

"*Buenas tardes,* ladies." He closed the parlor door behind him.

Diana started to speak, but her mother stopped her

again, "Not now, Diana. Later, please. My head is swimming with fatigue. I need to lie down."

Clenching her fists, Diana felt as if her head were swimming, too, swimming with fury and frustration. Who gave
him the right to question her abilities? To fob them off
with money, hoping to rid himself of their "inferior" female presence? Her father, indirectly, had given his life
for the formula.

Even if she had to fight both her mother and Seguín
for what was rightfully theirs, she was prepared to do so.

Two

Diana settled her mother in their room, loosening her corset and shuttering the windows against the mid-afternoon sun. After kissing Elizabeth on the cheek, she sat on her own bed and started to unbutton her blouse. Half-way down the bodice, she stopped.

She wanted to get to the bottom of Seguín Torres' offer and assess its worthiness. She needed proof of her father's partnership, and the proof was in his room, among his papers. She dreaded entering the room, but there was no other way. Rising, she squared her shoulders and approached the connecting door.

The innkeeper had adhered to the letter of the law when her father was killed. He had sealed the room, pending arrival of the family. He had given her mother the key, and Elizabeth had entrusted Diana with keeping it. She hadn't expected to use it so soon. Her grief was too fresh.

Despite her determination, she wasn't fully prepared for the welter of emotions that assaulted her when she entered his room. Jamie had never been a tidy man, and his personal belongings were strewn about haphazardly. A familiar smell wafted to her. It was the scent of the bay rum he always wore.

She felt her stomach clench, and she clung to the door-knob for support. Seeing his things, smelling his cologne, it was as if he could return at any moment. The reality of his death overwhelmed her, as if a huge void had opened at her feet—a black chasm that threatened to suck her down, too.

Steeling her resolve, she wiped the moisture from her eyes and approached the desk in the corner. Her gaze was drawn to a thin piece of parchment, lying open in the middle of the desk. It was her last letter to him. She picked it up and turned it over. She didn't know what she was doing. Everything was an agonizing haze.

Her last letter to him. Heaven help her, could she bear this?

With an effort of will, she choked back the nauseating churn of anguish, but she couldn't stop the rush of tears. This morning, at her father's grave, she had been unable to cry.

Ignoring her streaming eyes, she put the letter aside and riffled through the untidy stack of papers on the desk. At the bottom of the stack, she found what she was searching for: the formula. Her father had written to her about the basic elements of the process, and she understood the chemical reactions.

Seating herself in a chair, she stared at the paper for a long time. Her father's discovery was brilliant. The process accomplished three important things: it cut the time necessary to pound the silver ore with salts and mercury, it halved the amount of expensive mercury to be used, and it produced a purer silver. His notes outlined the steps and intermediate experiments.

Wiping her eyes dry, she concentrated on committing the process to memory. She stored each chemical compound and step carefully in her mind. When she was certain she had it all memorized, she gathered the papers together. Finding a sulfur match in a tin box, she started a fire in the potbellied stove. Feeding each piece of paper into the fire, she watched as their edges curled black before the flames consumed them.

Satisfied that she had protected her father's process, she stood back and dusted her hands. Now she would search for papers showing her father's connection with Seguín Torres. If she intended to fight him, it would be necessary to offer proof of the partnership, preferably signed by both her father and Seguín. If she didn't find anything, she had the letters her father had written, but she doubted they would be sufficient without Seguín's written agreement.

Bending down, she retrieved a pair of pants from the floor. Reaching inside a pocket, she found a small, heavy bag. Hefting it in her hand, the contents of the bag clanked metallically. Curious, she undid the drawstring and dumped it on the bed. Gold and silver *pesos* gleamed at her. She had learned the local currency during their trip from Veracruz. There was approximately one thousand *pesos*.

Straightening, she realized Seguín hadn't lied about the loan to her father. This was the proof, wasn't it? She hadn't really thought Seguín was a liar, did she? Did she believe he was dishonorable? Or was he was just another arrogant male who belittled women and strove to keep them in their place?

She was practical enough to realize a woman working at a silver mine in México would be in danger. But she refused to let him scare her off because she was a woman. When they reached an agreement, there would be compromise on both sides, not just hers.

The shining coins, scattered among the rumpled bed-clothes, bothered her. Something wasn't right. With her limited understanding of Spanish, she had learned from *Señor* Gutiérrez that her father had been killed in a robbery attempt. Why had the murderer left behind such a sum of money?

Puzzled, she gathered the coins together and returned them to the pouch. Where would they be safe? If her father had been accosted in this room and stabbed to death, was anyone safe here? She shivered, thinking of it.

A knock on the adjoining door startled her. Already jumpy, she hastened to lift her skirts and secure the pouch in the folds of her petticoats.

Her mother, voice muffled by the door, called out, "Diana, are you in there?"

Surprised that Elizabeth had awakened so quickly, she replied, "Come in, Mother."

There was a pause. "I'd rather not. Please come out. I want to speak with you."

"I'll be there in a minute, Mother."

There was no answer. She heard retreating footsteps.

Returning to her task, she searched the pants thoroughly, finding nothing but a comb and handkerchief.

When the adjoining door opened abruptly, Diana watched as her mother's eyes widened in pain. Elizabeth's hand flew to her breast, and she clasped the doorknob tightly, just as Diana had done earlier. Understanding her mother's shock, she dropped the pants and rushed to her side. Elizabeth slumped against her.

"Come, Mother. Close the door. You're not ready for this."

Her mother gasped, "No, I'm not. It's overwhelming."

Diana helped her mother to a chair, and Elizabeth sat down. She asked, "Feeling better?"

Elizabeth gazed at her, taking in what she knew were her tear-stained cheeks and red-rimmed eyes. Shaking her head, her mother replied softly, "You're not ready either, despite your stubbornness."

"I know it's . . . hard. But Mother, it's important that I verify Mr. Torres's claims. I was trying to find—"

Raising her hand, she stopped her with, "Enough. It can wait until later. I've wonderful news." Her mother's voice held the first hint of hope since they had reached México City.

"Do you remember your father wrote us the Yorks were here? They've sent a message inviting us to luncheon tomorrow. Their invitation is an unexpected blessing. It makes me feel less alone. Mr. York will look after us."

Feeling the awful shroud of grief lifting for one brief instant at this welcome news, Diana hugged her mother. The Yorks were here. In the aftermath of her father's death, she had forgotten they were in México, too.

Herbert York manufactured and sold mining equipment, and he had made a fortune doing it. Acquainted with her father for years, he had suggested her father come to México. Mr. York was one of her father's staunchest supporters, believing, as she did, that Jamie was brilliant.

Sarah, their daughter, had been her playmate and best friend from childhood. She couldn't wait to see Sarah again.

And Mr. York could help them with Torres and the partnership. Not that she doubted her ability to deal with Seguín, but Mr. York was a shrewd and influential businessman.

Her mother interrupted her galloping thoughts with, "Come and lie down, Diana."

"But Mother, I haven't finished—"

"You can finish later," her mother interjected. "You should see the strain on your face. Please, for me, go lie down before supper."

"All right," she acquiesced. Just knowing she would see the Yorks tomorrow made her search for evidence less urgent.

The private carriage delivered Diana and her mother to the York's residence. In this crowded city, the size of the York's home was impressive. It rose for three stories, and covered a city block. The architecture was Spanish Colonial with a white stucco facade and red-tiled roof. The driveway was bricked, and a graceful porte-cochére extended from one side of the house.

They were greeted warmly by the two York women, who were waiting for them under the covered entrance. Diana had imagined herself rushing into Sarah's arms, but when she saw their home, she felt reticent. Sarah must have felt uncertain, too, because she also held back.

Mary York had aged gracefully. She was an elegant lady with silver-gray hair worn upswept to enhance her intelligent features. Her bright blue eyes were warm, and her smile genuine. Sarah was a younger, brown-haired version of her mother.

Diana was awed by her friend's beauty. Sarah possessed perfect features and a flawless complexion. She was dressed in the latest fashion. Despite their correspondence and Diana knowing Sarah had grown and matured, she wasn't ready for the beautiful young lady standing before her.

It was Sarah who made the first overture, moving to her side and lacing her arms around Diana's waist. Forgetting her reticence, she returned the gesture, hugging Sarah tightly. Giddy with excitement at being reunited with her friend, she looked forward to spending time with Sarah. In spite of the years and miles that separated them, they had maintained a certain closeness, opening their hearts to each other in long, rambling letters.

With Mary leading the way, they walked through a massive, tiled foyer flanked by two curving staircases. Sailing along, Mary chattered nonstop, making a valiant effort to bridge the years separating the two families. She led them onto a large patio, centered by a tinkling fountain. The patio was lush with tropical trees and blooming flowers.

The acidic tang of orange and lemon trees, intermingled with the sweeter smells of jasmine and gardenias, filled Diana's senses. She spied the bright green feathers of a hummingbird as it darted among the fragrant blooms, so quick that her eye could scarcely follow its path.

A wicker table and chairs were artfully arranged among stands of banana trees with baskets of potted ferns suspended from the limbs of a blooming mimosa tree. A royal blue parrot stood tethered to a perch.

Enchanted by her surroundings, her gaze wandered, snagging on the antics of the parrot. It was sidestepping back and forth along the perch, stopping occasionally to turn its head sideways and stare at them with an unblinking eye.

There was a loud squawk, and the parrot screeched, "Pretty lady, pretty lady."

Diana blushed. She could have sworn the bird had looked directly at her, but then she realized Sarah was standing there, too, watching the bird.

"That's Sam," Sarah explained. "He's a pest, but we love him." She laughed.

The parrot seemed to know he was the center of attraction. He puffed out his chest and preened his feathers with his beak.

Sarah laughed again. "You see what an old reprobate he is. Shall we be seated, Mother?"

"Please. We could stand here and watch Sam, and I'm certain he'd love the attention, but I'm famished," Mary declared.

The meal that followed was both delicious and exotic. They began with a delicate squash-flower soup, followed by chicken breasts covered in a rich *mole verde* sauce. Spicy rice and beans with corn tortillas accompanied the meal. They finished with a creamy *flan* and strong coffee.

After the meal was over, the animated chatter died away while everyone sipped their coffee. Mary seized the moment and reached across the table to take Elizabeth's hands in her own, murmuring, "I can't believe Jamie is . . . gone. He was so looking forward to your arrival." She shook her head. "I don't understand how it could have happened. It's a respectable *posada*. Robbers don't usually break into hotels."

Diana had been wondering the same thing. Unless someone had known her father had a large sum of money. But how? Who would her father have confided in? And the money hadn't been taken; it was hidden beneath her skirts.

"I can't believe it, either," Elizabeth responded. She fiddled with her coffee cup. There was an awkward silence before she continued. "I was accustomed to being away from Jamie for long periods of time. It feels as if he could return tomorrow." Her voice caught on a sob, and Mary put her arms around Elizabeth.

With her own eyes stinging, Diana winced as the anguish knifed through her for the hundredth time. Taking a deep breath, she pushed the pain away and turned her attention to Sarah, forcing herself to ask, "What do you think of México?"

Sarah's blue eyes were filled with compassion, but she managed to answer lightly, "It's not France, but it's an interesting country." She laughed again. This time, her laughter sounded brittle, and Diana realized her friend wanted to comfort her but didn't know how.

"Everyone thought Maximilian would stabilize México, but I don't think he has the strength of character to rule. He listens to his advisors and Carlotta, his wife, too much.

"Now there's a strong character—Carlotta. At least she seems decisive, whereas Maximilian blows hot and cold. Have you heard about his latest *faux pas*? He has decreed that any Juáristas who resist his rule are to be declared outlaws. If caught, they're to be executed within twenty-four hours without appeal."

Diana caught her breath at the thought of such vicious reprisals.

"And it's rumored that the last part, about the executions, wasn't really his idea, but—"

"Sarah, please, they'll have plenty of opportunity to become acquainted with the politics here," Mary interrupted smoothly. "They've just arrived, and under the circumstances, their plans must be disrupted." Shifting her attention to Elizabeth, she inquired, "Have you thought what you will do next?"

"No. That is . . . you're right. There's been no time to consider. We do have some business to conclude but then . . . ?" Elizabeth finished lamely.

Pausing with her coffee cup raised, Diana knew this was the opening she had been waiting for. Their "unfinished business" was uppermost in her mind.

Before she could speak, Mary entreated her mother, "Selfishly, we'd like for you to stay, at least for a while. We've missed you so much, and it would be wonderful to catch up on old times. We seldom have the treat of other Americans here, although there are rumors that Maximilian is welcoming ex-Confederates. He's giving them land to settle."

Sarah shot her mother a sharp look.

Mary smiled at her daughter and admitted, "You're right, love. I stopped your discussion, and now I'm prattling about politics." Emitting a small sigh, she explained, "In this country, you'll learn politics are woven into the fabric of daily living." She dabbed at her mouth with a linen napkin. "Back to your plans. I insist you stay with us. We'd love to have you, and we have plenty of room."

Elizabeth brightened at the suggestion. "That's most gracious of you, but we couldn't impose—"

"Nonsense, what are old friends for? I won't take no for an answer." She inclined her head toward Diana and Sarah. "Just look at their eyes, shining with excitement."

Her mother glanced at them and smiled. "You've convinced me, Mary." She took Mrs. York's hands in her own and squeezed them. "I can't thank you enough. I do want to leave that awful hotel. It's too painful with Jamie's room there, and I don't feel safe, either."

Mary patted her hand. "Don't worry another minute. I'll send my *mayordomo* tomorrow for your things. Can you be ready?"

"Of course."

"I can't wait to show you México City. There's a wealth of entertainments here. The theater, opera, even balls at Maximilian's palace," Mary offered.

"It's very kind of you, but I don't think it would be proper. After all, we're in mourning," Elizabeth demurred.

"At least let Diana go. She's young, and will want amusement. Carlotta is renown for her lavish balls. When she first came to México, she gave one every week. Now she doesn't give them quite so often." Hesitating, she murmured, "But you must do what your conscience dictates, Elizabeth. I understand."

"Diana, do you want to go to a royal ball?" her mother asked.

Shrugging, she replied, "I'll have plenty of amusement, visiting with my dear friend." Her gaze sought Sarah's.

Sarah squeezed her hand, saying, "Let me convince her."

"I'll leave it in your capable hands," Mary replied. "And I want you to reconsider, too, Elizabeth. It will do you good to get out. Carlotta's balls are quite entertaining, watching the French look down their noses at the Mexican aristocracy."

Diana was tired of hearing about the balls and entertainments in México City. She had more important matters to discuss. "Mrs. York, my mother mentioned we had unfinished business," she ventured. "I wonder if Mr. York could help us?"

"Of course. What's this about?"

"It involves the partnership my father had with a Mr. Torres."

"Yes, Herbert spoke of it to me. I'm certain he can help you."

"Thank you. You don't know what a burden you've lifted from me."

Sarah turned to her with a question in her eyes, obviously curious to know more. Diana silently mouthed "later" to her friend.

"Good. Then, it's settled. You'll move in tomorrow," Mary declared.

The rain was a stroke of fortune. It had driven the guard inside. Ignacio had waited patiently, knowing his time would come. His cousin, a chambermaid at the *posada*, had left the window open for him. It was an easy climb to the second story room, and this time there would be no one to interrupt him.

Murdering a foreigner, who was in league with the devil that had killed his sister, hadn't bothered him. He would murder many times over to avenge her death. *Poor Esmeralda*, he thought, missing her on this rainy night.

He knew what he was looking for. Don Carlos had instructed him: papers, any papers, with symbols and writing covering them. He felt confident he would find what he sought.

Moving in the shadows, he kept to the right of the open gutter running down the street. Directing his gaze at the window, he shrugged the rope from his shoulder, uncoiling it and forming a loop. His gaze scanned the wet stucco wall, searching for the rooftop cornice he had used before.

He looked right and then left, down the street. The guard had abandoned his post, and everything was quiet. The houses had their windows shuttered, and no one moved along the street.

Ignacio tossed the loop at the cornice. It was a small target, two stories high. It took him several tries before he managed to settle the rope over its top. Pulling the rope taut, he tugged hard on it. The loop slipped, and then caught. He tested his weight against it, and was gratified to find the rope supported him.

A door closed with a reverberating thud in the shadowed street.

Abandoning the rope, he slipped around the corner of the building. His heart pounded. Had the guard come back?

Listening carefully, he realized the steps were receding, echoing in the opposite direction. When everything was quiet again, he moved from his hiding place and grabbed the rope. The night was waning. He must make haste.

Before he ascended, he stroked the small onyx figure at his throat. His great-grandmother, who had been a high priestess in the old religion, had given it to him and promised it would bring luck.

Swinging himself up, he groped for toeholds in the crumbling stucco of the building. Hand over hand, he pulled himself up the rope until he reached the terra-cotta ledge. When he tugged at the window, it opened easily.

Crawling inside, he carefully sought the floor with his feet. The room was black as a tomb. He stood very still for several moments, allowing his eyes to adjust to the gloom. After a time, he was able to make out faint shapes in the darkness.

He hesitated, listening for human sounds or movement. The room was silent. Reaching inside his pocket, he fetched a rough-shaped rock about the size of his fist. It was wrapped in a scrap of cloth, another legacy from his great-grandmother. He had placed the rock in the sun for two days, and now it gave forth a soft glow, like a shuttered lantern. He used it as a torch, cautiously moving it over surfaces while he advanced through the room.

The first shape that caught his attention was a desk. It would be the perfect place for a paper with symbols. After a hasty search, he was disappointed to find it was empty, except for some gnawed pencils and pieces of blank paper.

His shoulders slumped. He had been certain he would find the secret there. Maybe the foreigner had been clever. Maybe he had hidden his secret under the mattress. A surge of excitement swept through him.

Moving swiftly, his former caution abandoned, he advanced toward the bed. His foot struck something hard and metallic. The object skittered across the floor, coming to rest with a sharp, clanging noise. Bending over, he searched for it in the darkness, infuriated with his carelessness. A brass cuspidor lay overturned on the floor.

A shaft of bright light blinded his eyes.

Diana had sat bolt upright in her bed when she heard the noise from next door. She had been lying awake, unable to sleep. Lighting her bedside lamp, she had grabbed it and rushed to the adjoining door. The key was still in the lock. She opened it without considering the danger.

Her light washed over a hunched figure. The figure straightened, and like a butterfly pinned to a cork board, he was trapped in the lamp's beam for a frozen instant. His face was menacing, dark, and swarthy. His eyes gleamed, and there was a long scar running down his right cheek.

Frightened, but unwilling to show it, she shouted, "You! What are you doing?"

The intruder's eyes glittered. He didn't answer. Instead, he drew a knife from his belt and advanced slowly, menacingly, toward her.

Reacting on instinct, she screamed at the top of her lungs and snatched the water pitcher from the bureau.

She flung the heavy, clay ewer at the stranger's head with all her strength.

The man ducked and cursed under his breath.

The clay pitcher fell with a heavy thud against the stucco wall.

It was her turn to be angry. She had missed, and he still wielded a wicked looking knife. Panic replaced anger as she frantically searched for another weapon to use. The lamp? She might burn up in the ensuing fire, but it was her only chance.

She pulled her arm back, and then she heard the sounds. If throwing the pitcher had proven ineffectual, her screaming must have had the desired effect. There were doors slamming and footsteps in the hallway.

He stopped advancing and listened with his head cocked to one side. Obviously not liking what he heard, he whirled around and sprinted toward the window. Before she could react, he had one leg outside the open window, and then he disappeared over the windowsill. She heard him climbing down the outside wall.

Rushing to the window, she watched as he sprinted away. With the danger past, she slumped against the window frame, gazing into the frightening night, trying to regain control of her emotions.

Her mother's voice, filled with alarm, called from the adjoining room, "What's wrong, Diana? Are you all right?"

Elizabeth opened the door and stood on the threshold, her sleepy face creased with concern. She carried another kerosene lamp. The room was suddenly drenched in light.

"I caught a man in Father's room," Diana gasped. Spying the overturned cuspidor, she lifted it. "He upset this and I heard him. I rushed into the room, and he pulled out a knife." She pointed to the corner. "I threw the pitcher at him, but he—" Allowing the cuspidor to drop from her hands, she covered her face. The shock was wearing off, and she realized how vulnerable she had been.

Her mother put the lamp on the bureau and placed her hand on Diana's trembling shoulder. Elizabeth's voice was gentle when she asked, "And then what, Diana?"

Diana lifted her face. "My screams awakened the hotel, and he must have heard people moving around . . . like I did . . ."

There was a pounding on the door, and *Señor* Gutiérrez insisted, "Open up. Is something wrong? We've heard shouts."

"What does he want, Diana? I don't understand Spanish," her mother asked.

"He wants to know what's wrong, and for us to let him in."

Her mother gazed pointedly at their nightgowns. "I don't know what to do, Diana. We're not dressed for visitors."

Smiling wanly at her mother's Southern sense of propriety, she replied, "Under the circumstances, I think we should let him in."

Hesitating for an instant before she agreed, her mother said, "All right. Let me get our wrappers." She disappeared into their room.

"Just a minute, *Señor* Gutiérrez." Diana moved to the hallway door. "We're not properly dressed."

After they'd donned their wrappers, Diana unlocked the door and let the innkeeper and his eldest son, Jorge, into the room.

In halting Spanish, she explained the incident and asked the questions that had been bothering her about her father's murder. She wasn't completely surprised to learn that her description of tonight's intruder was the same as Jorge's. They had both noticed the jagged scar on the man's face.

The man she had confronted had killed her father. She was certain of it. Suddenly, her legs turned to mush and gave way beneath her. She sank onto the edge of the bed.

Señor Gutiérrez sent his son to fetch the authorities. Two men in khaki uniforms ornamented with braid and medals arrived quickly. They took a description of the intruder, but offered little hope of catching him. The leader of the two agreed with her that it was probably the same man who had broken in both times. Their solution was for the McFarlands to move from the *posada* as soon as possible.

She explained they were moving in the morning. They appeared satisfied with her answer, and left with a promise to contact the McFarlands if they found the intruder. *Señor* Gutiérrez and his son bid them goodnight, as well.

Through it all, her mother sat huddled in a chair, her face a study in bewilderment and anguish. Elizabeth hadn't understood a word of what had been said.

After the others were gone, Diana moved to the corner of the bed and faced her mother. Taking Elizabeth's hands in her own, she explained what had transpired.

"Why did he come back?" her mother asked, fear making her voice tremble.

"Because he didn't get what he wanted the first time."

"You mean—"

Diana nodded. "He must have been after the formula. It's the only thing that makes sense. Both times, he hasn't taken any valuables, even ones lying in plain sight." She paused and added, "I meant to tell you. I found the money from the loan Mr. Torres mentioned. I've hidden it in my things. At least, we won't go to the Yorks penniless."

"That's good. And that means Mr. Torres wasn't lying."

Her mother's statement surprised Diana. She hadn't thought her mother possessed doubts about Seguín. She was beginning to have other doubts about him, as well. Her father had written that the formula was a secret. Who else would have known to break in? Could Seguín be behind the nocturnal visits? Did he want to get the formula for himself without paying for it? Could he have had her father murdered?

"Diana," Elizabeth interrupted her troubled thoughts, "what are you going to do about Mr. Torres's offer?"

"I need to do more research. And I want to talk to Mr. York as well as an attorney, too."

"You're not really planning to work at the mines, are you?" Her mother shook her head. "I don't think that would be—"

"Of course not, Mother," she cut her off. "But I don't want Mr. Torres to swindle us, either. It's not fair. Not after Father's hard work, and what happened."

It was on the tip of her tongue to tell Elizabeth her suspicions, but something held her back. Tomorrow they would move to the Yorks, where they would be safe, but she would need to deal with Torres. She knew how her mother worried. It was better not to upset her.

"I hope you know what you're doing, Diana. I thought his offer was most generous."

"Please, Mother, trust me."

"Only if you promise not to be so impetuous. Tonight, you put yourself in terrible danger, rushing into this room. You must be more careful, dear. The authorities will catch the man and bring him to justice."

"Yes, Mother. I'll try to be careful." She wished she shared her mother's naive trust in the efficiency of the authorities, but after talking with them she didn't feel very hopeful.

"I assume the man didn't get the formula. That it's safe?"

"No, he didn't find it. I failed to mention it to you before, but I . . . destroyed all of Father's papers. I memorized the formula. It's only in my head. I did it for safety's sake."

"It seems there are several things you failed to mention to me, Diana." Her mother's voice held a note of hurt.

"Only because I didn't want to worry you."

"I appreciate your concern, but in the future try not to keep me completely in the dark."

"Yes, Mother."

"One thing more. I know you have an excellent memory, but please write down the formula. You can give it to Mr. York for safekeeping."

"All right, Mother," she dutifully replied. A tiny frisson of fear chased its way down her spine. Did her mother think something might happen to her?

Elizabeth leaned forward and patted her hand. "Quit thinking such black thoughts, dear—although, after what's happened during the past few days, I can't blame you." She sighed. "You've been very brave, Diana, all things considered. Don't add this extra burden to yourself. Write it down."

Rising to her feet, she declared, "I'm glad that's settled. I'm going to bed, and you should, too. We need to rise early and pack."

Diana followed her mother to bed, but after listening to Elizabeth's gentle snoring for an hour, she realized she couldn't sleep. Her nerves were still jangled from the encounter with her father's murderer, as well as her suspicions about Torres. She was wide awake.

Wanting to finish what she had started the day before, she rose from her bed and crept quietly to the adjoining door. Letting herself into the room, she lit the kerosene lamp. Someone had to pack her father's things, anyway, and she didn't think her mother was up to it.

Discovering some empty boxes beneath the bed, she sorted through her father's belongings. In his wallet, she found a miniature of her and Elizabeth and a folded piece of paper. The paper proved to be a note payable to Seguín Torres for one thousand *pesos*, signed by both her father and Torres. She didn't find a partnership agreement.

Could her father have been so trusting as to only have a verbal agreement with Torres? It would make her position that much more difficult. The lack of anything in writing would also make it easier to steal the formula. It was revealing that Seguín had committed the loan to paper, but there wasn't a scrap of evidence about the partnership.

Possession was nine-tenths of the law, at least in the States. She wasn't certain about Mexican law, but if her suspicions about Seguín were correct, she would give the formula away before she sold it to him.

When the boxes were filled, she moved them into her room. Glancing around the empty room, she sighed. Another piece of her father gone.

Three

Diana exited the hired hack and paid the driver. With her packing finished before daybreak, she had rushed out to select a marker for her father's grave. It was still early, and she hoped the Yorks' *mayordomo* hadn't arrived yet. Entering the hotel, she hurried toward the stairs.

A hand grasped her elbow. Startled, she spun around and came face to face with Seguín. When she tried to wrench away from him, he tightened his hold on her. Glancing around, she was dismayed to find the lobby empty.

In her most imperious voice, she grated out, "Let go of me, or I'll call for help."

Before she could carry out her threat he retorted, "Really, *señorita*, there's no need. You can't avoid me forever. You'll have to deal with me eventually." He dangled a piece of paper before her eyes. "You can't put me off. You owe me money."

Diana knew what he said was true. Stiffly, she nodded. Acting on her reluctant acquiescence, he propelled her into the dark *sala* and closed the door behind them.

"Now to business." He thrust the piece of paper at her. "I trust you found a duplicate note among your father's belongings."

She scanned the paper he held. It was an exact copy of the note she had in her reticule. She nodded again and drew away from his touch. This time he let her go.

"I've never known you to be so silent," he observed.

His closeness was disconcerting, but at least he wasn't touching her. She took a deep breath. Her suspicions from last night returned full force. It had to be he. There wasn't any other explanation. She wondered if she could surprise him into admitting his guilt.

"I don't know what to say. I can't believe you have the effrontery to face me. Not after last night."

He raised his eyebrows in question. "Last night? What happened last night?"

"Don't play games with me, Mr. Torres. I know you sent the man."

Seguín's forehead creased, and she could read the bewilderment in his eyes. When he wanted her to know his feelings, his eyes could be very expressive. The man was a consummate actor, she decided.

He lifted his hands and held them out, palms up. "I don't know what you're talking about. How can I defend my innocence if I don't know what crime I've committed?"

She turned away from him. It was hopeless. He wasn't going to admit the truth to her. It would be tantamount to confessing he had her father killed. Maybe that hadn't been the way he planned it. Maybe he had merely wanted to steal the formula, and his "henchman" had been too quick with a knife, like last night.

No, that couldn't be right. Why was she giving him the benefit of the doubt? Only with her father out of the way would he own the formula exclusively.

"Forget it. Let's discuss business." She faced him. "I found the note but nothing else concerning the partnership, except what my father wrote us. As far as I'm concerned, the formula is ours to do with as we please. We don't have to sell it to you or even accept a partnership." She took a deep breath. It was a long shot, but she had to try. "That is, unless you have a contract or some other document signed by you and my father, stating that—"

"I don't."

How convenient, she thought, *nothing in writing to link him with my father, except the debt.*

"Isn't that strange? I thought you and my father had an agreement."

"We did, but we hadn't finalized the terms. That first day when I met you and your mother, I had returned from the mines to discuss it with Jamie. Unfortunately, I learned—"

"That my father was dead, leaving two 'helpless' women as his heirs. You thought you could take advantage of us, didn't you?"

His head was thrown back, and his obsidian eyes gleamed. She thought she saw the corners of his mouth quirk. He had one finger hooked in his belt, and his hips were thrust forward. His stance suggested a cocksure arrogance, while at the same time it set her heart pounding. She hated what he did to her, how her body responded to his. Even now, she was having trouble pulling her gaze away from his loins.

"No, I don't want to take advantage of you, Diana."

"Then why do you press me so, waving my father's debt in front of my nose—"

He closed his eyes for one brief moment. For the first time since she had met him, he appeared unsure of himself, almost embarrassed.

"The formula means a great deal to me. More than mere money. I can't explain why it means so much. You'll have to take my word." He paused and continued in a softer tone. "You're right, I shouldn't have threatened you with the note, but I was afraid you would take the stand that you have. That you wouldn't sell to me for any amount of money. I can't let that happen."

If she didn't know him better, she would have believed he was begging. But that was ridiculous. He was an arrogant and ruthless man, and probably the murderer of her father.

Angry at herself for almost feeling sorry for him, she declared, "And you'd be right. After what you did last night, I wouldn't sell the process to you if you were the last person on earth!"

Seguín's mouth thinned, and he raised one hand. For a brief moment, she thought he would strike her, but instead, he pulled his fingers through his hair. "Damnit, Diana. I don't know what you mean. I wish you would tell me what I'm accused of."

"It wouldn't do any good. You would never admit it."

His jaw tightened. "It's not about the partnership, is it?"

"No."

"This isn't a ploy to wring more money from me, is it?"

"No. I might have considered that at first, but not now."

"And the note?"

"The note isn't dated, Mr. Torres. There is no term to it. I will repay you when I dispose of the process elsewhere."

"The hell you say!"

She lifted her chin. "And how will you stop me, Mr. Torres? I have no intention of cheating you. You'll just need to be patient."

"I don't intend to wait upon 'your good graces', *Señorita* McFarland. I have rights, too. I'll consult my attorney and see what can be done to collect my note."

"You do that."

Even though her words were brave, she wished she had consulted with Mr. York about her rights. As soon as they were settled at the Yorks she would talk to him, tell him the whole sordid story and get his assistance. In the meantime, she refused to give Seguín an inch. Nervous over the gamble she was taking, she licked her lips and swallowed. Her throat felt like a desert.

His fathomless ebony eyes followed her movement.

With a sensuous slowness, his tongue slid out, and he wet his lips, too. His gesture was laden with intimate promise. "I bet you've never been kissed by a man, Diana, much less courted by one. I don't know what Jamie was thinking, raising you to wear the pants in the family."

Rage swallowed her. She couldn't believe her ears, that he would stoop to personal insults to intimidate her. Her hands clenched into fists. She placed her balled fists on her hips. It took all of her self-restraint not to hit him.

She couldn't bear his arrogance a moment longer. Trembling with fury, she advanced on him. Her action must have startled him, because he backed up a step.

"You presume to tell me how I should be! To pass judgment on me! Well, take a look at yourself, mister. Only a sneaking, two-faced coward would have done what you did, sending someone to my father's room to steal the formula. Climbing through the window in the middle of the night to take the only legacy he left us!" Her voice crept higher. She recognized the hysterical note in it, but she didn't care. "The man you sent pulled a knife on me, and you have the gall to face me today as if nothing has happened. You're vile, you're—"

"Wait a minute." He held up his hand as if to ward off the blows of her words. "Let me understand what you're saying. Someone got into your father's room last night, and you saw him?"

Her breathing was ragged, and her stomach felt as if it'd been pounded with a meat cleaver, but she felt imminently better, having gotten it off her chest, having put him in his place. He wouldn't hear any more details from her, though. She wouldn't give her suspicions away.

"I didn't see him." She cringed inwardly as she told the lie. She didn't like to lie, even when it was necessary. "It was dark."

"Did he get the formula?"

"You should know the answer to that, Mr. Torres. You're here today because your hired thug returned to you empty-handed."

"I did *not* send the man." He grated the words out one by one, obviously wanting to emphasize his innocence. "Someone else must have sent him."

"Who, Mr. Torres?"

Her question stopped him. He appeared to be considering it carefully. Shaking his head, he admitted, "I can't tell you, Diana." Taking a step forward, he grasped her shoulders and spoke forcefully, "What you've told me places you in the gravest of danger."

Shrugging his hands off, she retreated a step. "Don't touch me. And please, Mr. Torres, spare me your show of concern. I want to know why you can't tell me."

He let his hands fall to his sides and avoided her question. "How can you be so certain the intruder was after the formula? He could have been just an ordinary thief."

Diana stared at him. He returned her gaze without flinching. "Good try. Do you believe that?"

"No."

"At least you're honest enough to admit it."

Pausing, she counted to ten silently, willing her breathing to return to normal. Once her emotions were under control, she stated flatly, "I believe we've arrived at an impasse. You're not going to convince me that you had nothing to do with my late night visitor. And I'm not going to convince you to leave us alone. You want something I have, and I owe you a debt."

She moved to the door and placed her hand on the doorknob. "I propose we avoid these encounters in the future and rely upon our attorneys to come to a resolution. *¿Entiende, Señor* Torres?" Without waiting for his answer, she opened the door and slipped into the lobby.

The cathedral bells were calling the faithful to mass when Seguín crossed the Zócalo, the central plaza of México City. He had just concluded two visits, one with

Pancho, the guard who had been outside the *posada* last night, and another with *Señor* Gutiérrez.

Pancho had admitted to abandoning his post to get out of the rain. He had believed he could watch the *posada* from inside a *pulque taverna* across the street. He reported seeing a man fleeing and trying to catch him, but the man had too much of a head start. The authorities had come soon after that. Seguín had fired Pancho on the spot.

Señor Gutiérrez's information was more interesting. Based on his eldest son's description and Diana's, the authorities had established it was the same man who had broken in before. The same man who had murdered Jamie.

Diana had lied to him.

He had made her angry enough to tell him about last night's incident, but not angry enough to disclose her suspicions about him. Probably she had some crusading notion of tying him to Jamie's murder and watching him swing.

Unfortunately, he couldn't explain who was really behind her father's murder because she would hate him, anyway. He was damned if he did, and damned if he didn't.

Only two good things had come from the frustrating interviews. Diana had confirmed what Gutiérrez's son had remembered—the man possessed a jagged scar down his right cheek. It wasn't much, but it was something to go on. And the McFarlands were moving in with the Yorks. They would be as safe there as anywhere in México. Herbert York employed his own personal guards. Seguín would have his men periodically check the York mansion and try to earn the confidence of the guards.

Through his business contacts he knew of Herbert York, but had never met the man. Seguín preferred to purchase his equipment from a Mexican company. There were already enough foreigners swarming over his country.

Patriotism aside, he suddenly wished he had done business with York instead. He had a feeling Mr. York might be the only person who could convince Diana to put aside her personal grievances and accept his offer.

"This is your room, Diana." Sarah opened the door and indicated the spacious room with a sweep of her arm.

Diana walked into the beautifully appointed bedroom. It was larger than the two rooms at the *posada* put together. Decorated in cool mint green and white, its spacious interior soothed her. The huge canopied bed, the dressing table, and the *armoire* were fashioned from blond oak, polished to a bright sheen. Soft throw rugs lay scattered about, covering the tile floor and lending a cozy atmosphere. There were even a small fireplace and a bookshelf filled with leather-bound volumes. A separate dressing area lay behind a gaily decorated screen.

Twirling around with her arms outstretched, she gushed, "It's wonderful, Sarah! How can I thank you enough?"

Her friend laughed. "I haven't shown you the best part yet."

"There's more?"

"Come and see."

Sarah led her to the bookshelves. On the other side of them, tucked into a corner, was a door. "Guess where this leads?"

"I don't know. The Garden of Eden?"

"Better yet." She flung the door open. "It leads to *my* room."

Squealing with delight, Diana breathed, "It's perfect! We can stay up all night gossiping, and no one will be the wiser."

"I thought you'd approve."

Taking her friend's hands in her own, Diana said, "You don't know what this means to me, Sarah. After the past few days, I feel as if I'm losing my mind."

"I can understand. Father's gruff and exacting at times, but I couldn't bear to lose him." Her blue eyes brimmed with compassion.

"It's not only that." She released her friend's hands and walked toward the bed. Giving into an uncontrollable urge, she flounced down on it, sinking into the feathery softness. "How long until we have to dress for dinner? I've been dying to tell you everything, but there's been no time."

Sarah consulted an exquisitely crafted watch pinned to her shirtwaist. "At least two hours. Mother suggested that you rest, but if you'd like to talk I'd be more than happy to oblige." Her friend's eyes shone with anticipation.

"You're incorrigible, Sarah."

"No worse than you, Diana."

She laughed for the first time since she had learned of her father's murder.

Joining her on the bed, Sarah tucked her legs beneath her, Indian fashion, and urged, "Tell me everything. But please, start at the beginning. Some of your letters were so rambling."

Snatching up a pillow, she swatted at Sarah. "How can you say such a thing? Your letters weren't exactly literary treatises."

Deflecting the pillow with a quick feint of her arm, Sarah promised, "I won't tease you anymore. I'm all ears."

Pausing for a moment, Diana marshalled her thoughts. Making a conscious effort to start at the beginning, she poured out her story. Starting from the letters they had received announcing her father's partnership in a silver mine to her latest, acrimonious encounter with Seguín Torres, she told her friend everything, including her fears and suspicions.

Sarah listened intently, stopping her from time to time to clarify a point. When she finished, Sarah stared at her for a long time and then opened her arms. She went willingly, and they embraced. Patting her back, Sarah crooned, "You've had a rough time."

Diana felt her eyes filling with tears. Her friend's comforting words and embrace had broken through her self-imposed reserve. It was good to have someone to lean on. It was hard to always be the strong one.

She wiped at her tears with the back of her hand. Sarah released her and pulled a handkerchief from the pocket of her voluminous skirts. "Here, take this."

Obediently, she dabbed at her eyes and blew her nose.

"I know some things about Seguín Torres that might interest you," Sarah announced.

"Really?"

"Yes, although I don't think my information will erase his guilt."

"I thought so!"

"It's not as simple as you think, Diana. Now it's your turn to listen. His story is an involved one. And remember, I'm repeating gossip, so not everything I know might be true, but it should give you a better idea."

"As you said, I'm all ears."

"And I'll try to start at the beginning."

She drew a deep breath. "Seguín Torres was born to the *criollo* aristocracy. After the Spanish were evicted from México during the revolution, most of the country's wealth and power fell to the *criollos*. Seguín's father owned several silver mines. Seguín was an only child. When Seguín was four or five years old, his father died. The silver mines were left to Seguín's mother, to be held in trust for her son when he came of age. After a proper period of mourning, the young widow remarried another wealthy *criollo*. Her new husband owns a huge rancho, just south of México City."

Diana couldn't help but ask, "How do you know this?"

"It's common gossip. México thrives on two things— politics and gossip. And the two are hopelessly intertwined.

When you attend social gatherings, you'll see what I mean."

"There's a point to this?"

"Of course. Just listen and you'll understand."

"All right."

"Good." Sarah patted her hand. "Where was I?" She paused, smoothing her hair. "I remember. Seguín's mother remarried and gave birth to another son, Seguín's half-brother." She stopped again, and her brow furrowed in concentration. "I don't remember his name, but it's not important. Seguín had been away at school. When he returned home, at about fifteen or sixteen, there was a horrible scandal about him. I've never been told the details, probably because I'm a *gringa,* and it wouldn't reflect well on the *criollo* aristocracy."

"What's a *gringa?*"

"It's not a nice term. It's what they don't call us to our faces but it means a *Norté Americaño.*"

"Oh." She felt curiously out of her element. Just because she had learned Spanish, she had thought she could survive in this strange land. Now she wasn't so certain.

"Right after the scandal, Seguín's mother died of a fever. And when the will was read, she had disinherited him because of the scandal. His stepfather lost no time in kicking him out."

"Then what did Seguín do?" She felt a twinge of pity for him.

"I'm not sure. This is where the rumors start, but people say he went north and joined the Juáristas."

"The revolutionaries?"

"Yes. And he vowed revenge on his stepfather for taking away his birthright. Some years later, as the rumors tell it, he won a silver mine in a card game and started the beginning of his mining empire. Over the years, he's bought more mines, until he and his stepfather are the principal owners in México. There are a few others who own mines, but they're small potatoes."

"So, Seguín needs my father's formula to drive his stepfather out of business and exact his revenge." She made the connection.

"Precisely."

She groped for the corollary. "And it wasn't Seguín who tried to steal the formula and killed my father. It was his stepfather."

"I don't know for certain, but it would be my guess. My father doesn't do business with Seguín, but he knows about him. Except for his hatred of his stepfather, Seguín appears to be honest and fair, with his employees as well as his business associates. I don't think he would have lent your father the money and then had him killed. That doesn't make sense to me."

Diana buried her face in her hands, trying to gather her thoughts. She hadn't really considered it that way before. Why would Seguín complicate matters by helping her father bring his family to México? He must have meant to honor the partnership.

"It doesn't really matter, does it?" She raised her head. "Even if it *was* Seguín's stepfather, he should have warned my father of the danger and protected him." The nauseating realization of her father's unnecessary death swept over her. "It doesn't matter," she repeated, "Seguín's hands are bloody, too."

"I think Seguín feels responsible, and that's why he's being so secretive. It's also why he's eager to buy you out and send you home."

"Yes, that's it." She lifted her eyes and captured Sarah's gaze. "What should I do?"

"I can't answer for you, Diana. You need to talk to my father. He can counsel you from a business perspective."

From a business perspective. Diana repeated the words in her head. How cold they sounded. Her father, unwittingly, had been ensnared in a bitter fight, a game of life and death.

And she was left to do the right thing, to make sense of this madness.

Herbert York, like his wife, was attractive. He had silver gray hair and blue eyes, too. He had kept fit, and carried himself with dignity. With two such handsome parents, it wasn't any surprise Sarah was so beautiful.

Diana's interview with Mr. York turned out to be almost as informative as her conversation with his daughter. She told him an abbreviated version of what she had related to Sarah, focusing on the business perspective, as Sarah had put it.

After she finished talking Mr. York rose from his desk and paced behind it, his arms folded behind his back. After a few moments he murmured, "I understand your concerns. Unfortunately, what my daughter told you is correct. Seguín and his stepfather own a majority of the silver mining interests in this country. Don Carlos, Seguín's stepfather, won't purchase the formula from you."

"Why not?"

"He's a tightfisted man. I know him. I do business with him. He would prefer to get it by devious means."

"If what Sarah believes is true, Don Carlos is directly responsible for my father's death. I wouldn't sell to him, anyway."

"You must approach this with your head, Diana, not your heart. What happened to your father was unfortunate, but nothing you do can bring him back. I know Jamie would want you to secure your financial future."

Cold dollars and cents. All of this was about money. Her father's death wasn't important.

"What about the other mine owners?"

"They're too small to pay you a fair price. Only Torres will give you what it's worth."

"What if I return to the United States and sell it there?"

"That's an option," he agreed, "although you'll need contacts in the industry to get a fair hearing. When we return to the States, I could help you. You can always sell it in the States, even if you sell it here as well. There's no patent limitation between the two countries. But it might be some time before you realize any money in the States. You'll need working capital."

What about the money she already owed Seguín, a voice in the back of her head nagged? She and her mother had spent part of it, paying the hotel bill and buying her father's marker. Of course, she could borrow the money from Mr. York, although she hated to impose on his hospitality further. And if what he said was true about needing contacts in the States—probably because she was a woman. Then it could be months or years before she saw any money from the formula. How would they support themselves?

Her head spun with the complications. No matter how she twisted and turned, she felt trapped.

"Despite my belief Seguín is indirectly responsible for my father's death, you would have me sell the process to him?"

"Not so fast, Diana. First, I would go to a Mexican attorney and learn how long you have to repay your father's debt. Next, I would make inquiries as to how much a ten percent partnership in Seguín's mines would bring. Say over the next five years, or perhaps even three years."

"Why such a short time?"

"Because the political situation in México is bound to deteriorate soon. The French won't stay forever, and then it's anyone's guess what will happen. My family will leave when the French pull out. Your father would have been forced to leave, too. You need to consider everything and weigh your options."

Diana hadn't remembered Sarah's father this way, so calculating, appearing unmoved by her father's death. She had always thought of him as a champion of her father and his brilliance. But today she saw him in a different light. From his point of view, everything revolved around money—forget the human blood and sacrifice.

She surmised that he was trying to look after her family the best way he knew, but his approach wasn't very comforting. She wanted to cry out: *what about my father's sacrifice, his innocent death?* Restraining herself, she focused on the business at hand.

"Can you direct me to a good Mexican attorney?"

"Certainly."

"What about estimating the profits my father would have made from the partnership? Over the next three or five years?"

"That will be easy. I have excellent industry contacts."

Rising to her feet, she ended the interview. "Thank you for your help and hospitality. My mother and I are indebted to you."

Seguín had waited for two weeks, and his patience was at an end. He had received no word from the McFarlands. When he consulted his attorney about the promissory note, he had been told the usual term was six months. To enforce it, he would need a court order from a judge. He hoped that wouldn't be necessary. With the passing of time, he assumed Diana's raw emotions had eased, and that she would see reason.

From one of his most trusted men he had learned an alarming fact: a scar-faced man had been spotted, watching the York household. It was imperative the McFarlands sell to him now and leave México.

When he rang the bell at the front gate, he was surprised by the ease he gained entrance. He waited only a few minutes before the Yorks' *mayordomo* ushered him inside. The house appeared empty as he followed the servant through an impressive foyer and onto the patio.

Diana was seated on a stone bench surrounded by the lush vegetation of the patio. A mosaic-tiled fountain tinkled behind her. A blue parrot paced on a perch. He had expected her to receive him formally in the *sala,* but somehow the patio suited her better.

She looked different from the way he remembered her. He realized she wasn't wearing spectacles. Her hair, which had been pulled back in a severe bun before, was loose, falling about her shoulders. And her drab, buttoned-down attire had been replaced by a light muslin gown, cut low in the front.

Staying seated while he approached her, she didn't look at him until he prompted, "Diana, thank you for seeing me."

Her eyes lifted to meet his. They were wondrous eyes, set wide in her face. Their hazel pupils reflected an array of colors: green, blue, gold, and all the shades in between.

She hadn't uttered a word of greeting, and his chest constricted painfully at the thought that she still held him responsible for her father's death. Wanting to dispel the tension between them, he bowed and reached for her hand. She jerked it away and hid both her hands behind her back. Her reaction reminded him of the guilelessness of a child.

He retreated, waiting for her to speak.

Lifting her chin, she stared past him. "I thought we had decided not to see each another again."

"I can leave if you're opposed to our meeting, but I came because I have important information."

She freed her hands from behind her back and knotted them in her lap. "Tell me."

The setting sun formed a golden nimbus behind her head, catching the gleaming highlights of her glorious hair. How could he have thought she was unattractive? She was a goddess. Her beauty hit him like the swift kick of a mule.

Even as he admired her newfound beauty, he realized his attraction went deeper. He was drawn to her spirit and fire. He had missed their verbal sparring since she moved from the *posada*. Jamie had been right—there was something to be said for an intelligent woman. His mother had been intelligent, he remembered. He surprised himself, thinking of his mother. He had tried to put her from his mind.

The silence became awkward, and he pulled his thoughts back to the present. "Diana, the last time we spoke, I warned you about the man who broke into your father's room. I realize you were frightened and angry, and didn't want to listen. I wish you would listen now. I've learned he's still watching you, lurking about the York residence. You must be careful."

She rose to her feet and moved away from him, facing the fountain, with her back to him. His words must have affected her because he could see the tenseness in her bare shoulders.

Leaning over, she trailed her long, tapering fingers in the water. He shivered. The lazy arcs she traced on the surface of the water made him think of how her fingers would feel moving over his skin.

Her voice was low when she finally inquired, "How do you know this?"

"I've had a man watching the York residence, too."

"Who gave you the right?"

"I feel it's my responsibility."

Turning from the fountain, she retorted, "Then why don't you catch the man?"

"We're trying, but he's elusive. Even if we do catch him,

someone else will replace him. You must be careful. Don't go out alone."

"You could have saved yourself the trouble of coming, Mr. Torres. I've already seen him from the Yorks' carriage, and I realize he must be after the formula. It seems you're not the only one who wants it."

"So, you believe me now, that I didn't send the man to your father's room?"

She shrugged.

He studied her. Her demeanor struck him as strange. She seemed remote, uncaring. Always before, she had been combative. He suspected her relaxed posture was because she felt safe with the Yorks, but he didn't want her to become complacent.

"Don't minimize this danger, Diana. Don't feel too safe."

"I'm careful. It's obvious the man isn't going away. What more can I do?"

"Sell me the formula."

Laughing caustically, she tossed her head. "How would that keep me from harm? Just selling the formula to you won't stop some unscrupulous character from forcing me to relinquish it to him, as well."

"I know. You must leave México at once." Logically, Seguín knew it was the safest course of action but when he spoke the words he almost wished he could take them back. If she left, he would never see her again.

"Mr. Torres, look around you." She flung her arm in an arc that encompassed the house and patio. "My mother and I are happy here. The Yorks are old friends. We have no plans to leave."

"You can't stay." He shook his head. "I'll be more than happy to arrange for an escort to Veracruz."

"I'm afraid that's impossible. Even now, my friends and mother are shopping for ball gowns. We've been invited to the Emperor's New Year's ball."

"Are you going?"

Drawing her brows together, she bit her lip. "I don't see that's any of your business, whether I go or not."

"I know it's not my business, but would you mind answering me?"

"Yes, I plan to attend the ball. I think a ball given by royalty should prove interesting."

"*Sí*, the Imperial balls are amusing, but Maximilian's reign, or lack thereof, is another danger to your family. His government is on the brink of collapse. The Juáristas grow bolder each day. Your family should leave before the civil war starts."

A shadow crossed her face, and her eyes widened. His argument appeared to have found its mark.

"I was afraid of that. I sensed the unrest, and Mr. York mentioned it, too." Her eyes narrowed speculatively before she added, "I'm certain your information is more reliable, considering your past association with the rebels."

Startled by her allusion to his background, he wondered what game she was playing. For the moment, he was willing to play along with her. He wanted to know where she was leading.

She moved to a camellia bush and plucked a shell-pink blossom. Seemingly absorbed in examining its delicate petals, she asked, "You were a Juárista, weren't you?"

If he were honest with her, would she begin to trust him? Making a sudden decision, he admitted, "*Sí.*"

"Juárez was the President of México before Maximilian. Is that right?"

"*Sí.*"

"Were you forced to hide when the French came?"

He closed his eyes. He didn't like to remember those days, when he was starving and frightened, wondering if he would live long enough to see the next sunrise. He forced the old memories back and opened his eyes.

"We hid in the north, along the border to your country,

where Juárez remains hidden from the French army to-day."

"Is that where you learned to speak English?"

Her questions were leading nowhere, as well as being of a personal nature. They should return to the issue at hand.

Suppressing his exasperation, he replied evenly, *"Sí.* At one point, we crossed the border to Texas to flee from the French army. For several months, I worked as a cowhand on a ranch. I learned English to survive." He hesitated, but couldn't resist the opportunity to turn the tables on her. "Where did you learn Spanish?"

"From books."

"Then that explains your, ah—"

Her lips quivered for a brief instant, and then she broke into a smile. The beauty of her face was dazzling when a smile softened her features. He felt his pulses race, and his stomach muscles tighten.

She finished the sentence for him. "Awful accent."

"I'm sorry. I didn't mean to give offense."

Twirling the camellia in her hands, she reached up to tuck it behind her ear. The simple lifting of her arm stretched the dress tight across her breasts. His loins stirred, heavy with aching desire.

Pulling his eyes from her bosom, he murmured, "I've enjoyed chatting, but you're avoiding the subject. You must sell me the formula and leave México."

"I'm not ready to sell."

"Diana, you can't put it off indefinitely. I still hold the promissory note."

"I have six months."

"Who told you that?"

"Mr. York's attorney."

She had decided to fight him.

Her stubbornness pushed him beyond the limits of his patience. Without thinking, he closed the gap between them in two strides. He grasped her shoulders and shook her.

With her eyes wide, he glimpsed the fear flickering in their depths. The sudden realization that she might be afraid of him pierced his heart. He didn't want to hurt her. *Madre de Dios,* he wanted to protect her.

Releasing her shoulders, he folded her into his arms. He buried his head in the spun-gold glory of her hair. It smelled of lilac water and the fresh scent of camellia. She didn't pull away from his embrace. Her arms encircled his waist, and she nestled against his chest. He could feel the soft swell of her breasts, and the ache in his loins grew stronger.

He cupped her delicate chin in his hands and pulled her face to his. He murmured *"La rubia,"* under his breath, and then his mouth captured hers.

Seguín savored the sweet, warm fullness of her lips, molding his mouth to fit the sensual curve of her lips. With tongue tip, he traced the contour of her mouth, stroking gently. She opened to him, and he insinuated his tongue within. The heated, honeyed essence of her hit him like a thunderbolt, and his senses reeled. Cherishing her mouth, he explored tenderly, sharing and giving. He wanted to please her, to break through the barriers she had erected between them.

His manhood rose, turgid with heated need. *Por Dios,* how he wanted her. All of her. She was so sweet, so infinitely sweet. And because she was sweet, he knew he must control himself. He didn't debauch virgins.

Gently, he broke off their kiss and stepped back. She swayed slightly in the circle of his arms. Her eyes were shut, her lips swollen from his kisses.

He stroked the sculptured curve of her spine through her muslin gown. Her eyes flew open. She pulled away from him. Her cheeks were tinged pink, and she took several unsteady steps. Keeping her eyes averted, she sat down on the stone bench again. She traced an imaginary pattern on the flagstones of the patio with the toe of her slipper.

Without looking up she whispered, "I think you'd better leave."

"At least think about what I've said, will you? And give my regards to your mother."

She nodded. He thought he detected the bright sparkle of moisture on her eyelashes. That he might have made her cry hammered at him. He couldn't be certain. Her head was lowered.

He waited as the minutes ticked by. He didn't know why. She had already told him to leave.

When he turned to go, her voice stopped him. "You were right that day at the *posada,* Seguín. I've never been kissed before." She brushed her fingers across her lips as if she couldn't believe it. "You said I acted like a man." She raised her head and her gaze found him. "Why did you kiss me now? To convince me to sell you the process? To appeal to my feminine vanity?"

Silently, he cursed himself for the ugly things he had said to her that day. She sounded so wounded and vulnerable. He knew what it felt like to believe no one wanted you.

"I want the process. I admit it. But not that much . . . not enough to make love to—" He stopped and ran his hand through his hair in agitation. She probably wouldn't believe what he was going to say. "I kissed you because you look so lovely with the sunlight shining on your hair. Because I *wanted* to kiss you, Diana. It was as simple as that."

His words had a profound effect on her. He watched as the slow flush crept up her neck, turning her cheeks as pink as the camellia nestled in her honey-blond hair. She lowered her head again.

A tense silence, like the one at the beginning, stretched between them.

"One thing more, Seguín. I know you didn't send the intruder. I know your stepfather did. Why didn't you guard my father against your enemies? Why did you allow him to be murdered?"

How had she found out? The Yorks probably. Gossip was the lifeblood of México, and the Yorks were well connected. The truth was out. She knew. With the secret revealed, came a strange sense of relief.

"I didn't mean to endanger your father, Diana. I'm sorry. I wish there was something I could do."

"I don't think I can forgive you."

"I understand."

Seguín waited, but she didn't respond. Her eyes were fixed on the flagstones.

He left the quiet house.

Four

They crowded into the Yorks' two broughams. Diana and Sarah filled the lead brougham with their huge, bell-shaped ball gowns. Elizabeth and the elder Yorks followed them. Their route took them along the new avenue Maximilian had constructed from the center of the city to Chapultepec. The broad, eucalyptus-lined boulevard overflowed with carriages, all headed toward the palace and the ball.

When they reached the bottom of the hill of Chapultepec, the crush became ferocious. Drivers and carriages jockeyed for position on the steep, narrow drive leading to the castle's entryway.

It was the middle of the afternoon. Sarah had explained to Diana that the Empress Carlotta's balls always started mid-afternoon and ended in the early morning hours of the next day.

"Look at the gardens, Diana." Sarah leaned across the brougham and pointed. "Aren't they lovely? Carlotta styled them after the gardens of her Italian villa."

Diana glanced out the window. Laid out beneath towering cypress trees that were hundreds of years old, the landscape was manicured to perfection. Dark green shrubbery punctuated by flame-colored poinsettias served as the backdrop. Stone benches, statuary, brick pathways, whimsical gazebos, fountains, and waterfalls invited exploration.

After what seemed like hours in their cramped quarters, they reached the courtyard of the palace and descended from the carriages. The view was magnificent. México City lay before them and the snow-capped volcanoes.

Following liveried butlers, their party climbed a short, stone stairway to the ballroom. It occupied the western wing of the second floor.

Her first glimpse of the ballroom almost took her breath away. Acres of vivid tapestries covered the walls, interspersed with huge, gilt-framed court portraits. Glittering chandeliers dripped from tall ceilings, holding thousands of candles. Groupings of *ormolu* furniture offered luxurious comfort for weary guests. A twenty piece orchestra occupied the far end of the room on a raised platform.

But the splendor of the room paled before the opulent display of ball costumes. The women's dresses were huge and bell-shaped like her own, made from yards of taffetas, silks, organzas, and velvets in all the colors of the rainbow. The gowns were flounced and bowed, covered with ribbons, and ruched with lace.

The men's fashions rivaled those of the women. The least flamboyant wore gray cutaway coats with silver cravats or black frock coats and white ruffled shirts. Some men sported velvet brocaded waistcoats, and a few were decked out in multi-hued satins.

French Imperial officers and Austrian Hussars dazzled the eye. The French officers were garbed in gold and scarlet uniforms, covered with medals and ribbons. The Hussars sported gold and white uniforms with satin sashes across their chests and medallions on heavy linked chains around their necks.

Jewels twinkled like a thousand stars. She glimpsed emeralds the size of birds' eggs. Huge crosses, made of square-cut rubies and sapphires, dwarfed their owners. Ball gowns and coiffures were liberally laced with diamonds. Enormous ropes of pearls dangled over exposed bosoms. Even the officers' ceremonial sword hilts were encrusted with glittering gemstones.

Self-consciously, she glanced down at her own green taffeta ball gown and touched the single strand of her grandmother's pearls. She had never cared much for balls, feeling ill at ease with meaningless flirtations and gossipy small talk, but her discomfort increased a thousandfold in this glittering assemblage.

Herbert steered them to a sheltered alcove where there were several unoccupied chairs. A liveried footman appeared, as if by magic, and brought them champagne. Herbert gallantly took turns dancing with each of the women, until it was Diana's turn. When he asked her to dance, she politely refused.

Sarah urged her to reconsider, but she held firm. She hadn't had much practice at dancing. What if she tripped over her own feet?

Her friend didn't press her. Instead, she whirled away in the arms of a French lieutenant, chatting easily in his native tongue. Watching her self-assured friend, she felt a twinge of envy. Educated in Europe and accustomed to lavish entertainments, Sarah exuded poise. Beside her, Diana felt like a country bumpkin. Taking a sip of the bubbly champagne, she wished she had remained behind, curled beside her fireplace, reading a book.

Better yet, she wished she were home in the States, where life was safe and predictable. Thrust into a strange land and the awesome opulence surrounding her, she felt like a fish out of water. Homesickness overwhelmed her. She wanted to go home, but she hated to leave Sarah. It was wonderful to be reunited with her old friend, even if they didn't have much in common.

When they were children, the difference in their social positions hadn't been important. Now as young ladies, it loomed between them, making Diana feel like a poor relation. At the same time, she felt guilty, too—guilty for having disloyal thoughts, especially after the Yorks had done so much for her family.

She wondered how her mother felt. Elizabeth had surprised her by putting aside her mourning to attend the ball. She suspected her mother had relented to please Mary.

Reminded of her father's passing for the thousandth time, she felt the sudden urge to put México behind her and get on with her life. She decided to probe her mother's feelings and press forward with Mr. York to sell the process in the States.

Taking another sip of champagne, she grimaced at the sweet-tart taste. Even the effervescent wine didn't suit her. Carefully, she placed the half-filled glass on a table beside her and retrieved a handkerchief from her reticule. As she wiped the lingering taste from her mouth, her fingers accidentally brushed against her lips.

An image of black, hooded eyes rose in her mind. Her lips tingled, thinking of his taste, the texture of his mouth on hers, and the heat simmering between them.

Shaking herself, she recovered her thoughts, and when she returned to them she wondered if she were being completely honest with herself. Why this sudden urge to flee México? Was she merely homesick, or was it something else?

Jamie had raised her to be ambitious, to make her own way in the world, not depending on some man to marry. Was it really the difference in social positions that bothered her, or was it Sarah's ease with the opposite sex? Did she want the austere life her father had planned for her? Or had Seguín Torres' kiss made her yearn for a very different kind of life?

Her parents had never been especially loving, and her father's volatile temper had driven them further apart. Mary and Herbert York, on the other hand, were devoted to each other. She sensed their mutual love in the way they touched each other often. Her parents had never touched.

She hadn't noticed the difference in the two marriages when she was a child, but now she couldn't help but notice. Was there more to marriage than a passionless union, built upon duty? She hadn't considered the possibility before, but living with the Yorks had opened her eyes.

And Seguín had affected her more than she cared to admit, opening a whole new world of passion and desire.

As if her thoughts had conjured him up, at that moment she glimpsed him across the crowded ballroom. His licorice-colored eyes met hers. He smiled and sketched a small bow. Then he extended his arms toward her. It was a silent invitation to dance. Obviously, he didn't want to approach her unless he was assured of her acceptance.

In an exaggerated gesture, she shook her head, refusing him.

His smile dissolved, and he shrugged elaborately.

Purposely turning her attention from him, she focused on the dizzy whirl of dancers, but her thoughts strayed back to him. She was surprised to see Seguín at the ball. She remembered him asking if she would attend. Surely, he hadn't come because of her.

As hard as she tried to eradicate him from her mind, she failed. She couldn't stop studying him, covertly, from the corner of her eye.

Handsome in everyday clothes, he was magnificent in formal attire. Dressed severely in black with a plain white shirt and a gray cravat, he didn't need brilliant fabrics or jewels to enhance his potent masculine allure. The cutaway coat emphasized his broad shoulders, and the stark power of his muscular legs was evident in his close-fitting pants.

She closed her eyes, remembering the tenderness of his kiss on the patio again, the hot, aching sweetness. When she opened her eyes, he was gone, melted into the crowd.

Disappointed, she returned her attention to the dance floor.

Sarah spun by, in the arms of a French captain this time. No one had asked her to dance except Mr. York and Seguín. Edging into the shadows, she wanted to sink into obscurity. When she slipped behind her mother's chair, the music ended abruptly and the dancers glided to a halt. An expectant hush fell over the crowd, and a fanfare of trumpets sounded.

There was a flurry of liveried servants and the emperor and empress entered. The royal couple took their place on the canopied dais at the opposite end of the ballroom, across from the orchestra.

They commanded the entire room's attention. Trumpets sounded again. Diana welcomed the diversion and she gazed at them openly like the rest of the crowd, curious to view a royal couple.

Maximilian was tall and slight with a luxuriant blond beard. His jacket and pants, exquisitely tailored, were charcoal gray and fit his spare body as if molded to him. Underneath his jacket was a white, pleated shirt. Against its stark purity, he wore a huge collar of golden links, the emblem of his office.

Carlotta was gowned in ice-blue satin, her dress unadorned. The severity of her gown provided the perfect foil for the magnificent diamond necklace gracing her throat, and a diamond tiara nestled in her dark hair. The Empress's features weren't exactly beautiful, but she possessed a strong, arresting countenance.

Watching and listening, Diana found herself intrigued by royal protocol. Maximilian rose and lifted his right arm, a formal gesture of welcome. Carlotta, in turn, rose and welcomed the guests, too, wishing them a happy new year.

After that, various persons were selected and led before the dais. One by one these guests were formally presented to the emperor and empress. Brief conversations ensued, but she was too far away to hear the words. At the beginning and end of each interview, the men bowed and the women curtsied before the royal pair. The presentations lasted more than an hour.

When she felt as if she would drop from exhaustion, the presentations ended. Maximilian took his wife's hand, and they rose. Facing the crowd, he bowed and she curtsied. Then they descended from the dais and officially opened the ball by dancing the *quadrille d'honneur* in splendid isolation, sweeping across the marble floor.

Trumpets sounded for the final time, signaling the end of the dance. Double doors to the right of the dais were thrown wide, opening into an immense banquet hall. Encouraged to find their places at the dining tables, guests streamed into the room.

The dinner proved to be as lavish as the ball. Dozens of courses were offered, served on Sèvres china trimmed in gold. The food was French and delicious, accompanied by copious amounts of fine wine. Unfortunately, the sumptuousness of the meal failed to impress Diana. Separated from her party and thrust between a shy Mexican youth and an aging French colonel, she felt completely out of her element.

She attempted polite conversation in Spanish with the limpid-eyed youth on her left. His replies were monosyllabic. The French colonel on her right was of another stamp entirely. Extremely voluble, he spoke only French. Her knowledge of French was limited to a few phrases. Their lack of a common language didn't stop him from leering at her throughout the endless dinner, even though he was old enough to be her grandfather.

During one of the dessert courses, she felt a sudden pressure on her leg. Glancing down, she found the colonel's hand on her thigh. Horrified, she raised her eyes to his. As she opened her mouth to hurl imprecations at him, he caught her gaze and winked lasciviously. Snapping her mouth shut, she realized he wouldn't understand her outrage. She didn't want to make a scene. Instead, she leapt up and loudly excused herself in both English and Spanish.

Sarah was seated at a long table on the opposite side of the room. When Diana passed by, she managed to get her friend's attention. Sarah must have sensed her agitation, because she rose and excused herself.

Once she knew Sarah was following, Diana headed for the balcony. The thought of fresh air was imminently inviting.

When Sarah joined her at the balustrade overlooking the city, she said, "You should have seen your face in there, Diana. What did the old goat do?"

Not surprised that her sophisticated friend had guessed the reason for her agitation, she replied, "He put his hand on my thigh. It was disgusting!"

Sarah laughed. "You know what they say about Frenchmen."

"I'm sure you've had lots of practice dealing with them since you studied in Paris. But I've never—"

"Don't say it. You did the right thing. But don't think you've dampened his enthusiasm." She grinned. "They love a challenge."

If she hadn't known how Sarah loved to tease, she would have been upset by her reaction. As it was, her friend always managed to see the comic side of things, and her merriment was infectious.

Diana's disgust and humiliation faded away, to be replaced by a wry sense of irony. Previously, she had felt like an unwanted wallflower. Now that someone had paid attention to her, she was incensed. Her emotions were volatile, to say the least.

"Too bad the other fellow, the young Mexican, was so

shy," she remarked. "He seemed nice, and I would have enjoyed practicing my Spanish with him."

Sarah leaned over the balustrade and peered at the courtyard below. "Yes, it's too bad he didn't speak with you. I'm certain he has some fascinating stories to tell. I wonder if it was shyness or discretion on his part."

"What do you mean?"

"The shy young man is José Blasio. He's Maximilian's private secretary."

Drawing a long breath, Diana shook her head. Her lips quivered. "Just my luck the old goat was the one to notice me . . . not someone fascinating."

Their eyes fastened onto one another, and simultaneously, they burst into gales of laughter. Falling into each other's arms, they clung together as waves of hilarity washed over them.

Laughing until their sides hurt and their eyes watered, Diana remembered her earlier misgivings about Sarah and decided envy had prompted them. Her friend hadn't changed. If their social positions separated them, it was her own sense of inferiority that inserted the wedge. Silently promising herself she would try to do better, she hugged Sarah tightly, reveling in their friendship.

When they stopped laughing and moved apart, Sarah commented, "You really should dance. The ball will go on for hours. There will be fireworks at midnight, but if you don't dance you'll get awfully bored."

"I'm not much of a dancer," she protested.

"All the more reason you should practice." Sarah twined her arms about Diana's waist, urging her, "Come on, try for me. I hate to see you bored."

With a sudden flash of insight, she wondered if her friend was using boredom as an excuse to encourage her. Sarah was shrewd, quick to guess people's feelings. Did her friend suspect her insecurities? she wondered.

Making a face to cover her embarrassment at having her doubts uncovered, she allowed Sarah to lead her.

Once inside, she was appalled to find the French colonel chatting with Herbert. Unfortunately, Herbert spoke impeccable French, and their conversation sounded lively. She hung back, hoping the colonel would disappear, but he didn't budge. With a sinking heart, she realized he was waiting for her. Forcing herself to approach her party, she suddenly craved being ignored again. Better to be a wallflower than slobbered over by some old goat!

She had decided to refuse to dance with him when Mary leaned over and whispered it wasn't wise to snub a French colonel—particularly an officer who was directly under General Bazaine, the commander-in-chief of the emperor's army.

Caving in under pressure, she accepted the inevitable and accepted his offer to dance, adroitly avoiding his roving hands. Sarah whirled by and winked, grinning wickedly. She grimaced in return, noticing that this time her friend had abandoned the French officers for a Mexican *criollo*. The young man was strikingly handsome. And he looked vaguely familiar, although she couldn't remember being introduced to him.

When her dance with the colonel ended, she was relieved to find that he appeared frustrated by her reticence. Bowing, he murmured some French words, leaving her abruptly. Before she had a chance to savor her escape, an Austrian officer asked her to dance. After that, a steady stream of men approached her. She'd never been popular before. Her sudden desirability came as a surprise. It was both exhilarating and nervewracking at the same time.

Seguín followed Diana's progress around the floor. Each time he found her, she was on the arm of another man.

Her desirability was no surprise to him. Once she was drawn from the shadows, her success was assured.

La rubia. Her blond hair shone as the finest spun gold in the light of a thousand candles. Her emerald-colored gown caught the deep forest glints in her hazel eyes and magnified them. Her skin was the palest ivory. Her vivid coloring and patrician features needed no tawdry jewels to enhance their beauty.

Even the plain dress suited her. She stood out from the crowd, like a graceful swan among a crush of preening peacocks. The simplicity of her attire only served to heighten the perfect symmetry of her willowy figure.

He felt his guts knot. Why was she dancing with every man who asked her, when she had refused him? He hated the way they swarmed to her, the way they placed their hands upon her body. He closed his eyes, willing the images to go away.

With an effort of will, he forced away the disturbing thoughts and focused on his purpose. He wondered what had happened to Manuel. Posing as his valet, Manuel, one of his men, had accompanied him to the ball. He had brought him to help guard Diana.

As if on cue, Manuel returned from scouring the grounds and whispered some words into his ear. Seguín knew his efforts were rewarded when Manuel told him what he had found in the Imperial gardens. Turning, Seguín followed him to the balcony doors.

Hesitating, he glanced back, hoping to catch one last glimpse of Diana. But it wasn't Diana that his gaze found. His glance settled on a young man dancing past him—Gilberto Aguirre, his half-brother. Seguín hadn't realized Gilberto was home from Europe. He must have just arrived. Gilberto's dancing partner also caught Seguín's eye. It was Sarah York.

* * *

Sarah wondered if she had drunk too much champagne. Her face felt flushed, and dizzy waves of giddiness washed over her. Clinging to the broad shoulders of her dancing partner, she was surprised at herself. Champagne was a known quantity. She knew better than to overindulge.

He has wonderful eyes, she found herself thinking, gazing at her partner. *And sensual lips,* she told herself, studying them, wondering what they would feel like. The scent of sandalwood and his own musk titillated her, filling her senses. Her giddiness heightened, making her wonder what was wrong with her. She had danced with hundreds of men, but no one had affected her like this.

Her partner had introduced himself. His name was Gilberto Aguirre. His introduction had identified him as a member of the Mexican aristocracy, and as Seguín Torres's half-brother. She told herself she had accepted his invitation because she was curious about him and might learn something to help Diana. But with his strong arms around her and his handsome face close, she wasn't so certain of her motives.

Hoping to draw him out, she asked, "Do you come to the Empress's balls often?"

Sable-brown eyes found hers, the irises ringed by tiny golden flecks—such marvelous eyes, she couldn't keep from noticing again.

He licked his lips, and her gaze followed the quick movement. She had been kissed many times by a variety of suitors. Some kisses had been quick, chaste pecks. Other kisses had been deep, with the men insinuating their tongues into her mouth. From the latter, she had recoiled. The intimacy of tongues had proven distasteful to her. Now, she wasn't so certain.

"I've been away for years, studying in Europe. I confess this is my first royal ball in México." He smiled at her. It was a tender smile, filled with promise. Promise of what? She didn't know.

"Where did you study?"

"Mostly in Spain, at a monastery school."

"Oh, are you intended for the priesthood?" Even as she spoke the polite question, her mind rebelled. She couldn't picture him in vestal robes.

He grinned, looking like a mischievous boy.

"Not the priesthood, but my father wanted me to have a strict education." Pausing, his gaze swept her.

With his gaze on her, she warmed. A heated flush spread through her limbs, traveling from her torso to her neck and then her face. It had been a long time since a man had made her blush.

When she was younger, she had experienced what her parents called "puppy love"—a strange, unnerving experience of craving a young man, only to realize when she shared time with him that her attraction waned and the relationship became tedious.

Her parents' relationship was her ideal. After twenty years of marriage, they were still in love with each other. She wanted the same passion for herself. None of her suitors had passed the test, but this man was different. They had only exchanged the briefest of words, yet she could sense he was unique.

He interrupted her thoughts. "You were educated in Europe, too, weren't you?"

"Yes, at the Sorbonné."

"Ah, Paris. Lucky you. I visited on holidays."

Surprised by his honesty, she smiled. Lowering her eyes, she tried to fight his magnetism. Casting about, she noticed what she had avoided before . . . his attire. His jacket and pants were glove-tight, fitting his body as if painted on him, accentuating his muscular chest and powerful thighs, leaving very little to the imagination. She wondered at his choice of clothing. Was this the new rage in Europe? Had she been stuck in México too long?

Their dance ended and he grasped her elbow, propelling her to one side of the ballroom. Before she could excuse herself, an auburn beauty approached and cooed, "Gilberto, you've come home at last. It's been too long."

Lifting his shoulders in an apologetic shrug, he grasped the auburn beauty's hand and bowed low. "Rosa, what a pleasant surprise. Give my regards to your parents." Kissing her hand, he promised, "I'll call at your hacienda later."

As soon as he had dismissed Rosa, a green-eyed woman with midnight black hair appeared. From behind him, she covered his eyes with her hands and challenged, "Guess who?"

He formed his boyish grin and started guessing.

Sarah had seen enough. Pivoting on her heel, she strode across the ballroom floor, making for the balcony. Fresh air beckoned her—anything to clear her head and senses.

Leaning over the balustrade, she stared into the black night, thinking about him. The too tight clothes suddenly made sense. He was a self-styled Don Juan.

She had met plenty of Don Juans in Europe, and none of them appealed to her in the least. Most of them were insufferable cads, arrogant in their good looks. She had to admit he possessed the requisite looks for the part. Earlier, she had almost fallen under his spell. How could she have been so foolish? Her parents had raised her better than to swoon over a pretty face!

Silently chiding herself, she put him from her mind and wondered where Diana was. She hoped her friend was dancing, but at the same time she wished Diana was with her now. She wanted to tell her about Gilberto.

Turning from the balcony with the purpose of finding her friend, she ran straight into the muscular chest of Gilberto. His strong arms caught and steadied her, holding her longer than necessary.

Incensed by his forwardness, she pushed her hands against his chest, demanding, "Let go of me."

He dropped his hands, and his handsome face creased in bewilderment. "What's wrong?"

"I didn't give you leave to touch me."

"But you're the one who ran into me. I merely caught you."

"And held me longer than necessary."

His grin was back, and despite her best intentions she returned it. Her anger melted away.

"You can't fault me for holding you, Sarah. It's very pleasant to have you in my arms. You didn't seem to mind on the dance floor when I held you. In fact—"

Her face burned, remembering the way she had clung to him earlier. He obviously remembered it, too. "Dancing is different," she managed, feeling like a clod. Where had her wit gone? She searched her mind, but couldn't think of one slicing remark.

"Not so different, *mi amorcíta.*"

"Don't call me 'your love.' I'm not your love, and I don't have any intention of being added to your . . . your . . . harem!" Her wit was back, and she felt gratified for its speedy return.

Throwing his head back, he roared with laughter, white teeth gleaming against his dark skin. "You're jealous! I share one dance with you, and you think you own me. That's it, isn't it?"

"That's not it, you arrogant cad. It just so happens I don't like your type."

"What type is that?"

"A ladies' man."

"*¿Pérdónme?*"

"A Don Juan, a Lothario. You know." She stamped her foot in frustration, trying to make him understand, wondering if he was playing with her or if he really didn't understand the English phrases. Either way, she felt ridiculous, talking about such things with a strange man.

"I accept the compliment, but you give me too much

credit. Those women were childhood friends, glad that I've returned home. I'm sorry I ignored you." He went down on bended knee before her, his hands clasped in supplication. "I humbly beg your pardon and want to ask you—"

His mock pleading was too much. Taking advantage of his awkward position, she swept past him, almost running to find her party in the ballroom.

The deep timbre of his laughter followed her. She would never forgive him for mocking her.

The New Year, 1866, had begun. The fireworks were over. The Yorks were fatigued and ready to go home. Sarah had joined their party, red-faced and out of breath. Diana longed to ask her what was wrong, but she decided to wait until they were alone in the carriage. Something in her best friend's face warned Diana that she wasn't in the mood for explanations.

Stifling a yawn, Diana waited patiently while good-byes were exchanged. Her feet were aching. She had never danced so much in a single night. Finally everyone was ready to leave. She followed her party downstairs and into the courtyard.

A large crowd of people waited impatiently for their carriages. Remembering how long it had taken them to ascend the hill, she sighed. It might be a long time before their carriage appeared.

Sarah had pushed ahead with her father to send a runner to fetch the two broughams. Mary and Elizabeth stood in front of her, their heads close together, gossiping about the ball. She wished Sarah hadn't rushed off. Again, she wondered what was wrong with her friend.

The mob closed around her, pushing and jostling to get to the front of the line. She was in the thick of it, trying to stay with her party, when she was roughly elbowed. Her breath expelled in a hard rush, and she doubled over, unsteady on her feet. Someone shoved her again. This time, the jab came from behind. She stumbled several feet before righting herself.

Muttering under her breath about the rudeness of the mob, she found herself on the outskirts of the throng. She couldn't see her party. They had been swallowed by the crowd. Straining to locate them, she rose on tiptoe, and turned her head from side to side, searching. The flickering torches, ensconced in wrought iron embrasures, proved inadequate. The faces of the crowd were shadowed, and she could barely see two people ahead of her, the crush was so great.

When she stepped back into the throng, a hand descended on her mouth and jerked her head back cruelly. An arm like a steel vise encircled her waist.

Panic surged through her, and she started to struggle, muffled screams rising to her throat. The arm around her waist loosened for a split second, and she surged toward freedom. But in the next instant, her hopes were dashed. She felt the prick of something sharp under her breast.

The stench of onions and garlic assaulted her as a harsh voice hissed, "Don't fight. I've got a knife."

Fear rose within her like a living thing, choking and suffocating her. Her heart thudded in her ears. Despite the warning she struggled, and the grip on her waist tightened. A low curse assailed her, and a searing pain burned beneath her right breast. Tears of pain and fright streamed from her eyes.

She stopped fighting and went limp.

Five

Darkness closed around Diana. The man pushed her forward relentlessly. She moved without thinking, her mind a blank, washed clean of thought by the raw power of her terror. Thrashing through the manicured bushes she had admired earlier, her abductor cursed each time he was forced to stop and loose her voluminous skirts from clinging branches. Her fragile slippers were worn through, and rocks slashed at her unprotected feet, causing her to stumble and falter.

Their nightmare flight went on and on, seemingly without end, until she glimpsed the dark outline of a tethered horse against the night sky. Her abductor grunted and stopped short. He withdrew the knife from beneath her breast, sheathing it.

A greasy, balled-up rag replaced the hand clamped over her mouth. She gagged, and for a brief instant she was afraid she wouldn't be able to breathe. He yanked her hands behind her back and tied them together with a coarse rope. She winced from the abrasion of the rough cord against her wrists.

With surprising strength, he heaved her onto the waiting horse's back. Mounting behind her, his arms encircled her waist.

A bright light split the gloom. She squinted into the

light, trying to make out its source. Relief flooded her body when she realized who held it.

Seguín!

He was standing with his back against a tree. In one hand, he held a lantern, in the other, a pistol. Slowly, he squatted down, keeping the gun trained on them. Placing the lantern on the ground, he straightened up.

His voice was sharp when he demanded, *"Déjala ir."*

Her abductor tensed. Sensing his hesitation to obey Seguín's command, she prayed he would have no choice but to comply. He had sheathed his knife, and she didn't think he had a gun.

She heard Seguín's pistol cock.

Tightening his grip on her, the man lifted her from the saddle. Before she knew it, she was hurtling through the air.

From the corner of her eye, she caught a blur of movement. Her abductor sped away, the darkness closing around him. With her hands tied, she couldn't break her fall. In a blur of motion, she saw Seguín drop his gun and rush forward. She landed on top of Seguín, and they fell together to the ground. Stunned and with their limbs entwined, they lay still for several moments. Winded from the fall, craving air, she gasped. A burning pain seared her. It hurt to breathe. Panting in shallow gulps, she tried to force air into her starving lungs.

Slowly, Seguín pulled himself into a sitting position and shifted her to his lap. His movements jarred her, and her entire body felt bruised. Rolling from beneath her, he retrieved the lantern. With his sudden movement, a muffled moan rose to her throat.

He pulled the awful gag from her mouth. Finally free of the filthy thing, she felt as if she were going to vomit. Afraid of what that violent movement might cost her, she fought the rising nausea, clamping her mouth shut and swallowing several times while he untied her hands.

"Did you see him?" she asked. Her mouth felt dry and foul. It was difficult to speak, but she had to know.

"I saw him. He had a long scar running down his right cheek. He's our man." His face was grim. "I didn't want him to get away. Now we have to worry about him coming back again."

She thought she saw a ghost of a smile cross his face when he added, "It's hard to do two things at once."

"Like catch me and shoot at the same time?"

"Something like that."

The pain had subsided while she kept still. Testing herself, she tried to sit up. Agony shot through her body, wrenching another low moan from between her clenched lips.

He shook his head. "Don't move, Diana." He placed the lantern closer to her. "I want to examine you for injuries. It hurts to move, doesn't it?"

"Yes."

"I need to feel for broken bones."

His words were innocuous, but his eyes burned into hers. The garden was quiet around them, hushed and expectant. Not even the insects stirred. A soft breeze played across her heated skin, bringing the sweet fragrance of a night-blooming flower. She understood what he was asking.

She nodded.

Searching for broken bones, his hands moved over her limbs. "Where does it hurt most?"

But his touch didn't bring pain. Instead, it raised gooseflesh on her. Embarrassed by her body's reaction, she closed her eyes, accepting his gentle probing.

"Diana, you must tell me where it hurts," he repeated, prompting her.

"It's difficult to pinpoint. I feel as if I've been stomped by a wild bull." She caught her breath and admitted, "Seguín, it hurts to breathe."

"I was afraid of that. I'll need to loosen your gown and unlace your corset. You might have broken some ribs when he threw you from the horse."

She didn't know how to respond. His hands on her limbs had awakened every nerve ending in her body. How would she feel if he touched her chest . . . would she be able to withstand the sweet torture? Feeling the heat rise to her cheeks, she turned her face away.

"Wouldn't it be better if you took me to a doctor? I mean—"

Tenderly, he cupped her chin in his hand and turned her face to his. Their eyes locked. "I don't advise it. I think I should examine you before I try to move you." Shrugging, he kept his tone light. "We'll try it your way, first."

He managed to get his arms under her shoulders and knees. When he lifted her off the ground, the pain flared. She gritted her teeth against it. Rising in a half crouch, she dangled from his arms. The pain lanced through her like a hot poker. She tried to stop her reaction and failed.

She screamed.

Seguín cursed under his breath and slowly lowered her to the ground. Red-black dots swam before her eyes. Her entire torso felt as if it were on fire.

"We've tried it your way. I want a look at your ribs. Your modesty is secondary, Diana. I must—"

"I understand," she interrupted. "You're afraid one of my lungs might be punctured."

Surprise lit his hawk-like face.

"I was raised in rough and tumble mining towns. I've seen a lot of accidents."

Nodding, he replied, "I'll be gentle."

Unsheathing his knife, he quickly slit the thin taffeta of her dress down the front. Peeling the fabric back, he cut until her torso was freed from the confines of her gown. Swearing softly at the boned fortress of her corset, she waited while he considered what to do next. Her corset was laced in the back, and she knew he was thinking of the pain it would cause to turn her.

His lip was clamped between his teeth and his brow furrowed, and she sensed his genuine concern. His concern touched her, deep inside where precious little had ever reached before. Tenderness welled within her, and her eyes stung with tears.

Ignoring the difficulty of moving, she raised her arm and brushed back a stray tendril of his sable hair, offering, "I think you can open my corset if you're careful to cut the fabric between each of the stays."

Grunting in response, he ran his hands over the corset. She shivered from his touch. Carefully, he located a thin line of fabric webbed between the thick whalebone stays. Slowly and methodically, he sheared the fabric in two places on either side of her chest. The corset fell from her body. Blessed breath rushed into her lungs. She breathed again, more deeply this time, and experienced a low throbbing pain in her left side. She prayed she hadn't punctured a lung.

"What's this?" He pointed to a red gash beneath her right breast.

"Our *friend* got carried away with his knife. It was his way of keeping me from struggling."

He didn't respond to her explanation.

A nightjar called in the distance. A lazy wind lapped her body. Covered by only a transparent camisole, she felt his gaze hot upon her flesh. The lantern gleam burned in the depths of his obsidian eyes. Without a word, he lowered his head and kissed the wound through her camisole.

She shuddered at the intimate touch of his lips. Her nipples hardened, pouting and begging for his attention.

Lifting his head from her chest, he devoured her with his eyes. She felt the quickening beat of her heart, and the heady liquid warmth his gaze brought her. Longing rose within her, a longing to be in his arms, to bury herself in his strong embrace.

Seguín groaned deep in his throat as if affirming their unspoken, mutual need. Lowering his head again, he found her lips. His mouth crushed hers, insistent with need, hot with desire.

Responding, she felt herself unfold, like a cactus flower in a brief rainstorm. She melted into his embrace, greedily exploring his mouth with tongue tip, wanting all of him, drawing him into her mouth. Their tongues danced together, twined in intimate contact, tasting and taunting.

She ran her hands over his face, craving the rough abrasion of his male skin, savoring the hard lines of his lips, desiring the rough plundering of his tongue.

His heady masculine scent surrounded her, filling her nostrils, drowning her senses with a nameless yearning. Her almost naked breasts were crushed against the hard planes of his chest. Her nipples tingled from the pleasurable contact. Raw waves of shimmering heat washed over her.

Circling his tongue with hers, he left her with one last promise. Then he withdrew and kissed her hard on the lips. She closed her eyes, cherishing the feel of his mouth against hers. His kisses trailed downward, his tongue like velvet heat upon her neck.

Tracing the line of her throat, he paused at the hollow of her throat to worship there. Blowing his hot breath on her tender neck, he eased the scorch by gently licking the sensitive hollow. Entranced by the sensation, she melted against him.

Boldly, his lips and tongue moved downward. He kissed the deep cleft of her bosom, running his tongue along the side of one breast. Her heart pounded in double-time, and her skin tingled. Time stopped when he took her breast in his mouth, wetting the thin fabric with his tongue, circling and licking.

Groaning with the too bright flame of passion, she felt lightning flash through her body, and her bones melted. Hot streams of liquid fire scorched her, centering in the core of her being. She felt an exotic, pulsating need grow between her thighs, in that most intimate and female place.

He moved his mouth from one breast to the other. For a split second, the abandoned breast hurt with a sensitized pleasure-pain. Then his hand came up to cup it and soothe the aching need while his mouth worked its magic on her other breast.

Her fierce longings intensified. She was melting, floating, craving more . . . wanting to be closer. The strange feelings engulfed her and carried her along on a tantalizing torrent. She was drowning, drowning in the too poignant pleasure of unleashed desire.

Reaching up, she curled her fingers in his coarse hair and pulled him nearer. She arched her back and greedily thrust her breast into the heated adhesion of his mouth. Unexpected agony eclipsed the pleasure. Her fingers dug into the back of his neck, and a ragged gasp escaped her lips. Despite the torment of her injuries, she didn't want him to stop. Not now, not ever . . .

He must have heard her involuntary gasp because he lifted his head from her breasts. When he did so, she felt bereft. Hungry with need, hungry for his touch, she was pinned to the earth by her injuries.

His eyes were wild, reflecting his need, but his face was stamped with shame. "Diana, forgive me. I—"

"Don't."

The silence stretched between them, as taut as a strung bow. Her body felt heavy, full of unquenched longings. Vaguely, she recognized the powerful feelings as passion. What else could they be? This overwhelming need to touch and be touched.

She watched the swift play of emotions across his hawk-like face. He was fighting for control, and within seconds he mastered himself. His polite mask slid in place. His eyes were black and bottomless, no longer reflecting the fire burning within.

"Diana, I haven't finished." His voice sounded thick with unresolved emotions. "If it's your ribs, I must bind them so I can move you."

Nodding, she shut her eyes, delivering herself into his hands.

She felt him lift her camisole from the bottom and bunch it beneath her breasts, ironically preserving a modesty she no longer cared about. His fingers gently probed each rib, one by one. At certain places, pain overwhelmed her, despite his careful touch. She bit the inside of her cheek to keep from crying out again.

Apparently satisfied, he took his hands from her.

Her eyes flew open. He stood up to remove his jacket and shirt.

"What did you find?" She asked.

With his shirt off, he methodically tore it into wide strips of cloth. The lantern light bronzed his naked chest. She stared openly at its smooth expanse, lightly dusted with black, curling hair. His powerful muscles bunched and corded with the effort of ripping the cloth. Mesmerized by the sheer animal magnetism radiating from him, she yearned to explore his masculine beauty, to run her fingers and tongue over his warm flesh.

"Good news. Only one rib seems to be broken, although others might be cracked. I see no evidence of internal injuries." His practical answer jolted her back to reality. "That damned corset may have served a worthwhile purpose. It probably protected your ribs from the fall."

He finished tearing his shirt into pieces. The long strips wafted in the breeze as he gazed down at her. "If I can bind your ribs with these strips, I think it will be safe to move you. The binding may hurt a bit. Can you stand it?"

"Of course."

But she had overestimated her stamina. The movements to lift her so he could pass the cloth beneath her body and the tightness of the bindings were an agony. The red-black dots appeared again and grew thicker. A buzzing began in her ears. When he was halfway through with his task, she knew she wouldn't be able to stay conscious much longer.

With the last bit of her strength, she reached up and wiped the perspiration from his brow. Worry etched his strong features, and she glimpsed the reflection of her own pain in his eyes. Accepting the unfamiliar sensation of someone caring for her, she allowed the feeling to flow over her, washing out the pain, bringing blessed relief.

"Thank you, Seguín."

Staring down at her inert form, he realized it was a blessing that she had fainted. He could finish the bindings without hurting her further. Then he would return her to her mother and the Yorks. They must be crazy with worry.

He finished the bindings quickly. While he was considering how to move her without more pain, he heard a crashing in the underbrush. His hand went for his pistol, and he drew it. Reloading quickly, he leveled the muzzle at the direction of the sound.

Manuel rode into the clearing.

With his guard's sudden appearance, he remembered Diana was half-naked, and he covered her with his discarded jacket.

"Took you long enough. What happened?" he barked at the man, disappointed to see Manuel was alone. The scar-faced man must have gotten away.

"I waited at the bottom of the hill, as you instructed. But he never came." He peered around the small clearing and asked, "Did he get away?"

"Sí. He got away while I was saving *Señorita* McFarland."

"I thought you sent me to guard the only way down."

"I told you to cover the customary path. Unfortunately, it's not the only way. There's an old aqueduct opening on the opposite side. It's mostly filled with rubble. I never dreamed the *bastardo* would know that way out."

"La señorita," Manuel ventured, staring at the limp, unconscious figure on the ground. "Is she—?"

"No, she's alive. But she's hurt. She has one broken rib, maybe more. Dismount, and between the two of us, we'll take her back to the castle."

"Her friends have missed her. I passed several search parties when I came up the hill."

"I'm not surprised," Seguín responded shortly. "I'll carry her in my arms, but I want you to take her legs so they don't dangle. Keep them straight. And carry the lantern so we can see where we're going."

"Sí, Señor Seguín."

"Let's go."

"Ouch!" Diana yelled.

The flinty eyed doctor didn't hesitate. He continued to bind her ribs with meticulous precision. He had given her some laudanum to ease the pain so he could attend her, but her chest felt as tender as a boil.

The Yorks had sent for their own personal physician, Doctor Cabrera. He seemed imminently competent, and he even spoke English, but his bedside manner left a great deal to be desired.

Her mother and Sarah hovered at the foot of the bed. When the doctor finished, he ignored his patient and turned instead to Elizabeth.

"Give her another dose of this." He indicated the laudanum in a brown bottle. "I gave her enough to deaden the pain. It's more effective to tape the ribs when the patient is upright, rather than limp. Although," he shrugged, "whoever bound your daughter's ribs did a fair job of it.

The extra dose of laudanum will make her rest. She'll need to stay in bed for five weeks to heal, particularly the one rib that's broken. She has several others that are cracked."

Five weeks . . . it sounded like a prison sentence to Diana. She remembered other times, with the usual childhood illnesses, that she had spent in bed. Those weeks had been agonizing. The hours had dragged by . . . but five weeks. She had never been in bed for five weeks.

The doctor snapped his black bag shut and rose. "One dose, each morning and night. Make certain the bindings don't loosen. Call on me if there is a problem. Otherwise, I will check on her three days hence." He tucked his bag under his arm and reached inside his jacket, pulling out a small square of stiff paper. "Here's my card, where I can be reached. Is there anything else?"

"No, Doctor Cabrera. Thank you for coming so quickly," Elizabeth said.

Taking her mother's hand, he bowed over it. "My pleasure, *Señora* McFarland. Please, keep her quiet."

"I will, doctor. Carmen will see you to the door. Goodbye."

Bowing again, this time to Sarah, he murmured, *"Hasta la vista."*

Following the doctor's orders, her mother moved to her bedside and poured a draught of the laudanum. Diana drank it down, grimacing at the bitter taste. Elizabeth placed a chair next to her bed and seated herself.

Sarah moved to the other side of her bed and took her hand, squeezing it reassuringly.

"Does it hurt much?" her mother asked.

"Not now. Just a steady throbbing, but that should go away soon." She glanced at the bottle beside her.

"Yes, well, we must follow the doctor's orders." Her mother hesitated for a moment and then said, "Diana, do you want to tell us what happened? We were beside ourselves with worry."

"Yes, please tell us," Sarah echoed.

Diana stifled a yawn with the back of her hand. It was full daylight now, but her eyes were scratchy from lack of sleep, and she could feel the beginning effects of the drug.

"Mother, Sarah, I know you're upset. But couldn't it wait? I'm so exhausted." Burrowing deeper into the pillows, she hoped they would take the hint.

Sarah appeared to understand, squeezing her hand again and kissing her cheek. "I'll be back after you've rested."

"Thank you, Sarah. We'll talk then."

Her friend smiled and withdrew, but her mother remained.

She yawned again. What was wrong with her mother? It wasn't like Elizabeth to ignore her pleas. When she had been afflicted with the measles and then the mumps, her mother had been the gentlest of nurses, catering to her every whim.

Elizabeth cleared her throat, venturing, "Diana, I know you're tired, so I'll try to keep this short. How did that Torres man find you? And why did you allow him to . . . to . . . undress you . . . ? It was humiliating, in front of the Yorks, to see you like that. He pawed you and then let everyone see you undressed!"

Forcing her eyelids open, she stared at her mother in open astonishment. "He didn't paw me! He tried to move me without binding my ribs. The pain almost killed me. You heard the doctor. What he did was necessary."

Feeling only the tiniest twinge of conscience at withholding part of the truth from her mother, she rationalized the omission. He had *touched* her, and it had been the sweetest thing she had ever known. But her mother wouldn't understand how she felt.

Elizabeth had been strictly reared in the Southern tradition. Her father had been a Presbyterian minister. Knowing what she did now, Diana wondered if her mother's upbringing had driven a wedge between her parents, rendering their marriage dry and lifeless.

Her mother's lips thinned. Diana realized her vehement response had wounded her mother, but she refused to take the words back. Elizabeth should be thankful Seguín had saved her, instead of condemning him.

"I can't understand why you would defend Mr. Torres. I thought you didn't trust him. And I'm beginning to share your distrust. I find it very odd he always turns up. It's as if he's shadowing you."

She smiled to herself, remembering Seguín's words on the patio. He *was* having her watched. He had admitted it.

Trying to put two and two together, her drugged mind fumbled for answers. How had he known where to intercept her abductor? He had asked if she planned to attend the ball, and when she arrived he had been there, too, but he hadn't mingled with the other guests. She couldn't remember him dancing with anyone, either. Why had he gone?

He had asked her to dance, though. The memory warmed her. And he had been there, ready to stop the scar-faced man, to protect and keep her from harm. Realizing what he had done, her unresolved feelings about his part in her father's death shifted. It was difficult to blame him any longer. He was trying so hard to safeguard her.

And she didn't believe it was guilt that drove him. Maybe at first, but not now. She remembered his eyes burning into hers, his tender touch, his genuine concern for her injuries.

No one had ever looked at her like that before. No one had ever touched her with desire. No one had ever found her attractive before.

She *was* desirable. The thought rose in her mind, soothing her aching body and spirit with the strongest balm possible.

"Diana," her mother prompted, drawing her from her private thoughts.

"Yes, Mother?" Her tongue felt thick in her mouth. It was difficult to speak. The edges of her vision blurred. She tried hard to focus on her mother's face.

"I apologize for my earlier . . . unkind words. It's just that you're my only daughter and I worry—" Her mother paused, obviously groping for the right words to say. "I'm certain Mr. Torres only did what he had to do. I still can't understand how he knew where to find you."

She couldn't tell her mother that Seguín feared for their safety, that he was having them watched. Elizabeth would panic. And they couldn't leave México now. She wasn't fit to travel. The doctor had ordered her to stay in bed for five weeks. If she told her mother, Elizabeth would be a nervous wreck the entire time.

Hating herself for the lie but forcing herself to concoct a reasonable answer, she explained, "I saw Seguín at the ball. When he rescued me, he told me he was in the courtyard when the man grabbed me. He followed us and scared the man away."

"Why would anyone want to abduct you? It wasn't the same man who . . . who broke into Jamie's room, was it? Is this about the formula?"

Diana closed her eyes. She should have expected her mother would guess the truth. She couldn't face her mother and keep lying to her, but she couldn't tell her the truth, either.

"Seguín suspected robbery as the motive," she muttered. "There was a king's ransom in jewelry at the ball. The man must have grabbed me because I was alone. The crowd pushed past me. I got separated from you . . . and . . ." Her words trailed off. She couldn't talk any longer; her tongue was too thick, and her conscience felt like a dead weight, dragging her down.

Elizabeth must have understood her difficulty, because she didn't press. Instead, she kissed Diana's forehead and patted her shoulder. Diana heard the rustle of her skirts as she rose, reverberating in her head as if from a faraway place, down a long tunnel.

"I'm glad Mr. Torres saved you, Diana. Rest now."

Not waiting for an answer, her mother left her alone, closing the door softly.

Wincing at her mother's trusting words, she despised lying. But she doubted Elizabeth could face living in danger. What if the scar-faced man tried to grab her mother the next time? The frightening thought pierced the gray mist shrouding her. Shouldn't her mother be warned?

Lurching up, she opened her mouth to call Elizabeth back, but no sound came forth. Her bones felt hollow, unable to support her, and she flopped onto the pillows. Her last rational thought was that she must ask Sarah for advice.

Six

Sarah wrinkled her nose. The smell in her room was cloying. Roses covered every available surface. White roses intermingled with yellow roses, sprays of pink rosebuds nestled next to full-bloomed red ones. Their collective fragrance overpowered the room, reminding her of a funeral parlor.

Gilberto Aguirre had certainly outdone himself. Clasping her hands together, she paced the room, considering. Why was the man so adamant about winning her regard?

Since the night of the ball, a dozen roses had arrived every day for her, along with invitations to balls, supper clubs, theaters, and various parties. She had turned down each one with a short but polite note. She couldn't bring herself to throw out the roses. He must have emptied every flower shop in the city.

Pursuing her had become his passion, it seemed. She was practical enough to know his pursuit had nothing to do with her desirability as a woman, much less as a person. To a man like Gilberto, a self-styled Don Juan, she presented an irresistible challenge. He pursued her because he couldn't have her.

Amused by her daughter's dilemma, her mother had advised her to go out with him. Once Sarah accepted an invitation, it was Mary's belief, his ardor would cool. Unfortunately, Sarah wasn't so certain her mere acceptance would be enough. She feared he would want to vanquish her, too, leaving her panting at his feet, like his other conquests. The thought made her sick.

There was a knock on her door, and she said, "Enter."

Her maid, Carmen, appeared and executed a quick curtsy. Before she could explain her errand, Sarah directed, "Take some of these roses to *Señorita* Diana. There're too many of them in here."

Diana's room already held numerous bouquets, but Sarah hoped she wouldn't mind a few more.

"*Sí, señorita,*" Carmen replied, pausing before she added, "There's a gentleman caller for you. He's in the southern parlor."

"Who is it?"

Carmen offered a silver tray with a single calling card on it. Scanning the lavish script, she half-suspected whose it would be, and she was right. The name on the card read: Gilberto Aguirre. She had wondered how long it would take him to get tired of exchanging polite but cold notes. He struck her as a man of action, not a man of patience, and he hadn't disappointed her.

"Please tell him I'll receive him in a few minutes."

"*Sí señorita,*" Carmen repeated and bobbed her head. "I'll return for the roses." She pulled the door shut behind her.

Moving to the mirror over her dressing table, Sarah placed several bouquets on the floor. Gazing at herself in the looking-glass, she found it difficult to focus on her appearance. Conflicted emotions pulled at her. She had thought she would welcome his inevitable visit as an opportunity to put him in his place, telling him to stop sending invitations and roses. Instead, she found herself wanting to follow her mother's advice and go out with him.

What could she possibly be thinking? The man was a womanizer, bent on conquest. Why did she want to go out with him?

Because he intrigued her, the thought bloomed in her mind, like one of the overblown roses he had sent. Because she found him just as much of a challenge as he must find her. Because victory over such a Lothario would be sweet.

The game could prove fascinating. The Lenten season had almost arrived, and México City was infinitely boring at this time of year. What better way to pass the time? The idea appealed to her; a challenge always did. She would use all of her wit and charm to infatuate him, only to drop him when he was ensnared. That would put him in his place better than mere words.

Applying a subtle amount of rouge to her cheeks, she smiled to herself. Let him experience the scorn of a woman. It would do him good.

Entering soundlessly on slippered feet, Sarah found him in the southern parlor. He didn't realize her presence. He stood with his back to her, gazing out the windows. Unlike most men, he wore his hair short. His curly brown hair fit his head like a cap, reminding her of Michelangelo's David.

An unladylike urge seized her, gazing at the back of his head. She yearned to run her hands through that close-fitting cap of curls, to ruffle his perfect appearance, to leave her indelible mark upon him.

What was wrong with her?

He was dressed in a blue chambray shirt. His shirt was tucked into gray trousers. No sign of skintight clothes this time. In fact, the casual clothes appeared draped on his frame. Compared to the bold effrontery of his evening clothes, his loose-fitting attire accentuated the male sleekness of his body. He reminded her of a golden cougar, all bone and muscle and sinew.

Sensing her presence, he turned from the window, exclaiming, "You're here!"

"Yes. You seem surprised. I sent my maid to announce me. Didn't she tell you?"

"She said you would come, but I didn't believe her."

"Why not?"

"Because you've refused all my invitations with polite notes."

"Perhaps I didn't care for the amusements you offered."

His face drew into a scowl, but even scowling, his features were beautiful, compelling and utterly masculine . . . but beautiful. He advanced a step. "I've invited you to a score of entertainments. No one dislikes everything. I think you dislike me."

"What a statement to make," she countered, wanting to turn the tables and put him on the defensive. If he thought he could play on her sympathies and make her feel sorry for him, he underestimated her. "Are you always so blunt when you pay a social call? What happened to polite conversation?"

The hint of a smile played about his lips. His golden cat eyes widened. She felt her heart rise to her throat. It was difficult to draw air into her lungs. Why did he have to be so devastatingly handsome?

"Speaking of courtesy, will you offer me a seat?" He pulled a gold-fobbed pocket watch from his trouser pocket and consulted it. "It's almost teatime. I forgot to have lunch. Could I trouble you for some refreshments?"

Covering her mouth with her hand, she tried to hide the smile that had sprung to her lips. He was incorrigible. Tit for tat, like a perfectly planned chess game, he knew just what to say to retake the offensive.

Affecting a nonchalant attitude, she waved her hand dismissively. "Of course. Please be seated. I'll ring for Carmen to bring the tea things." Moving to the bellpull beside the door, she gave it a vicious yank and then turned with a false smile plastered to her lips, explaining, "I didn't expect you to stay. I know you must be a very busy man. I wouldn't want to keep you from anything . . . or *anyone* more important."

This time, he narrowed his gold-flecked eyes and studied her openly. Feeling the force of his gaze upon her, she stared back, refusing to give an inch.

She was entranced. His eyes mesmerized her. Ringed by thick, black lashes, they were almost decadent in their appeal. No man deserved such gorgeous eyelashes.

"*Con permiso,* after you." He indicated the satin-brocade couch beneath the window and bowed, waiting for her. He had just thrown her words back in her face again, proving his good manners. No gentleman would sit down before a lady was seated.

Why hadn't she thought of that? She must keep her wits about her. If she were going to execute her plan, she had to defend herself against his wiles. She couldn't stand around admiring his good looks.

Inclining her head in recognition of his perfect manners, she gathered her skirts and perched on one end of the sofa. He seated himself at the other end. Carmen appeared and Sarah sent her for refreshments, but not before she glimpsed the flirtatious admiration in Carmen's gaze when it rested on Gilberto.

For a moment, she wondered if she could go through with this. When they were alone, their verbal fencing proved entertaining, just as she had imagined it would be. But put Gilberto within one hundred feet of another female, and she suddenly felt like an unwanted appendage. Could she face going out in public with him? Face hordes of admiring women, all throwing themselves at his head?

As if he could read her mind, he asked, "What entertainment interests you? Since you don't object to *me*, I assume my offers weren't enticing enough. What do *you* like to do, Sarah?"

"With you, you mean?" she hedged, knowing perfectly well what he meant, trying to buy time. Her mind scram-

bled for some place where they could go while avoiding
the fair sex.

"*Sí*, with me," his words were edged with irony. "If it
would make you feel more comfortable, I'll speak formally
to your father—"

"That won't be necessary," she cut him off, "my family
is quite modern. They allow me to choose my friends."
She paused, an idea forming in her mind. "I love to ride.
Perhaps we could go riding in the park."

His handsome face fell, but he recovered quickly and
smiled. "I had hoped to take you somewhere more . . .
fashionable. But if you wish to ride in the park, I'm eager
to accompany you. Do you have your own mount? If not,
I can get one for you."

"No, that won't be necessary. I own a thoroughbred
mare. She's always in need of exercise."

"Say tomorrow then, after luncheon?"

"That will be perfect."

"We'll go to Alameda Central. There are plenty of bridle
paths there."

She was familiar with the park, having ridden there before. It was a huge place in the middle of the city, filled
with tropical flowers, copses of trees, and numerous fountains. The park was so large a rider could ride for a mile
or two without seeing another human being. For a public
place, it was the perfect choice. Her heart lifted at the
thought.

Carmen interrupted her thoughts with the tea things.
Along with the traditional tea the huge silver tray held
urns of coffee, as well as creamy hot chocolate, the favorite
afternoon beverage of México. There were glazed cakes,
small sandwiches, crusty meat pies, several kinds of
cheeses, and a variety of fruit. Carmen had outdone herself.

When she dismissed the maid so she could serve them
herself, Carmen left slowly, with many backward glances

at Gilberto. Sarah had to admit he handled the situation well, ignoring the maid completely, seemingly oblivious to her "come-hither" looks.

"What can I pour for you?" she offered.

"Coffee, please."

"Not chocolate?" She was surprised. Most *criollos* preferred cocoa to tea or coffee.

He wrinkled his nose. When he did that, he looked like a mischievous schoolboy, young and appealing, not like a Don Juan. She suddenly wished he *were* different. Along with his looks, he possessed wit and charm, and sophistication mixed with an exuberant maleness. It was too bad that he knew it.

"Chocolate doesn't leave much room for food—too rich and sweet. Coffee goes better with food. I learned to drink coffee when I visited Italy. They're coffee crazy." His hand hovered above the stack of plates. "May I help myself?"

"Please do."

She poured his coffee and then her tea. "Do you care for cream or sugar?"

"No thanks, just plain."

Leaning forward, she offered the cup and saucer. He set down the half-full plate and reached for the coffee. Their fingers brushed. Her skin tingled. Heat flashed through her. She felt a wave of giddiness sweep her, and her head felt suddenly light. Bewildered by her reaction, she realized the sensations were familiar. She had felt the same way at the ball when he held her in his arms.

Dropping her gaze to cover the blush creeping up her neck, she fumbled for her own cup and saucer. Not knowing what she was doing but needing to do something, she dropped three lumps of sugar into her tea.

Watching the brown sugar sink into the brown tea, she shook her head. She hated sweet tea. One lump was her limit. Grasping a lemon slice, she wrung it dry, hoping to offset the sugar.

She was playing with fire. The thought blazed its way through her mind. If his mere touch affected her so, how could she hope to vanquish him? Wouldn't she, like his other conquests, be the one to be vanquished? For the first time in her life, she felt unsure of herself.

Taking a sip of the tea, she grimaced. Her confusion had produced a syrupy concoction resembling the hot lemonade her mother gave her when she had a sore throat. Holding her breath, she gulped down the remainder and started over with a fresh cup, taking just one lump this time.

The deep bass of his voice broke the silence. "One lump or three, which is it? I didn't think anyone drank tea with three lumps. Might as well have chocolate."

"It's all the rage, sweet tea is. Haven't you heard?" she inquired, her voice as syrupy as the tea he denigrated. Her words were flippant, but inwardly she cringed.

Placing her cup and saucer on the table, she clenched her hands into fists and hid them in the folds of her skirts. It took all of her self-control to not grit her teeth, too. Amazed that he had noticed her mistake and too quick correction, she promised herself to be more careful in the future. He was more observant than she gave him credit for. Most Don Juan types were too self-absorbed to notice the actions of mere mortals.

"You don't let fashion lead you, do you, Sarah? You reverted to the tea you like, and you chose a most unfashionable outing. I think you have a mind of your own and follow the dictates of your own conscience. I like that quality. It's refreshing."

His compliment surprised her. Most men didn't like strong-minded women. Her father was an exception. He adored his wife's levelheaded strength, and he encouraged his daughter to form her own opinions, too. That someone like Gilberto would admire her independent mind was unusual. And somewhat suspect, she decided.

Murmuring her thanks for his kind words, she studied his face for signs of duplicity. If he was as good as she thought he was at charming women, wouldn't he be adept at complimenting them? The usual compliments hadn't worked on her at the ball, she remembered. As quick as he was, wouldn't he have sensed that and changed his tactics?

She couldn't find a trace of guile in his face. In fact, he appeared to be wholeheartedly enjoying the food. He hadn't lied when he said he was hungry. She watched as he devoured three meat pasties, several slices of cheese on wafers, a handful of sandwiches, and two slices of cake.

When he reached for an apple to top off his repast, she couldn't help but remark, "I'm glad you like the refreshments."

Smiling at her, he took a bite of the apple and then offered it, saying, "Care to join me?"

Images of the original sin from the Bible flashed through her mind, played in reverse. This time, it was the man offering the forbidden fruit. As quickly as the errant thought came, she pushed it away, silently chiding herself for her fancifulness.

"No, thank you. I'm not hungry."

"A pity. You must give my compliments to your cook. It was delicious." He wiped his mouth with a linen napkin and requested, "Could I have some more coffee?"

"Certainly." She took his cup from the table, eager to avoid touching his hand again.

He forestalled her effort by taking her hand in his. "You don't really believe I'm a Don Juan, do you? Other than my ungentlemanly enjoyment of your good food, I hope I've proved I'm parlor trained."

This time, the flush started at the tips of her toes and worked its way up. Snatching her hand from his, she silently cursed the telltale blush she knew must grace her cheeks.

"I would expect a Don Juan to be, as you put it, 'parlor trained.' Your battlefield must be ballrooms and parlors and—"

"If you believe that, why did you agree to go out with me?"

"Because you're a challenge."

Even as the words popped from her mouth, she knew she had made a tactical error. It was the first completely truthful statement she had uttered that afternoon.

And it was too revealing, too revealing by far.

When Sarah visited her, Diana voiced her fears about the man who had tried to abduct her—the man who was her father's murderer. Asking for her best friend's advice, she couldn't decide whether to tell her mother and alarm her or keep quiet, hoping for the best.

Sarah listened carefully and then offered, "Why don't I explain your situation to my mother and have her caution Elizabeth? My mother has a way with words. She's not nearly so blunt as I am."

"What do you mean, Sarah?"

"What I meant is, my mother could warn Elizabeth about how dangerous México City is, without admitting the specific danger you're in."

"Do you think that will work?"

"I think it's your only choice, until you decide what you're going to do about the formula. If you tell your mother now, I'm afraid she'll force you to decide before you're ready."

"Would that be so bad?"

Sarah's gaze sought her best friend's face. Their eyes met and held. "You need time to get over your father's death, Diana. You and he were very close."

"You know me so well." Diana shook her head. "You're

telling me I should reconcile myself to selling to Seguín, aren't you?"

"I don't see any other solution, unless you get a loan from my father and have him help you sell the formula in the States. You said you had considered that."

"Yes, and discarded the idea." Diana pulled away from her and wiped her eyes with a handkerchief. "According to your father, that could take months, and nothing is ever certain in business. I just can't accept—"

"We're going over the same ground, Diana. I understand your reservations, and I sympathize. Only you can make the decision. I'll have my mother talk to Elizabeth. When you make your decision, you can tell her everything. In the meantime, we won't allow any harm to come to either of you."

Gazing at Sarah's earnest face, she realized how lucky she was to have Sarah as a best friend. But as lucky as she was in the choice of her friends, the rest of her life was a mess. And Sarah had just reiterated what she didn't want to hear: the burden lay squarely on her shoulders.

"Damn Seguín Torres and his hideous stepfather, anyway," Sarah declared vehemently.

Not surprised by her friend's use of profanity, she knew Sarah was more worldly than she, having lived in Europe. Diana, on the other hand, raised with strict Southern propriety, would have never dreamed of using such a word.

"I've waited years to see you again, and we can't enjoy each other with this cloud hanging over us," Sarah continued, frowning. "You go to one ball and look what happens. Not to mention, your fath—" She stopped herself and bit her lip. "What's more, you need to leave México as soon as possible. Selfishly, I don't want you to go, but I know you must."

"I don't want to leave you, either. I do get homesick sometimes," she admitted. "Then I think how dull it would be without you, and I wish things were different."

Pausing, she couldn't pass up the opportunity to tease her friend. "I'm surprised you would condemn Don Carlos Aguirre. After all, you spent most of yesterday afternoon with his son."

Sarah's eyes widened, and she opened her mouth. After a moment, she shut it again and grinned, conceding, "Yes, I did. How did you know?"

"Mother told me. Have you learned anything useful about Seguín? Anything that would help?"

"No, I haven't had time. I'm trying to lay my traps carefully."

"What do you mean?"

"Gilberto Aguirre isn't your garden variety suitor."

"I had already figured that out," she replied, glancing at the mounds of roses in her room, overflow bouquets from Sarah. "Does he own a flower shop, as well?" She couldn't keep from smiling at her own joke.

"Please, don't," Sarah gasped. She wrapped her arms around her waist, and laughter bubbled forth. Infected, Diana joined in.

When their giggles finally died away, Diana asked, "Seriously, what do you mean by 'laying traps'."

"Did you get a look at *Señor* Aguirre?"

"Briefly, when he was dancing with you. I noticed he looked familiar, and later, I understood why. He reminded me of Seguín."

"What did you think, other than he resembled Seguín?"

"He's very handsome. Is that what you mean?"

"He's very handsome," Sarah repeated, adding, "and he knows it, too. The man is a self-styled Don Juan. Women literally hang all over him." Her voice was laced with disgust.

"So?"

"I can't stand his type. He's an affront to womanhood. I want to take him down a notch or two."

"Thus, your traps?"

Sarah's lips quirked into a sly smile. She nodded. "I intend to win his affections and throw him over, but not before I 'pump' him for information about your Seguín."

"My Seguín? Hardly *my* Seguín. He's not *my* anything," she corrected too quickly.

Sarah's eyes narrowed. Diana sucked in her breath. Had she "protested too much?" Realizing her friend was already onto her, she felt an overwhelming urge to confide everything. Everything—including the way Seguín made her feel when he touched her—but not before she heard more about Gilberto.

"I think you've already won his affections. Just look at this rose garden, and I haven't seen your room yet. It's outrageous and decadent."

"Pah." Sarah dismissed the roses with a wave of her slender fingers. "Conquest tactics, that's all the flowers are. Gilberto knows his business."

"And his business is seducing women?"

"It would appear so."

"Are you sure you know what you're doing? Don't do it for my sake, please. If you can't stand the man, don't have anything to do with him. It's not worth it."

"It's not just for you, Diana. I *want* to do it. It's the challenge. He's an intriguing man, although it's too bad he knows it. I enjoy crossing swords with him." Her eyes shone. "I'm going riding with him this afternoon."

There was more here than Sarah cared to admit, Diana surmised, more than a mere challenge. Could Sarah be falling in love with Gilberto and not realizing it? Diana could empathize with her. Her own feelings for Seguín were far from clear.

A knock on the door interrupted her thoughts, and she called out, "Come in."

The door opened and Mary sailed into the room. "How are you doing, Diana? I promised your mother I would look in on you. Elizabeth is resting." Her gaze fell on

Sarah. "I see my daughter is keeping you company, but I don't want you to overdo. You must rest, too."

"I feel fine," she demurred. "Sarah and I haven't talked in days. I was too sedated."

"I know, dear," Mary patted her shoulder. "But I promised your mother you would rest before luncheon. And I need Sarah's help. Could I borrow her for a while? Sam got loose again, and Sarah is the only one who can coax him from the trees."

She started up, worried about Sam. The sudden movement sent a shooting pain through her right side. She subsided against the pillows with a groan.

Mary clucked her tongue, chiding, "You shouldn't make any sudden movements, Diana. Remember what the doctor said?" Bending down, she pecked her on the cheek. "You see, you do need your rest." Turning to her daughter, she asked, "Sarah, do you think you can catch him?"

"I'll try."

"He won't fly away, will he?" Diana inquired.

The Yorks' patio wouldn't be the same without Sam. The doctor had promised her that she could visit the patio for some fresh air in a week or so. It was one of the few things she had to look forward to, and Sam's antics would enliven her outing.

"No, dear, don't worry." Mary patted her shoulder again. "Sam's wings have been clipped. He can't fly far. It's not Sam we're worried about. It's his annoying habit of dropping things on people's heads when he's loose. It's not safe to go on the patio with Sam lurking in the trees."

New laughter bubbled in Diana's throat. She glanced at Sarah and caught her friend gulping hard, her mouth held tightly. She realized Sarah was suppressing a giggle, thinking about Sam, the mad bombardier.

"I'm glad his wings are clipped. I miss Sam."

"But first, you must rest and get stronger," Mary urged.

"Carmen will bring your lunch in an hour. Doze until then."

"Yes, ma'am."

"Sarah, are you coming?"

"Yes, Mother," Sarah acquiesced, but behind her mother's back she made a face. Leaning down, she placed a sisterly kiss on Diana's forehead and whispered, "We'll talk more later."

Seven

"Damn you, Sam, why won't you come down? I've been patient, but now I'm late for an appointment." Sarah shook her fist. "Blasted bird." Her voice, although full of frustration, wasn't loud, but it was loud enough for Gilberto to hear. Her profanity didn't shock or surprise him. He remembered her spirited response on the balcony at the ball.

Bemused, he watched her strain, trying to grab the parrot. Her split riding skirt hugged her bottom like a second skin. It was a nice bottom, he decided, one of the nicest ones he had ever seen, and he considered himself an authority.

His gaze traveled upward, skimming her form, approving of her rounded hips and slender waist. He leaned against the doorway, happy beyond his wildest dreams, content to watch her graceful, if agitated, movements.

She must have sensed his presence because she pivoted abruptly on the ladder and faced him. Her sudden movement upset its balance, and it swayed precariously. Acting on instinct, he started forward, his arms outstretched. For one terrifying moment, she clung to the ladder's lurching surface, alarm suffusing her features.

Just as the ladder slid sideways, he caught her in his arms. She grabbed his shoulders and twined her arms around his neck. Her tight hold reminded him of their dance at the ball. She had held him that way then, as if she never wanted to let go. He savored the moment, realizing she wasn't thinking, only reacting.

Wishing they could return to that first time, before she had decided he was a Don Juan, he wondered if she would ever trust him. To give her credit, it *was* true he had desired many women. Women had filled an empty place in his life, making him feel, if only for brief moments, wanted.

They all paled before the figure in his arms. He didn't desire just *any* woman. He desired Sarah York.

Gazing down at her closed eyes, with her eyelashes laying like filigreed lace against the porcelain perfection of her face, he felt a surge of protectiveness flood him. He could cradle her in his arms forever, watching the play of sunlight on her toffee-brown hair, inhaling the lavender scent of her.

Her eyes flew open, their sky blue depths searching his face. As if awakening from a dream, she struggled in his arms, pushing against his chest with open palms and demanding, "*Señor* Aguirre, put me down."

Obediently, he lowered her to the ground. As if he possessed a contagious disease, she backed away until the ledge of the fountain stopped her retreat.

"You're early," she blurted.

"I told you I was eager."

Ignoring his provocative words, she explained, "I'm trying to catch Sam. He's a parrot, you know."

Suppressing a smile, he lifted his head and located the bird in the branches of a mimosa tree. Preening his feathers with his curved beak, Sam didn't appear to have a care in the world.

"Want me to help?" he asked.

"Would you?"

"Not until you thank me for catching you." He grinned and wagged his finger at her. "Where are your manners, *Señorita* York?"

The pink flush suffusing her flawless complexion was

much more becoming than the spots of artificial rouge she used, he decided, watching the evidence of his remark find its target.

Turning her back to him, she raised her head and shaded her eyes with her hand, appearing intent on finding the elusive bird. As if an afterthought, she offered, "Thank you, Gilberto. You saved me from a nasty fall."

"My pleasure."

"What would you suggest?"

Her words were innocent, he knew, but the other meaning leapt into his mind. His groin tightened in response. Struggling for self-control, he inquired, "To catch Sam?"

"Yes, do you have any suggestions?"

"Look at me when you talk to me." The sound of his voice was harsh, even to his own ears. He hadn't meant to demand her attention, to admit his need, but it was too late.

She turned to face him. Azure lightning blazed from her eyes. With her shoulders thrown back, and her chin pointed at the sky, her posture shouted a challenge.

"As Your Highness wishes." Scorn sharpened her words. "I was trying to keep my eye on Sam."

"I'm sorry," he found himself saying, against his better judgment. Hastening to cover his momentary lapse, he changed the subject, returning to the pursuit of the parrot. "Have you tried food to lure him down?"

"I tried his favorite fruit, banana, before lunch. He ignored me."

"Do you have a—"

Something hit his head with a loud smack. A streak of blue flashed by. He raised his hand and massaged the spot. "What the—?"

For one suspended moment, she looked as stunned as he felt. Their eyes held. And then she doubled over, holding her middle and shrieking like a banshee.

Chagrined, he crossed his arms and stared at her, wanting to shame her for her unladylike reaction. She must have noticed his displeasure, because she covered her mouth with her hand, and her sapphire eyes held an amused but pleading note.

Uncrossing his arms, he rubbed the tender spot on his head again. Her laughter had subsided to giggles, but her bright blue eyes crinkled with mirth. He couldn't resist her. The silliness of the situation struck him. He grinned, trying to restrain the fizz of hilarity bubbling through him. She hiccupped, and another giggle escaped. Not able to stop himself any longer, he laughed openly.

She joined him. He didn't know who closed the distance between them. It might have been he. He hoped it was Sarah. They fell into each other's arms and laughed until their sides ached.

It was definitely Sarah who recovered and pulled away, observing, "Diana was right. Sam is a mad bombardier. That's why we must catch him."

"Who's Diana?"

"My best friend." She smoothed back her hair. "Your half-brother is Seguín Torres?"

Surprised by the question that seemed to come from nowhere, he admitted, "Yes."

"Are you close?"

"What are you getting at, Sarah? I thought you wanted to catch Sam."

"I do. I was just wondering."

What had prompted her inquiries? What did Seguín have to do with catching the parrot? Not wanting to spoil their newfound closeness, he decided to humor her.

"Seguín was away at school while I was growing up. We aren't close."

Remembering the scandal when his half-brother returned home, he frowned. It was a sore point with him, an unresolved issue. He wished his brother hadn't left. He wished he could have helped him. When he tried to tell

LOVE ME ONLY 119

his mother what he knew, she was already too sick to do anything.

"So, you and your brother have lived apart?"

"Mostly," he admitted, "but he came home for a short time. Then our mother died, and he went away." Even after all these years, he found it difficult to talk about. "I wanted to know Seguín better, but I didn't have the chance." Pausing, he searched his memory. "I remember him playing with me when I was very young. He was patient." Gilberto closed his eyes, as if remembering something from a long time ago. "And he was very strong. I remember that. He used to take me in his arms and swing me over his head, telling me to fly like a bird."

He opened his eyes. Sarah's gaze captured his, her eyes shimmering with compassion. He didn't want her pity. That hadn't been his objective. She had asked about his half-brother, and he had tried to explain their relationship to the best of his ability. That was all.

But it wasn't all, he admitted to himself. He didn't know why she had questioned him about Seguín. It probably had something to do with her best friend . . . Diana. It wasn't her reason that mattered. What mattered was that he wanted to open himself to her, to explain his feelings and garner her understanding.

He had spent most of his life hiding his feelings from other people, and from himself. Burying himself in the pursuit of women, he had longed for his mother. Pathetic as that sounded, it was the truth. His mother had died when he needed her the most. Sometimes, in his blackest moments, he blamed Seguín. After all, hadn't she gotten sicker when she learned about the scandal?

And then he remembered the truth he had discovered as a child. The truth no one wanted to hear. The truth about his father, which he didn't want to believe, either.

Shaking himself, he pushed the bad memories aside.

"Are we going riding, or do we need to catch the 'mad bombardier' first?"

"We need to catch Sam."

"Do you have a net or piece of cloth? Maybe we could corner him."

"Pretty lady, pretty lady," came the falsetto shriek from nearby.

Turning in unison, they spied the bird perched on a camellia bush, two meters away.

"I think he's tired," she observed.

"I believe you're right."

They approached the bird together. Sarah went left, and he went right. When they reached the camellia bush, Sam submitted readily, hopping onto Sarah's outstretched arm.

Coaxing the parrot with soothing words while she grasped him behind his wings, she took him to his perch and tethered him. Gilberto followed her, keeping in the background, admiring her expertise with the bird.

Once Sam was secured, she declared triumphantly, "Let's go riding."

Pivoting quickly on the balls of her feet, she ran into his arms. He hadn't meant to move so close behind her, or had he? He told himself he wanted to be nearby, in case Sam tried to get away. But that wasn't the truth. The truth was he wanted her in his arms.

Having accomplished his goal, he felt his self-control snap. From the very first moment at the ball, he had dreamed of kissing her. Unable to withstand the temptation any longer, he lowered his mouth to hers.

Her lips were warm and lush. For a moment, she held back, her arms limp at her sides. Sensing her distrust and wanting to overcome it, he moved slowly, melding his lips against hers, exploring the sensitive corners of her mouth with tongue tip.

Tentatively at first, her arms came up, and then they encircled his neck, pulling him closer. When she ran her fingers through his hair, he groaned, deep in the back of his throat. Encouraged, he became bolder, probing gently with his tongue against the tender seam of her mouth.

Sighing and leaning against him, she opened her lips, accepting his intimate invasion. She tasted of honey and lemon, sweet, then tart. *So like Sarah*, he thought, his mind a blank page, rewriting history.

Twining his tongue with hers, he savored the soft, nubby velvet feel of her. At first, slow and aching, they explored. But with each touch, each stroke, their joining escalated, becoming feverish. Greedily, they swallowed each other, craving more.

Never before had a woman excited him so much. Never before had he wanted a woman with such complete abandon. And never before had he dreamed about . . . forever.

As if from far away, a sound intruded—a rude, barking sound. Immersed in kissing Sarah, he dismissed it, thinking the parrot was making a fuss. The sound returned, encroaching on their private moment, demanding attention.

Breaking off their kiss, she retreated a step, blushing crimson. He reached for her, but she backed away again, shaking her head and cutting her eyes to the entrance of the patio.

Recovering his senses, he turned and followed her gaze.

Carmen stood at the door to the patio. "*Señorita* Sarah, *Señorita* Sarah, your mother wishes to speak with you."

Seguín grabbed Juan Martínez and gave the man a bone-crushing hug. He was glad to see his old friend and partner. He had been away from Juan and his mining operations for too long.

Stepping back and studying the older man, he realized that Juan never seemed to age. To Seguín, he looked the same as he had when he befriended him years before. The

only change was a few more strands of silver in his friend's
grizzled hair and thick beard. The broad features were the
same, the lines etched around his mouth no deeper. And
Juan hadn't run to fat, either. He still carried his powerful,
short frame proudly.

Smiling, Seguín slapped him on the back. "It's good to
be here, *amigo*. How's the mine? I would have come sooner,
but—"

"*Mi hijo*," Juan interrupted, "business later. Sit. I will
fetch my best bottle of *tequila*. We will drink a little, talk a
little. The mine, she's not going anywhere." He flashed a
grin, his teeth largely obscured by the lush growth of his
beard.

Juan busied himself by clearing a spot on the dusty table
that served as his desk. The table contained a jumble of
items associated with silver mining: ledgers, weights, bottles
of acids, pouches of ore samples, dishes of salts, vials of
mercury, and bars of silver lay scattered across its surface.

As he seated himself at the corner Juan had cleared, his
gaze fell on the silver bars, recently poured. Reaching
across the table, he grasped them and hefted them in his
hands. Taking a magnifying glass from the clutter on the
desk, he studied them closely. Disheartened by what he
saw, he realized that little, if any, progress had been made.

His partner returned with a bottle, two-thirds full of an
amber liquid, two shot glasses, and some lime slices. Placing the glasses on the table, he uncorked the bottle and
poured three fingers into each glass. He put the bowl of
limes between them and sat down.

Seguín savored the fiery liquor in silence, chasing each
sip by sucking the acidic juice of the limes. Juan drained
his shot and refilled both their glasses.

Nodding toward the bars of silver, Juan observed, "No
luck, *mi hijo*. Luis has tried his best, but he's unable to
duplicate *Señor* McFarland's process."

"I'm not surprised."

Luis, a competent but unimaginative chemist, had been trying since Jamie's death to unlock the secret of the formula. Seguín had sent a message to Juan to set Luis on the task, using the limited information Jamie had told him about the process.

He hadn't expected Luis to succeed, but after his first acrimonious encounter with Diana, he needed to try something. Even if they succeeded, he would pay her for the formula. It was the honorable thing to do. If she remained stubborn and refused his offer, he hoped to salvage something by working on his own.

Since the night he rescued her, his thoughts had veered from obtaining the formula to . . . Diana. He couldn't erase her from his mind. Over and over, he remembered her sweet lips, the softness of her skin, the smell of lilac in her glorious, golden hair. At night he woke, covered with sweat, tossing and turning in his bed. Feeling as if he were going mad, he decided to pay a visit to the mines, hoping he could erase her from his thoughts.

"It doesn't matter, Juan. I believe I'll own *Señor* McFarland's process in a few weeks."

Something told him Diana would be willing to sell now, but he almost dreaded seeing her. He had sent her a note asking after her health, and then left town. He wanted to see her and he needed to talk to her, but at the same time, he dreaded facing her.

Juan nodded and saluted him with his drink. "Congratulations *mi hijo*. I know how much the process means to you. And not a moment too soon, either. I hear rumors of war coming. If we are to drive Don Carlos out of business, we must do so before the war." He shrugged. "After that, who knows what will happen?"

He returned the salute and belted down his *tequila*. With the war coming, Diana and her mother were at even greater risk. She must leave México as soon as possible, but every time he thought about her leaving, his insides knotted. He was afraid of seeing her, but even more afraid of never seeing her again. Where would this craziness end?

"What about the other part of my message? Have you found out anything?"

Cocking one bristly eyebrow at him, his partner declared, "None of your men betrayed you, Seguín. I am certain. The threat came from without, not from within." The older man leaned forward and tapped his temple with a stubby index finger, admonishing, "Think, Seguín, think. Other than your stepfather, who would want to see you ruined, brought low?"

Dropping his hand and shifting back in his chair, he advised, "You must always keep your enemies in the forefront of your mind, *mi hijo*. It is when you least expect them that they attack."

Pausing, Juan raised his glass and drank down the entire contents. He brought a lime slice to his lips and sucked it down to the peel. His eyes watered from the *tequila*.

Seguín waited patiently, not bothering to answer Juan's rhetorical question. It was the older man's way—slow, deliberate, sometimes even circuitous, he never lost sight of his ultimate goal.

Dashing the tears from his eyes with the back of his hand, Juan spat out, "Ignacio Hernández. The viper your stepfather took in. The brother of the girl who ruined your life with her lies. He is the one. He murdered *Señor* McFarland."

Suddenly, it all made sense. Ignacio, the sullen orphan boy, whose weapon of choice was a knife—who, when he was barely fifteen, sustained a jagged scar on the right side of his face in a vicious fight with a man much older and larger. Before he and his sister, Esmeralda, came to the rancho to live, they had been raised by their grandmother, an Indian sorceress, trained in Indian cunning. It was no wonder his men had trouble capturing him.

And he *was* an enemy, too, as Juan had pointed out. Ignacio had never believed his innocence with regard to

Esmeralda. While he was still living at home, he had half-expected Ignacio to stab him to death in his sleep.

It all fit, and it also explained the tenacity of Jamie's murderer, something that had bothered him for weeks. No hired thug working for money would have been so persevering. But Ignacio would persevere, until he fulfilled Don Carlos's bidding and ruined him.

Seguín's blood boiled and roared in his ears. An innocent man was dead because of an old hatred. If Ignacio wanted revenge, why hadn't he faced him, man to man, and exacted his vengeance, instead of involving innocent people? Because that wasn't Ignacio's way, he remembered. Ignacio had always been furtive, sneaking about the rancho, intent upon his own secret missions.

Lashed by frustration and unable to contain his fury, he leapt to his feet and paced the small room. "I don't know how you found out, Juan. I should have suspected Ignacio before, but it's been years—"

Stopping himself, he ran his hand in agitation through his hair. "That's no excuse. I should have been on my guard against all my enemies. You're right, *mi amigo*."

"Do not whip yourself, *mi hijo*. You cannot undo the past, only safeguard the future. *Señor* McFarland's death was ordained by God."

Shaking his head, he muttered, "I wish I could accept that, but I feel Jamie's blood on my hands." Halting his pacing, he faced the older man. "And what about Jamie's family? Ignacio tried to abduct his daughter. She's abed with broken ribs from his 'gentle handling.' The nightmare continues."

"Find him and kill him. Don Carlos will be hard pressed to replace him."

"You know our men are trying. It's not that easy."

"Set a trap."

He considered the idea, turning it over in his mind. It was a good idea. Unfortunately, he didn't need to ask who the bait would be . . . Diana. Sighing to himself, he didn't think he could bring himself to involve her again. Better to get her out of the country and then deal with Ignacio.

"One thing bothers me. How did Don Carlos or Ignacio find out about the formula and its value? Jamie didn't talk, did he?"

"Yes, in a way, *Señor* McFarland did talk. But so did you."

"What?" His voice was sharp. As much as he loved Juan, this entire situation exasperated and infuriated him, to say nothing about his concern for Diana. He was through waiting for his old friend to get to the point.

"The *posada*, Seguín. Did you and *Señor* McFarland discuss the formula at the *posada*?"

A vision of the dark and dusty *sala* rose in his mind. It was where he and Jamie had discussed their partnership and the new process.

"Is *Señor* Gutiérrez on my stepfather's payroll? I could have sworn he was innocent of—"

"Not Gutiérrez. It was the chambermaid, Maria Hernández—a cousin of Ignacio's. According to my sources, Ignacio has been watching you for a long time. It was an unfortunate coincidence that Ignacio's cousin worked at *Señor* McFarland's *posada*. Unfortunate, indeed." Pausing, Juan combed his fingers through his beard. "She must have overheard you talking. Don Carlos understood the significance, and sent Ignacios after the formula. I don't think they planned to kill *Señor* McFarland, just to steal the formula. It was the will of God," he repeated.

Juan's fatalistic outlook wasn't news to Seguín. His partner had always been like that. It didn't keep the older man from fulfilling his duties to the best of his abilities, but it did keep him from worrying about matters he couldn't control. Seguín wished he could be more like Juan.

"I shouldn't have spoken with Jamie there. But I got careless because I was in a hurry to come to the mines. Remember when we had the cave-in?"

His partner nodded.

"Always before, I was careful to talk where no one could overhear us, like in the park. One slip and—"

"Your enemies take advantage," Juan finished for him. "It is an old story, *mi hijo*. Wars have been won by such errors. But no one is perfect, either. No one can see into the future."

"I guess not," he replied, not convinced. As if more information would take the sting from his error, he asked, "How did you uncover this?"

"I have eyes and ears everywhere . . . and old favors outstanding. It took me time to put the pieces together, but it was well worth the effort, wouldn't you say?"

"*Sí,* I can't thank you enough. I owe you one."

"You owe me nothing but your friendship and respect."

Juan leaned back in his chair and took another sip of *tequila.* His eyes narrowed, considering Seguín thoughtfully. "This daughter of *Señor* McFarland, is she beautiful?"

"I hadn't noticed." He lowered his gaze, hating to lie to Juan. He trusted him with his life, but sometimes his partner overstepped the bounds.

Along with his fatalistic tendencies, Juan was an incurable romantic, married to the same woman for thirty-some years. They had twelve children and twenty-three grandchildren, at last count. His partner definitely believed in the institution of marriage, and he had been after him to get married for years, but marriage was out of the question. He didn't trust women, not after what his mother had done.

"She's a thorn in my side, is what she is," he muttered darkly.

"Sit and drink," Juan thumped the table. "Between your pacing and my drinking, I'm getting dizzy."

Obeying, he sank into his chair and lifted the bottle, filling his glass to the rim. Downing the liquid fire, he devoured most of a lime, too. Although he seldom drank, he knew liquor could bring forgetfulness. And he desperately needed to forget the way Diana's arms had clung to him, the softness of her breasts, the tiny moans she made in the back of her throat. . . .

"I think this thorn is also a rose, no?" His partner slurred the words, but his meaning was clear. "I hear it in your voice *mi hijo*. You can't fool old Juan. You've never given so much as—" He tried to snap his fingers and missed, grinning at his failure. "As . . . as a fig for a woman. But this one is different, no?"

Seguín glanced at the bottle; it was almost empty. He couldn't help but notice that Juan's eyes had glazed over. Night had fallen outside the rude shack that served as their mining office. He would inspect the mines tomorrow, and oversee the production of the silver. Juan would nurse his hangover and forget tonight had happened. Or would he?

Sighing, he realized it was no use; drunk or sober, Juan knew him too well. Dropping his head into his hands, he admitted, *"Sí,* she is different."

Diana threw the embroidery hoop across the room. She had never cared for needlework, anyway. It was just another diversion to make her forget the slow march of time. Removing her spectacles and placing them on the bedside table, she rubbed the bridge of her nose and sighed.

She had passed four long and dreary weeks of confinement. She was almost at her wit's end. Having read every book of interest in the house, whether in Spanish or English, she had no idea how she would fill the last week.

Reaching underneath her pillow, she pulled the note from its hiding place and smoothed it out. It was a simple note, short and to the point, wishing her a speedy recovery and promising a visit. It was signed by Seguín Torres—no closing, just the name. Reading it for the hundredth time, she could detect no hidden message, no double meanings.

How could a man who had intimately touched her send such an impersonal note?

There was a knock on her door, but before she could respond Sarah swept in, dressed in her evening clothes. She wore a blue silk moire gown, the shade exactly matching the color of her eyes. Her light brown hair, braided into a thick coronet on top of her head, was woven throughout with tiny blue ribbons.

Begrudgingly, Diana had to admit she looked lovely, and tonight there was a special sparkle to her eyes, a luminosity transcending her mere features. Morosely, she realized her friend's obvious joy made her own misery more complete.

"To what do I owe this visit, Your Majesty?" She couldn't keep the sarcasm from her voice.

"A bit testy tonight, are we?"

"I don't think so, not considering how you've neglected me."

Perching on the edge of the bed, her voluminous petticoats rustling like leaves scurrying before the wind, Sarah grasped her hands and murmured, "Forgive me."

"I don't know why I should," she replied, still pouting. "I never see you. In the morning you're busy with your toilette, in the afternoon it's riding with Gilberto, and you go out with him every night. Occasionally, it would be nice if we could spend some time together."

"What about the other night? The night I stayed in and we played chess?"

"Sarah, that was eight nights ago!"

Releasing her hands, Sarah covered her face. Her voice trembled with penitence. "I didn't realize the time passing. I've been horrible and selfish. You have a right to be angry with me."

"It doesn't matter." A dark depression settled over Diana.

"But it does. I want—"

"Have you learned anything about Seguín from Gilberto? Have you conquered the famous Don Juan yet?

When does he get vanquished, as you put it? I would think you would have trapped him by now." She knew the tone of her voice was sarcastic, but she couldn't help herself. It was as if her best friend had betrayed her, having so much fun going out.

Rising, Sarah pointed her chin skyward, her mouth pressed into a thin line. "I can see this conversation is going nowhere. I'll come later when you're feeling better."

"I feel fine, Sarah. And it won't hurt to keep Gilberto waiting a few minutes. It might even pique his interest further." Purposely softening her voice, she asked, "You're not going to answer any of my questions?"

She ticked the questions off, one by one on her gloved fingers. "Well, let's see. First, you asked about Seguín. I talked to Gilberto about his half-brother, but he wasn't able to tell me much. They lived apart most of their lives, what with Seguín away at school and then turned out of the household."

"I see."

"As for Gilberto, I think he's totally infatuated with me," she said with a small, triumphant smile. "I can vanquish him anytime I want."

"But you won't."

"How do you know that?"

"I can see it in your face. You're gloriously happy."

"Why wouldn't I be? He's been the perfect gentleman. Oh, he's stolen a kiss or two, but that's not so unusual." She stopped, hesitating, as if she had said too much.

Diana's ears pricked up, and she hoped Sarah would continue. This was what she had been waiting for, an opportunity to talk with her best friend about men and courting, subjects she didn't dare broach with her mother. Sarah was experienced in such matters, and she hoped her friend could shed light on Seguín's actions.

"He's very charming and witty," Sarah continued, "not like most men who talk endlessly about themselves."

"What about his Lothario tendencies? Has his eye roved?"

"No, not once. At first, I wouldn't go in public with him because I didn't want to be humiliated if he encouraged other women. But he proved my fears to be groundless. In fact, he *discourages* old friends, especially if they're women, from speaking with us."

"He sounds too good to be true. Be sure you don't fall into your own trap."

Sarah's face colored immediately, and Diana realized her sally had hit the mark. Her best friend was in love, and she didn't even know it—or at least, she didn't want to admit it.

Flustered and obviously wanting to change the subject, Sarah pointed to the crumpled note, asking, "What's that?"

"A note from Seguín."

"Have you made your decision yet?"

"I think so. Your father gave me some more ammunition." But it wasn't the kind of ammunition she wanted. It merely centered on business, and what a partnership should be worth.

"That's good."

Detecting a polite but impatient note in her friend's voice, she decided to release her. "You'd better go. It's getting late."

Leaning down, Sarah brushed her lips across her forehead, promising, "Tomorrow. We'll talk tomorrow night. I'll stay in, and we'll gossip to our hearts content."

"I'll look forward to it."

Watching Sarah cross the room, she wondered if she would be able to talk openly with her best friend. How could Sarah help her sort her muddled feelings when her friend didn't understand or accept her own?

Eight

Sarah pressed her fists against her temples, willing her throbbing headache to go away. Stretched flat on her bed with the room darkened, she had done everything to ease the pain, even taking some of her mother's headache powders. Unfortunately, nothing had worked.

Sighing to herself, she attributed her headache to the late nights she had been keeping with Gilberto. Even after he brought her home she found it hard to sleep, feeling restless and strangely exhilarated at the same time. Customarily an early riser, she found sleeping late difficult.

A rap sounded at her door, and with a sinking heart she knew who it would be. Her expectation was confirmed when Carmen opened the door and announced Gilberto's arrival.

She had been trying to banish the headache so she could go riding with him. Knowing she would be poor company, feeling as bad as she did, she told Carmen to say she wasn't feeling well.

Bobbing her head, the maid withdrew. With the closing of the door, she remembered she wouldn't be seeing him tonight, either, because she had promised Diana. A feeling of desolation swept her. It was ridiculous, and she hated to admit it, but twenty-four hours without Gilberto seemed like a life sentence.

Tossing and turning on the bed, her desolation turned

to desperation, heightening her restlessness. Sitting up in bed with a start, she realized she hadn't explained to Carmen that she would be unavailable tonight, too. It didn't seem fair to keep him dangling, to have him come around this evening just to be turned away again.

Rationalizing her sudden change of heart, she decided it wouldn't hurt to see him for a few minutes and explain the situation. After all, Carmen wasn't exactly the most tactful of servants, and she didn't want him to get the wrong impression.

Swinging her legs over the side of the bed, she winced from the sudden movement. She had the granddaddy of all headaches. Ignoring the pain in pursuit of her mission, she forced her wobbly legs to move swiftly, descending the stairs to the foyer in a gallop, hoping to intercept him before he left.

When she reached the south parlor she was surprised to hear voices from within. She had expected to run into him on his way out, not find him still in the parlor. Who could he be talking to? Her father was at his work. Her mother and Elizabeth had gone to the *modista* to have new gowns fitted.

Noticing that the door stood slightly ajar, she strained to see inside, but the opening was too small. Placing her hand on the doorknob, she had started to enter when she heard the distinct male rumble of his voice. A perverse kind of curiosity stayed her hand. She didn't push the door open. Instead, she pressed against the wall and listened.

"You're very lovely, Carmen, and I'm flattered by your interest, but I don't think—"

"I can make you very happy, *señor*, give you much pleasure," Carmen's sultry voice interrupted. "You don't want that cold, *Norté Americaño* bit—"

"You forget yourself, Carmen," he stopped her, his voice harsh with warning. "She's your employer, and you owe her respect."

"*Lo siento.* I apologize." The words were proper, but the voice pouted. "You are much man, *señor,* and need a willing woman in your bed. I wouldn't cost much, just a room and some clothes."

Rage poured through Sarah's veins, hot and molten, like lava. Clenching her fists, she dug her fingernails into the palms of her hands, trying to restrain the emotions overwhelming her. She wanted to lash out, to strike something, preferably . . . someone.

How could Carmen, her own maid, do such a thing? Proposition her—her what? He wasn't her fiancé. In reality, she had no hold on him, and *she* certainly wasn't going to sleep with him for the price of a cheap room and some rags.

Holding herself very still, she closed her eyes and concentrated on her breathing. With her breath coming in short, quick pants, and her heart thumping against her chest, she felt as if she had run a mile. When her breath returned to normal and the pace of her heart slowed, she tried to be objective about the situation. If Gilberto needed a mistress, why should she care?

Who was she fooling? She did *care!* The realization struck her like a lightning bolt. She wouldn't stand for him dallying with her maid.

"I don't need anyone in my bed." His reply penetrated Sarah's self-absorption.

His response surprised her. Half-expecting him to accept Carmen's offer, she realized he wasn't the Don Juan she had originally thought. And as she had told Diana, his conduct toward her, both private and public, had shown a rare devotion.

She had misjudged him miserably.

A thought wormed its way into her mind, a thrilling thought. He cared about her, too. She wasn't just another one of his conquests.

"I can't believe you don't want me, *señor.* Take a closer look . . . or perhaps a taste," Carmen's voice offered.

"I need to take my leave, and you should cover yourself," he declared firmly.

Having heard enough, she burst into the room. Startled, both Gilberto and Carmen stared at her as if she were a ghost. Carmen's hands flew to her naked breasts, and she frantically plucked at her blouse to cover herself.

Gilberto, his eyes wide and his mouth open in astonishment, sputtered, but no intelligible words came out. If she hadn't heard their previous conversation, she would have been hard-pressed to not think the worst.

As it was, she felt decidedly smug, knowing what had *really* transpired. If she hadn't cared for him so much, she might have been tempted to leave him dangling, making him think she suspected the worst. But the time for games was over. Completely trusting him for the first time, she wanted to throw herself into his arms and rain kisses on his handsome face, not add to his discomfort. And the female in her savored the triumph, too, knowing he had turned down a half-clad woman to remain loyal to her.

As for Carmen, she possessed no compunctions whatsoever. Turning to her maid, she declared, "You're fired. Be out of the house by sunset."

Carmen's pretty face registered shock, and then fury suffused her features, twisting them into an ugly mask. Raising her fist and shaking it, she shrieked, "Not so fast! I've seen you two together, stealing kisses. I don't think your parents would approve, *Señorita* York," her voice sneered. "My silence for my job," she negotiated.

"No!" Both Sarah and Gilberto responded in unison.

As they turned to each other, their gazes held and their determination solidified.

"Get out," Diana ordered.

"I'll go, but I won't go quietly," Carmen threatened, crossing the room and slamming the door.

For a few seconds, they stood still as statues, staring at the closed door. The silence grew oppressive. Unspoken thoughts simmered between them.

She waited for him to speak, suddenly ashamed she had eavesdropped at the door, unwilling to admit her distrust and jealousy.

"Nothing happened, Sarah," he blurted. "It wasn't what it seemed."

"I know," she replied and flew into his arms.

Not hesitating for a second, he folded her against his chest and rested his chin on her head. His voice was gruff. "I'm glad you understand. I didn't think you would—"

"Don't." She reached up and placed her fingers lightly against his lips, stopping his words.

There was no need for him to explain himself, and she didn't want to spoil the moment by admitting her earlier, jealous doubts. All that mattered was they had weathered the storm and were together.

His gaze found hers, his golden tiger's eyes burning with desire, promising a passion that made her shiver. Dipping his head, he buried his face in her hair, murmuring, "I love you, Sarah. *Por Dios*, I've never loved another."

Her heart swelled, hearing the words she had craved for so long, not even realizing she wanted them. Threading her fingers through his crisp curls, she whispered, "And I love you *mi amorcito*." She purposely used the term of endearment he had spoken that first night at the ball.

With his lips soft against her temple, she trembled. Nuzzling his neck, she traced lazy patterns with her tongue against his bare skin.

Groaning, he trailed feathery light kisses down her cheekbone and across her nose, settling on her mouth. His lips were firm and warm, tasting of his beloved coffee. Sighing her surrender, she opened to him, and he slipped his tongue inside her mouth.

She felt a wave of spiraling dizziness, a breathlessness of

indescribable pleasure. Her body went liquid, and her insides quivered. Clinging to him, she wished they could be even closer. Torrid visions played through her mind, visions of their naked bodies entwined.

Need pulsated through her, fired by the sensual touch of his tongue against hers. Throbbing with desire, she felt her need centered between her thighs, in that most private, female part of her. Feverish for him, she returned his kisses, their tongues dancing together, imitating their ultimate joining.

Breaking their kiss, his lips strayed downward, tracing a silken cord of desire across her trembling neck. Gently, his hands pulled back the fabric of her blouse, his fingers fumbling with the buttons.

An image of Carmen offering her naked breasts to him rose in her mind. The thought that he wanted *her,* wanted to taste her naked breasts instead, possessed her, thrilled her.

With his head bent, she buried her face in the crisp waves of his hair, inhaling the exotic scent of him, a mixture of spicy cologne and his own special musky essence.

His lips against her skin felt like warm velvet, brushing the tops of her breasts, setting them on fire, leaving them tingling with sultry promise. Her nipples hardened pleasurably, drawing into tight points, begging to be noticed, begging to be touched. His fingers strayed south, as if in response to her unspoken need, brushing her nipples through the silken covering of her camisole. The callouses on his fingertips, rubbing against the silk, sent tiny shock waves through her.

She had dreamed of what it would feel like to have a man touch her breasts, but her girlish dreams hadn't prepared her for the aching pleasure-pain, the swelling fullness of her breasts responding to the symphony of his fingers.

Groaning, she arched against him, reveling in the hard

length of him, pressed against her abdomen—evidence of his reciprocal need, his desire for her.

A door slammed in the distance, barely penetrating her consciousness but producing a profound effect upon Gilberto. Abruptly, he pulled away. His sienna eyes glittered, passion smoldering in their depths. Breathing hard, he felt his chest rise and fall rapidly.

Her gaze sought his, a silent question in her eyes.

His bronzed face turned a shade darker. Reaching out, he tenderly rebuttoned her blouse, pleading, *"Por favor,* forgive me, Sarah. I did not think. You were so sweet and giving." Pausing, he added, "But it wasn't my intention to seduce you. I don't want you to think I'm . . . that I would take advantage of . . ." His words, thick with emotion, dwindled away.

Far from being outraged by his advances, she had welcomed them. Confused and not knowing how to respond, she straightened her blouse and smoothed its pleated front, tucking it into the waist of her skirt.

Hadn't he told her that he loved her? Or had she dreamed it?

They had shared kisses before, many kisses, but none so urgent and feverish as this. She ached with unfulfilled desire, trembled with unquenched need.

Didn't he want her as much as she desired him? Or were they back where they had started, seeing each other as a diversion?

Forcing a normalcy into her voice she didn't feel, she said, "Carmen told you I had a headache and couldn't go riding." Hesitating, she took a deep breath and explained, "I can't go out tonight, either. I came down to tell you I have a previous—"

"I want you for my wife, Sarah," he declared, cutting short her explanation.

She lifted her head. Their gazes locked. His eyes pleaded. With his square chin thrust forward, he looked as if he expected her to reject him. Despite his defensive posture or maybe because of it, she realized he was serious. He wanted to wed her, to join their lives together.

Glancing down, she spread her fingers wide, ostensibly studying her fingernails. Her numb mind struggled to respond. She felt as if she were in the eye of a hurricane, buffeted by a maelstrom of emotions: first, jealousy, then triumph, followed by passion, and now, the ultimate commitment.

Clearing his throat, he offered, "You don't have to answer right away. Think it over."

Think it over. The phrase repeated itself in her mind.

She had never considered marriage with Gilberto. The thought hadn't entered her mind. She had imagined them in bed together, though, just moments before. Would she have compromised herself, giving herself to him?

Marriage was another thing entirely. Marriage meant they would share their lives together, raise children. Thinking of her parents, she remembered their secret smiles meant only for each other, their affectionate embraces, and their devotion.

Then she knew. As if the heavens had opened and a chorus of angels trumpeted the message, she knew. It was right. They were right. They belonged together, just like her parents. She had said she loved him, and she meant it. Beyond the bright flame of their desire, she enjoyed being with him, talking and laughing, sharing and caring.

And there was a special quality in Gilberto that tugged at her, an almost boyish appeal, begging for her love.

He had changed for her. Deep inside, she knew he had. When she met him he had reveled in his attractiveness to women. Now, he shunned other women. Had his earlier conquests been shams, a flurry of meaningless affairs to fill the emptiness within? She had thought he seduced women to feel powerful. Now she knew better. It was as if

he were a changeling from a fairy tale, waiting to be awakened. Waiting to be loved.

She lifted her eyes to his.

"You honor me," she said, the love unfolding in her
heart, filling her with unspeakable joy. "I accept your pro-
posal." Her heart brimmed, and her voice dropped an
octave, "I love you, Gilberto." Repeating his earlier vow,
she said, "I've never loved another."

His eyes shone bright, too bright, shimmering with un-
shed tears. It was a revelation, a new and different aspect
of him. He was sentimental, romantic, and vulnerable. Her
eyes burned, too, her heart touched by his response.

As if she were a fragile piece of precious china, he took
her hand in his. Lowering his head, he turned her hand
over and kissed her open palm. Shivering from the feel of
his lips upon her flesh, she rushed into his arms. He cradled her there, murmuring sweet love words.

Embracing hungrily, they lingered in each other's arms.
Closing her eyes, she wanted this moment to last forever.
She had never felt so complete before, so blissfully happy.
Savoring her newfound joy, she nestled in his strong arms,
wishing they could be married tomorrow.

The sound of his voice jolted her, as if awakening her
from a trance, returning her to the world of reality and
the necessary arrangements to be made.

"I'll go and tell my father first, if that's acceptable with
you. When I return, I'll ask your father for his permission."
With his innocuous words, fear thrust its dagger into her
heart, cruelly bleeding away her innocent bliss.

For the past few weeks, she hadn't thought about his
family. Seguín and his connection to Diana had receded
from her mind. She had concentrated on Gilberto. Thinking back, she understood Diana's feeling of being abandoned by her. She had been falling in love, and she didn't
know it. Gilberto had become an obsession, blocking out
everyone else.

But his father was Don Carlos Aguirre, she reminded herself, feeling the dagger turn. And Don Carlos was reputed to be a cruel, unfeeling man. He had stripped his stepson of his birthright and turned him out.

"Will your father have me as a daughter-in-law?" She had to ask.

"Of course," he replied easily, kissing the top of her head. "He's been wanting me to marry. He'll be happy I'm going to settle down."

His words were reassuring, but she couldn't help but wonder if Don Carlos would want his only son to "settle down" with *her.*

"I hope you're right."

"Don't worry. If you would like, I'll ask your father first."

"No, go home and tell your father. I'll prepare the way with my family."

"You are *not* going to marry Gilberto Aguirre, and that is final," Herbert York thundered, pacing the close confines of his study.

"But Father, you didn't oppose my seeing him." Sarah sat in one of the overstuffed leather chairs and watched her father's agitation with genuine bewilderment. "Surely you would have—"

"We trusted your judgment, dear," her mother interjected. "Your father and I never dreamed you would consider him as a serious suitor." Waving her graceful hands, she emphasized her point. "Just days ago you were laughing at him for showering you with roses. How could you be taken in by his smooth talking?"

To say that she hadn't expected her parents' negative reaction would be an understatement. In the matter of choosing suitors, her parents had always been liberal and open-minded. She still couldn't believe their opposition, thinking if only she said the right thing, they would understand she loved Gilberto and wanted to be his wife.

"It wasn't like that, Mother. He didn't 'take me in,' as you put it. I fell in love with him, and he fell in love with me. It's as simple as that."

"You fell in lust, you mean." Her father rounded the corner of his desk and pointed his finger at her, his harsh accusation scorching the air between them.

Gasping, she stared at him. How could he say such a thing to her? Not a particularly religious man, he had never been particularly judgmental, either. This wasn't like him.

"Now, Herbert," her mother moderated.

"Don't 'Now Herbert' me, Mary. You heard what the maid said. It's disgusting to think my daughter would—"

"Kiss a man?" Sarah finished defiantly. "What's so wrong with that? I've been kissing beaus since I was fifteen."

Swinging his attention to his wife, he demanded, "Is that true, Mary? Is our daughter a wanton? Did you know about this?"

"Herbert, Sarah has always been open with me. She's exchanged a few chaste kisses with several of her suitors before, but—"

"Chaste kisses. Hah! If you had heard that maid's graphic description of what went on with our daughter and Gilberto Aguirre, you'd be alarmed, too. Their bodies entwined and their mouths open. It's disgusting," he repeated, pounding his fist into the open palm of his hand. "How could you have raised our daughter to be so shameless?"

Mary's hand flew to her chest. "Me? I raised her to be shameless? How could *you* say such a thing to me, Herbert York?"

Closing her eyes, Sarah willed herself to remain calm.

Her parents seldom snapped at each other, and a part of her felt guilty for causing them distress.

She had expected her father to be scandalized after speaking with Carmen. It didn't take a fortune-teller to guess the maid would make the most of her story, wanting to punish Sarah for firing her and Gilberto for spurning her. She had been prepared to explain the motivation behind Carmen's vicious accusations, and she had naively believed her announcement of marriage would soften the blow, too. But she was stunned at the vehemence of her parents' objections.

"I'm sorry, Mary." Her father tugged at his sideburns in obvious frustration. "I didn't mean to blame you. The blame lays squarely on Sarah's shoulders." As he faced her, his gaze pierced her with righteous indignation. "I know we raised you better than this. I can't believe you allowed yourself to be degraded and—"

"Wait a minute, Father," she broke in, unable to stand his ugly accusations any longer. "I kissed the man I plan to marry. I don't find that degrading. And furthermore," she gave voice to her thoughts, "Carmen denounced me from spite because I fired her after she *offered* herself to Gilberto in our parlor."

"Offered herself?" Mary gasped. "You don't mean—?"

"Yes, I do."

Her father pounced, obviously hoping to discredit him. "What did Gilberto do?"

"He refused her, several times," Sarah replied.

"How do you know he refused her?" His voice dripped with skepticism. "Because he told you he did? Or did Carmen offer herself in front of you?"

"Not exactly in front of me. I saw them, but they didn't know I was there."

"You eavesdropped?" her mother guessed.

"Yes."

"Then you don't trust him either, do you?" he concluded triumphantly.

Shaking her head, she knew it would be impossible to make him understand the confusing path her emotions had taken before she allowed herself to admit her love for Gilberto. Instead, she stated flatly, "It's not like that, Father."

And she didn't want to pursue the subject of Carmen further. As far as she was concerned, it was a side issue. The important issue was why her parents, and particularly her father, were so opposed to her marrying Gilberto.

Before she could marshall her thoughts, he challenged, "So, you want us to believe Carmen lied out of spite. You didn't kiss Gilberto?"

"I kissed him, Father. I freely admit it. I love him." Desperate to know the reasons for their objections, she blurted, "Why are you against Gilberto—because he's Mexican?"

Herbert drew back in pained astonishment, looking as if she had slapped him. His distinguished features turned to stone. If anything, the look on his face became sterner than before.

"It's not his nationality I'm against, Sarah." He paused, as if considering his words carefully. "I hope that in our travels around the world I've proven to be an open-minded man, judging each individual on his own merit. I wanted to instill that same unbiased trait in you, Daughter."

"But you have, Father, that's why I'm so surprised—"

"Stop," he commanded, holding up his hand. "I haven't finished. This is important, and you have a right to know my objections." As if movement would help him to explain, he retreated behind his desk again and resumed pacing.

"It's not his nationality I object to, but the politics of his native land. México, where you will reside if you marry him, is a troubled country. When the French leave, there will be civil war."

"There was a civil war in the United States," she countered.

"Yes, there was, *one* civil war." His gaze found hers, drilling into her, willing her to see his side. "But you know your history, Sarah. How many civil wars and presidents has México had since they declared their freedom from Spain?"

"I'm not marrying his country, Father, I'm marrying the man," she protested.

Her mother reached over and patted her arm, chiding, "Let him explain, dear."

Sinking deeper into the chair, she felt her heart sinking, too. Her father wasn't just enraged over Carmen's vicious accusations. His objections went much deeper than that. Her earlier hopes dwindled away, to be replaced by a dejection so heavy she felt as if her heart had dropped to her toes.

"I don't want to worry about my only daughter living in such a dangerous place. Your mother and I will never have another moment's peace. As soon as the French pull out, I'll conclude my business and return to the States. I'd hoped you would find a suitable American to marry, preferably from our circle of friends. There are any number of young men who—"

Stopping himself, he shook his head. "We'll talk about that later. Another objection I have is his unsavory family. You know that history, too, Sarah. It was you who explained it to Diana when she first came here. The thought of Don Carlos as your father-in-law makes my blood run cold. How can you think of marrying the son of a man who had your best friend's father murdered?"

His words were a low blow, but they were the truth. How could she think of marrying Gilberto, knowing what she did about his father?

Gulping back the nasty taste filling her mouth, she admitted, "I don't like who his father is. But I've never felt this way about another man. I know we're *right* together. Somehow, I'll have to accept Don Carlos."

"But Don Carlos will never accept you. I have it on good

authority. He wants his son to marry the daughter of the family who owns the neighboring rancho. Gilberto's father cares for nothing but furthering his empire. I know the man. I've done business with him."

So, her forebodings were true. Gilberto would meet with just as much resistance as she had, maybe more. Desperation overwhelmed her. She felt tied down, like Sam tethered to his perch.

"And furthermore," he continued relentlessly, "I don't like Gilberto's reputation, either. He's a ladies man, quick to seduce every woman in his path. What kind of a husband would he make? Could you be happy with him, knowing he kept several mistresses?"

"He's not like that anymore. He's changed," she defended him.

"Pah! Changed, you say. A leopard doesn't change his spots. He might be hiding his true nature to court and marry you, but after you're married, then what? He'll resume his old ways. Women always think they can change men, but it's a fantasy. The man you marry is the man you'll live with the rest of your life. If you don't believe me, ask your mother."

"He's right, dear," her mother agreed. "This is the most important decision of your life, Sarah. Who a woman marries, more than anything else in the world, defines her happiness." Leaning forward, she wrapped her arm around Sarah's shoulders, adding ammunition. "Just look at poor Elizabeth. I loved Jamie. Your father and I both did. But as a husband he was careless and unfeeling, busy pursuing his dream. Elizabeth loved him and she mourns him, but she was never happy with him."

"It's not the same," Sarah denied. Despite her defiant words, with her mother's arm around her shoulders, her heart ached, thinking of the anxiety she was causing them. The tears she had proudly held back spilled over, and she covered her face with her hands.

Tightening her hold on Sarah's shoulders, Mary soothed, "We want what's best for you, dear. Please try to be reasonable."

Raising her head, she dashed the tears from her eyes with the back of her hand. Gazing at her mother for a long time, she noticed the worry lines crisscrossing her mother's usually smooth forehead. Turning from Mary, she met her father's eyes. His earlier sternness had softened to be replaced by a look of troubled concern.

She dropped her gaze to her lap, conflicting emotions pummelling her. How could she oppose them? They loved her so much. Her father's arguments had merit, too. The thought of living in México wasn't exactly appealing, and she knew that Don Carlos, even if she overlooked his hideous crimes, wouldn't accept her. And the whisper of that old doubt about Gilberto's character nagged at her. Had he really changed? Would he be a faithful husband?

Closing her eyes, she tried to picture Gilberto's face, searching her memory for clues to his true nature. Remembering, her feelings returned with a rush, making her heart pound, filling her with unspeakable longings. She missed the taste of him, the touch of his skin, and the strength of his arms. Yes, she desired him, but her feelings went deeper than that. She could talk to him, tease him, exchange ideas. Their conversations were never boring, and she never tired of being around him.

She had had many suitors. Not one of them had known her, not one of them had cared to know her. She was just another pretty face with the promise of a large dowry and the right background. With Gilberto, it wasn't like that. With him, it was different. He needed her, she sensed it. He loved her for herself, not for what she represented.

As if from far away, she gazed at her parents again. They were waiting, hoping they had convinced her.

It was all so painful. She had never been in opposition to them before, at least, not in serious opposition. There had been minor rebellions along the way, to test her wings, but nothing that couldn't be resolved with a few words. They had raised her with an open-handed attitude, allowing her to form her own opinions and trusting her to make wise ones.

This time was different. They were locked in opposition. There was no middle ground. Despite their arguments to the contrary, something told her she would regret giving up Gilberto. He was the other half of her, the person she wanted to share her life with. She would never feel this way about another, no matter how suitable her father might deem someone else to be. Wise enough to know her decision wouldn't be an easy one, she accepted the difficulties that lay ahead with resignation.

"What if I refuse to accept your decision? What if Gilberto and I elope?"

She heard the sharp intake of their breath, almost as if they had rehearsed it together. Ironically, her parents had given her the model of what to expect from her life mate. If she and Gilberto were ever faced with a similar situation, she knew they would act the same, experiencing the same feelings in unison.

"I can confine you under guard, Sarah. You know that." Her father's voice grated, filled with frustration.

"Please, dear, don't do this," Mary pleaded.

"What if I escape your guards, Father?" She pushed ahead stubbornly, ignoring her mother's plea, wanting to know what she and Gilberto faced.

"If you elope with Gilberto, I'll have no recourse." His voice sounded weary, laced with pain. "I'll call him out and kill him."

Nine

Opening her eyes to the sunbeam slanting across her bed, Diana realized it must be mid-morning. She had slept later than usual. Her sleep had been troubled last night, with worry about Sarah.

After supper the night before, when she had been lying in bed waiting for Sarah to join her, she had heard raised voices and slamming doors from downstairs. Tempted to investigate, she wanted to leave her bed and find out what was wrong, but something held her back. After all, this wasn't her home. What right did she have to interfere in the Yorks' personal affairs?

Sarah had appeared, after what seemed like hours. Her friend's face was tear-streaked, and her eyes puffy. She apologized for not spending the evening with Diana, saying something had come up. Diana had tried to extract an explanation from her, but she begged off, promising to explain everything tomorrow.

Tomorrow was here, and the hour advanced. Where was Sarah, and what was wrong? For that matter, why was her breakfast tray so late? Where was Carmen?

As if in answer to her thoughts, there was a knock at her door. The Yorks' stout cook, Felicia, entered, bearing her breakfast. Murmuring an apology for the lateness of the meal, Felicia plumped the pillows behind Diana and helped her to sit up.

It was on the tip of her tongue to question Felicia, but she remained silent. She didn't know Felicia very well, and she felt odd interrogating her. The cook's round face held no clue, either. Her features were carefully composed, and she avoided Diana's eyes.

Dismissing Felicia with her thanks, she halfheartedly picked at the lukewarm eggs. Even the tea was cold. Something was definitely wrong. Having been patient for so long, she decided she wouldn't wait any longer. Placing the tray on the bedside table, she threw back the covers and rose to her feet.

So far, so good, she thought. There was no pain when she moved around. In fact, she was almost healed. Doctor Cabrera was due to return at the end of the week and examine her. Based on his previous visit, she expected him to pronounce her well and allow her to resume normal activities.

And it wouldn't be a moment too soon. If she had to stay in bed much longer, she would go stark, raving mad.

Using the bedposts to steady her progress, she moved carefully, as if she were an old woman. Her body was healed, but every time she exerted effort she was reminded of how weak she had become, forced to remain in bed. Tottering from the bed to the *armoire,* she searched through stacks of neatly folded clothing for something to wear.

When she located her favorite day dress, she had to stop and lean against the *armoire,* to catch her breath. The remainder of her toilette—washing her face and hands, dressing, and brushing her hair—dragged out endlessly with frequent pauses so she could rest.

At the last, when she was struggling to twist her hair into a knot atop her head, she was startled by another knock on her door. *Just my luck,* she thought, *Carmen finally comes when I no longer need her.* But it wasn't Carmen who entered her room without waiting for a summons. It was her mother.

Elizabeth didn't bother to offer the conventional greeting. "Diana, what are you doing?"

"I'm getting dressed, Mother."

"I can see that, but Doctor Cabrera hasn't released you from bed. I don't want you to hurt yourself."

"I'm fine. Just a little slow." Shoving the last hairpin into the lopsided loop of her hair, she told herself it didn't matter if she looked picture-perfect this morning. She just wanted some answers.

Turning to face her mother, she asked, "What's going on? Sarah came up last night but wouldn't tell me anything. I know something is wrong. And where's Carmen?"

Elizabeth didn't answer. Instead, she grasped Diana's shoulders and turned her again to face the looking glass. With sure fingers, she undid her hair and reknotted it atop her head. Several seconds passed while she watched her mother's deft hands, her impatience building. Had someone died? What could be so awful that everyone was going out of their way to keep it from her?

"It's Sarah," her mother finally spoke. "She wants to—"

Another knock sounded at the door, interrupting her mother. Spying Elizabeth's reflection in the mirror, she saw the expression of relief cross her face. Exasperated by the untimely intrusion, Diana snapped, "Come in."

The door opened and Pedro, the Yorks' *mayordomo,* appeared on the threshold. Bowing low, he murmured, "*Señora* McFarland, *¡buenos días!*" Turning to Diana, he continued, "A gentleman to see you, *Señorita* McFarland. He gave his name as Seguín Torres. He doesn't have a calling card," Pedro sniffed in disdain. "I told him you were confined to bed." His gaze swept her, ostensibly noting she was no longer in bed. Stiffly carrying out his duty despite the altered circumstances, he finished, "I didn't know if you were receiving visitors."

Her pulse leapt in response. Seguín was here, and he had come to see her, just as his note had promised. She didn't care if he had come for the formula. She wanted to see him. Her earlier questions fled from her mind, eclipsed by the tumult of her yearning.

"Yes, I'll see him," she responded quickly.

Leaning forward, she gazed at her reflection in the mirror, grateful her mother had fixed her hair. There were dark rings beneath her eyes, witness to the restless night she had spent. And her skin looked sallow, pale and lifeless from weeks of lying in bed. Pinching her cheeks for color, she almost wished she had some of Sarah's rouge.

Her mother cut short her excited thoughts. "Do you think it's wise to see him? I don't think you should be out of bed."

"Mother, if I don't get out of this room, I'll scream. I've been down to the patio before, and it didn't hurt me. My ribs feel fine. I'm just a little weak." Facing Elizabeth, she insisted, "If you would help me down the stairs, I can manage from there."

Elizabeth's expression looked doubtful, but she must have read the silent plea in Diana's eyes, because she nodded. "I guess it couldn't hurt. But only if you promise to sit quietly."

"I promise."

Pedro, who had been waiting patiently at the door, cleared his throat. Understanding his unspoken question, Diana responded, "Pedro, show *Señor* Seguín to the patio." When she said the word *patio,* memories of their first kiss flooded her senses. She didn't know if she should see him there. It might make their meeting more awkward than it would already be. And the sun would magnify the flaws in her face.

When had she become so vain, she wondered?

Changing her mind, she amended, "No, Pedro, not the patio. Where do the Yorks usually receive guests?"

"In the south parlor."

"Please, I'll receive him there."

"As you wish." He bowed again and disappeared.

Diana entered the parlor on her mother's arm. She looked pale and tired. Her breath came in short, quick pants, bringing two bright pink spots to her otherwise wan cheeks.

Seguín's heart constricted, looking at her. She had been thin before. Now she was almost ethereal, a whisper of her former self. All this suffering, and all because of him. How could he ever hope to right the wrong he had unwittingly done?

Guilt crashed down on him, and with it a sense of protectiveness. He had felt that way the night Ignacio abducted her, too. She brought out the tender side of him, the side he thought he had buried with his mother. A voice in the back of his mind warned him not to feel, to block the tenderness welling in his heart—warned him of the danger of trusting again, particularly a woman.

There followed the perfunctory greetings, to both mother and daughter. *Señora* McFarland hovered for a few minutes, obviously concerned for her daughter's welfare. After a pointed glance from Diana, she took the hint and withdrew, leaving them alone.

Rushing to fill the awkward moment, once they were alone, he proffered the package, offering, "This is for you."

Surprise animated her drawn features, and she accepted the bundle, wrapped in plain brown paper. "Thank you. How thoughtful."

Plucking at the string holding it together, he noticed that her fingers trembled. Was she that weak? His first impulse was to help her, but he didn't want to get too close to her, to take the chance of touching her.

Por Dios, if he touched her, he didn't know if he would
be able to stop. Remembering the last time he had been
with her, the night he rescued her, he relived the silky
warmth of her skin, the puckered buds of her breasts. His
loins grew heavy, taut with aching desire.

No, it wasn't a good idea to touch her.

With that thought in mind, he took a chair across from
her. Several feet separated them.

After some initial fumbling, she undid the string and
pulled back the paper. Drawing forth his gift, she unfurled
it, gasping, "It's so beautiful! What a wonderful shawl."
Raising it to her face, she brushed it against the skin of
her cheek, saying, "And so soft, too."

"It reminded me of your eyes," he admitted.

That was why he had bought it. Made of the softest
lamb's wool, the strands were dyed a rainbow of colors:
blue, green, turquoise, gold, and the subtlest shading of
lavender.

She raised her eyes to his. *Those eyes,* he thought, *her
luminous eyes,* made more pronounced by the thinness of
her face. Would he ever be able to forget her eyes? Or her
hair, the spun-gold glory of it?

"Thank you," she repeated, "it was kind of you to think
of me."

He shrugged, embarrassed she had drawn such an un-
guarded response from him. Desperate to cover his blunder, he spoke again without thinking. "You're not wearing
your spectacles." He felt utterly foolish, once the observation had left his mouth. After all, she hadn't been wearing
them that day on the patio or at the ball. Why had he
asked her now? Because the shawl reminded him of her
eyes? But to almost admit such a thing to her was far too
revealing. He could bite his tongue in two.

With a tiny smile, she replied, "I only need them for
reading or embroidery."

Then why had she worn them when he first met her, he

wondered. To hide behind her intellectualism? To deny the feminine side of herself? As much as he had liked and admired Jamie, he didn't approve of the way he had raised his daughter. It had made her strong, but something else, too. For lack of a better word, the term "wary" rose to his mind.

"Are your ribs healed?" he asked, desperate to turn the conversation into less personal channels. "What does the doctor say?"

"He said I'm almost well. My ribs feel fine, although I'm weak from being in bed. I'm certain when Doctor Cabrera returns, he'll find me healed."

"That's good."

"Yes. I've hated being confined to bed. It's so boring."

Remembering his first encounters with her, as his fiery adversary for the formula, he wasn't surprised she chafed at being bedridden.

"And you? You've been well?" she inquired politely.

"Yes, thank you."

After what had transpired between them the night he rescued her, he found their stilted conversation ridiculous. But he shouldn't complain, he reminded himself—better that they maintain a polite distance.

"I want to thank you for rescuing me that night. I don't know what would've happened if you hadn't been looking out for me."

"It was the least I could do, considering."

"Have you caught the man?"

Her abrupt question surprised him, although it made perfect sense. Feeling guilty again and strangely powerless, he admitted, "No, we haven't caught him. But I know who he is."

"Who is he?"

Grinding his teeth, he wished he didn't feel compelled to answer. She had every right to know. "He's a cousin of my stepfather. His name is Ignacio Hernández."

"Knowing who he is—won't it help to catch him?"

"It should, but he's very clever. He was raised by his grandmother's people, Aztecs. They can be crafty when stalking prey."

She gasped. "Prey! What a way to put it."

"I'm sorry," he apologized, raking his fingers through his hair, wishing he were anywhere but where he was, wishing the bright Aubusson carpet at his feet would leap up and carry him away—like the fabled flying carpets of the stories in the *Arabian Nights*. "I didn't mean it like that—"

"I understand," she interrupted. "I just wish you would catch him."

"It wouldn't matter, Diana. My stepfather would send someone else."

Even as he said the words, he knew they were only part of the truth. No hired thug would be as tenacious as Ignacio. Ignacio hated him, and believed he was the reason for Esmeralda's death. But he wouldn't recant. She must understand the danger. The night at the ball had been a close thing. And she couldn't stay locked in the Yorks' house forever. A reckoning must come.

As if she could read his thoughts, she replied, "I know what you're trying to say." Pausing, she worried her bottom lip with her teeth.

His eyes narrowed, watching her. What would he give to feel the sharp prick of her teeth against his mouth? To taste the sweet honeyed essence of her innocence again?

"Sarah is seeing Gilberto, your half-brother. I worry about it."

She spoke as if her remark fitted with her previous comment, as if the two were woven from the same cloth.

Confused at first, he pieced the threads together. His stepfather was a monster in her eyes, and rightly so. For her best friend to be seeing Don Carlos's son was alarming. He couldn't agree with her more.

"I'm sorry to hear that. I wouldn't recommend my half-brother as a suitor for anyone."

"Oh, why is that?"

Was she playing with him? Wasn't the answer obvious? Or was she trying to elicit information from him? Probably the latter, and he was glad to oblige.

"I would warn your friend against Gilberto. He's charming and handsome, but that's where his finer qualities end," he stated flatly, the old bitterness rising to the surface. "He's a womanizer. He'll hurt *Señorita* York."

"Thank you for being so honest," she replied.

Was there a hint of mockery in her voice? He hoped not. He had been painfully honest with her, and he didn't like to talk about his so-called family. It brought back too many ugly memories.

"Seguín, I'm prepared to sell you the formula."

Her declaration caught him off guard. He had expected a spirited debate from her at least, not this quiet surrender. Peering at her closely, he wondered if she were even weaker than she appeared. Surely, her mother wouldn't have allowed her to meet him if her health were in serious danger. Would she?

"Say something, Seguín," she demanded, with a nervous laugh. "I feel as if I'm carrying the conversation by myself."

"I'm gratified you're willing to sell me the formula," he managed to reply. Knowing he should stop there, he didn't understand what drove him to ask, "Why this change of heart?"

Dropping her gaze, she combed her fingertips through the threads of the shawl. An involuntary shudder gripped him, remembering the night when she had threaded her fingers through his hair, drawing close to him despite her injuries, hungering for his mouth on her breasts.

Tearing his eyes away from her hands, he stared at the top of her head, trying to gather the scraps of his shredded control. Half-formed feelings slithered through him, like secret serpents, entangling and confusing his thoughts.

He should feel triumphant, knowing he would finally get the formula. But he didn't. Disappointment weighed at him, dragging him down. As much as he dreaded his passionate response to her, he craved it, in spite of himself. For the first time in a long time, another human being had touched him, penetrated his self-imposed wall of stoicism. He cared deeply about her; it was as simple and as complicated as that. Thinking of her selling the formula and leaving México blackened his mood, filling him with despair.

Lifting her head, she gazed at him. "I changed my *mind* because it's the right thing to do. My father would have wanted it this way." Pausing, as if for emphasis, she continued, "I know my father wouldn't *blame* you, and I can't continue to do so." As if speaking to herself, she added, "Revenge can eat you up."

"I'm relieved you've made your decision. After the sale, you'll be leaving with your mother?" He tried to keep his voice light, hoping she wouldn't detect his despondency.

"Yes, we'll be going as soon as possible. Then you won't need to worry about our safety."

"Bueno, bueno." He felt as if his features had frozen into place, so awful was the effort it took him to remain outwardly composed.

"There is one thing more, Seguín." She cocked her head and smiled a brittle smile. Her hazel eyes glittered. The fire in them reminded him of the Diana he knew before her "accident."

"I want more money for the formula. My father would have expected that, too." When she squared her shoulders against the satin of the couch, he recognized the gesture. Each time she decided to go into battle with him, she squared her shoulders. The gesture touched him, and bittersweet memories coursed through him.

"Of course. I want to be fair," he murmured, amazed at the turn of the conversation. Even ill and weak, she was a fierce adversary. That part of her hadn't changed. She never failed to astonish him. Admiration mixed with desire was a potent brew. Desire exploded within him. He ached to take her in his arms.

"Mr. York made some inquiries on my behalf about your mining operations. He determined what my father's partnership interest would have brought, over a few years' time." Her hand strayed toward the bellpull. "I've put together some figures. If you would like to see them, I can send for the accounts."

He shook his head. "No, that won't be necessary."

And it wasn't necessary for her to prove the worth of her father's interest. Cringing inwardly, he realized he had forgotten about his original offer to Diana, when all he had cared about was owning the formula and sending the McFarlands home. Then he had started to worry about her safety, and the price he had offered, or even obtaining the formula, had become secondary.

Agitated by thoughts of his earlier mendacious spirit, he leapt to his feet and strode to the curtained window, looking out at the cobbled driveway curving before the house. He half-expected her to speak, but she didn't. Silence stretched between them like an empty desert.

Determined to rectify his earlier selfishness, he turned. "I'm prepared to triple my first offer."

She gasped, and her pale cheeks colored, as if she were embarrassed by his offer. "I don't want your pity, Seguín, or guilt money." He started to respond, but she held one thin hand up, palm out, as if to ward off his quick words. "I want to forget the past and do what is right. Double your previous offer is right. No more than that."

His heart expanded within his chest, making him feel as if he would burst from wanting her. She was so damned honorable, so damned noble! If only all women could be so . . .

Pulling himself away from that particular emotional precipice, he replied, "As you wish, Diana. I will have my attorney draw up the papers. When they're ready, I'll notify you. Is that satisfactory?"

"Yes, more than satisfactory. Shall we shake on it?"

Resigning himself to purgatory, he nodded and strode forward, enfolding her paper-thin hands in his own. The mere touch of her boiled through him like a summer storm. Lightning streaked along his veins and his thoughts raced, imagining them together, pressed skin to skin, locked in passion.

Their gazes met and held. The tremor in her hands was slight, but he felt it.

She cared about him, too, he sensed. But they were doomed, doomed to be apart, doomed to etch their own solitary paths on earth, far from each other.

Dropping her hands abruptly, he bowed low, taking his leave.

Watching Sam pace the short confines of his perch, Diana digested Sarah's anguished outpouring. Of all the things she had half-expected, half-feared to hear, her friend's confession stunned her. Sarah was in love with Gilberto Aguirre and wanted to marry him—despite her parents' wishes to the contrary.

Gazing at her sophisticated friend, she couldn't quite relinquish her surprise. As hard as she tried, she couldn't picture Sarah and Gilberto as a couple. And Seguín's words of caution haunted her, reminding her of Sarah's earlier, similar assessment of Gilberto. Could her worldly friend have fallen into her own trap?

"Sarah, I know you're distressed by your parents' opposition. But I can't blame them. *You* told me Gilberto is a

Don Juan. How can you marry such a man? And his father is a murderer. You told me that, too." She spoke the words with trepidation, realizing they wouldn't convey the support Sarah desired. Even so, she had to say them. She had to be honest with Sarah about her doubts, too. After all, if she didn't express her concerns she wouldn't be acting as a real friend.

Her best friend's eyes filled with tears, and she looked away. Diana's heart went out to her. The last thing she wanted to do was hurt her.

"I was wrong about him, or he's changed." Sarah almost sobbed. "I swear to you, Diana, he hasn't looked at another woman since we've been together. As for his father—" She shrugged, admitting, "I have no excuse. I love him despite his father." She raised her eyes, pleading, "Don't condemn me because I do. I can't help myself."

Recoiling from her best friend's casual dismissal of Don Carlos's crimes, she hated her for a moment, realizing Sarah's self-absorption. But her obvious sincerity touched Diana. *Who can command the longings of her heart?* Diana asked herself. As hard as she had tried, she couldn't tame her own unruly heart.

Sympathizing, she drew Sarah into her arms. "Are you certain you love him? That he can be faithful to you?"

"I've never been more certain of anything in my life."

Stroking Sarah's hair from her brow, she soothed, "Then you must fight your parents for his love. It's as simple as that." With a twinge of regret, she wished it could be so simple for her.

She loved Seguín with all her heart, but parental opposition wasn't the problem. The problem was Seguín. It was obvious he desired her, although at times she even doubted that—she wasn't beautiful like Sarah. Seguín certainly wasn't in love with her, though. Of that she was certain. She just hoped Sarah knew what she was doing, and that Gilberto really loved her.

"I will fight," Sarah breathed, pulling away and pinning Diana with her gaze. "I'll need your help, too. Promise me."

Feeling as if she were putting her neck in an unknown noose, she replied with her unruly heart, not her head. "I'm your best friend, Sarah. I would do anything to help you."

"So, you've fallen in love, eh?" Don Carlos's words were clipped. Gilberto could sense that his father disapproved but was holding himself in check. That was unusual. His father possessed a hideous temper, and he didn't like to be crossed.

"*Sí*, Father, I've never loved another woman before." He then appealed to his father's view of women. "The others were mere diversions, you understand."

"*Yo entiendo*. I understand, Gilberto." His father paused, reaching for his half-filled glass of Madeira and taking a sip. "But you must think with your head, *mi hijo*, not your nether parts." Splaying his stubby fingers across the well-worn desk, he punctuated his words by stabbing the old wood with his index finger. "You're *criollo* aristocracy, and you should marry into the *criollos*. A Protestant wife." He snorted. "How can you consider such a thing? Your children will be neither fish nor fowl."

"That's not true. I know Sarah will convert to Catholicism for me."

"Then she's spineless, with no beliefs of her own." His father's tone was scathing, meant to belittle.

"Father! How can you say such a thing, not knowing her? She's not spineless, but I know she would be accommodating."

"Accommodating?" He harrumphed loudly. "Accommodating your birthright, you mean."

Having heard all he could take, Gilberto pushed himself

to his feet and paced to the terrace door, gazing out at the overgrown rose garden, a legacy of his mother.

He was furious, but like his father he realized it was important for him to maintain his composure. If he lost his temper his father would follow suit, and nothing would be accomplished. Once they exchanged angry words, he knew Don Carlos would become even more entrenched.

Turning on his heel, he took a deep breath and avoided looking directly at his father. Don Carlos prided himself on being a great hunter. Gilberto allowed his gaze to wander over the stuffed trophies in the study—dead, collared animals with their heads sticking out from frames, their fake eyes glassily staring. Shuddering, he lowered his head and tried to blot the forms from his mind. He refused to serve himself up as a specimen, like the vanquished animals on the walls, bowing to his father's dictates. He would fight with every weapon at his disposal.

Approaching Don Carlos's desk, he took up the earlier thread of their conversation. "Sarah York isn't after my birthright, Father. You must know that. You do business with her father, Herbert York, and he's a very wealthy man. Sarah is his only child."

Don Carlos took another sip of wine. "I don't doubt she will bring a handsome dowry. But what kind of dowry? Land is the only thing that endures, that restores itself, over and over. Señor York is not wealthy in land. His wealth is in machinery, which rusts and decays, and paper currencies that become worthless as one ruler usurps the other."

"What are you driving at, Father?"

"You deserve a wife with a large dowry but a dowry of land. You've known for a long time I've an informal agreement with Señor Figueroa. His Maria is perfect for you—an only daughter, too, who will inherit the neighboring rancho. Eventually, your lands, like your lives, will be joined together, to nurture future generations." His father spread his hands expansively, admitting, "I regret I only have one son to carry on my name. I had wanted a houseful of children, but your mother was sickly and she died before her time."

A chill ran through him at his father's offhanded remark. He spoke of his wife as if she were a brood mare, good for only bearing children. Surely, his father had cared for his mother. Hadn't he?

The question slipped out before he thought better of it. "Why didn't you remarry?"

Don Carlos smiled wolfishly from beneath his thick moustaches, bragging, "Just because I didn't remarry doesn't mean I've remained celibate. I have several *bastardos* carrying my blood. But it's not the same thing." He shook his head.

"No, a wife is important to a man's stature. She is a reflection of him. Her background, her breeding, her beauty, and her dowry all must be perfectly suited to his station in life." He twirled the almost empty glass of red wine between his fingers. "Unfortunately, I haven't found another match like your mother. I refuse to settle for second-rate, Gilberto, and I can't allow you to, either. You must chose your future wife with care."

The unspoken conclusion hung between them: because Sarah was a Norté Americaño and a Protestant, she was second-rate in his father's eyes. Anyone other than Maria Figueroa would be considered second-rate.

His father had already decided who he would marry, and Don Carlos didn't allow challenges to his authority. Ever. It was one of the reasons he had been willing to study in a strict monastery school in Spain. As strict as the monks had been, he had instinctively known they couldn't equal his father in bone-crushing iron will.

He had been away too long, he realized suddenly. He had forgotten how hard his father was to deal with. Cursing himself silently, he knew he should have planned this interview more carefully. Instead, he had blundered into it like a lovesick schoolboy.

"I will not stand in your way if you want to marry this Sarah York," Don Carlos said, surprising him, holding out the velvet glove before it changed into a cruel vise. "But I cannot support you. Your future wife's dowry will have to suffice, or you will need to make your own way in the world."

Gilberto's heart plummeted at this final ultimatum. Fighting down fast-rising panic, he searched for a way out. Without his birthright, what could he offer Sarah? She, who was as accustomed to wealth and luxury as he was? He could work for her father and make his living that way, but it would unman him. He would feel like the lowest scum, a man who lived off his wife.

"I'm your only son, Father, as you pointed out. Who would you leave your lands and mines to, if not to me?" He hated the incipient plea in his voice.

Smiling maliciously, Don Carlos leaned back in his padded leather chair. "To Mother Church, of course. It would assure my place in heaven, would it not?"

Trying to gather his wits, he didn't doubt for a moment his father would carry through with the threat. An image of his half-brother, Seguín, rose in his mind, and he finally felt his brother's pain, at having his birthright stripped from him, whether it was deserved or not. But Seguín hadn't given up. He had fought back, against the indomitable will of Don Carlos.

If he were to call himself a man, he could do no less.

He loved Sarah York and wanted her for his wife. Nothing would ever change that. Years apart wouldn't dim their attachment, either.

Where there was a will, there was a way. The old saying flooded his thoughts suddenly, echoing through his mind. After all, he *was* his father's son. He could be just as tenacious as Don Carlos. And what he hadn't gained by a direct approach might still be attained by indirect means.

"I understand your position, Father. Given the heavy responsibilities of my future union, I hope you'll understand if I remain a bachelor for a time longer."

Without waiting for an answer or asking to withdraw, he bowed and exited the room, pulling the heavy oak door behind him.

Ten

Diana signed her name to the documents that *Señor* Hildago, Seguín's attorney, had prepared. Her mother followed suit. Mr. York's attorney, acting on behalf of the McFarlands, had already reviewed them and given his approval.

Seguín had brought the papers to the Yorks' home. They had been presented in both Spanish and English for their convenience, courtesy of Seguín. After the signing, the exchange of monies took place, part in gold and silver and part in a letter of credit to be drawn on a bank in San Francisco, where they had determined to settle.

The Yorks' permanent home was in San Francisco, and Diana didn't want to be separated from them again, although she secretly wondered how Sarah's love affair with Gilberto would turn out. As hard as it was for her to picture Sarah and Gilberto as a couple, it was doubly hard for her to imagine her friend living in México for the remainder of her life.

Putting herself in Sarah's place, she wondered how she would react if Seguín declared his undying love and asked for her hand in marriage.

Would I be willing to remain in México? she asked herself. Without being put to the test, she couldn't know for certain, but something told her she would be willing to live anywhere, so long as she was with the man she loved.

Surprised by her feelings, she remembered Elizabeth lamenting the places her father had taken them to live. She had thought her mother loved her father and was willing to follow him anywhere. But when she looked back on the times Elizabeth had chosen to return to her parents' home instead, Diana knew that wasn't true.

Did love wear out? she wondered, rendered threadbare by the difficulties of daily living? Or was there love, and then another kind of love—the kind of love that transcended the petty hardships, taking joy in everyday events, in the simple pleasure of being together? Because she hadn't lived the love she felt in her heart, she couldn't know with certainty.

And because her examples of matrimonial love were so different, it was a difficult question to answer. Her mother and father had lived one kind of life, torn apart by her father's erratic ambitions, which had led to failure in his lifetime. The Yorks, as a couple, had lived at the opposite end of the spectrum, enjoying their worldly travels. Had their happiness stemmed from Mr. York's success, or would they have been happy together even if he had been a failure, like her father?

She didn't know, and she would probably never know. It was as if each life, like a snowflake, was totally different from all others, and every couple's joy was unique, peculiar only to them and the way they loved each other.

Deep in thought, she felt the male rumble of Seguín's voice interrupt her musings, pulling her back to the present. Blinking, she glanced around. The south parlor was deserted, except for herself and Seguín. Her mother, the two attorneys, and the Yorks, who had acted as witnesses, had dispersed, leaving them alone.

Knowing he had spoken when she hadn't been listening, she inquired, "Pardon me?"

"I wanted to wish you luck and success when you return to the States."

"Thank you, that's very kind. And it was thoughtful of you to have the signing take place here. You made it very convenient for us."

"I'm happy to be of service."

A door closed softly in the distance, a clock chimed, and the faint chatter of birds on the patio reached her ears. The silence between them was alive, too, teeming with unspoken words.

Closing her eyes for one brief moment, she took a deep breath. How could she face this, knowing that she loved him and would never see him again? Should she tell him how she felt?

No, that was a silly thought, she admonished herself, pushing the urge away. What good would it do? He didn't return her love. She wasn't even certain that he liked her. After all, it was easy for him to be polite and considerate, having gotten what he wanted—the formula. Her mind rebelled against that thought, too, knowing it wasn't quite fair. He had rescued her, and brought her a beautiful shawl.

Guilt. The word reverberated through her. His actions had been predicated by the guilt he felt over her father's death. Why couldn't she accept the fact and move on? Over time, she would forget him, wouldn't she? She might even find someone else.

He looked tense, too, she noticed, with his arms crossed over his chest, accentuating the corded muscles of his forearms which strained against the cloth of his cutaway coat.

How she longed for him to take her in those strong arms, to kiss her with the ferocious passion she knew he possessed. Her heart galloped in her chest, and her fingers tingled with the rushing of her blood. It was all she could do to keep from throwing herself in his arms.

"You plan to settle in San Francisco?" It wasn't really a question. He knew her financial arrangements. It was just a polite ploy to ease the awful silence between them.

"Yes." She didn't elaborate. Her throat felt tight, and her eyes burned. If he didn't leave soon she would humiliate herself by breaking into tears.

Taking the initiative, she brushed her forehead with the back of her hand, apologizing, "You'll have to excuse me, Seguín. I'm still not very strong, and I feel a blinding headache coming on." Reaching for the bellpull, she offered, "I'll ring for Pedro. He'll be happy to show you out."

"No, that won't be necessary." He bent to retrieve his hat from the table where he had placed it earlier. "I know the way out," he replied, advancing on her with his hand outstretched.

Expecting him to shake her hand, she reluctantly reciprocated, offering her right hand. But he didn't shake it. Instead, he bowed low and brushed a kiss across the back of her flesh.

His touch was the most sublime torture of all. Remembering how she had invited him to touch her on every other occasion, she thought what a fool she had been. With his departure from her life, she couldn't bear it. Not this time.

Jerking her hand free, she almost ran from the room, choking back her sobs and muttering, *"Adiós,"* in farewell.

Slowly, Seguín settled the flat-brimmed hat on his head, pausing to cock it at a particular angle, using the gilt-edged mirror hanging over the rosewood desk as his guide. His movements were jerky, barely controlled. He avoided looking at the reflection of his eyes in the looking glass.

He had wanted to take her in his arms more than anything else in the world. His mines, the formula, and his plan for revenge on his stepfather had all paled before that desire, obliterated by the aching need he felt. It didn't make any sense, and it would have solved nothing, but there it was. The need still throbbed through him, simmering in his veins, straining his nerves until he felt as if they would snap from the awful power of it.

Head down and fists clenched, he fought it. With every fiber of his self-control, he fought it.

She ran from me, a voice whispered in the back of his mind, bringing a measure of release, a small surcease from suffering. *It's over. She sold me the formula. If she welcomed me before, it was as a curious, uninitiated virgin, wanting to taste the heady wine of passion. The experiment is complete. I'm dismissed, a closed chapter in her life. She's eager to return to the States.*

And would I want it otherwise? the same voice probed.

No, of course not, he reassured himself, breathing more evenly now. There was no place in his life for Diana. She came from another world, another culture, a different viewpoint. Besides, he had vowed to avoid attachments, particularly with women. One betrayal was enough.

The betrayal by a mother of her son.

"It's not a rumor, Mary. It's a fact. I have it from the best sources. Napoleon is withdrawing his troops," Herbert York declared.

Dropping her knitting, Mary reached for her husband's hand and squeezed it. "You knew it was coming. Don't worry. We'll get away safely."

"I hope so," he muttered, retrieving his pipe from an ashtray. "There are so many business details to attend to before we can leave." As he filled his pipe with tobacco, she couldn't help but notice that his movements were unsteady, barely controlled.

"How can I help?" she found herself asking, alarmed at her husband's obvious agitation. Herbert, who planned for every possible calamity, was seldom agitated about anything. It worried her to see him this way. Was the situation more dire than he would admit, or was increasing age making him more cautious?

"Start packing and prepare to close this house. And send word to shut up our house in Cuernavaca, too. Alert the McFarlands to be ready to sail for home. I'm glad they've finally concluded their business."

"Yes, that's one less worry," she agreed.

"What about our daughter?" He broached a subject they had avoided for the past few days. "Have her wild inclinations been tamed yet? I haven't noticed Gilberto Aguirre at our door to beg for her hand." He snorted.

Mary kept her peace, not wanting to inflame him further. Gilberto Aguirre had called yesterday, asking for Sarah. Following her husband's wishes, she turned him away, instructing Pedro to say he was no longer welcome at their home.

It had upset her to do this. She didn't like being uncordial to anyone. She had almost talked to him herself, thinking to explain the situation. Upon careful reflection, she had thought better of it. What could she have said? Her explanations would have been far more painful than a mere dismissal.

Her heart went out to Gilberto, as well as her daughter. She remembered what it felt like, that first rush of love, and she sympathized with them. Even worse, with Herbert at work during the days, these unpleasant tasks fell to her. She didn't like being their daughter's jailor. For all of her daughter's life, they had been close. Now Sarah had withdrawn, shutting her out.

"I think we should give her a little freedom," she moderated. "After all, we'll be leaving soon and—"

"A little freedom?" he bellowed, removing the pipe from his mouth to stare at her in amazement. "A little freedom," he repeated, "to elope with Aguirre while our backs are turned? I think not!"

She didn't want Sarah to elope with Gilberto. On that

point, she agreed with her husband; the young *criollo* was totally unsuitable. Despite Sarah's obvious commitment to Gilberto, she found it hard to believe their daughter would defy their wishes.

"You said yourself he hasn't shown himself," she pointed out, allowing herself a small lie, hoping to soothe her husband's concern. "And it's doubtful he will, either, because, as you also said, his father would never allow the marriage."

"Don't use my words against me, Mary," he groused, puffing hard on his pipe.

"Oh, Herbert, don't be so hard. This is our daughter we're talking about."

"That's why I'm not taking chances. She's not just our daughter, she's our *only* child."

"Yes, dear, I suppose you're right to be careful," she subsided. But her heart didn't agree.

The harder they bore down on Sarah, replacing their will with hers, the longer it would take for her to get over Gilberto Aguirre. If they gave her some breathing room, Mary was certain her daughter would do the right thing.

Ignacio stared at the mounted heads on Don Carlos's walls. The old religion taught that animals possessed the spirits of the dead. Animals were to be revered and worshipped, not massacred without honor.

Waiting for Don Carlos, he wondered why he had been summoned. Before he arrived at an answer, his employer opened the door and strode into the room.

Slapping him on the back, the don shook his hand and offered, "Take a seat, Ignacio. Make yourself comfortable."

"I'd prefer to stand, Don Carlos."

"Suit yourself." The don heaved his bulk into a wide

leather armchair and said, "I guess you want to know why I sent for you."

"*Sí, Señor Don.*"

"You've been watching the McFarland girl, haven't you?"

"*Sí.*"

"But no luck?"

"No. Since the 'accident' after the ball, she has remained inside under guard."

"And you haven't been able to penetrate the guard, to get to her and obtain the formula?"

"I have become friendly with some of the guards, and I believe I could get into the house at night. But then what? I need time and privacy to 'convince' her. There are too many people about. Her mother, the Yorks, the servants." He paused and stretched his hands, palms up. "I thought it better to be patient. She must leave the house sometime."

"*Sí,* but 'sometime' might be too late. I've heard rumors that she has already sold the formula to Seguín. He will probably start undercutting my price within the next few weeks."

Ignacio didn't respond. There was nothing he could say. He had done his best.

"It doesn't matter if Seguín has the formula, so long as we have it, too," the don observed, helping himself to a cigar from the humidor on his desk. "Does it?"

"Why won't you let me kill him, *Señor Don?*" he asked, his soul burning for retribution, for the long-awaited revenge of his sister's death. "Then our worries would be over."

"Not quite." Don Carlos rolled the cigar between his fingers. "Juan Martínez would oversee the production. He's Seguín's trusted partner."

"I'll kill him, too."

The don laughed, a short, hoarse bark. "You can't kill

everyone off, Ignacio." He shook his head. "No. Now that Seguín has the formula, the only way is for us to obtain it as well. After that . . . you can do what you want with Seguín. But the first time the McFarland girl goes out, bring her to me. I'll get the formula from her."

"What about her friends, the Yorks? Won't there be reprisals if I bring her here? I had thought to take her to my place in the capitol and frighten her a little. It should take only an hour or so to—"

"Let me take care of the Yorks," Don Carlos interjected. "Bring her to me."

"*Sí, Señor Don,* as you wish." He bowed and half-turned toward the door. "Is that all?"

"One thing more, Ignacio. You've been watching the York household. Since my son returned to the capitol, has he visited or gone out with the York girl, Sarah?"

"No, he went to the house once, but was turned away. One of the guards told me he used the cook to carry messages to *Señorita* York."

"Listen carefully, *mi amigo,* because this is of premier importance." The don raised his voice to make his point. "It is as important as the formula and Seguín. *¿Entiende?*"

Ignacio drew himself up and gave the don his full attention. "*Sí,* I understand. What do you want me to do?"

"My son must not see *Señorita* York. If he does, hire men and take him prisoner. Bring him to me. Can you do this?"

"*Sí,* Don Carlos. I will do as you say."

Some promises were made in heaven. And then there were other promises that were made in . . .

Closing her eyes, Diana leaned against the brougham's padded squabs. It was her first outing since her "accident," and the rocking of the carriage made her queasy. How would she fare on the long trip home, she wondered. And how could she leave Sarah behind in such a dangerous and precarious situation?

Sarah, despite being held a prisoner in her parents' home, was determined to stay in México and marry Gilberto. Gilberto had managed to smuggle a note to Sarah, through the staid cook, Felicia. His note hadn't been particularly promising. He was having just as much difficulty with his father as Sarah was having with her parents.

Sarah had admitted that her father intended to "call out" Gilberto if they eloped, which made Diana's errand that much more foolhardy. If she hadn't already given her word, she would have refused to take Sarah's note to Gilberto. No, if it meant Sarah's ultimate happiness, she would make the sacrifice.

With Seguín gone from her life forever, she knew the anguish of giving up the man she loved. Sometimes, it was all she could do to rise in the morning and face the empty day ahead.

Gilberto's note had begged Sarah to elope with him in the hope that his father would accept the marriage once it was done. That still left Mr. York, but Sarah believed her parents would relent, too, once they were married.

Diana shook her head. Somehow, despite Sarah's optimism, she had grave doubts that the two fathers would give in so easily. Because Sarah was a Protestant and Gilberto was Catholic, they would be married by a magistrate, not in the church. It would be too easy to obtain an annulment, Diana realized.

For Sarah's sake, she hoped their elopement was the answer, but for her own sake, she hated leaving her best friend behind in México.

The covered brougham lurched to a halt. The door opened and a large, beefy hand reached inside, offering assistance. The hand was attached to the red-haired arm of Gustave Wolke, a man Mr. York had recently hired.

According to Sarah, Gustave was Austrian, a farmer's

son who had joined the Austrian mercenaries. Military life hadn't suited him, and Mr. York had hired him as a bodyguard for the family. Standing six-foot-six in his stocking feet, his mere size daunted most people, making him the perfect guard.

Diana had asked him to accompany her because his size and strength made her feel safe. Sarah concurred with her decision, explaining he seemed to be slow-witted and tight-lipped, as well as capable of speaking only his native tongue and a little French. Sarah felt it was doubtful he would report Diana's "detour" to the Yorks.

"*Mercí*, Gustave." She thanked him when she found herself on solid ground, standing before the steps to Gilberto's town house.

Straining to make herself understood in limited French, she explained she was leaving a note for a friend before they continued to the market to buy embroidery thread.

Gustave bobbed his head and said nothing. She swept past him, climbing the front steps and grasping the brass knocker. Banging the knocker, shaped like a lion's head, she prayed and held her breath.

After a few moments, the door opened and the *mayordomo* stood on the threshold. Switching to Spanish, she explained that she had a confidential letter for *Señor* Gilberto Aguirre. The *mayordomo* offered to take it for her, but she refused. Sarah had warned her that all of the Aguirre servants couldn't be trusted.

Despite her reluctance to carry out this mission, she realized her heart was pounding in her chest, waiting for the *mayordomo's* answer. If he refused or if Gilberto wasn't at home, what would become of Sarah's plans?

After what seemed like hours but could have only been a few seconds, he bowed stiffly and stood back, allowing her to enter the house. Turning, she waved at Gustave and reassured him that she would only be a minute.

Standing at attention beside the carriage, he inclined

his head and looked straight ahead. It was eerie, she thought briefly. The man was almost not human.

Following the servant down a long, dark corridor, she was ushered into what appeared to be a parlor. Having never been inside a Mexican home before, she found the atmosphere odd.

The room was virtually empty except for several tall mirrors, dark religious paintings, and two long mahogany tables laden with wax flowers and wooden statues of saints. Four straight-backed, uncomfortable-looking chairs completed the ensemble. The tile floors were bare, and there was no fireplace. Despite the austerity of the furnishings, she noted that the room was equipped with its own reliquary niche, complete with a plaster Madonna and votive candles.

Hearing the scrape of steps behind her, she turned to face Gilberto Aguirre. After dismissing the *mayordomo* and pulling the massive, brass-bound door shut, he greeted her. "Thank you for coming. You are *Señorita* McFarland, Sarah's friend, aren't you?"

They had met only once, that fateful night at the ball, but she felt as if she knew him. He looked so much like Seguín. She knew she shouldn't stare, but she couldn't drag her gaze from his face.

The eyes and hair were different, she observed. Seguín's eyes were dark pools of obsidian, and this man's eyes were lighter, more caramel-colored. Gilberto's hair, in contrast to Seguín's long, straight black mane, was curly, fitting his skull like a monk's cap. But the sculpted planes of their faces were the same. Too much the same.

Her breathing felt ragged, and her stomach knotted. In years to come, would she be haunted by Seguín's face, the features of her best friend's children carrying the same unmistakable stamp?

Shaking off the premonition, she replied, "Yes, I'm Diana McFarland, Sarah's friend." Opening her reticule, she drew forth Sarah's letter and offered it. "Sarah sent me with a reply."

"Her parents are against our marrying, too." It wasn't a question; it was a statement. He took the folded paper from her hand.

"Yes, they are. Sarah can't leave the house."

"I see." Fixing her with his tawny eyes, he stated flatly, "I guessed as much when I was turned away. But my note must have gotten through, or you wouldn't be here?" This time, it was a question.

"Yes, Felicia, the cook, smuggled it in."

"*Sí*, the cook. I waited outside and followed her to the market. I was desperate, and paid her handsomely. I hope she's discreet."

Recalling the placid features of Felicia, she assured him, "I believe she is."

Knowing that the longer she stayed the more suspicion it might arouse, she excused herself with, "I must be going, *Señor* Aguirre. Sarah's letter will explain everything, even the signal she has prepared if you can execute her plan."

At her words, his golden eyes gleamed and his mouth stretched into a wide smile. Fleetingly, she wondered if he had doubted Sarah's loyalty, thinking the letter would refuse his suit, because of her parent's objections. That such a handsome and charming man would be anxious about Sarah's loyalty surprised her. It was in that instant she intuitively knew Gilberto Aguirre loved her best friend with all his heart.

Sighing to herself, she was glad, silently rejoicing that Sarah had found true love. Her earlier doubts fled, too, and she was ready to help her best friend to marry him.

Bowing, he replied, "I understand your haste. I can't thank you enough for coming. You're a true friend to Sarah, and I hope you will become a friend of mine as well, in the future."

He tucked her arm into the crook of his arm and offered *"Por favor,* allow me to escort you to the door."

"I can't believe I let you talk me into this." Diana reached up and pushed aside the shutter covering the brougham's window. Peering out, she watched the dark countryside flash by.

"Don't be such an old woman," Sarah chided. "After all, you did *promise.*"

"I know I promised, but I've already fulfilled my vow, going to Gilberto with your letter," Diana groused unnecessarily, realizing she was committed to seeing her best friend married to Gilberto. If only the plan didn't seem so impetuous, so utterly dangerous.

"Not quite. There's more if you mean to honor your promise." Sarah giggled, obviously giddy about her impending elopement.

"But to be a . . . what did you call it?"

"A 'diversion'."

"I don't think Gustave is capable of being diverted," Diana noted caustically.

"Even Gustave can be. Use your feminine wiles. Just get him to drink some beer and slip him this powder." Leaning across the lurching carriage, Sarah placed a small vial in her hand. It was filled with a white powder.

"When and where is this supposed to happen?"

"Next door to the beer brewery, there is a small lace shop. I'll step inside to look at the lace. I'm supposed to meet Gilberto there at noon, when the sun is directly overhead. While I'm looking at the lace, you must get Gustave to drink some beer. The other servants claim beer is his one weakness. It shouldn't be too hard."

"Sarah, this is ridiculous. Won't Gustave wonder why we didn't wake him all afternoon? Why we let him sleep for hours?"

"Don't worry. We'll say we were shopping and forgot how late it was."

"What about the man steering the boat?"

"Bribe him with the money I gave you."

"I hope this works. I wanted to be your maiden of honor. Instead, I'm a 'diversion'."

Giggles erupted from Sarah again, and she covered her mouth with her hand. She must have seen the hurt look on Diana's face, because she reached out and hugged her. "I know you wanted to see me married, but this is the only way I'll have time to be alone with Gilberto."

As soon as the words left her mouth, Sarah blushed, telltale crimson staining her cheeks. Suddenly flustered, she released Diana and leaned back.

Noting the high color of her friend's face, Diana couldn't help but wonder what it would be like to honeymoon with her own husband. What would it be like if she could have one brief afternoon in Seguín's arms?

"How did you get your mother to agree to this outing?" Diana asked, worrying about the danger of their hasty plan.

"I told her I wanted to show you the floating gardens before we left México."

"And she agreed?"

"Yes, Mother is very sympathetic. I think she understands how I feel. I wish she could convince Father."

Diana gasped. "You don't mean she knows you're eloping, do you?

"No, no, nothing like that. She believes I'll uphold their wishes. But she hates for me to be a prisoner."

"Then you're deceiving them both?"

"Yes. To have Gilberto, I'm willing to deceive them both."

She registered the steely conviction in her friend's voice. She wished she were as brave as Sarah, going after what she wanted. But then, it wasn't the same for her. Seguín didn't want her for a wife . . . or anything else.

Knowing the die was cast and she would need to go through with the plan, she inquired, "What's this place called?"

"Xochimilco. It's a perfect place to be married. You'll see. It's so romantic—like glimpsing a piece of ancient México before the *conquistadors.*"

"But, Sarah, it's so far away. We'll be late returning. Your father will have a seizure."

The brougham hit a bump, was airborne for a few moments, and then landed with a bone-shattering crunch. Diana clutched her seat and muttered, "And the roads are terrible, just like all Mexican roads."

Their gazes met in silent agreement. Diana vividly remembered the horrible condition of the roads from the coast, when she and her mother had arrived. Winding through swamps, jungles and mountains, the roads were nothing but rutted tracks, full of holes and entire sections that weren't passable. More than once, the passengers were forced to walk so the public coach could move forward.

Sarah must have read her mind, because she reached across the bouncing space and clasped her hand. "Don't worry, everything will be fine. You'll see."

Releasing her hand, Sarah rummaged through the picnic basket they had brought and tossed a mango to her. "Chin up. Have something to eat. It'll make you feel better."

She caught the mango. Foraging in the picnic basket, she found a paring knife and began peeling the exotic fruit. Lifting her head from the task, she inquired, "How far is Xochimilco?"

"About thirteen miles from the center of México City."

"What's so special about this place?"

"Have you seen pictures of Venice, Italy?"

"Yes."

"Remember the canals and boats? Xochimilco is like that, but instead of floating through a city you float through gardens. It's enchanting. A leftover from Aztec México."

"Sounds intriguing."

"There's more. Would you like to hear it?"

Diana nodded.

Leaning forward, Sarah explained eagerly, "Before the Spaniards came, the Aztec capitol was where the center of México City is today. The capitol stood on an island in the middle of a lake, connected to the mainland by a causeway. The outlying areas were lake or swamp. But the Aztecs were ingenious. To make more land for farming, they drove stakes into the shallow parts and filled the space with dirt and debris. Then they raised produce on their man-made land, and took it to market in canoes. The Spaniards came and eventually drained most of the lake. Xochimilco has remained as it was before."

"That's fascinating. Where did you learn this?"

"From Papa's history books. Unlike someone I know, I don't just read novels."

"I don't just read novels," she defended herself, "but while I was convalescing I couldn't seem to keep my mind on anything serious."

Sarah smiled, and she smiled back. Despite the danger she was happy for her friend, and excited, too. But she couldn't quite squelch the uneasy feeling that their plan would somehow go awry.

Her friend must have read the concern on her face, because she admonished, "Quit worrying. Everything will go right. You'll see." Beaming at her, she added, "After all, this is my wedding day."

"You promise to return before sunset? No matter what?"

Sarah repeated their favorite vow from childhood. "Cross my heart and hope to die."

"Xochimilco is on the way to Cuernavaca, and Cuernavaca is where Maximilian and all the wealthy Mexicans keep summer homes. In fact, we have a summer home there, too, although we seldom use it," Sarah mused, half to herself.

"You're not thinking of going to your summer home after the . . . ?" Diana couldn't finish her thought out loud. Feeling like a third wheel, she found it hard to talk about Sarah's impending honeymoon.

She hadn't confided to Sarah about Seguín, the night of her rescue, although she had intended to. The time had never seemed right. Now that she was leaving México, what did it matter?

"No, it's too far. I hope Gilberto has found a suitable place close by." The high color returned to Sarah's cheeks, and she covered her embarrassment by retrieving a mango for herself from the picnic basket.

Silence filled the carriage as they peeled and ate their fruit, throwing the refuse from the brougham's windows for the birds.

"Do you still worry about that awful man who tried to abduct you?" Sarah asked abruptly.

Surprised by the unexpected question, Diana considered for a moment before responding, "Not really. I've been locked in the house for so long, he's probably given up. At least, I hope he has." She wasn't sure if she believed it, not after what Seguín had told her, but she didn't want to add her own burdens to their already hazardous undertaking.

Sarah nodded absent-mindedly, biting into the mango and mopping at the juice with her handkerchief.

Pushing the carriage's shutter back to throw out a remnant of the fruit, Diana declared, "It's getting light out."

"We'll be there soon. We can eat our breakfast *al fresco*, while drifting through the gardens."

Knowing their time alone together without Gustave's

watchful eye upon them was drawing to a close, she admitted, "I'm happy for you, Sarah. But I'll miss you terribly
when I leave for the States. It seems I've just found you,
only to lose you again." As hard as she tried, she couldn't
keep the wistful note from her voice.

"I'll miss you, too, Diana. But it's not forever. You'll be
living in San Francisco, close to my parents. Gilberto and
I will come to visit. You'll see."

Their gazes met and locked. She noticed Sarah's eyes
looked as watery as hers felt. Without speaking, they both
leaned forward and hugged again, not caring how sticky
their hands were, covered with the juice of the mangos.

Eleven

The floating gardens of Xochimilco proved to be as enchanting as Sarah had promised. They hired a boat for the day. It was shaped like a flattened-out gondola, much wider than the boats Diana remembered from the pictures of Venice. The carriage driver remained on shore. Gustave accompanied them.

They floated through a labyrinth of water passageways, dotted with tiny islands. The vegetation grew thick and tropical. Flowers covered every inch of land. Even the gondolas were decorated with them. Each morning, the boat owners and their wives wove hundreds of fresh blossoms onto arched trellises over their boats. The effect was spectacular. Riotous color assaulted the eye, and the flowers' mingled scents filled the air.

Brilliant birds flashed overhead. Diana recognized the familiar parrots, parakeets, canaries, and toucans, but there were myriad other less familiar species as well. Sarah pointed out the iridescent feathers of a kingfisher and a large heron that was standing, one-legged, searching for its breakfast amid the watery reeds.

They drifted and stopped and moved on. The tame contents of their picnic basket were forgotten as they sampled exotic offerings from the native vendors. Fiery stuffed peppers, tortillas filled with pork and eggs, *tamales* containing raisins and spices and meats, as well as a veritable cornucopia of fresh fruit, were all theirs for the tasting.

Gustave, however, appeared suspicious of the native foods. At Sarah's bidding, he satisfied his hunger from their picnic basket.

Along with sampling the food, they drifted from island to island, stopping to admire the Mexican handicrafts for sale. Pottery and jewelry crowded cheek by jowl with clothing and saddlery. Silver utensils and decorative items gleamed beside wooden and onyx carvings. Crude native paintings adorned large sheets of bark or fragile, dried banana leaves. The paintings, like their surroundings, were brilliant with color, depicting flowers, birds, and curling vines.

Music, too, eddied around them: Mexican folk songs sung by an impromptu chorus, the plaintive strumming of Spanish guitars, the eerie flute notes and drumbeats of Indian chants, and the frenzied rhythms of fiesta music wafting on the breeze.

They looked and exclaimed and ate their way, for three hours, straight through breakfast and lunch. As the sun grew higher, even though it was only late March, the tropical heat made them uncomfortably warm, and they retreated to the canopied shade at the back of the boat.

"*Señor* Gondolier," Sarah called out, "isn't the beer brewery nearby? My friend and I are thirsty."

"*Sí, señorita,* I will take you there," the boat owner replied.

Diana glanced at Gustave, who was sitting at the opposite end of the boat, wanting to gauge his reaction. Unfortunately, he showed no reaction, and then she remembered that he didn't speak Spanish.

The distinctive, yeasty aroma of beer filled the air. Rounding the corner of an island, they spied another larger island. On it were several small shops, nestled beside a long, palm-thatched shed housing several huge oaken vats and a strange looking apparatus made of tubing, suspended above a fire. To one side, Diana spied the tiny lace shop Sarah had designated as the rendezvous point.

Looking up, she found the sun shining directly overhead. Turning her gaze to Gustave, she was gratified to see that his interest was riveted on the beer brewery. In fact, his nostrils fairly quivered with the heavy smell of brewing malt. Relieved that Sarah had been correct in her assessment, she took a deep breath and told herself she could do this.

"Gustave," Sarah directed in French, "fetch us two pints of beer, will you? Oh, and get one for yourself, too. You must be thirsty."

The Austrian bodyguard rose to his feet, rocking the boat and bowing awkwardly. "As you wish, Mademoiselle, I will fetch your beer." Shaking his large, red head, he declined Sarah's offer with, "Thank you, but I had better not indulge myself, Mademoiselle. Water will do for me."

Diana's heart plummeted to her shoes with Gustave's refusal. Sarah captured her gaze and winked, obviously trying to bolster her courage. Diana wished she shared Sarah's never-failing optimism. How on earth would she convince him to drink the beer?

Her mind spun in circles, thinking of ways. In the meantime, with Gustave gone, she found the vial of sleeping powder in her reticule and pushed it up the sleeve of her dress, ready for use.

Gustave returned with their pints of beer in earthen mugs. Diana stared down at the murky depths of hers and grimaced. She didn't like the taste of beer, anyway, and from the looks of it this beer promised to be particularly vile.

On the other hand, Sarah attacked her beer with gusto, leaving a thin moustache of foam on her upper lip. Wiping her mouth with a handkerchief, she said, "That was great. It really quenches your thirst."

Raising her hand, she shaded her eyes, gazing at the island. As if she had just noticed it, she exclaimed, "There's a lace shop! Just what I've been looking for. Diana, do you want to look at the lace with me?"

Knowing her part in this crazy drama, Diana shook her head. "Not now. I'm a little tired, and I need to finish my beer. You go on ahead."

When he helped Sarah alight from the boat, Gustave looked confused, swinging his head in Diana's direction and then in Sarah's. Diana understood his confusion. He had been instructed to keep an eye on both of them, but if they split up, what should he do?

"Mademoiselle Sarah, shouldn't I go with you?" His voice sounded hesitant. "Mademoiselle Diana will have the gondolier, and I'm supposed to—"

"Do as you please," she replied lightly, as if the decision held little interest. In stark contrast to her airy words, her movements were determined and even hasty. She was already halfway to the lace shop before Gustave had digested her answer.

Diana could have throttled her best friend. They hadn't discussed this possibility—that Gustave would leave the boat to trail after Sarah.

"Eeek!" Diana screamed. "Gustave, a snake, a snake!" She pointed to the shallow water beside the boat.

At her scream, both the gondolier and Gustave started forward. The boat owner brandished his pole as if it were a club.

When they reached her, she moved to the opposite side of the boat and shrieked hysterically, in both French and Spanish, "Get it, get it! Oh, I can't look. Please get it." Purposely she turned her face away and covered her eyes with one hand. With the other hand, she slipped the sleeping powder into her beer.

With her eyes carefully averted, she heard the men rummaging about, muttering under their breath, obviously mystified by what had frightened her. The boat rocked, and water splashed as they stomped around, searching.

Finally, Gustave said, "Mademoiselle, we can find nothing. Would you please turn around and show us where you saw the snake?"

She turned and pointed at a spot on the water, admitting with a shrug, "That's where I saw it. I guess it swam away."

Even though she spoke in French, the gondolier must have understood. He left her to Gustave, muttering something about a crazy woman.

Gustave shook his head and started to follow the gondolier to the front of the boat, but she stopped him by tugging on his coat sleeve and pleading, "Please don't leave me. What if it creeps into the boat?" Lifting her head and staring warily at the flowery canopy overhead, she added, "It could be hiding in the flowers."

"Mademoiselle—"

"Please, Gustave, just sit with me for a few moments until I'm not afraid." Regaining her seat, she patted the cushion beside her, giving him her most coy look.

"As you wish, Mademoiselle Diana." He acquiesced, and sat beside her.

Retrieving her mug of beer, she declared, "This scare has made me thirstier than before."

Gustave eyed the beer she held as if it were made of pure gold. His tongue snaked out, and he wet his lips. Obviously tempted, he glanced away, a stern look settling on his countenance.

So far, so good, she thought.

Taking the tiniest sip of the beer, she made a face and spit it out, exclaiming, "Pah! This beer is awful. It's so . . . so bitter." Thrusting the beer at him, she commanded, "Here, you take it, Gustave. Please get me some water."

Obediently, he took the beer and rose to get the water. When he returned with the water skin, he asked, "What should I do with the beer?"

"Why don't you drink it?" She held her breath, hoping he would take the bait.

"I don't know if I should. I'm guarding you and Mademoiselle Sarah, and I need to—"

"Then dump it out," she interrupted, wanting to force his hand. "Although it seems a pity to waste it."

"*Oui,* mademoiselle, it does." She watched the conflicting emotions play across his face. "Maybe a sip wouldn't hurt. I'm awfully thirsty, too."

Gingerly, he brought the mug to his lips. In tandem, as if offering silent encouragement, Diana tilted the water skin to her mouth and drank deeply.

Pausing, he wiped his mouth with the back of his hand. "It's not so bitter, mademoiselle, at least not for me." He tipped the mug back and drank deeply, finishing it. "One mug shouldn't addle my wits," he declared after the fact, as if giving himself belated permission.

Diana exhaled. It was the first deep breath she had taken since this drama began playing itself out. Returning the water skin to him, she arranged her skirts carefully so as to cover her limbs and reclined against the cushions as if she were going to take a nap. From half-closed eyes, she kept a sharp watch on Gustave.

He managed to navigate the distance to replace the water skin without any trouble. Then he stared at the lace shop as if he were planning to go after Sarah. Just when she was at her wit's end, he sat down with a thump, cradling his big head in his hands.

"I feel funny." His words were slurred.

Like a delicate flower in the noonday sun, the giant man seemed to wither, slowly crumpling to the rough planks of the boat. When a harsh snore emerged from his lips, she wanted to jump up and down with joy and relief.

The gondolier caught her eye and shrugged, murmuring, "Big man, little stomach for liquor."

"Señor Gondolier, please take me to the opposite side of the garden."

"The other, *señorita?* We're going to leave her behind?"

"Just for the afternoon." She approached him with the bag of coins in her hand. "I need your cooperation and silence. You will, of course, be paid your usual fee for the boat, as well."

The boat owner took the bag from her and hefted it in his hand. Obviously pleased with the weight of it, he smiled and nodded.

"I now pronounce you man and wife," the magistrate intoned flatly. The hurried ceremony had taken only a few minutes to perform.

Expecting him to add the final statement with, "You may kiss the bride," Sarah was disappointed when he directed instead, "Please step this way and sign the registry."

As if he could read her mind, Gilberto squeezed her hand and winked. Taking some small measure of relief from his encouragement, she obeyed, and trailed after the two men. Their two witnesses, the ladies who owned the lace shop, giggled behind their hands.

Now that the deed was done and all that remained was for her to pen her name beside Gilberto's in the blotched, ink-stained registry, the enormity of what she had done pressed down on her. And the surroundings, coupled with the dry, matter-of-fact ceremony didn't help.

The back room of the lace shop was dank and dusty, filled with stacks of lace and lace-making tools, as well as mounds of other fabrics and half-finished goods. Instead of the white satin wedding dress she had envisioned for herself, she wore a gray muslin day dress, covered with tiny, embroidered pink flowers.

Gilberto had been thoughtful enough to purchase her a beautiful lace veil from the shop owners. It covered her

Here's a special offer for Romance readers!

Get 4 FREE Zebra Splendor Historical Romance Novels!

A $19.96 value absolutely FREE!

Take a trip back in time and experience the passion, adventure and excitement of a Splendor Romance... delivered right to your doorstep!

Take advantage of this offer to enjoy Zebra's newest line of historical romance novels....Splendor Romances (formerly Lovegrams Historical Romances)- Take our introductory shipment of 4 romance novels -Absolutely Free! (a $19.96 value)

Now you'll be able to savor today's best romance novels without even leaving your home with our convenient and inexpensive home subscription service. Here's what you get for joining:

- 4 BRAND NEW bestselling Splendor Romances delivered to your doorstep every month

- 20% off every title (or almost $4.00 off) with your home subscription

- FREE home delivery

- A FREE monthly newsletter, *Zebra/Pinnacle Romance News* filled with author interviews, member benefits, book previews and more!

- No risks or obligations...you're free to cancel whenever you wish...no questions asked

To get started with your own home subscription, simply complete and return the card provided. You'll receive your FREE introductory shipment of 4 Splendor Romances and then you'll begin to receive monthly shipments of new Zebra Splendor titles. Each shipment will be yours to examine for 10 days and then if you decide to keep the books, you'll pay the preferred home subscriber's price of just $4.00 per title. That's $16 for all 4 books with FREE home delivery! And if you want us to stop sending books, just say the word...it's that simple.

4 FREE books are waiting for you!
Just mail in the certificate below!

If the certificate is missing below, write to:
Splendor Romances, Zebra Home Subscription Service, Inc.,
P.O. Box 5214, Clifton, New Jersey 07015-5214
or call TOLL-FREE 1-888-345-BOOK

FREE BOOK CERTIFICATE

Yes! Please send me 4 Splendor Romances (formerly Zebra Lovegram Historical Romances), ABSOLUTELY FREE! After my introductory shipment, I will be able to preview 4 new Splendor Romances each month FREE for 10 days. Then if I decide to keep them, I will pay the money-saving preferred publisher's price of just $4.00 each... a total of $16.00. That's 20% off the regular publisher's price and there's never any additional charge for shipping and handling. I may return any shipment within 10 days and owe nothing, and I may cancel my subscription at any time. The 4 FREE books will be mine to keep in any case.

SP0599

Name _____

Address _____ Apt. _____

City _____ State _____ Zip _____

Telephone ( ) _____

Signature _____
(If under 18, parent or guardian must sign.)

Terms and prices subject to change. Orders subject to acceptance by Zebra Home Subscription Service, Inc. .
Zebra Home Subscription Service, Inc. reserves the right to reject or cancel any subscription.

A $19.96 value.

FREE!

No obligation
to buy
anything,
ever.

SPLENDOR ROMANCES

ZEBRA HOME SUBSCRIPTION SERVICE, INC.

120 BRIGHTON ROAD

P.O. BOX 5214

CLIFTON, NEW JERSEY 07015-5214

AFFIX
STAMP
HERE

head and reached halfway down her back, woven of gossamer threads, delicate as a spider's web.

A spider's web. Why had she thought of the veil in those terms, she wondered. Was it because she felt suddenly trapped in an impossible situation. While planning for their secret union she had felt confident, daring. But now, facing the reality, her nerves failed her.

What have I done? the voice in her head cried. *Defying my parents to marry a man I barely know, who can't promise me a future. Sneaking back home after the ceremony, married but not really married, to continue this charade until our parents are forced to recognize the union.*

With a shaking hand, she signed the register, writing both her maiden name and her new married name beside Gilberto's bold scrawl. *Aguirre,* her new name was *Aguirre.* But was it really? Gilberto's father didn't want her to belong to his family. To Don Carlos she was an unlanded *gringa,* worthy of his contempt.

And what about her father? Had she misjudged him? When she admitted her marriage, would he accept it? Would her mother help to convince him? Or would he demand a duel with her new husband, as he had threatened?

Thinking about her father and Gilberto facing each other with pistols was too horrible to contemplate. A sob rose to the back of her throat and lodged there. *What have I done?* The tortured question reverberated through her mind.

Gilberto captured her shaking hand in his, holding it tenderly for a moment before he raised it to his lips. His full mouth brushed her skin, bringing a shiver of pleasure. His eyes sought hers—warm, golden-colored eyes, shining with promise, shining with their future.

How could she have doubted the rightness of their marriage? There was no other man for her. With one touch, he banished her misgivings. If she had to move heaven and earth she would remain beside him for the rest of her life, forsaking all others.

There followed a flurry of meaningless gestures. The two shop owners produced a pitcher of beer from the brewery and poured mugs for them all, toasting them on their wedding day. Sarah barely tasted the liquid, politely taking a sip. Gilberto paid the magistrate and dispatched him. After much hugging and tearful congratulations, they took their leave, slipping through the back door of the tiny shop.

Her new husband led Sarah along a primitive path, snaking through the lush gardens until they reached the end of the island. Crossing a rickety, wooden bridge, they sped across another island and another bridge. Finding themselves at the edge of the gardens, they hurried along yet another path, this one fainter than the others.

Gilberto brought her to a clearing. In the middle of the clearing sat a thatched hut, a one room hovel. A few scrawny chickens scratched at the doorway. She guessed it belonged to one of the gondoliers.

Sweeping her into his arms, he carried her across the threshold, kicking the wooden gate that served as a door, shut behind them. Gently, he lowered her to her feet and kissed the top of her head.

Leaning against him, it took a moment for her eyes to adjust to the semi-darkness of the tiny place. The floor was hard-packed earth, but it had been swept clean. A scarred table and rickety chairs huddled beside the hearth. The table held a basket. Their wedding feast? She wondered.

Two straw mattresses were piled in the corner. She shuddered to think of the vermin living there. The center of the hut had been cleared to make room for an enormous feather mattress, covered with a bright, woven counterpane.

Crossing to the mattress, her new groom threw back the counterpane, revealing snowy-white linen sheets, strewn with flower petals. Their exotic scents rose in the air, a cloud of sweetness filling the sour little room. She recognized gardenia petals, camellias, hyacinth, jasmine, and honeysuckle.

I will fashion my ladylove a bower of flowers and lay down beside her there. . . . The half-forgotten line of the sonnet rose in her mind.

She didn't know if those were the exact words, but it didn't matter. Her new husband had done this for her, to sweeten the ugly little room, to 'make pretty' their harried, rushed union. Her heart squeezed, and tears rose to her eyes.

Shrugging, he admitted, "It isn't much . . . but it was the best I could do. We have this place for the afternoon."

Threading her arm through his, she drew close, so close she could feel the heat emanating from his body. "It's wonderful," she breathed. "A scented garden for us—" She couldn't go on. The words clogged in her throat.

How many times had she dreamed of their wedding night . . . or afternoon? Heat suffused her, starting at her toes and spreading through her torso, bringing a telltale flush to her face.

Now, faced with the intimacy she had so longed for, she felt suddenly shy. She had had countless suitors and kissed many of them. Beyond that, she was as innocent as a newborn babe, whereas Gilberto was—by all indications—very experienced.

Would he be disappointed in her? And if he were, would he regret their hasty, secret marriage? Would he rue the day he had defied his father and gambled his birthright? A new kind of fear fluttered in her chest, stretching its wings, enfolding her in the darkness of doubt.

"Would you care for something to eat? I had a picnic basket prepared for us." He cleared his throat, and looked unsure of himself. Even in the dark hut she saw the answering blush on his countenance. The realization struck her. He was just as uncertain as she was. Knowing this gave her new courage.

"I'm not hungry, Gilberto, at least not for food." She surprised herself with the sultry invitation.

His arms were suddenly around her, and he slanted his mouth across hers. This was what had been missing from their arid ceremony. The potent promise of their attraction for each other, the passionate pledge of their hearts. With their mouths joined, she knew they hadn't made a mistake. They were meant to be together, to share their lives as one.

Savoring the wonderful texture of his full mouth pressed against hers, she reveled in the malty taste of their wedding toast on his lips. Their mouths fit together like two pieces of a puzzle, perfect mates, sensitive flesh against sensitive flesh.

As he opened his mouth their breaths intermingled, their souls tentatively touching. With reverent care his lips moved over hers, nipping, caressing and soothing. His tongue tip worried the seam of her lips, demanding entrance, seeking a joining. Their tongues touched, and heat simmered in her veins. With his tongue exploring the inner recesses of her mouth, she gave herself over to him, shuddering with unspeakable pleasure.

Their tongues mated and danced, advanced and retreated, in the age-old rhythm of love. She rubbed her tongue along his, reveling in the hot, velvety nap of him. He opened his mouth wider, drinking her in, devouring her with his mouth. Lifting his mouth from hers, he poured kisses over her upturned face, trailing with sensuous promise down the column of her throat.

Pleasure pulsed through her, hot, pure, sweet-as-honey pleasure. The pleasure mounted, spiraling through her, turning her blood to fire, her bones to jelly. She ached for him. Passion overrode the pleasure, advancing on stealthy feet, making her want . . . making her need. Turning her thoughts into mindless impulses, she existed only to feel, only to desire.

Pressing closer, she dug her fingers into the curling crispness of his hair, pulling him closer and closer yet, coming home, burrowing into his body, wanting him nearer and nearer.

Clutching each other as if they were drowning, they sank to the fragrant mattress. His fingers were at her throat, hurrying down the corridor of buttons on her dress. Her own hands were shaking, hastily untying the cravat at his throat and undoing his collar buttons.

When a triangle of his chest appeared, matted with brown hair, she buried her face there, softly moaning, raining tiny kisses over the salty, musky expanse of his chest. He groaned deeply in answer and parted the top of her dress, slipping her arms from the fabric, allowing it to pool at her waist.

The air touched her bare shoulders. Her breasts were covered by only a thin chemise. She felt his eyes on her, burning through the flimsy fabric. He bent his head and kissed the hollow of her throat. Her pulse leaped there, echoed by another pulse . . . lower . . . at the juncture of her thighs.

His lips strayed, soft and warm, worshipping her throat and shoulders. She anticipated his touch before she felt it, the murmur of angel's wings against her breasts, the sensuous slide of silk over sensitive skin. Her breasts tightened and stretched, filled with their own life, their own longing. Her nipples peaked, hardening like new berries.

A whisper of cloth, the satiny slide of fabric, and her breasts were bared. His hands covered them, circling and stroking, teasing the strutted nipples into harder points, filling her with a yearning so bright, so hot, she felt as if her blood had caught fire.

His lips returned to her throat, lingering, idolizing. Hot and wet, his tongue teased downward, perfect counterpoint to the rough yet smooth surface of his mouth. When he circled her nipple with his tongue, she gasped. Desperate for the heated abrasion of his mouth, she arched her back, pushing her nipple into his mouth.

He accepted her offering, returning her frenzied need with a frantic passion of his own, sucking her deeply. Streamers of pleasure-pain streaked through her, centering at the most intimate, feminine part of her. She felt as if her heart had stopped beating, and at the same time it seemed to be pounding from her chest.

Her hands ripped the shirt from his back, and she traced her fingertips over him, memorizing the texture of his skin, the finely sculpted muscles of his chest. Plaiting her fingers in the crisp mat of his chest hair, she found his flat, male paps and circled them, tentatively, wanting to pleasure him as he pleasured her. To her surprise and delight, they responded like her own nipples, puckering and peaking, begging for her touch.

Groaning, he slipped his tongue into the sensitive valley between her breasts and murmured, *"Por Dios mi amorcita,* you're driving me wild. I don't know if I can wait."

"Then don't."

His hands were almost rough, shaking with his need, when he pushed her to the mattress and removed her dress and undergarments. She lay naked beneath his searing gaze, clad only in her silk stockings and garters.

Stretching her arms above her head, she arched her body as if in silent invitation, savoring this newfound female power she held over him. His eyes touched her everywhere, drinking her in, and she gloried in it, feeling wanton and bold.

When she moved, the exotic scent of the flower petals surrounded her, mingling with the erotic musk of their arousal. She felt as if she were floating on a cloud of heavenly enticements. Every sense she possessed sharpened to a fine point. Every nerve in her body jangled with barely suppressed anticipation.

"Aren't you going to get undressed?" Her silent invitation became a spoken one.

In one stroke, he shed his pants and stood before her . . . in all his male glory. Echoing his bold gaze, she allowed her eyes to wander over him. He was hers, a young David, awesome in his nakedness.

Her gaze rested on his familiar, achingly handsome face, trailing down the powerful column of his neck to the broad sweep of his shoulders. She feasted on the sculpted planes of his chest, and the washboard flatness of his abdomen. Skirting the tapering V of his chest hair, she noted the muscled hardness of his thighs and calves.

Raising her eyes, she finally allowed herself the sensuous exploration of gazing at the essence of him . . . the part that desired her the most. Turgid and filled with his need, it rose from the brown curls between his legs. A tiny drop of moisture glistened on its head.

Suddenly, she ached to hold that part of him. To touch him intimately. As if he had read her thoughts, he lowered himself to the mattress beside her.

She's so lovely, so much lovelier than I had dreamed, he thought, astonished by the beauty of her body. Her milk-white, pink-tipped breasts were perfect, soft and round and wondrous. The span of her waist was tiny, tapering into long, slim legs, covered with the sheer silk. He shuddered, thinking of her legs wrapped around him, the silk sliding against his naked flesh.

But the most private part of her riveted him—light brown curls, dewy with her own essence. The tender, rose petal flesh of her woman's mound beckoned him. It was the gate to heaven, the bridge to their oneness and ultimate union.

"You're beautiful, Sarah." His voice was husky, thick with desire. "The most beautiful woman in the world."

Throwing her arms around his neck, she snuggled close to him, pressing her bare skin against his and murmuring into his chest. "And you're the most handsome man in the world, Gilberto." Pausing, she teased, "Unfortunately, you know that already."

Shuddering again from the sensual slide of her naked flesh against his, he feared he wouldn't be able to contain himself, that he would spill his seed before he had shown her a woman's pleasure. Fighting down the almost painful arousal, he growled low in his throat.

His mouth found her nipple, and she gasped her delight, raking her fingernails over his back. Laving and suckling, he worshipped her breasts, his head dropping lower, licking downward to the sensitive curve beneath her breasts. What his mouth had abandoned, his fingers sought, playing with her breasts, cupping each in turn, as his tongue traced southward.

Pausing at her navel, he sipped the nectar there, the hot, sweet salty moisture of her. She lurched up and buried her fingers in his hair, moaning, "Gilberto, Gilberto, I feel . . . I want—"

Needing no further encouragement, his mouth trailed lower and lower still, nuzzling the satiny curls, dipping his tongue into the honeyed essence of her. She went completely still, galvanized by his intimate touch. His lips found the nub of her passion and he suckled it, laving it with tongue tip. The erotic scent of her desire filled his nostrils.

Bucking her hips, she pressed herself against him, crying out, "Oh, Gilberto, I never dreamed . . . I . . . I . . . my love . . . my love." And then she convulsed with ecstasy, her legs going rigid, clamping down on his shoulders. Her hot, slick moisture spilled forth, signaling her readiness, confirming the fulfillment he had so painstakingly given her.

Unable to wait a moment longer, he rose above her and parted her thighs. Driving himself into the very core of her wet, molten center, he trembled from the force of his own passion. Bringing himself up short at the barrier of her maidenhood, his gaze found hers. "Am I hurting you?"

"No, no. It's, it's—" she moaned, and she answered him more fully by bringing her legs up and gripping him. His self-control spent, he plunged deeper, breaching the last barrier.

She lunged, and gasped. He glimpsed the briefest flicker of pain in her eyes. Lowering his mouth to hers, he drew the pain inside himself, wanting only to bring her joy. As if in answer to his prayers, she seemed to open herself more fully, drawing him deeper within.

He began the slow rhythm, the achingly bittersweet mating. She followed him, matching her movements to his, giving and taking, bestowing and accepting.

Lava, white-hot, poured through his veins, pounding at his temples. The pleasure was so intense, he thought he would die from it. And when she convulsed beneath him again, he did die, a little—died and ascended to heaven, a heaven filled with the rapture and wonder of his only true love . . . his wife . . . his Sarah.

He floated to earth, pillowed in her arms. Turning to the side, he brought her with him. His sex was still deeply embedded within her. They lay side by side, melded together by their mutual fulfillment and the joy of being together.

Snuggling deeper into his arms, she sighed. Her hands reached up and cupped his face tenderly. Brushing his lips with hers she murmured, "I want us to be like this forever, my love."

Cradling her against his shoulder he replied, "So do I."

"Don't make me go home alone, Gilberto." He sensed the sudden tenseness in her.

And he understood the plea beneath her simple statement. She wanted to abandon their earlier plan, to return to their respective homes and confront their parents with the fact of their marriage. His first inclination was to protest, to convince her they should carry through with the plan. The more he thought about it, though, the less certain he felt.

What if her parents and his father still refused to listen? What if the Yorks kept Sarah prisoner again? This time he doubted there would be a reprieve. This time they would make certain she sailed with them for the States. The only way to stop them would be with force, and he didn't want to use force.

How could they hope to build a life together if there was bad blood between him and Sarah's parents? Confronting her parents together would make it difficult for them to take her from him, although there was the chance her father would go through with his threat and challenge him to a duel.

He weighed the options. Something told him not to let her go.

"I agree, Sarah. We'll go to your home first and tell your parents. After that, I'll take you to my home. As my wife, my father will accept you."

Feeling a tremor pass through her, he tried to remain calm, not wanting to reveal his own trepidation. He didn't know if she trembled at the possibility of confronting her own parents, or his father. He didn't ask, either, because he didn't want to know. Despite Herbert York's posturing, he feared his father's reaction far more.

Twelve

The sun had buried itself in the trees when Diana returned to the lace shop. Gustave hadn't stirred all afternoon. He lay snoring at the bottom of the boat when they reached the rendezvous point. She prayed he would stay asleep until Sarah was safely back in the gondola. After that, she hoped it wouldn't be too difficult to rouse him. If it were, would he guess that he had been drugged? She hoped not.

The gondolier beached the boat with a soft crunch on the shore of the island. Diana noticed that the brewery and shop were deserted. She guessed everyone must still be at afternoon *siesta*. That was better for their plan—the fewer witnesses, the better. She hoped Sarah would come quickly because it was getting late.

"*Señor* Gondolier, we will wait for the other *señorita*," Diana directed. "She should be along soon."

He bobbed his head in silent agreement and stuck his pole in the shallow lagoon beside the boat. Seating himself on the prow, he found the water skin and took a long drink.

Nervous, but wanting to appear composed, she regained her seat on the cushions and knotted her hands in her lap. Her nerves jangled and jumped. The waiting was awful. What if Sarah didn't come back? What if she decided to run away with Gilberto now? What would she tell Gustave? Even worse, how would she explain to Sarah's parents, who had been so kind and helpful, that she had helped to deceive them?

She squirmed on the cushions—praying Sarah wouldn't put her in such a position—but if her friend loved Gilberto as much as she appeared to, Diana knew how difficult it would be for Sarah to leave him after only one afternoon.

Given the same circumstances, could she leave Seguín?

Fortunately, she didn't have time to answer that question because the bushes parted and Sarah and Gilberto strode into view, their arms entwined. Diana was surprised to see Gilberto. She had thought Sarah would return to the boat alone. It was a good thing Gustave hadn't wakened.

Waving, she studied her best friend covertly. Did the passage from maiden to woman leave a visible mark, she wondered? Other than disheveled hair and two high, pink points on her cheeks, her best friend looked the same as before.

"Gilberto is returning with us," Sarah called from the shore.

"What?" she gasped, startled by the change in plans.

"We decided it would be best to confront our parents together, Diana," Gilberto explained.

"Are you sure that's wise?" Once the words were out, she could have bitten her tongue. It wasn't her business how they announced their marriage.

Sarah and Gilberto glanced at each other. A silent communication passed between them. It was Sarah who replied, "We don't want to take the chance of being separated again."

"Raise your hands, *Señor* Gilberto," a harsh voiced commanded from behind the couple.

Shocked by the unexpected intrusion, Diana strained to see who had spoken, but the man was hidden from view. What could it mean? Had Don Carlos or Sarah's father had them followed? Her already overwrought nerves thrummed, and panic filled her, making her heart thud.

Slowly, Gilberto lifted his arms. Sarah whirled around to see who it was.

The same harsh voice ordered, "Raul, Felipe, escort the *señorita* to the boat. Bring the other *señorita* from the boat to me."

The Spanish words jumbled in Diana's head, taking their time to settle and make sense. Terror streaked through her at their meaning. Her heart pounded harder, as if she had been running for a long time. Briefly, she thought of throwing herself over the side of the boat. Only one thought kept her in place: it must be some kind of mistake. *What could they want with me?*

In the next instant, she knew. The hidden man moved from the bushes into view. It was the scar-faced man! The man Seguín had called Ignacio.

She held her breath and closed her eyes. This couldn't be happening to her, could it? Opening her eyes, she found that the horrible nightmare hadn't gone away. At pistol point, Ignacio searched Gilberto for weapons, finding only a knife. The part of her mind still functioning registered Ignacio's use of a gun this time. She had thought his weapon of choice was a knife.

What was she doing, theorizing about the weapon Ignacio was using? What was wrong with her? *Think, think,* she commanded her frightened brain. She had to find a way out of this. Biting her lip, she welcomed the pain. It cleared her mind.

Because Sarah twisted and struggled, the other two men were forced to drag her to the boat. Ignacio finished his search and quickly looped a rope around Gilberto's outstretched wrists. The gondolier had risen from his seat, his face a study in bewildered astonishment.

When the two men roughly tossed the shrieking Sarah inside the boat, the gondolier stood to one side, his face averted. One of the men said, "Take her back as soon as we get this one." He jabbed a dirty finger in Diana's direction.

The gondolier avoided her eyes and shrugged his acquiescence. Sarah half-rose from the bottom of the boat. The other man, who hadn't spoken before, pushed her down, warning, "Stay down or it will go harder with your friend."

Sinking to the planking, Sarah turned her face to Diana. Abject misery shone from the depths of her eyes, and a silent apology. Shaking her head, Diana put a finger to her lips.

The man who had spoken to the gondolier—Raul or Felipe, she didn't know which—nodded and said, "This one is smart. She knows not to give us trouble."

"Hurry up," Ignacio commanded from the shore.

The men touched the pistols at their belts and glanced at each other. As if in silent agreement, they left their guns where they were and advanced upon her.

Purposely shifting from one foot to the other, Diana started the boat rocking. The men swayed, trying to regain their footing and cursing at her to stay still. Acting as if she were stumbling, she fell on top of Gustave, who lay at the bottom of the boat between two of the seats. She hoped the men hadn't seen him.

Gustave grunted, and his eyes flew open. At first, his gaze was unfocused, staring past her, but after a few seconds, he appeared amazed to realize she lay on top of him, her face inches from his own.

The men grabbed her arms, pulling her off Gustave. At the last moment, they noticed him, and their faces reflected shock. Shaking his huge, red head, Gustave leapt up, growling deep in his throat.

Raul and Felipe retreated a step, clutching at their pistols. Gustave didn't hesitate. He grabbed the one on his right and heaved him over his head. Before the man could pull his gun, he landed with a splash in the water. The other man retrieved his pistol and aimed it at Gustave.

Diana kicked him in the shin as hard as she could. Surprised, he grabbed his leg. Gustave turned and seized him. The pistol went flying, and the second man landed in the water.

A curse rang out from shore. Ignacio, brandishing his gun, started toward the boat. Gilberto, with his arms tied behind him, lunged at Ignacio, falling on him from behind. The pistol discharged as Ignacio hit the ground. The bullet passed overhead with a shrill whine.

Sarah rose from her seat and rushed to the front of the boat, but Gilberto bellowed from the shore, "Gondolier, get them out of here! Sarah, don't worry about me. Get to safety. I'll come for you later."

Retrieving his pole, the gondolier backed the boat up quickly. It jerked and bobbed. The two men in the water stood up and sloshed toward them. As quick as the boat's retreat was, one of their attackers managed to grab the side.

Reacting on instinct, Diana lifted the first object she could find—the half-filled picnic basket. Bringing it down with all of her strength on the man's fingers, she was gratified to hear a sickening crunch. The man yelped and clutched his hand, raising it to his mouth and sucking his fingers. The other one—the first one Gustave had thrown in the water—still had his pistol. He raised it and pointed it at them.

Her heart filled her throat, staring down the black barrel. There was a ping and puff of smoke, but nothing discharged. Relief flooded her. The powder must have been wet.

Gustave rushed to her side, as if to protect her from further harm. It was then that they heard Sarah sobbing.

She stood at the prow of the boat, crying out, "Gilberto, Gilberto!"

Following her gaze, Diana stared at the receding shoreline. Ignacio had freed himself from the still bound Gilberto, and held him at knife point. The other two men
sloughed their way through the water to join them. Sarah's
husband had sacrificed himself so they could get away.

So I could get away, she reminded herself. Ignacio hadn't
wanted Sarah—just her and Gilberto. Not regretting her
narrow escape, knowing how her friend must feel, she felt
her heart go out to Sarah.

Moving to her side, she took Sarah in her arms and tried
to comfort her.

"You did well, Ignacio, bringing Gilberto to me as I instructed," Don Carlos congratulated him. "But the girl
slipped through your fingers again, eh, *mi amigo?* That is
not good. My mines are already feeling the effects of
Seguín's new process."

"I tried, Don Carlos," Ignacio replied. How could he
have known the two men whom he hired would be totally
ineffectual?

"You'll need to do better than 'try,' Ignacio, or I'll be
ruined. Who will take care of you then?" The don's tone
of voice was soft, but Ignacio recognized the steel beneath
his words.

"The York house is too well-guarded, *Señor* Don, but my
sources tell me the Norté Americaños will be leaving for
Veracruz shortly. I could take the *señorita* while they're on
the road."

"Do your sources say whether they're going by public
coach or private escort?"

"A private escort of about ten guards."

"Too risky. Too many men." The don shook his head.
"And I don't want anything to stop the York girl from
leaving México. As soon as she's gone, my son will be
forced to listen to reason."

Ignacio digested Don Carlos's answer and asked, "What would you have me do?"

"I've given the matter considerable attention, and I've come to the conclusion that the most direct way is the best. Forget the McFarland *gringa.*" Pausing, he gazed directly at Ignacio. "I want you to infiltrate Seguín's mining operations and learn the production method. That way, we don't need the formula, just the method." Reclining in his leather armchair, he smiled, obviously satisfied with his plan.

"But Seguín only hires miners from families who have worked those mines for generations," he protested. "We've tried before to penetrate his operations without success. It's a close-knit society. And besides, Seguín knows me."

"Break the barriers down with money." The don tossed him a heavy bag of coins, which he caught with ease. "Loyalty goes only so far. One of the mine workers is bound to need extra gold."

Sarah was inconsolable. She cried for days. Between crying bouts she begged her parents, especially her father, to find Gilberto. She confessed to their secret marriage and even admitted its consummation.

As inconsolable as Sarah was, her parents were equally unmovable. The secret marriage held no weight with them. Herbert York declared it a sham, easily dissolved. He made inquiries and found that a Mexican civil ceremony wasn't even recognized in the States. That was good enough for him. They were going home, and Sarah was going with them. If a child should come from that one illicit afternoon, they would present Sarah as recently widowed.

Diana did her best, trying to comfort and reassure her friend. They had gone over the incident and come to the conclusion that Ignacio, acting on behalf of Don Carlos, had orders to take Gilberto so he couldn't be with Sarah. They surmised he had wanted to abduct Diana too, for the same old reason, to wrest the secret of the formula from her.

They huddled together, sharing Sarah's abject misery, while the house hummed around them. The preparations for leaving México hastened forward; they were scheduled to sail from Veracruz at the end of the month. The arduous trip overland would take at least ten days before they reached the port city.

Furniture and chandeliers, draped in linen cloths, made the York home look like a way station for an assortment of ghosts, imparting an echoing emptiness even before their departure. Trunks and valises filled quickly, piled in neat stacks in the corners of rooms, constant and silent reminders.

With sluggish movements, Diana gathered together her few possessions. They were scheduled to leave for Veracruz in two days. It was the first opportunity she had had to start packing. Sarah, exhausted, was sleeping fitfully in the adjoining room.

She was glad her friend was finally resting. Sarah looked like a shadow of her former self. Her beautiful face was ravaged by tears, and her stylish dresses hung on her, as if they were castoffs from some other woman. Days had turned into weeks, and she had been filled with an almost maniacal frenzy, seldom eating or sleeping, only wanting to pace and cry and talk about Gilberto.

Diana pressed the back of her hand to Sarah's forehead. Did her skin feel feverish? She didn't know. She was too exhausted herself to think straight. When Sarah's parents refused to help, Diana had been Sarah's only solace. She had tried to keep pace with her best friend, to be there for her, at any time of the day or night, and it had taken its toll.

Beyond the physical stress of comforting her, Diana experienced Sarah's anguish as if it were her own. Before, she had been able to keep her hopeless yearning for Seguín at bay, but with her friend openly grieving for Gilberto, it was as if Sarah's tears swept away the barriers she had erected. Her own sorrow rose up, an answering tide-flood, to join and mingle indiscriminately with Sarah's.

The half-hidden door between their rooms slid back, and Sarah plunged through the opening. Her eyes were red and puffy, and her hair fell in lank strands around her shoulders. Her dress, in which she had fallen asleep, was creased and rumpled. But her face was wreathed in the most glorious smile Diana had ever seen.

Dropping the nightgown she had been folding, she rushed to Sarah and put her arms around her. Gazing at her friend's joyous expression, she experienced a frisson of uneasiness. Why was Sarah so happy, so suddenly? Could her grief have pushed her over the edge?

Pulling apart from their embrace, Sarah clasped Diana's hands. "I know how we can get help!" Releasing her, she turned to pace the room, her movements jerky and barely controlled. Diana's concern for her friend's sanity deepened as she watched her anxiously.

"I can't believe we didn't think of it before." Pivoting suddenly, she faced Diana and shook her index finger at her. "You should have thought of it. You're in love with him, aren't you? Just like I'm in love with Gilberto. It came to me in a dream, and I understood." Rushing back into Diana's arms, she softly chided, "Diana, why didn't you tell me before?"

Bewildered by her outburst and more than a little frightened for Sarah's sake, she held her friend tight, patting her back and trying to soothe her. Knowing she must answer her friend but dreading it, she responded, "Think of what, Sarah? Tell you what?"

Grinning mischievously, Sarah said, "Don't play coy with

me, Diana McFarland. The only person who can help us
is Seguín Torres. And you're in love with him, too," she
added. "I can't believe you didn't send for him sooner."

Diana opened her mouth, but no words came. Half-
formed feelings ricocheted through her, a welter of emotions vied with one another, each one scrambling for
supremacy. She felt pulled in too many directions, confused and distraught.

Was her friend a little mad? There was bad blood between Seguín and his half-brother Gilberto. How could
Seguín help them? Better yet, why would he want to? And
how had Sarah guessed that she loved Seguín?

There had been a time, before her friend became involved with Gilberto, when she had wanted to confide in
Sarah. But the moment had passed. Other situations had
commanded their attention. Despite her silence, Sarah
had somehow divined the truth.

"I know what you're thinking, Diana," she rushed
ahead, not waiting for an answer. "Seguín won't help us
because he hates Gilberto." She shook her head. "But
that's where you're wrong. He will help if *you* ask him."
Grinning again, she continued, "I've seen the way he looks
at you . . . and the way you look at him. If I hadn't been
so wrapped up with Gilberto, I would have realized
sooner."

Grabbing her shoulders, Sarah shook her, as if to waken
her from a self-induced trance. "Just think, Diana, we
could be sisters in every sense of the word. You and Seguín
married, and Gilberto and I. You would stay in México,
too." Releasing her, she asked, "Why did you sell him the
formula and send him away? Why didn't you fight for your
love, as you told me to do?"

"It isn't like that," Diana managed to croak. Despite her
guarded reply, Sarah's words had affected her. The tiniest
bud of hope sprouted in her heart. *Had* Seguín looked at
her in a special way? And if he had, could Sarah have

misinterpreted his look? She knew he desired her. Could that be what her best friend had seen?

If she sent for him and he came, she would at least get to see him again, wouldn't she? She doubted he would help them, knowing the way he felt about Gilberto. That wouldn't really matter, though. She would see him again. A crust of bread was better than nothing at all, wasn't it? And if he agreed to help them, what would it entail? Would they stay with him in México, trying to find Gilberto?

Would Seguín become their protector, irrevocably linked to them for a time? Endless days and nights of being with him beckoned to her, stretching before her with shining promise. Was she a little mad, too?

"What do you mean—'it wasn't like that'?" Sarah demanded.

"Yes, I'm in love with Seguín," she admitted slowly. "I can't believe I love a man who was involved with my father's death, but I do." Her voice caught. She covered her face with her hands.

Gently, Sarah pried her hands from her face. "Don't, Diana. Seguín didn't want your father killed. You know that. The worst thing he did was to underestimate his stepfather."

"Your father-in-law," Diana pointed out.

A visible tremor shook her friend, but she squared her shoulders and lifted her chin. "Now you know how I feel. I couldn't believe I had fallen in love with a man whose father is a monster, either. But I couldn't help myself. Gilberto is not like his father. He's gentle and wise and thoughtful. Don't let what Don Carlos did stand in the way of loving Seguín."

"It's not that." She turned away, embarrassed to confess. "Seguín doesn't return my feelings, Sarah. Unlike with you and Gilberto, there have been no words of love spoken between us, no plans for a secret marriage. When I sold him the formula and sent him away, he went willingly."

Sarah's forehead creased, and she pursed her lips. Diana could see her turning over this new piece of information.

"Seguín doesn't love me, Sarah. All he wanted was the formula." Her voice was barely a whisper. Just saying the words shot an arrow of pure anguish through her heart.

Her best friend's countenance cleared, and she wrapped her arms around Diana. This time, it was Sarah's turn to console and comfort. "I don't believe that. I think he cares for you. Either he doesn't realize it, or he doesn't want to admit it."

Despite her best intention to crush any futile hope about Seguín's feelings for her, Diana's heart lifted, listening to her friend's reassurances.

"Send for him," Sarah urged.

"What if he won't come?"

"He will come."

"Will your parents allow him to see me? After Xochimilco, I don't think they trust me, either."

"Make up some excuse—use the formula."

"All right. I'll send for him."

And he did come, despite the thinness of her pretext.

Diana had contacted him through his attorney, explaining she needed to discuss selling the formula in other countries. The Yorks and her mother had paid scant attention to her unusual request, as caught up as they were in the final preparations for departure.

This time she met him on the patio, just as she had done the first time, that long-ago day before the ball. She had chosen the patio for two reasons: there was less chance of listening ears, and the house was a mere shell, stripped of its contents, with all the parlor furniture draped.

When he strode onto the patio in the late afternoon, her heart skipped a beat. Was his hair a little longer? The lines around his mouth a little deeper? His broad shoulders still blocked out the setting sun, she noticed. And his walk . . . did anyone else walk like him—on the balls of his feet, like a big cat ready to spring?

He approached her, and she rose from her seat. Sweeping the flat-brimmed hat from his head, he bowed and murmured, *"¡Buenas tardes!* Diana."

Why did her name sound like a caress when he spoke it? Shivers ran up her spine, and at the same time her hands began to perspire. She wanted to rush into his arms, to drag her fingers through his carefully plaited queue, freeing his midnight mane to fall about his shoulders. She wanted to crush her mouth against his, drinking in the bittersweet taste of his lips. She wanted—

Did Sarah feel like this when she was with Gilberto?

Words failed her. How could she possibly ask him to help with their outlandish plan? Why did she allow Sarah to drag her into such craziness? She knew the answer without thinking. Because Sarah never asked anything that wasn't in her own heart. Even if he turned her down, she had seen him one last time. It was enough. It was more than enough.

Obviously baffled by her silence, he cleared his throat. "You wanted to speak to me about selling the formula in other countries? I thought the documents made it clear that—"

"They did." She wet her lips. "I had another, more private reason for summoning you."

His obsidian eyes glittered. She thought she caught the briefest flicker of some unidentifiable emotion, and then it was gone. Silently, she cursed their black depths.

"I'm at your disposal." His generous lips quirked into a half-smile, and he bowed again.

"Please, take a seat." She regained her seat on one end of the stone bench.

"Gracias."

He seated himself at the other end and crossed his legs.

Her gaze feasted on him, watching his powerful thigh muscles bunch beneath the black, corded fabric. Her throat closed again, and it was difficult to catch her breath.

Quickly, she averted her eyes, taking in Sam's deserted perch. The parrot wouldn't be going with them. Mary had decided the trip would be too difficult for him. A friend of hers had taken the eccentric bird yesterday.

How to start? It really was a fantastic request. Fighting down her nervousness, she found that her practical nature came to the rescue. She must start at the beginning.

"Sarah York, my friend, has fallen in love with Gilberto Aguirre, your half-brother."

"And does my brother return her affections?" he asked coolly.

She had thought her bald statement would surprise him, and cause a reaction. As usual, Seguín remained singularly composed.

"Yes. In fact, they were secretly married by a magistrate several weeks ago."

"I thought your family and the Yorks were returning to the States."

"We are, but Sarah doesn't want to go. She wants to stay in México with Gilberto. The problem is that Gilberto was—"

"Let me guess," he interjected. "The Yorks are keeping Sarah as a prisoner, and my stepfather has taken Gilberto away."

"How did you know?"

"Rich and powerful men have peculiar ways of protecting their offspring—like planning their lives for them. My stepfather has wanted Gilberto to marry the daughter of the neighboring *hidalgo* for years. I'm certain Herbert York has a suitable match picked out for his daughter, as well." His lips quirked again, and he raised one ebony eyebrow. "You see, not being a member of society can have its compensations."

His gaze rested on her. How intense his hawk-like eyes were. How filled with bitterness he was. Why did she love this unapproachable, prickly man? What crazy chemistry drew her to him? But he *had* come as soon as she sent for him. Was Sarah right? Did he, in his own unfathomable way, care for her?

"Can you help us?" she asked, desperate to say it and get it over with.

He laughed, throwing his head back and exposing the corded muscles of his neck. Tiny drops of perspiration glistened on his smooth bronze skin. She quelled the urge to run her tongue over his throat, lapping at the salty essence of him. Closing her eyes, she fought the potent, physical pull of him.

Besides, he was laughing at her, wasn't he? She summoned all of her offended sensibilities and fashioned a scathing answer.

Before she could say anything he stopped laughing and observed, "Always my forthright Diana. No beating about the bush, no sweet talk for you." Pausing, his gaze flicked over her, resting for a long moment on her mouth. This time she read the message there . . . pure, undiluted desire.

Heat spread through her, sweeping from her toes, through her body, spreading its warmth across her face. Not wanting him to see her blush, she leapt to her feet and crossed to the fountain, keeping her back to him.

"Don't make fun of me, Seguín, this is serious."

She heard the scrape of his boots on the tiles. He grasped her shoulders and spun her around, bringing her up against the hard planes of his chest.

"This is serious, too," he echoed as his lips found hers.

His warm mouth devoured, greedily sucking the very breath from her. Before she could even kiss him back, he had his tongue inside, stroking and caressing the inner recesses of her mouth. Parting her lips in frantic surrender, she sought his tongue with her own, twining and thrusting with a rapacious hunger that equaled his.

Her hands went up and locked behind his neck, glorying in his mouth on hers, the touch of him along the length of her body. Strange, fluttery sensations chased through her abdomen, dipping and swirling, making her want to press closer into his embrace, to push her pebble-hard nipples against the welcome abrasion of his shirt.

The core of her turned liquid, and she felt as if she were flowing into him, like two rivers joining, mingling, rushing to the sea.

He lifted his mouth from hers to shower kisses over her upturned face . . . and throat . . . and neck. When his fingers found the buttons at the collar of her shirtwaist, he stopped abruptly and raised his eyes to hers, his hands frozen.

As if she had suddenly caught fire, he stepped back and thrust his hands into the pockets of his trousers. It was his turn to not look her in the face. His eyes sought the tiles at their feet and remained there, as if he were memorizing the blue and red pattern of them.

"You see how it will be, if I help you." His voice sounded husky, rough with desire. "When I'm near you"—he paused and ran his hand through his hair in obvious agitation—"I can't make promises, Diana." Finally, he lifted his eyes and snagged her gaze. "It's as simple as that."

What was he trying to say? That if he helped them, the price would be her body? A voice in the back of her mind whispered that she didn't care. Even more, she wanted him with a passion that equaled or surpassed his. But pride intervened, cautioning that she shouldn't hold herself so cheaply. If he only desired and didn't love, it would be a joyless joining. Wouldn't it?

But he couldn't be so crass, another part of her argued. Could he?

She met his gaze and studied him openly. He was silent,

but this time his feelings were clearly discernible. For a brief moment he opened himself to her, and she read the confusion there—the jumbled yearnings he felt, desire, tempered by uncertainty, even a little fear, perhaps. Most daunting of all was the wariness she found in his eyes—an unwillingness to be drawn to her despite the strong pull of their attraction. He couldn't have explained himself more clearly if he had spoken volumes.

So, those were the terms, she realized. He wanted her, but he didn't like wanting her. And if his desire overcame his common sense while they were together, it would be nothing more than desire fulfilled—nothing more, nothing less.

She shivered, and the realization left her cold in the tropical heat. With the chilly realization came the question: *Why is he afraid to feel anything deeper than passion? Afraid to love?* She wanted to know. No, that wasn't quite correct . . . she desperately *needed* to know.

As women have from the beginning of time, she prayed she could change him. Time with him would give her knowledge, and that knowing might provide the key.

Suddenly, Sarah's desperate need for Seguín's help became secondary. She wanted him, but not just for today. Not just for a passing physical release. What had Sarah said? "Why don't you fight for his love, as you told me to do?" It was a fair question. More than that, it was the only question. She had thought they would be parted forever, but circumstances had thrown them together again. Surely, fate had a reason.

"I understand, Seguín," she finally answered. "I'm aware of the dangers, but I still want to go through with it."

He nodded, and a strange, strangled kind of hope leapt into his eyes. "We'll need to plan."

"Yes."

"I'll have to take you and Sarah to a safe place while I

try to find Gilberto. I could take Sarah alone, then—" He stopped, his meaning obvious.

"I've made up my mind. I'm staying with Sarah until she's rejoined with Gilberto."

Nodding again, he replied, "It will be easier away from here. Mr. York has the house heavily guarded. When do you leave for Veracruz?"

"Tomorrow."

He expelled his breath in a rush and stated flatly, "Doesn't give us much time. Will you be going by public coach or private escort?"

"Private escort."

"How many guards?"

"I'm not certain, but I would guess about ten men."

"Will you stop at the usual way stations for the night?"

"Yes, I overheard the Yorks planning the trip. They said it would take at least ten days."

"Plan for the second night. I'll come then. Be dressed and pack as lightly as possible. Take only what you can carry on horseback." He paused, asking, "You both ride, don't you?"

"Of course." She allowed herself a small smile.

"*Bueno.* Dress in sturdy clothing and boots. We'll be riding in the mountains."

"We'll be ready."

Brushing her lips lightly with his, he promised, "I'll be there."

Suddenly, she wondered if anyone were watching them. Before, when they had kissed long and passionately, she hadn't cared. Now, with the plan at stake, she worried their intimacy would prove their downfall.

He stroked one finger down her cheek. She quivered from his tender touch. Another promise, she wondered? A promise of what was inevitable between them? A joining of the flesh, and nothing more.

But she would make it more, she railed silently.

Striding from the patio, she watched him go, savoring his predatory prowl. Just looking at him turned her insides to mush.

Thirteen

Gilberto stared at the dank, oozing walls. Taking a scrap of pottery, he etched another mark beside the cornhusk mattress that served as his bed. Another sunrise—viewed through the tiny, barred window at the opposite side of his cell—another day. There were already nineteen marks on the wall.

He hated to think how many more there would be before he or his father gave in. *Correction,* he mouthed silently—how many more marks before his *father* relented? He had no intention of giving in to his father's demands.

Shaking his head, he combed his fingers through his hair and rose to make his morning ablutions. A handful of tepid water sluiced over his face completed his toilette. Next, came exercise. He paced the length of the tiny room, three meters, turned and paced the width, two meters. Turning again, at the third corner, and a fourth time, he completed the square, bypassing his bed, which was pushed against the wall.

Avoiding the dangling manacles attached to the wall beneath the window, he marched past them. When he had first come to this cell, he had been surprised to find the manacles, shocked that the room even existed.

As a boy, he had heard whispered tales about this room and the punishments enacted here upon recalcitrant workers or servants. He had never believed the stories.

Was his father really so cruel? And when would his father's patience run out? So far there had been no threats, except continued incarceration if Gilberto didn't sign a paper annulling his marriage to Sarah and become betrothed to Maria.

Since he had no intention of agreeing to the demands, he wondered what tactic his father would use next. It didn't matter, he reassured himself. Nothing could make him give up Sarah.

Diana's bottom stung. They had ridden most of the night, and glancing at the sun she judged it to be mid-morning already. Seguín hadn't exaggerated the roughness of terrain they would cover. Her horse was coated in white lather, and she could hear his labored breathing. Still they climbed. The mountains were all around them, and they had entered a secluded canyon that slanted upward toward the far peaks.

She guessed they must be getting close to their destination, because at the mouth of the canyon several of their escort had veered off, and she had glimpsed other men, standing guard along the canyon walls. If nothing else, they should be safe here.

Their escape had proven to be surprisingly easy. Mr. York's guards had slept through it. When she asked Seguín how he accomplished it he had winked, boosted her into the saddle, and whispered that it was a Juárista secret.

With a swat to her horse's rump, they were off, at first covering the miles at a hard gallop, and later at a fast lope. She glanced over at Sarah, and was surprised to find her friend looking ill. Her mouth was drawn in a thin line, and perspiration had soaked through the brim of her hat. A grimace of pain crossed her features, and Diana became concerned.

Reining her gelding close to Sarah's mount, she asked, "What's wrong?"

"Nothing. I hope we're almost there." The words seemed to cost her an inordinate amount of effort, coming from behind clenched teeth.

Something was wrong, but Sarah wouldn't admit it.

Kicking her faltering mount, Diana made it gallop after Seguín. Since the sun had risen, she had kept well behind him, wanting to avoid looking at him. Handsome on foot, he was magnificent on horseback. Controlling his horse, a wild-eyed, black stallion, with the pressure of his muscled thighs and loose reins, he reminded her of some mythical creature, a centaur of old. Just watching him on horseback made her feel like butter left too long in the sun.

Closing the distance, she pulled up and cantered alongside. He gazed at her with an unspoken question in his eyes.

"How far to where we're going?" she asked.

"We're almost there." He pointed toward the mountain peaks. "End of the canyon. Is there a problem?"

"No, just curious." She had started to tell him about Sarah, but decided against it. If they were this close, it could wait—she hoped.

Within a few minutes she spied the far wall of the box canyon. Glancing up, she saw a rock overhang at the rim of the canyon, looking like a huge curled lip. Beneath it, the canyon wall sloped inward, as if some giant hand had scooped it out. Perched halfway up the canyon wall, nestled under the overhang, stood a small house. A lazy wisp of smoke rose from its chimney and disappeared against the gray, limestone rock.

It must be their destination. She had to admit it was the perfect hiding place.

At the bottom of the canyon wall, a stream meandered, framed by drooping willows. Seguín led them into the thickest part of the willows. Hidden there was a crude lean-to and brush corral. Several horses milled in the pen, some of them drinking from the creek which wandered through the middle. Looking around, she realized Seguín had cleverly used the natural attributes to their fullest advantage.

Several of their guards rode up and took their mounts to unsaddle. Sarah slid to the ground, clutching her abdomen. Concerned, Diana rushed to her side.

Before she could ask again, Seguín was beside them, asking for her, *"Señorita* Sarah, are you hurt?"

"No, Seguín, not hurt. The ride . . ." she panted. Pointing to the canyon wall, she admitted, "I don't think I can make it."

Diana's gaze followed her friend's pointing finger. She found a steep, rocky path zigzagging up the canyon. It didn't look much better than a goat trail.

Exasperated and tired from the long ride, she blurted, "We're supposed to climb that?"

"Hideouts aren't necessarily convenient," Seguín muttered. Turning to Sarah, he said, "You don't have to climb it." With those words, he swept her into his arms and started up the path.

Miffed at his pointed answer and feeling a trifle ashamed for having complained, she followed behind like a tagalong puppy. At first, she nursed her offended pride but halfway up the rock wall she stopped, gasping for air. Glancing at Seguín's retreating form, she wondered how he was able to carry Sarah up such a steep path without pausing to rest.

He emerged from a cutback, several yards ahead, and her carefully reclaimed breath deserted her again. She had never had occasion to glimpse him from this particular view, straining upward, legs pumping, and with his flexed bottom in plain sight. The fabric of his pants fit him like a second skin.

From her vantage point, it didn't take much to imagine

how he would look, naked, from the back. Sinking to a rock, she removed her hat and fanned herself. Heat simmered through her, hot as a witch's cauldron. Just watching the taut, muscular form of his posterior made her nipples harden pleasurably. There was an answering tug in her nether regions.

Raising her hand to her forehead, she felt dizzy . . . dizzy with desire.

Loose rocks thudded on the path. Pulling herself together, she looked up. He stood directly overhead, on a portion of the trail that looped back on top of itself.

"Do I need to carry you up, too?" his voice taunted.

Rising to her feet, she dusted her riding breeches with her hat and then set it firmly on her head. Not deigning to answer, she placed one foot in front of the other and started up the trail again.

More rocks sprayed down, and she glimpsed his back before he disappeared. After about ten minutes of laborious climbing, she emerged at the top, panting, desperate to pull air into her lungs.

Bent over with her hands resting on her knees, she glanced around. The hollow where the house stood was larger than it appeared from below. Ten or twelve houses could have fit there. Behind the house, a spring bubbled from the rocks, forming a muddy pool, surrounded by ferns. There were two small outbuildings beside the spring. At the far end of the hollow, where the rock lip receded, there was another trail, snaking upward to the canyon rim. She wondered where it led.

The house was made of stucco, painted a grayish color instead of the usual whitewash. Natural camouflage, she supposed. The roof was made of thick thatch, and the chimney of the indigenous limestone rock. There was one door in the front; she guessed there would be another in back. Two windows framed the door, their heavy wooden shutters thrown back.

A diminutive woman with skin the color and texture of a hickory nut appeared in the open doorway and beckoned, "Come inside, *señorita. Bienvenidos.*"

Doing as she was bid, she entered the house, but having recovered her breath she didn't take time to inspect the interior. Instead, she asked, "Where did Seguín take the other *señorita?*"

"The second bedroom on the right. Your friend is sick, no?" The woman's face was a study in concern.

Promising herself to get acquainted later, she replied, "I don't know. I need to find out."

Nodding, the woman stepped aside, and Diana rushed to the bedroom with the woman close on her heels. She found Sarah ensconced in a brass bed, complete with eiderdown mattress. Somehow, she hadn't expected such comforts in this remote hideout, but she was grateful for them. Anything to ease her friend, who was still clutching her abdomen and frowning.

The problem appeared to be with Sarah's stomach. Diana thought back to the last time they had eaten, at the way station, the night before. It was true the tortillas had been greasy, and the *carne guisado* barely palatable, but she had eaten the same thing and she wasn't sick.

Seguín, who had been standing in the corner of the room as if waiting for her, stepped forward and said, "She wants you. I was going to make her more comfortable, but . . ." He shrugged. "Let me know if there's anything we can do." He inclined his head toward the woman who had welcomed her. "Lupita's sister is a *curandera,* a healer. I can fetch her within the hour."

Standing aside, she let him pass. He closed the door behind him. Turning her attention to Sarah, she approached the bed and took her friend's hand in her own. Sarah's hand was cold as ice, despite the perspiration beading her forehead.

Concern mounted in her, and she bent forward to gently

wipe the dampness from her brow. "Tell me, Sarah, what is it?" She urged.

Sarah bit her lip and averted her eyes, staring down at the bright patchwork quilt covering the bed. Silence stretched between them, a silence so thick that Diana felt smothered by it, desperate to help her friend.

"I think I'm pregnant, and trying to lose the baby. The cramps are—" She snatched her hand free and writhed on the bed, her hands like claws, clutching the too-bright quilt.

"Gone?" Herbert's voice sounded hollow, defeated. He shook his head. "Gone where?"

Mary sighed, her heart heavy, fear swamping her. How could their daughter, their own sweet Sarah, have done this? It was bad enough that she had secretly married Gilberto, and admitted to compromising herself. And now this. It was unthinkable, a nightmare come to life.

"Just gone." Her own voice sounded hollow, empty, devoid of emotion. She offered the scrap of paper to her husband. "Sarah left this so we wouldn't worry." She choked on the last word. Thrusting the note into her husband's hand, she covered her face with her hands. The initial shock had receded, replaced by tears.

"I've gone to find my husband, Gilberto," he read from the paper. "Diana is with me. Tell her mother. You won't be able to find us. Go home. I'll wire when I find Gilberto. Love, Sarah."

Moving into the lee of his arms, Mary sobbed there, wetting his perfectly starched linen shirt and not caring. "What will happen to her, Herbert? Alone with another girl in a foreign country—in the middle of a war? Oh, what will happen to our little girl?"

"She won't be alone," he declared gruffly, patting her on the back. "We're turning back to México City. You tell

Elizabeth, and I'll tell our guards." Pausing, he swore under his breath. "Those guards, where were they? Why didn't they stop her? I'll have their hides. First Gustave, and now—"

"Don't, Herbert," she cut him off. Releasing her hold, she stepped back and wiped the tears from her eyes. "Forget the guards. What is done is done. The important thing is to find her."

He nodded again. "You're right, Mary. The important thing is to find her," he echoed. "I'll hire an army of men to hunt for her. Don't worry, we'll find her," he promised.

Diana didn't explain Sarah's fears. She simply requested of Lupita, Seguín's housekeeper, that she send for her sister, the healer.

Seguín left to fetch the *curandera*. Afraid to move Sarah but wanting to make her as comfortable as possible, Diana loosened her riding breeches and unbuttoned her collar. She placed a cool compress on her forehead and pulled the covers over her.

Sarah lay under the covers, clutching her abdomen and moaning. Diana, feeling totally helpless, held her hand and stroked her head. After a few minutes, her friend went limp and fell into a fitful sleep. Agitated and worried, Diana paced the small room. Besides the luxurious bed, the furnishings were plain: a table with a water pitcher and basin and lamp, one ladder-back chair, pegs on the wall, and a chamber pot.

Unable to stand the waiting and knowing she wouldn't be far from Sarah, she decided to relieve her mind by exploring the house.

Stepping into the hallway, she glimpsed two other bedrooms furnished much the same as Sarah's. The first room contained a massive, walnut four-poster bed and matching armoire. She guessed that room must belong to Seguín. Moving down the hallway, she found what appeared to be a fourth bedroom at the back of the house. The door to the room was closed. She assumed it belonged to Lupita.

Retracing her steps to the front of the house, she discovered the sitting room she had so hurriedly passed through before. It was furnished with a worn, horsehair settee and two matching chairs. One wall held built-in shelves, filled with books. A table with a lamp and a reliquary niche completed the ensemble.

Off the sitting room, she stepped down into the kitchen. The size of the room astonished her. It comprised half of the house. The hearth was huge, too, taking up an entire wall by itself. That explained the lack of other fireplaces, she realized. The immense hearth, when properly fired, could easily warm the house.

As overwhelming as the hearth was, the focal point of the massive kitchen was a large, oak table with twelve carved-back chairs. Most of the chairs had been pushed to one side, and the table's surface appeared to serve as a preparation surface as well as a storage area.

Diana gazed at the jumble of flour and sugar bins, bowls of chopped vegetables and spices, whole plucked chickens, and an assortment of clay cooking pots. Bunches of peppers and clumps of herbs hung from the open rafters overhead. It was a mess, but a homey mess. The huge kitchen, warm and spice-filled, seemed to open its arms and welcome her.

She suddenly understood why it was the largest room in the house. As inviting as it was, no one would bother with the remainder of the house, except for sleeping.

Lupita, who was retrieving flour tortillas from the hearth's oven with a wooden paddle, dumped her load on a platter. Straightening, she caught Diana's eye and asked, "*Señorita* Sarah, does she need anything?"

As she tried to smile, Diana's face felt frozen when she thought of her friend's problem. "No, she's sleeping now. I just . . . I couldn't—"

"*Yo entiendo.* The waiting is the hardest thing." Lupita dusted her hands on her apron. "The house is small. If she awakens, we will hear her."

"Yes, four bedrooms, a sitting room, and the kitchen."

"You've been exploring. *Bueno.* The kitchen, she is *magnifico,* no?" Lupita bragged with a sweep of her arm. "*Señor* Seguín wanted it this way."

Diana realized she hadn't thought of Seguín in any domestic sense. That he would want a huge, welcoming kitchen was surprising. She would have never guessed it.

"So this is Seguín's home."

"*Sí,* when he's at the mines."

"The mines are close by?"

"*Sí,* on the other side of the canyon."

"That's where the other trail leads, the one going up to the canyon rim."

Lupita bobbed her head.

Wanting to know more and sensing Lupita was willing to talk, she asked, "Why is this place so inaccessible, so hard to get to?"

"Because a mine owner is always in danger." The housekeeper shrugged. "Is it not so? Men will do terrible things for the silver from the ground."

"I guess you're right."

The housekeeper's words reminded her of when Seguín, in that horrible parlor at the *posada,* explained how dangerous the mines were, not a suitable place for women. But she was here, against all odds, and she meant to see the mines and her father's process, too—just as soon as Sarah was better.

"You can't tell her, Seguín. She might lose the baby." Diana kept her voice low. They were standing in the sitting room, scant feet from the door to Sarah's bedroom.

Seguín had been gone for ten days, inquiring after Gil-

berto. During that time, Pilar, Lupita's sister, had nursed
Sarah. After examining her, Pilar had declared that Sarah
was in the earliest stages of pregnancy. According to the
curandera, the first three months were the most dangerous.
It was easy to lose a baby during that time.

Pilar had plied Sarah with herbs and prescribed bed rest.
Unlike Diana, who had secretly rebelled when she had
been confined to bed, her friend accepted the confinement willingly, desperately wanting to hold onto Gilberto's
child. Acting on Sarah's wishes, Seguín had left, the day
after they arrived, to find news of Gilberto.

"She wants to know, Diana. She sent me to find out. It's
wrong of you to withhold the truth from her."

"But—"

Her reply was cut short. The door to Sarah's bedroom
opened, and she stood, swaying, in the hallway, clutching
the walls for support.

Rushing to her friend's side, Diana chided, "You
shouldn't be out of bed. Remember what Pilar said."

"Let me be." Sarah's voice was sharp. She pushed Diana's helping hands away and tottered along the wall by
herself, clad in a long, cotton nightgown.

Entering the sitting room, she found her way to the
horsehair sofa and sank onto it. Turning to face Seguín,
she asked, "What about Gilberto? What have you found?"

Diana shot Seguín a pointed look, but he ignored it.
Instead, he stepped forward and knelt at Sarah's feet, explaining, "I don't want to distress you. The news isn't
good."

"I want to know," Sarah stated firmly.

"Don Carlos is holding him prisoner in the basement
of the *hacienda.* Rumor has it he won't allow Gilberto his
freedom until he signs a paper annulling your marriage
and agrees to become betrothed to the daughter of the
neighboring *hidalgo.*"

"I see. What if Gilberto doesn't agree to his father's terms?"

He stroked his chin as if considering. "Hard to say. Don Carlos might keep him locked up for some time." Hesitating for a moment, he added, "Knowing the situation and having time to think it over, I believe the wisest course of action would be for you to go home as planned, to leave the country."

"What!" both Sarah and Diana exclaimed.

Holding up his hand with the palm out, he pleaded, "Hear me out. I think if Don Carlos knew you had left . . . and I could make certain he knew, he would be more likely to free Gilberto. I still have contacts at my stepfather's *rancho*. I could get word to my half-brother that I would help him to leave the country, too. Then he could follow and join you."

"But Sarah can't travel now. You know that—" Diana reminded him.

"I understand," he agreed. "Pilar mentioned the safest part of a pregnancy is during the middle months. Perhaps we could wait until then. By that time, I think both my stepfather and Gilberto will be heartily sick of being jailor and prisoner."

Sarah nodded her head slowly. "It might work. But I don't know if my father would—"

"Accept Gilberto if he escaped to the States," he finished for her.

"Yes."

"Even if you're going to bear Gilberto's child?"

She blushed, admitting, "I hadn't thought of it that way."

"Speaking of your father, I heard he's returned to your home in México City, and he's moving heaven and earth to find you. I don't think his hired men will track you here, but you might consider writing a letter to let him know you're safe and cared for."

Turning to Diana, he added, "You might want to write your mother, too."

"Yes," she agreed quickly. "That's a good idea."

"He won't be able to trace the letter here?" Sarah asked.

"No, I'll see to that," he promised.

Diana summed up their discussion. "Then the plan is to wait until Sarah is out of danger and return to the States."

"Do you agree, Sarah?" he asked.

"Yes, it might work."

"*Bueno.* Now all you need to do is get strong," Seguín reassured her.

Sarah had responded to Pilar's care. For the past five days, she hadn't experienced any cramping, and she felt fine as long as she remained in bed and didn't exert herself.

Diana had been surprised to find that, even in Seguín's home, their contact was minimal. He woke long before she did, ate, and left the house to work at the mines. Most evenings he returned late, had supper alone, and went to bed.

Remembering the sensual promise of his words on the patio, she wondered if he were purposely avoiding her. He knew if they spent time together, the inevitable would happen. And now, with Sarah's pregnancy staring them in the face, she guessed he didn't want to tempt fate.

A part of her was disappointed, she admitted to herself. Living in Seguín's house without interacting with him was sheer torture. She found herself straining to hear the familiar scrape of his boots, hoping he would decide to come home early one evening and have supper with her. At odd times during the night, she wakened and listened to the silent house, imagining what would happen if she went to him.

The days dragged by, long and almost as empty as before. She read and played cards with Sarah. She helped Lupita in the kitchen. And she spent long hours sitting in front of the house, gazing over the canyon.

The view was magnificent, with the lofty peaks ringing them. Clouds played peekabo with the taller mountains. At sunset, the colors were a sight to behold, ranging from blood red in the path of the setting sun to darkest purple where the shadows of night encroached.

It was a peaceful time. It should have been a pleasant time. She and Sarah were safe and together. There were plenty of new books to read, in both Spanish and English. Lupita's cooking was excellent—so good, in fact, that she feared she was putting on weight. What should have been a peaceful interlude became a kind of torture because of her yearnings for Seguín.

Despite her longings, she couldn't fault him for his aloofness. To be close, as he had pointed out, would lead to further intimacies. And further intimacies could easily lead to . . . Sarah's condition. Instead of mooning over the man, she should pin a medal on him. He must have thought of it, too, and in all probability he held his natural desires at bay to protect her. Or was it to protect himself? The question rose, unbidden to her mind.

If they made love and she became pregnant, would he feel the responsibility to marry her? Lupita had made remarks about *curanderas* and their knowledge of women's bodies. Something to the effect that her sister could end a pregnancy as easily as she could save one. Was that true? And if it was, had Lupita guessed her secret, and in her own kind way was trying to help her?

But she couldn't bring herself to terminate a pregnancy, even if the opportunity were offered to her. She would want her and Seguín's child, no matter what the circumstances. But Lupita couldn't know that, could she?

Her tormented thoughts circled her mind, giving her

no rest, no peace. She needed something to take her mind off her hopeless situation. Sarah was doing well, and Lupita would be only too happy to watch her for a day. She wanted to visit the mines.

Diana woke long before daybreak and dressed quickly. Lupita, who took a long *siesta* in the afternoon, was already up, busily frying bacon and eggs.

Lupita covered her obvious surprise upon seeing Diana at such an early hour by handing her a cup of coffee and greeting her with, *"Buenos días."* But her curiosity got the better of her, and she observed, "You're up early this morning, *Señorita* Diana. Is there a problem?"

"No, nothing's wrong. Sarah is doing well, and I wonder if you would take care of her today. I rose early to go to the mines with Seguín."

Boots sounded on the tile floor behind her, and she swung around, coming face-to-face with Seguín.

"Did I hear my name?" he asked. His gaze rested on her for one brief instant, and then flicked away. "To what do I owe this unexpected pleasure, Diana?"

"I want to go with you to the mines today."

He accepted a cup of coffee and opened his mouth to speak. His forehead was creased, and his mouth turned down. She sensed he wanted to refuse her, but he must have changed his mind because he shrugged and his features relaxed.

"That's a good idea. It's only fair that you see your father's process being used. Firsthand knowledge might help you to sell it in the States."

Surprised by his easy capitulation, she murmured her thanks. They ate breakfast together while Seguín explained his mining operations.

"I control five silver mines, spread over twenty miles and five different mountains. The oldest and largest mine is closest. I'll introduce you to my partner, too—Juan Martínez," he offered.

The more they discussed the mines, the more eager she was to see them. In her excitement, she was able to eat only half of her breakfast. Feigning a patience she didn't feel, she forced herself to linger over her coffee, waiting for him to finish eating.

Wiping his mouth with a napkin and rising from his chair, he warned, "You'll have to climb another steep trail."

"I'm ready."

"*Bueno. Vengase.*"

They stopped first at the crude hut Seguín proclaimed as his mine headquarters. Upon entering the semi-dark interior, Diana was amazed at the filth and jumbled contents. This place made Lupita's kitchen look like a model of efficiency. She wondered how Seguín ever found anything.

A middle-aged, bearish looking man with a full beard rose when they entered and bowed formally.

Seguín introduced them. "This is Juan Martínez, my esteemed partner. Juan, I have the pleasure of presenting *Señorita* McFarland."

Juan approached and took her hand, shaking it vigorously. "It is indeed an honor to meet the daughter of a genius. Seguín tells me you're very intelligent, too."

Diana couldn't help herself. She blushed, feeling like a ripe tomato being held up for inspection. Despite her embarrassment, she managed to respond, "Thank you for your kind words. I'm happy to meet you, *Señor* Martínez."

"Ah, intelligent and possessing a silver tongue, too. And beautiful, as well." He nudged Seguín in the ribs. "You've been holding out on me, partner."

She didn't think it was possible, but more heat flooded her face, turning her from a tomato to a beet, she guessed.

Suddenly, she was glad for the dark interior, hoping the worst of her embarrassment would remain hidden.

"Diana wants to see everything. The refining room as well as the mine itself. We'll stop by after we're done," Seguín said.

"I'll be here." Juan gazed around the disorganized office and frowned. "Maybe a little tidying up might be in order, to receive your guest properly."

Seguín smiled, his even white teeth flashing in his bronzed face. Diana's heart beat a little faster, and her fingertips tingled. He was so handsome when he smiled. She wished he would do it more often.

Taking her elbow, he led her from the office into what seemed like blinding sunlight after the dark shack. But her attention wasn't on the bright sun; she was too busy savoring his touch on her arm. Where his fingers held her, she could feel gooseflesh rising. How long had it been since they'd touched? *Forever and a lifetime,* she thought, closing her eyes and remembering his mouth on hers.

His voice drew her back to the present, asking, "What do you want to see first? The mine or the refining room?"

"The refining room, of course."

"Your wish is my command."

She wished it were so.

Fourteen

Diana followed Seguín into an immense vaulted cave. A string of burros and mules wound from the mine tunnels, laden with chunks of rock. At the crushing bin, almost naked men, their skin glistening with perspiration, pounded the rocks, extricating the ore. Small boys scooped up the ore and dumped it into a huge, square trough filled with what looked like mud.

The waterfall outside the cave turned a waterwheel. The waterwheel powered an immense stone roller that pounded the silver ore into wet mud.

Seguín led Diana to the trough and explained, "This is the step where we add the mercury and salts. Using the chemical compounds your father perfected, we only need about half of the mercury we used before." He pointed to metal pipes, snaking from the trough. "When the quicksilver finally merges with the raw silver, we collect it in those pipes. Then it must be fired for eight hours in kettles before the mercury vaporizes."

"I thought it took twelve hours."

He gave her an admiring glance and observed, "You *do* know a lot about mining. It takes only eight hours now. That's the beauty of your father's formula. Less mercury, less firing to vaporize it. Cuts both raw material cost as well as labor."

Taking her elbow, he propelled her to a smaller vault

built into the side of the cave. It had a metal door and an elaborate lock. A mustachioed guard, holding a carbine, barred the entrance.

In deference to Seguín, the guard bowed and stood to one side. Stepping over the raised doorway, Diana followed him inside. It was like walking into Aladdin's cave. Crisscrossed stacks of silver bars gleamed in the smoky torchlight.

With a wave of his arm, he indicated, "The finished product. Thanks to your father's genius, each bar takes twenty to thirty fewer pesos to produce. A significant savings, and one we can use to undercut our competitors."

"You mean your stepfather, don't you?" She didn't know what made her prod him. After all, both he and Juan had called her father a genius, and Seguín, in particular, was being quite complimentary of Jamie, showing her how his formula was being utilized.

He didn't reply. Instead, he closed the heavy metal door behind them, shutting out the guard's presence. Snatching the torch from its embrasure, he buried it in the dirt, snuffing out the only light.

The darkness was so complete that she couldn't see her hand in front of her face. Stunned and bewildered by his abrupt reaction, she willed herself to remain calm. Standing still in the tomb-like blackness, her other senses sharpened. She could hear him breathing, close by.

Suddenly, he caught her wrists, gripping them firmly. His hot breath was on her face. "Why do you taunt me so, Diana the huntress? *La rubia,* the goddess of the golden hair. With your milk and honey body, soft to touch, but with the fire inside. Why do you taunt me?" he repeated.

Pulling her to him, he brought her up against the solid expanse of his chest. He slipped one hand free and grasped her chin, holding her jaw open. His mouth descended upon hers, burning her in a scorching kiss.

In the dark, her sense of taste heightened. She sampled

each nuance of his breath—the coffee he had for break-fast, the salty tang of bacon. Cocooned in the dark with him, she felt each touch, each brush of his flesh against hers, bring a shivering ecstasy. The skin of his face was rough, even abrasive—although he must have shaved just an hour before—but his full lips were supple, warm, and wonderfully soft. The hot gliding of his tongue brought a ripple of desire. Its texture was nubby and rough-smooth, inviting her exploration.

Had he meant all those things he said about her? She trembled with the pleasure of remembering them. No one had ever complimented her looks before.

He released her other hand and she strained forward, fingers twining through the queue of his black mane. His hands were on her bottom now, cupping it, bringing her against the rigid evidence of his desire. She clutched him to her, reveling in each thrust of his tongue, responding to each gyration of his male body.

They were completely alone, locked in the dark womb of their embrace. Only a few layers of clothing separated them. Would he make good his threat . . . or promise? Would her body be the price? If it were to be, she wantonly rushed to it—wanting him . . . wanting all of him.

Abruptly, he broke away and stepped back. She could hear his labored breathing. It played counterpoint to her thudding heart. Reaching forward blindly, she didn't un-derstand his sudden abandonment. Her hand brushed the cloth of his shirt.

"Don't," he hissed, twisting away and hating himself.

Por Dios, he had almost given in, almost admitted the deep feelings he had for her. Almost allowed himself to trust again. Not that she didn't seem deserving of his trust. She was strong and brave and loyal—everything a man could want. And she was *la rubia,* the flame of his passion, burning bright, beckoning.

That day on the patio, he had warned her this might

happen. Or had he warned himself? he wondered. It didn't matter. It was the same thing. That day a part of him had wanted it to happen. She had seemed willing, and he was consumed with wanting her. If he took her, would it quench the fire burning him up?

Sarah's pregnancy had made him keenly aware that satisfying his lust on her virgin body wasn't so simple a thing. What if he got her with child? Then what? Could he stand to give her and the child up? Could he play the domesticated husband? It was almost tempting, thinking of her swollen with his child—thinking of building a life together.

Almost tempting . . . until he realized he would have to trust again.

Gilberto threw his bound hands in front of his face when they led him from the dark cellar into the sunlight. The sun bore down on him, burning through the thin membrane of his eyelids. He stumbled along behind his father's men, surprised to find how weak he was even though he had exercised every day.

They shoved open the back door and dragged him through the kitchen. Luz, the cook, took one look at him and threw her apron over her face.

He grinned to himself. He must look a sight, he realized—dirty and bearded, with his usually short hair falling to his shoulders. It had been weeks since his father had locked him up. When he thought about the passage of time, his thoughts always returned to Sarah, and he wondered how she was. Would she be waiting for him? Probably not. By now, she would be on her way to San Francisco.

Thrusting him inside his father's study, the guards left him there. Again, his eyes were forced to adjust to semi-darkness. This was the room where it had all begun . . . the struggle to marry Sarah. As his eyes accustomed themselves, he realized his father was already there waiting for him like some malevolent Buddha, hunched behind his desk with his hands resting on the wide girth of his abdomen.

Sketching a shaky bow with his hands tied, he mocked, "I came as soon as I could. At your service, *señor.*"

"Don't be sarcastic, Gilberto. It doesn't become you." His father wrinkled his nose, registering the aromatic stench that accompanied him. "You're not the handsome ladies' man now, eh? They would all run screaming if they got sight . . . or a whiff of you." Don Carlos guffawed.

Not Sarah. The thought rose, unbidden, to his mind.

"What do you want, Don Carlos?"

"Don Carlos, you say? Rather formal for your dear *Papá*, eh?"

"Fathers don't lock up their sons, like beasts."

"The hell you say!" He slammed his fist on the desk, making the papers fly and the inkwell jump. "Fathers do that and more if their sons are disobedient."

Gathering some of the strewn papers, his father thrust them at him and demanded, "Are you going to sign this annulment or not?"

Lifting his bound wrists, he observed wryly, "I doubt it."

"Damn you! You're trying my patience sorely. You know what I mean. If I untie your hands, will you sign?"

"No."

His father's eyes bore into him, malice gleaming in their depths. Gilberto shuddered, wondering when he had become so twisted. Was it when his mother had died?

Don Carlos shrugged, appearing to regain his composure. "Then you leave me no choice. I'm sending you back to Europe. Back to the monastery, where you'll do six months' penitence. I'll obtain the annulment without your signature. When you return, you'll marry María Figueroa." He paused and added, "Do you understand?"

Returning his father's shrug, he replied, "I understand."

"You'll be taken to Veracruz under armed guard. There

will be another guard to accompany you on the voyage. You'll have no money, so escape will be useless."

Already a plan had formed in Gilberto's mind. A plan to escape and find Sarah. "May I take a bath?" he asked.

"Always the dandy, eh, *mi hijo?*" his father noted sarcastically. "All right, I'll send a bath to your room. You'll leave tomorrow, so I'll allow you to stay tonight in your room. But there will be guards, posted at your door and window. *¿Entiende?*"

Sarah sat up in bed. Far off, there was a rumbling noise as if a storm were coming. Rolling over, she pulled the pillow over her head and tried to fall asleep again. Sleep eluded her. Tossing and turning, she couldn't help but worry about Gilberto.

How was he? Was his father still holding him prisoner? Seguín said so, that there had been no change. But he wouldn't know if something happened until days had passed, and the word reached here.

More important, did Gilberto still love her? She wished she could tell him about the baby. She pounded her fist into the mattress and silently cursed both Don Carlos and her parents for their stubbornness. Would she and Gilberto ever be allowed to live together as man and wife?

Tenderly, she stroked her belly, imagining the new life lying there. Don Carlos and her parents couldn't deny them once they knew about the baby, could they?

She believed her parents would give in, but she wasn't so sure about Gilberto's father. Everything she knew about the man led her to believe he was totally ruthless, without conscience. Even Seguín avoided her eyes and questions when she asked him if the baby would make a difference with his stepfather.

Punching the pillow and rearranging the covers, she tried to shut her mind off, to drift back to sleep. It was no use. Confined to bed, she napped during the day, making it difficult to sleep through the night.

The rumbling noise came again. It almost sounded like thunder, but not quite. Maybe it was echoing off the sides of the mountains, making it sound strange.

She knew she wasn't supposed to get out of bed, but if she couldn't sleep what was the use? And she didn't feel like reading, either. A restlessness had seized her. Lupita prescribed hot milk when she couldn't sleep. If she were quiet, she could get her own milk from the kitchen and no one would know. Everyone else was sleeping. She decided to heat some milk and watch the storm roll in over the mountains.

Carefully, she slipped her feet over the side of the bed, as if testing the waters. Feeling for her wrapper in the dark, she located it at the foot of the bed and put it on. Fumbling for the matches, she lit the lamp and opened the door slowly, hoping the hinges wouldn't creak.

Passing through the sitting room, she realized she hadn't been in any part of the house other than her bedroom. As soon as she had arrived, they whisked her off to bed and there she had stayed, except the one time when she ventured out to ask about Gilberto.

A strong wind whipped through the open shutters just as she crossed to the kitchen. Her lamp went out. She cursed her bad luck. Should she turn back and get the matches from her room or fumble in the dark until she found some in the kitchen? Undecided, she took a tentative step forward . . . into nothingness.

Her feet flew outward. As she desperately grasped empty air, the lamp fell and shattered. She pitched forward, blindly trying to break her fall with her hands. The hard tile floor rushed up. She landed heavily, pain shooting through her abdomen and head.

The night became blacker, and from far away she heard a scream.

* * *

It was Diana who found Sarah, lying unconscious at the entrance to the kitchen. Sarah's scream had awakened her, and she came running. Kneeling beside her friend, she felt panic sluice over her, as if she had plunged into an icy stream. Not knowing what to do first, she felt for a pulse in Sarah's throat. She found it, like butterfly wings fluttering against the smooth skin.

There was a gash where Sarah's head had hit the floor, which must have brought on her unconsciousness. Afraid to look for other injuries before she got help, she rose to her feet and ran back down the hallway, shouting, "Seguín, Lupita, come quickly and bring your lamps! Sarah's been hurt."

Seguín emerged first, shirtless and buttoning the placket of his pants while trying to hold a lamp. Snatching the lamp from his hand, she registered the broad expanse of his muscular chest. If she hadn't been so afraid for Sarah and the baby, she would have savored this rare glimpse of his naked torso.

Lupita came next, her wrapper flapping around her, holding her lamp aloft. Her face was lined with concern, and she started to ask, *"Qué*—what—?"

Diana interrupted, "Sarah must have gotten up during the night and decided to go into the kitchen for something. She didn't know about the step down, and she fell. Her head's cut, and she's unconscious. I don't know—"

Sarah's groan from the kitchen cut her explanation short. They turned as one and raced toward the sound.

With three lamps to light the disastrous scene, Diana realized Sarah was hurt worse than she had originally thought. She appeared to be regaining consciousness, and with the return of her senses she clutched her abdomen and moaned.

A bright red spot stained the snow-white cotton of her nightgown.

Seguín saw and understood. Slowly and gently, he

slipped his arms beneath the writhing woman. Rising to one knee, he balanced there for a brief second, getting a firm grip on her. The muscles in his neck and arms knotted and strained as he rose, holding her carefully in his arms.

"Lupita, boil some water and cloths. Diana, help me to get her into bed." He barked the orders.

Diana trailed after them, fear about Sarah's condition sending icy fingers down her spine. Lupita headed for the kitchen's hearth.

When they had her settled as comfortably as possible, he declared, "I'm going for Pilar. It might take me some time. It's harder to get around at night in the mountains."

Diana's eyes met his, and she nodded dumbly. Concern and the touch of panic she felt were echoed in the midnight depths of his eyes. Despite the horrible situation, it warmed her to know he cared about Sarah and her baby. It was another rare glimpse into the complex man he was.

"Do you know anything about nursing?"

"A little. Remember, I grew up in mining camps."

"*Sí*, that's good. Clean the head wound with the boiled cloths. Then apply a cool compress to her head. Use the spring water out back. As for the other . . ."—he hesitated, obviously feeling out of his element—"try to staunch the blood with the boiled cloths." His gaze found hers again. "Do you agree?"

"Yes."

"*Bueno.*" And then he did something that surprised her. He brushed her lips with his. It wasn't a kiss of passion, as were the other kisses they'd shared. No, it was something more. A kiss of reassurance, a very human kiss, recognizing her as an equal mortal sufferer.

And it touched her, touched her heart and soul. If his errand hadn't been so urgent, she would have nestled in his arms, drawing strength from his caring.

* * *

It was over before Seguín returned with Pilar, although Diana didn't realize it. Or maybe she knew, but didn't want to admit it. Despite her best efforts to staunch the flow, Sarah kept bleeding.

When Pilar arrived, she took over and shooed both Diana and Seguín from the room, relying upon Lupita to bring supplies from the kitchen.

Relegated to unnecessary appendages, Seguín and Diana waited silently in the sitting room. The room lightened slowly with the coming dawn. A far off rumble broke the silence, sounding like thunder. Seguín's head jerked up, and he listened intently.

Roused from her despondent state, Diana asked, "What is it?"

He shook his head and avoided her eyes. "Probably just a storm in the mountains."

Something about his response bothered her; she knew he wasn't being truthful with her. She started to question him, but found she didn't care. Nothing mattered but Sarah. A part of her mind finally realized he was wearing a shirt. He must have donned it when he went to fetch Pilar.

Pilar strode into the room, wiping her hands on her apron. "*Señorita* Sarah lost the baby," she declared without preamble. "Her head wound isn't too bad. She's young and healthy. She'll recover fast."

"How fast?" Seguín asked.

Surprised by his abrupt question, Diana glanced at him, expecting an explanation for his unusual rudeness, but he ignored her, concentrating on Pilar.

"Two to three weeks."

"I see. Thank you for coming, Pilar." With those words he turned and strode from the room.

Her gaze followed his hasty exit. His sudden leave-taking made her feel even more empty and alone than before.

How on earth could she comfort Sarah? What could she say?

As if she had read her thoughts, Pilar offered, "When the cramping starts so early in a pregnancy, it's usually a sign something is wrong . . . with the baby."

"But you said the first three months are the most dangerous."

"*Sí*, I did. Because that's when nature usually corrects her mistakes."

"Mistakes, mistakes. What do you mean?" She knew her voice sounded hysterical, but she couldn't help herself.

Grasping her shoulders, the *curandera* shook her gently. "I didn't mean—" She expelled her breath and murmured, "How to explain?"

Twisting from her grasp, Diana covered her face with her hands. Moisture filled her eyes, leaking from the corners like rain.

"A seed is not always a baby, *Señorita* Diana. Sometimes, it will be nothing more than a seed. I do not understand why this is so, but I know it to be true. Many women lose babies . . . or seeds in the first three months. It's not uncommon."

"It's *uncommon* for Sarah," she grated out, her heart wrenching from the loss. This baby had meant everything to her best friend. It had tied her and Gilberto together irrevocably. And it had been a new life, uniting their lives, a promise for the future.

Now there was nothing but wasted dreams.

Gilberto grabbed the slop bucket and retched again. Clasping his stomach with both hands, he prayed for an end to this endless voyage. He had never possessed good "sea legs," and traveling under guard in the cargo hold, closest to the choppy waters of the Atlantic, only heightened his discomfort.

He wondered if his father had devised this extra torture to subjugate him further or if it was as his "companion" had explained—it was easier to watch a prisoner in the hold of the ship than in a cabin topside.

Either way, it didn't matter. He was miserable, and would remain so until they docked in Lisbon. Once his feet touched solid ground, though, it would be another matter . . . another matter entirely.

Patting the hidden pocket in the inseam of his pants, he reassured himself the diamond was still there, big as a pigeon's egg. His mother had given it to him on her deathbed. He had held it sacred, coming from his mother at such a time. If she were alive and understood how much he loved Sarah, he knew she would readily agree to his disposition of the rare stone. And he happened to be acquainted with a jeweler in Lisbon who would give him a fair price and ask no questions.

Escaping from the monks shouldn't prove to be too taxing. With the proceeds from the diamond, he would have more than enough money to sail to San Francisco.

Sarah lay in bed, staring out the window. It was all she did now. She barely ate and hardly moved. Her face had filled with fine lines, as if she were an old woman.

Diana and Pilar had said everything they knew how to say. Done everything they could think of doing. Even Seguín came to Sarah, at odd times, and tried to cheer her up. Nothing worked.

Lifting a dog-eared copy of Jane Austen's *Pride and Prejudice*, Diana inquired, "Sarah, would you like to hear the next chapter?"

"I don't care. Whatever you want," she replied listlessly.

Frustrated and worried about her friend's state of mind, she started to voice her concerns, but the rumble they'd been hearing for days diverted her attention.

She had sat for hours at the front of the house surveying the canyon for signs of storms, but the summer sky was like an overturned blue bowl. As hard as she searched, she couldn't find evidence of storms. The sound disturbed her, and she promised herself to ask Seguín about it again. This time, she wouldn't be put off so easily.

At that moment he entered Sarah's room unexpectedly. Glancing at the slant of the sun through the open window, she judged it must be late afternoon. He never came home before nightfall. After their kiss in the dark, he had taken to avoiding her again. For him to come home in the afternoon, there must be a serious reason.

Without speaking, he motioned for her to step outside. She glanced at Sarah, but her friend remained still as a statue, not noticing or caring about his sudden appearance. Following him from the room, she said, "I'll be back in a minute."

Sarah didn't respond.

Shutting the door behind her, she joined him in the sitting room.

"Yes, Seguín, what do you want?" she asked, forgoing the customary greetings.

"How is she?"

Diana shrugged. "The same."

"How long before she'll be able to travel?"

"I don't know about traveling. Pilar says she can start taking light exercise in two or three days. What's this about?" Remembering her earlier question, she added, "And what's that strange rumble we keep hearing? I've looked and looked, but I don't see any sign of a storm."

He pulled his hand through his hair. She recognized it as his customary gesture of agitation. The sense of unease that his unexpected appearance and abrupt questions had raised heightened, forming a tight knot in her stomach.

"The rumbling is what I came to talk to you about. It's not thunder. It's cannon fire. The war is creeping closer every day. The Juáristas will try to take the silver mines. The mines will provide them funds to keep fighting."

"But you're a Juárista, or you were one." Saying the words reminded her of that far off day on the patio. How young and naive she had been then. "Why would they take the mines from you?"

His lips quirked, as if in acknowledgement of her quick logic. "I'm not saying the mines won't be returned to me after the war for my loyalty to the cause. And I'm not saying we'll fight to keep them. But the fighting is all around us. The French are coming, too, and I have no connections with them. One of the villages where the miners live has already been destroyed. It's not safe for you and Sarah to remain here."

"Not safe here?" Diana replied, stunned. Seguín's eagle nest house seemed impenetrable.

"No, I don't want to risk it. Besides, now that Sarah's . . ." It seemed he couldn't bring himself to say the word. "Now that she's the way she is . . . and there's something else." He paused, obviously trying to marshall his thoughts. "Gilberto sailed from Veracruz for Lisbon, under guard. The imprisonment didn't work. He refused to give up Sarah, so Don Carlos sent him back to Europe. My stepfather bribed some officials to annul the marriage without the bride and groom's signatures."

"Oh, no."

"Oh, yes. Given the situation with Gilberto, and Sarah's condition, I think she should return to her family. And I don't want to endanger either one of you with fighting nearby. What do you think, Diana?"

Despite the bad news, it gave her a warm feeling to know he cared about her opinion. After all, it involved her . . . and Sarah. And her best friend was in no position to be making decisions. He *should* care what she thought. She doubted the old Seguín would have, though. In the wake of denying their desire for each other, were they becoming friends?

She remembered the kiss of reassurance he had given her the night Sarah lost the baby. It would seem an uneasy truce had been struck between them. This time, she couldn't attribute his consideration for her feelings to any secondary motive, either. He had the formula, and he had had plenty of opportunity to seduce her, too. He must know she was willing—too willing, for her own good.

Had Seguín begun to care for her as a person?

If he had, it could be the first step toward love. Not passion or desire, but the kind of love Sarah and Gilberto shared.

With her heart soaring with hope, she didn't want to answer him truthfully. The truth would snare her hope and return it to earth, to perish under the hot sun of reality. Considering Sarah's condition, she knew it was best they return to the Yorks. But if they did so, she would leave México, too, never to see him again.

Seconds ticked by, painful, wrenching seconds. In the end, she knew what her answer must be.

"Yes, I think Sarah should be with her parents." She paused, unsure, knowing she was asking too much—especially after all he had done for her and Sarah—but she couldn't help herself. It was the only way to keep her hope alive.

"Will you escort us to Veracruz?"

"My mines—" He gestured, before adding, "Herbert York is more than capable of—"

"He didn't do such a good job the last time," she interjected.

His night-black gaze snagged hers. A question, and then a sudden awareness shone there. Either he was being more open with her, or she had learned how to read him, because more often than not she knew what he was thinking.

Warmth flooded her. He understood the reason behind

her request. She was certain he would refuse. He had been avoiding her for weeks. Why would he want to continue the charade?

He surprised her by agreeing. "I'll escort you to Veracruz. After all, I promised you that once, didn't I? Juan will have to deal with the Juáristas. He's an old freedom fighter, too. That's how we met."

The heady wine of triumph flowed through her veins. She had never felt so utterly female before. As painful as it was to stay together, it must be just as painful for him to leave her as it was for her. She didn't trumpet her triumph, knowing that a fragile bond existed between them. Instead, she returned to the matter at hand.

"Who will tell Sarah, especially about Gilberto?"

Hesitating for the briefest moment, he replied, "We both will. I think she'll need both of us." He shifted his feet. "I think Gilberto will find his way back to México as soon as he can escape. I'll leave word at his father's *rancho* as well as here with Juan. When he returns, I'll help him to get to San Francisco."

"You would do that for Sarah and Gilberto? I thought you didn't even like your half-brother."

"Haven't I been helping since you asked me?" he countered.

She couldn't disagree with him. He *had* been helping her and Sarah. She just wished she knew why. Because he cared for her . . . wanted her? After their kiss in the mine vault, he had distanced himself again. She had hoped he would admit that he was helping them because of her. But she should know better than to expect that. Even if he did care for her, he would never admit it.

"Pilar, what's in the bundle?" Diana inquired, her curiosity piqued.

She had been expecting the *curandera*. It would be her

last visit to check Sarah's progress. Arrangements had been made, and Sarah had been told. They planned to leave for México City the next day.

Sarah, when told about Gilberto, had surprised them by showing no emotion. It was as if she no longer cared about anything. Diana was beginning to worry in earnest, and she prayed Sarah's parents would be able to reach her.

Lifting her arms, Pilar held them in a half-tilted position. Peeking from the bundle was the tiny, wizened face of a baby. The infant possessed a shock of dark brown hair and rounded cheeks. She couldn't see the color of the baby's eyes because they were squeezed shut, and its rosebud mouth trembled. It appeared as if the child might burst into tears at any moment.

"Oh, Pilar, what a beautiful baby!"

"*Muy bonito,* no? It's a boy, and he's two weeks old."

"But where did you get him?" She knew he couldn't belong to the *curandera* because she hadn't been pregnant. And Pilar possessed an old-young kind of face. Diana would have been hard pressed to guess her age. Had she hazarded a guess, she would have thought Pilar was too old to have a baby, and too young to be a grandmother.

"From the village that was destroyed by the French. He's an orphan. Both his parents were killed."

Shaking her head, Diana murmured, "Poor little fellow. May I hold him?"

"Of course. Here." Pilar held out the baby, and she tentatively stretched out her arms.

"I've never held a baby before," she admitted. "I'm an only child."

"It's not difficult. I'll show you." Directing her, Pilar said, "Put your right arm under his bottom like so, and cradle his head with your left arm." She took the infant, trying to follow directions but feeling inordinately clumsy as she did so. "Remember," Pilar counseled, "the important thing is to support the child's head."

When she finally had the baby securely tucked into her arms, she gazed down at him and was struck with awe. Even with his eyes squinted and his mouth twisted, he was beautiful. His chubby arms and legs churned, dimpled at elbows and knees. She noticed his fingernails, exact replicas of hers, but so tiny and fragile they appeared to be made from angel's wings. His toes resembled peas, small and round. He was perfect . . . so perfect.

A strange feeling stole over her. She could almost feel her heart expand in her chest, and an infinite sense of love filled her. Gooseflesh rose on her arms. The magic of the moment was indescribable, beyond anything she had experienced before. Could Sarah have known it would be like this? But Sarah was an only child, too. How could she have—

Like a thunderbolt from heaven, she suddenly understood why Pilar had brought the child. Raising her eyes, she caught Pilar's gaze. A silent communication passed between them.

"Let's show him to Sarah," Diana suggested.

Smiling and nodding, Pilar opened the door to Sarah's room.

They didn't say anything when they entered. As usual, Sarah sat propped against her pillows, gazing out the window. Diana leaned over the bed and placed the tiny bundle beside her. Sarah didn't appear to notice.

The cry that had been threatening to erupt finally found voice, and the infant released a lusty wail.

Sarah started and turned toward the sound. Her half-closed eyes flew open. Seconds ticked by as she studied the baby. The glazed look in her eyes faded, to be replaced by bright animation. A look of awe suffused her features, and she raised a tentative hand to push back the swaddling clothes.

Stroking her finger across the infant's downy cheek, she murmured, "Sssh, little one. It's all right. Everything will be fine. Your mommy will—" She stopped short, and her head jerked up.

Pinning both Diana and Pilar with her gaze, she asked, "Where's the baby's mother?"

"He doesn't have one. He was orphaned in the fighting," Pilar explained softly.

"Doesn't have—" Sarah mouthed. Her gaze returned to the child and then back to them. "Doesn't have a mother?"

"No, or a father," Pilar added.

"It's a baby boy, Sarah," Diana offered.

The infant's wails increased in intensity, and she scooped him up, hugging him close and murmuring low words of comfort. Diana and Pilar exchanged glances.

"Wha—what will happen to him?" Sarah inquired.

"I'll try to find a home for him," Pilar replied.

As she raised her eyes from the crying infant, determination and joy commingled on Sarah's face. An odd combination, Diana thought, but understandable, given the circumstances.

"He has a home," she whispered so quietly that it was difficult to discern her words over the baby's cries. Her demeanor left no doubt, though. She had taken the child into her heart as soon as she saw him.

Pilar beamed. Diana smiled, tears rising to her eyes.

"Seguín will be so pleased. Two women and now a baby to escort," Diana observed archly.

"Three women," Pilar corrected.

"What do you mean?" Diana asked.

"His wet nurse, Lydia, will need to accompany you. She lost her baby and husband in the fighting. She's been feeding him."

Sarah's face fell, and she turned her head away. "I suppose she wants to . . . to adopt him." Her voice quivered with ill-disguised pain.

Rushing to her side, Pilar placed a hand on her shoulder. "No, it's not like that. She has no husband, no way to raise him. She cares for him because—" Her voice faltered.

"I understand," Sarah replied. Her face had already brightened. "Of course he must have a wet nurse. I'll hire her. Is that what she wants, a job?"

Hating to intervene in this happy moment, this first glimpse of hope she had seen from her friend, Diana debated silently with herself. They were scheduled to depart tomorrow. If Sarah wanted to adopt the baby to replace the one she had lost, she agreed wholeheartedly. The positive effect the child had was already apparent. But they weren't just going to México City. After that, they would be continuing to the States. Would Lydia, the wet nurse, be willing to leave her homeland? It was an issue they needed to face because there was so little time.

"Pilar, we'll be returning to *Los Estados Unidos*. Will Lydia want to leave México?"

"I don't know. You must ask her. She's waiting outside. I believe the little *muchacho* needs her. I'll fetch her."

The baby's cries had undulated, rising and falling, reaching a heartrending wailing only to subside into whimpering hiccups.

"Needs her?" Diana queried.

"*Sí*, he cries because he's hungry," Pilar explained before leaving the room.

She felt foolish. Why hadn't she thought of that? The poor child cried because he was hungry. She and Sarah had a lot to learn about taking care of an infant.

Apparently undaunted by the responsibility, Sarah raised a face shining with happiness and declared, "We'll call him James Gilbert Aguirre. James for your father, and Gilbert for his father. Gilberto will be so pleased."

Touched by her friend wanting to name the child for her father, Diana crossed to the bed and encircled both Sarah and the baby in her arms. "That's sweet of you, but wouldn't you rather call him Gilbert James?"

"No, I want to honor your father's memory for all you've done, Diana. I know it's been hard since . . . since . . ." She paused and licked her lips. "But you've never wavered. You've stayed beside me and cared." She freed one hand from beneath the baby and squeezed Diana's shoulder. "I couldn't have done it without you. And you'll be his godmother."

Hot tears rose to her eyes, and Diana bowed her head. Gazing at the baby, she felt irrevocably linked, part of a triangle of caring. She, Sarah, and little James, they were a family. A strange family, but one, nevertheless, and she would do her best to be a good godmother.

"Thank you, dear friend," she said. "I'll be there for you both."

"I know. So, it's settled."

"Yes. I'm glad you're happy, Sarah."

Their tender embrace was broken when the door opened. Diana straightened to face Pilar and a young woman, who must be Lydia.

Sarah eased the awkwardness of the situation by speaking first. "You must be Lydia. I'm glad to meet you. I'm Sarah, and this is Diana." Lifting her arms with the whimpering child, she directed, "Please take him. He needs to be fed."

Bobbing her head in deference, Lydia approached the bed and took the infant.

"His name is James," Sarah supplied for Lydia.

Lydia retreated to the ladder-back chair in the corner and exposed one breast. Baby James greedily took her offering.

Pilar approached the bed and told them she had spoken

with Lydia. The young woman had no family, and she seemed willing to start a new life.

Sarah was pleased by the information. Diana was pleased for her friend. She couldn't help but wonder how Seguín would react to the news.

Fifteen

Seguín reacted better than Diana had hoped. He seemed to understand how much the orphaned child meant to Sarah, and he didn't complain when the baby made their trip miserable with his constant crying.

Riding into the environs of México City, she worried about baby James. It was obvious that traveling didn't suit him, and unfortunately he would be doing a great deal of it in the near future.

Besides worrying about the child, she wondered how Sarah's parents would accept the baby. It was difficult enough, her returning after running away—but with an orphaned baby in tow? She hated to think how the Yorks would react. And then, there was her own mother to deal with. She knew Elizabeth would be disappointed and hurt by her actions.

She dreaded the reunion and explanations.

When they reached the York home, bedraggled and weary, the reality of the situation wasn't as bad as she had feared.

The Yorks and Elizabeth were so happy to see them returned safely that they accepted them gladly. Diana sensed animosity between Herbert York and Seguín, though. Sarah's father didn't approve of Seguín's part in their running away.

Baby James, on the other hand, was welcomed with open

arms. Mary York quickly became attached to him, and Diana wondered why she hadn't had more children.

Despite the subdued animosity between them, Herbert and Seguín spent several hours together, discussing the best strategy for reaching Veracruz. The war had escalated. The public coaches to the coastal town had been suspended. As the French army evacuated to the coast, it became increasingly dangerous to travel there. Passage from México had become difficult to obtain. After much wrangling, Herbert declared he had booked space for them on a clipper ship called the Red Cloud. They would sail south to Panama, cross the isthmus, and continue, on the Pacific side, to San Francisco.

Thinking about their route made Diana realize her time with Seguín was running short. And he continued to avoid her. She had hoped, in his mountain stronghold, that given time he might learn to love her. That hope was fading. She had thought he had agreed to escort them to Veracruz to be near her, but with each passing day he had seemed more and more absorbed in the journey's success.

His abandonment made her bitter. It was as if he had betrayed a sacred promise between them.

Seguín assumed the role as the leader of their party. He was obviously determined they would reach Veracruz safely. He checked the preparations personally and spent long hours pouring over a map, choosing their route with care.

Holding several sessions with Mr. York's guards, who would accompany them, he went over last minute details and doled out duties for the trip. Despite Mary's and Sarah's protests, he limited them to one wagon for baby James and their baggage. He wanted them to travel light so they could avoid the main road. Explaining his strategy, he said he intended to lead them to Veracruz along coun-

try roads, so as to minimize their chances of encountering
roving bands of soldiers.

Once they were underway, Diana understood why
Seguín had been loathe to take even one wagon. The main
roads of México were bad, but the paths he chose were
infinitely worse, nothing more than faint traces through
the wilderness. The wagon rattled and lurched, sounding
as if it were coming apart at its joints.

Despite Lydia's best efforts to cushion baby James, the
movement and noise upset him. He cried almost continu-
ously, and refused to nurse. As the trip wore on, the baby
became thinner and more fretful, nursing only at night
when they camped.

Because the going was so rough and the wagon so slow,
it took them fifteen long and arduous days to thread their
way through the mountain passes and emerge at the edge
of the coastal plain leading to Veracruz.

The evening when they finally reached the flatlands,
Seguín called a halt and had the guards set up camp. Baby
James proved to be particularly fussy, refusing to nurse
even though they were no longer moving. Lydia had tried
everything to soothe him. Sarah had tried, too, but she
had a stomach ache and wasn't able to care for him.

That left his godmother, Diana. She worried about him,
as fretful and upset as he had been during the trip. Taking
him from Sarah's arms, she paced with him and crooned
a low, wordless lullaby.

Gazing down at the baby's red, puckered face, she suspected the problem was that he wasn't getting enough
sleep. She didn't know much about infants, but she knew
they required a great deal of sleep. Unfortunately, the
wagon's noise and movement kept him awake all day. His
accumulated discomfort from the journey had reached a
feverish pitch, and she feared he was ill from exhaustion.

Her heart reached out to him as she studied his thin,
pinched face. She knew they were getting close to Ver-

acruz, because they had left the mountains behind. She prayed silently he could endure the remainder of the trip.

After an hour of singing and pacing, the poor mite finally calmed and succumbed to exhaustion. He was so sweet, lying snuggled in her arms. Watching him sleep deeply, she felt torn over what to do. Should she allow him to sleep until he awakened on his own, or should she wake him to see if he would nurse?

Before she could make up her mind, she heard the crunch of boots and the jangle of spurs behind her. Turning, she found Seguín staring at her and the baby. His gaze was open. It was as if his eyes were reaching out to her and the infant in sympathetic understanding, a silent token of his caring.

Hurt and angry with him for ignoring her, she had taken to avoiding him, too. Staying in the rear with the wagon, where Lydia and baby James were, kept her removed from his unsettling presence. He usually took the lead and ranged far ahead of their party, scouting the route for dangers.

But tonight, he had sought her out.

Heaven help her, all she wanted to do was lay her head on his strong shoulder and let him comfort her. Against all logic, she longed to pour her heart out to him about her fears for the baby. But that was insane. He must have come to speak to her about something else . . . something to do with the journey.

He surprised her by saying, "Poor *niño*, he's had a rough time. Is there anything I can do?"

She shook her head, afraid her voice would betray the torment of longing and bitterness raging within her.

Leaning close, he brushed his knuckle over James' cheek. "Little Pepito, the journey won't last forever. You must be strong."

His gaze captured Diana's.

Diana realized he was sending her a message. *The journey*

won't last forever. It would be over sooner than they realized, and with the end of it they would part.

She had been a fool to expect anything more. All he had shown her was passion . . . reluctant passion. She must have misread the brushed kiss and the nuances of his glances. He didn't care for her, not in the way she had hoped. She didn't understand why he had helped her and Sarah, but he must have his reasons. Was guilt over her father's death still a factor? She had discounted it, but now she wasn't so sure.

If that were the case, he was more noble than she gave him credit for. Unfortunately, she didn't want his nobility. She wanted his love.

But wanting his love wasn't enough. He needed to want hers, too. She had thought there was hope for them. Her hope had died. Hurting, she decided to withdraw. The only way to armor herself against further hurt was to avoid him and forget about him. In short, to treat him as he had treated her.

A painful silence stretched between them, broken only by the croak of frogs in the coastal swamp surrounding the camp. So far, she hadn't spoken a word. It was better not to speak to him, she thought. Shrugging, she turned away.

She had decided to let James sleep until he awakened on his own. Thin as he was, she believed he needed rest more than milk. She hoped she was right. Without a backward glance, she strode toward the wagon where the baby's makeshift cradle was kept. Now that James was asleep, she realized how tired she was, too. She hadn't eaten supper. She had been too worried, and now she was past being hungry. Her pallet in the wagon beckoned.

Before she had gone more than a few steps, Seguín was beside her, placing his hand on her arm and saying, "Wait. Don't go yet."

His touch burned through the thin cotton of her sleeve,

awakening all the tumultuous yearnings buried inside of her. She stopped short and shook his hand off her arm.

"I must put James down. He needs to rest."

"*Sí,*" Seguín's voice at her ear was a whisper, light as a caress. "Diana, I'm worried about you. I want you to be happy. You're returning home—doesn't that make you glad?"

He was a snake, she realized. Everything he had done for her and Sarah was to absolve his conscience about her father. He wanted to tie her in a neat bundle and send her home, happy to be going.

How could she have been such an idiot to think he cared? She knew he had desired her, but when the reality of desire intruded in the form of Sarah's pregnancy, he had retreated quickly.

A snake, she repeated to herself, a low-crawling serpent.

At the same time, another part of her realized her assessment wasn't completely fair. He would have been a true cad if he had taken her and gotten her pregnant, only to abandon her, wouldn't he?

She didn't care. Why couldn't he love her, like Gilberto loved Sarah? The refrain had played through her mind so often that she was heartily sick of it. There was no answer. Drawing herself up, she lifted her chin and stared at him coldly. "What does it matter, Seguín?"

"It matters to me."

"Still trying to ease your conscience?"

"What do you mean?" His midnight-black eyes narrowed.

She expelled her breath. "Forget it."

He leaned dangerously close, his lips mere inches from hers. She realized he was going to kiss her, and she couldn't stand it. Just like the time in the Yorks' home when she had sold him the formula and thought she would never see him again, being near him was painful now, knowing they would part soon.

Exchanging intimacies would be torture.

Twisting away, she sprinted for the wagon.

Seguín felt gratified they had come this far without incident. They were only two or three days from Veracruz. Unfortunately, the final miles were the most dangerous stretch. French troops were all around them. He had scouted the area and seen several of their encampments. He knew he must push his party, on this last leg, as fast as they could travel.

Even as he urged them toward the relative safety of the port town, a part of him wanted the trip to last forever. Being near Diana was bittersweet. Not allowing himself to touch her or speak to her was a constant agony.

Not being around her would be an even greater torment. As long as he guided them, he could gaze upon her face from a distance and overhear her melodious voice. Just to know she was close by somehow eased the hollow emptiness in his soul. It wasn't enough, but it was something.

And then there was the baby . . . baby James . . . little Pepito.

He had never dreamed he could become attached to a baby, especially one that cried all day long. But he had. Poor little orphaned *niño*. He felt a strong empathy for the child. Seguín knew what it felt like to be without parents. He was amazed at the fierce protectiveness the child aroused in his heart—a protectiveness that echoed Diana's obvious love for the baby.

As he witnessed her tender care of James, she became the embodiment of the Madonna for him. When he watched her hold the baby in her arms, he fantasized she was holding his child. He dreamed of making a home with her, and siring a dozen children just like Pepito.

But I don't know how to be a husband and father, a voice

inside his head cautioned. *I wouldn't know how to trust, and without trust there could be no real love, no true commitment. Could there? At the first sign of trouble, I would doubt her, and question our relationship. It would never work. I would be sentencing us both to a living hell.*

He pushed the painful thoughts from his mind and concentrated on the job at hand. Pulling his black stallion up short, he rose in the stirrups and surveyed the party. The Yorks, *Señora* McFarland and Sarah, surrounded by the guards, were just ahead of him, but the wagon wasn't in sight, although the road stretched straight for a least a kilometer behind.

An alarm bell sounded in his head, and he spun his stallion around and spurred him into a gallop. Riding swiftly, he topped a rise and saw the wagon.

It was lying in the dust, tilted crazily to one side. The right rear axle was buried in the road. Estéban, the driver, examined the loose wheel, which had been thrown several meters. Lydia stood beside the wagon, holding the baby. Diana was there, too, standing beside the dun gelding she rode.

Seguín vaulted from his saddle. Surveying the damage, he wasn't particularly surprised the wagon had broken down. What was surprising was that it had lasted this long, considering the rough terrain. It was easy to see it was beyond repair. The axle had broken clean through, leaving a truncated piece of wood protruding from the middle of the wheel. They would have to continue without it.

"*Mi amigo,* staring at it won't help." He approached Estéban. "It can't be fixed. Not out here. We would need a blacksmith and the closest one is in Veracruz. We must continue without the wagon."

Making a decision, he ordered, "Estéban, take one of the wagon horses and catch up with the rest of our party. Bring back a mount for Lydia and yourself, and some rope.

We'll lash the baggage to the wagon horses. Tell the rest of our party to wait for us."

Estéban nodded and moved toward the dray horses. He unhitched the left horse and leapt onto him bareback, using the bridle to guide it. Saluting Seguín, he galloped over the rise after the others. Seguín watched him go until he was out of sight, and then he began unhitching the other wagon horse's traces.

The women hadn't said a word.

Turning to them, he explained, "While we wait, I'll see if I can rig a pack for the baggage. Diana, there should be some rope in the wagon. Would you get it for me? We'll use the rope Estéban brings back for the other wagon horse. We won't be able to carry everything. You'll need to think about what you can leave—"

The sharp report of a carbine shattered the air.

Dropping the horse's traces, he leapt astride the stallion. He urged his mount to the top of the rise. French soldiers covered the road, barely a kilometer away. Estéban was nowhere in sight. The shot could mean only two things: they had either captured or killed Estéban. Seguín shuddered.

Without knowing it, he had sent an innocent man into a nest of hostile soldiers. How had they appeared so quickly? His first instinct was to rush into the soldiers, firing heavily, to see if he could rescue Estéban. But cold, hard logic prevailed. He must leave Estéban to his fate in order to save the two women and baby. If the French found him, alone with two young and attractive women, they would kill him and rape the women for sport.

Pure, raw terror jolted through him. They had to get away. But how? His mount and Diana's horse could sustain a protracted chase, but not the wagon horse Lydia would be forced to ride. And then, there was the baby. Holding him would slow any rider down. His mind turned somersaults, searching for an escape. Seconds ticked by, the seconds of their lives, and no solution presented itself. He raised his head, and his gaze swept the area. The answer came to him.

The swamp.

Both sides of the road wound through a thick swamp. It was all around them. It was their only hope of escape. With a bit of luck, they could melt into its dense darkness before the French soldiers saw them. He realized the swamp was dangerous, a place full of quicksand, snakes, and voracious, disease-carrying insects.

It was the only chance they had.

Racing back to the women, he called out, "French soldiers are just beyond the hill. They've got Estéban, and we're cut off from our guard. We have to get away."

"But how? Where?" Diana's voice sounded strangled with fear.

Ignoring her question, he barked orders, "Get mounted." Pulling his stallion to a stop beside Lydia, he slid to the ground. "Lydia can you ride bareback?"

"*Sí.*"

"Give me the baby."

Lydia's eyes were wide in her face, panic clearly stamped on her features. As if in a daze, she handed James to him. He, in turn, handed the baby to Diana. Cupping his hands, he helped Lydia to mount the wagon horse's back.

The churning hoofbeats of the French troops drummed closer. They would top the rise in seconds. He remounted and stopped his mount beside Diana. Holding out his arms, he commanded, "Give me the baby."

Diana clutched James closer and muttered, "I don't think—"

"There's no time," he grated out. "Give me James."

She hesitated for a heartbeat, and then she handed him to Seguín. He tucked the baby carefully into the crook of his left arm, declaring, "The swamp. It's our only chance. Let's go."

"No!" Diana exclaimed. "Not the swamp."

A shot ripped through the silence, and a bullet whistled over their heads.

He didn't hesitate. He slashed both of the women's mounts with his quirt. Their horses sprinted forward. He spurred his stallion, riding close behind them, urging them faster. More shots filled the air, but they raced beyond the range of the bullets.

When they reached the dense thicket of the swamp, he breathed a momentary sigh of relief. But he knew they couldn't linger on its fringes. That would be too dangerous. They must go deeper, to lose and discourage their pursuers.

Knowing they had to navigate the swamp with care, he forced his mount to the front and directed, "Follow me. Make certain you stay behind me, single file. Don't stray off."

Glancing down at the baby, who was fussing, he clutched James tighter, hoping the warmth of his body and the slower pace would soothe the child.

Straining his eyes, he searched for the hillocks of solid ground threaded haphazardly through the bogs and mud. As he led them deeper into the primeval gloom, he prayed the French soldiers wouldn't follow them into the swamp because of the dreaded yellow fever.

At the same time, he offered a silent supplication to the Virgin Mary that they would be spared from that same deadly fever.

Night fell, and the thick gloom of the swamp deepened into total blackness. Seguín drove them relentlessly forward, inches at a time. They edged through the darkness like a blind man with his hands outstretched, searching for a familiar place.

Saw-edged palmetto leaves tore at them. Webs of Span-

ish moss clung to their faces, and voracious insects attacked them in swarms. The obscene sucking noise of their
horses' hooves in the mire mingled with the angry buzz
of the insects and the pitiful cries of the baby.

After what seemed an eternity to Diana, Seguín must
have been satisfied they weren't being followed. He found
a hillock of dry land and called a halt. The rancid smell
of rotting vegetation assailed her nostrils as soon as they
stopped, and the insects closed upon them . . . especially
baby James. When her eyes adjusted to the gloom, she was
horrified to find the insects settling on every inch of the
infant's exposed skin. They covered him like an oily blanket.

Swatting and twisting, Diana and Lydia tried to drive the
bloodsucking mosquitos and flies away. Tormented for herself and the baby, Diana begged Seguín, "We *must* start a
fire. The smoke might keep the insects away."

"No, we can't chance it. I think we've lost the soldiers,
but if they're still searching the smoke could lead them to
us." He loosened the girth on his stallion and jerked the
saddle free. "Besides, there's no dry wood here."

"But—"

"No, Diana. A fire is the least of our worries, and we
can't chance it." He handed her a canteen of water. "More
critical is that we have no food with us, and the swamp
water is full of disease. My canteen is only half full, so go
easy. Take a few sips. It's all we have."

Accepting his canteen, she realized she was both hungry
and thirsty. Taking a few sips, she passed the canteen to
Lydia.

When he had finished unsaddling his mount, he turned
to Diana's gelding, loosening the cinch and pulling the
saddle to the ground. Over his shoulder, he asked, "Lydia,
can you nurse the baby? At least one of us should eat."

Lydia complied silently, baring one milk-heavy breast to
the swarming mosquitos. Despite her stoic offering, James

refused her breast. The stings of the insects were obviously tormenting him. He writhed and thrashed in agony, screaming hideously.

Diana watched the infant's frenetic movements with a feeling of utter helplessness. She felt suspended in a nightmare . . . descended into a hell on earth. Anguish suffused her, mingled with horror.

Without thinking, she rushed Seguín and pummelled his broad chest with her fists, crying, "A fire! We must have a fire . . . something!" She hiccupped and then screamed, "I can't stand by, watching—"

He shoved her aside roughly, ignoring her hysterics. She stood there, clenching her fists and trembling violently, while he covered Lydia and James with the rough blanket from his stallion.

"Lydia, try to kill the insects remaining under the blanket but stay covered," he directed.

"Sí, señor."

Understanding penetrated Diana's panic-stricken brain, and she suddenly realized why he had been in such a hurry to unsaddle the horses. She relaxed a fraction, and her body stopped trembling. With half her mind, she listened to the muffled slaps of Lydia attacking the insects under the blanket.

After a few moments, the blows stopped and Lydia began crooning softly. Her shrouded figure swayed, rocking the baby, encouraging him to calm and nurse. Diana strained her ears, waiting hopefully for the baby's screams to cease while she slapped at the insects covering her.

Baby James's pitiful wails stopped, abruptly followed immediately by a loud, sucking noise. Lydia's voice was triumphant when she called out, "He's nursing, *señor.*"

"Bueno," Seguín responded, and before Diana could call further encouragement he seized her, pushing her to the ground.

Her mouth opened to protest while he sank to the

ground beside her and settled the blanket from the gelding over them, forming a thick tent like the one covering Lydia and the baby.

Once under the makeshift tent, he methodically squashed the remaining insects. Diana felt his hands move over her, searching for mosquitos and flies. Even though his touch was impersonal she trembled, and sobs crowded her throat. She felt overwhelmed, totally out of her element. The coarse blanket smelled nauseating, redolent of horse sweat, and its itchy coarseness suffocated her.

She felt the hysteria building within her again, blocking out rational thought. His touch was driving her wild with need, and the blanket was smothering her. Unable to breathe, she clawed wildly to get out, pushing against his rock-hard chest and moaning.

He grabbed her wrists and restrained her, holding her tight against him. "Diana! Be still." His voice was harsh. "You must stay under the blanket. It might be hot and hard to breathe, but the insects cannot reach us. *Por favor,* think!"

His words brought her back to her senses. The hysteria ebbed away. She forced herself to sit perfectly still, taking deep breaths of air, proving to herself she could breathe. The angry buzzing died away. The insects hummed outside their improvised tent, but she was no longer tormented by their savage stings. Her arms and face felt as if they were on fire from the earlier bites.

Ignoring her own discomfort, she called out, "Lydia, are you and the baby all right?"

"We are fine, *señorita.* Little James has suckled and fallen asleep." She paused and then said, *"Gracias,* Señor Torres. This blanket is uncomfortable but necessary. *Buenas noches."*

Heaving a deep sigh of relief, Diana replied, *"Buenas noches."*

A rustling noise came from the direction of Lydia and

the baby. She guessed Lydia was stretching upon the ground with James.

"We should do the same, try to rest." This time, both his voice and hands were gentle as he urged her into a reclining position. Lying close beside her, he managed to tuck the blanket around them and cover as much of their legs as possible.

Diana stiffened at their forced nearness, willing away the need for his touch, but his hand strayed to her hair and stroked gently. *"Mi rubia,* let me take care of you. I ask nothing more than to protect you. Try to trust me."

She fought the beguiling pull of his solicitude for her, but her hunger for him vanquished her resolve. The overwhelming needs she had kept at bay for months rose within her, and she found herself clutching him close. Seeking his reassuring comfort, she nestled her head into his shoulder.

Peace and happiness flowed through her as she snuggled into his strong arms. The horror of the swamp drained away, and she felt as if she had come home . . . at last.

Haggard and filthy, they emerged from the swamp the next day. Seguín had tarried at the edge of the dismal bog for hours to make certain no new danger awaited them on the road.

They found the charred remains of the wagon. It had obviously been looted and then burned. Gazing upon the wanton destruction, he turned to Diana and asked, "Do you have your money and sailing ticket?"

She lifted sad eyes from the burnt wagon. Patting her riding skirt, she reassured him, "My funds and ticket are sewn into the lining. Everyone carried their own, I think."

He breathed a sigh of relief. Despite everything, her money and ship passage were safe. It was one consolation, especially considering what they had been through. They all, including the baby, looked as if they had been in a torture chamber. The women's faces and arms were swollen and covered with angry red splotches, testimony to their hideous struggle with the insects.

Curious, he touched his own face, and his fingers pressed deep into the sensitive swelling there. He offered a silent prayer they wouldn't catch the deadly yellow fever.

Gazing down at the mottled, crimson welts on baby James' face, he prayed even harder, silently beseeching the Virgin to spare the innocent child's life. It surprised him, his sudden propensity to prayer. His mother had raised him as a strict Catholic, but with the events surrounding her death he had turned his face from the Church.

If you don't care about anyone, there's no need to pray. The thought flashed through his mind.

The baby was still fretful, tormented by the venom from the insect bites covering his body. Seguín feared he would be in even greater discomfort once they started moving. With the wagon gone it would be difficult to ride fast and hold onto the baby at the same time . . . unless—

An old memory flashed through his mind—a memory from his Juárista days—and he silently castigated himself for not thinking of it sooner. The Indian women who were camp followers of the Juáristas managed to keep their infants content when traveling by strapping the babies to their backs.

Inspired by the memory, he handed the infant to Lydia and bade her, "Watch." Removing the shirt from his back, he tore it, with the help of his teeth, into a rough triangle of cloth.

Gesturing for Lydia to return the baby, he wrapped James's small form in the cloth, bringing the short point through the baby's legs and snugly wrapping the longer part around the infant. Presenting his back to Lydia, he gave her James.

"Have you seen Indian women with papooses on their backs?"

"*Sí, señor.*"

"*Bueno.* Tie him tightly under my arms. I want him to be secure."

Diana spoke up, her voice full of concern. "Seguín, this is dangerous. What if he falls?"

"He won't fall if Lydia ties the knots tightly enough. Indian women carry their babies like this. When we reach town, we'll find a suitable rig so he'll be more comfortable. For now, this will have to do."

Lydia finished tying James to his back, and he tested the knots. Leaning forward, he shifted the burden into a more comfortable position. The baby, staring backward from his curious vantage point, quit fussing. Either the change or the warmth of Seguín's body appeared to have calmed him.

Diana circled Seguín and the baby, her head cocked to one side. She smiled slightly and nodded. "It just might work."

"Of course it will work. Now that we don't have the wagon to hold us back, I want to reach Veracruz by tomorrow night," he informed them.

Sixteen

They straggled into Veracruz late the next night. Hunger consumed them, followed closely by exhaustion. They had managed to buy a skimpy meal of rice and beans from a suspicious farmer, and they had slept for a few hours. Seguín was determined to get them to the port as quickly as possible. Once they were inside the town, the French wouldn't bother them.

Baby James, unlike before, was better off than the adults. He nursed readily and seemed to enjoy riding tied to Seguín's back. Nestled against the comforting warmth of Seguín and lulled by the rhythmic rocking of the stallion's canter, he slept easily, rousing only to be fed and changed.

Diana wished Seguín had thought of the papoose trick sooner for the baby's sake, but she couldn't complain. Against all odds, he had led them safely to Veracruz, just as she had known he would. She hoped the Yorks and her mother had also arrived unscathed.

For now, they were famished and exhausted. Seguín promised to make inquiries about the others on the following day.

He found a *posada* close to the waterfront and ordered baths, suppers, and ointment for their insect bites. Within an hour's time, Diana found herself luxuriating in a warm bath, her stomach pleasantly full of *cabrito* and rice. She watched over the rim of the tub as Lydia soothed baby

James with the ointment. After her bath, it would be her turn to apply ointment to the hundreds of insect bites covering her body. She sank deeper into the bathtub and washed her hair, feeling grateful to have returned to civilization and to know the pleasure of a bath and a real bed.

As hard as she tried to forget, Seguín's closeness in the swamp haunted her. Tender and unselfish, he had protected her against her agonies and fears. It was the caring side of him that she had fallen in love with. The physical attraction had always been there, from the first time she had seen him. But her love had grown slowly, nurtured by the thoughtfulness he had shown her and Sarah . . . and even the baby.

It didn't matter where his motives stemmed from. As hard as he tried to hide it, he possessed a tender side. He was certainly capable of loving. Why couldn't he learn to love her?

Climbing from the tub of water, she stretched her naked body with languorous ease. Every nerve in her body tingled with sensual awareness, remembering his hard body pressed against hers in the swamp.

With the aid of Lydia, she anointed herself with the ointment. After the bites were properly cared for, she found the crushed nightshift in her saddlebag. The remainder of her clothing had been lost with the wagon. The filthy clothes she and Lydia wore had been washed and hung to dry on the window ledge. They were stained and torn. Not possessing needle and thread, they had done the best they could. They would need to purchase new clothing before they boarded the ship.

She yawned, but she wasn't really sleepy. Pretending to go to bed, she climbed into the narrow cot and pulled the covers to her neck. She watched impatiently while Lydia finished readying James for bed and a fresh tub of water was brought for her.

After the better part of an hour, Lydia finished her toilette, blew out the lamp, and settled for the night. Diana lay perfectly still in the darkness, inches from the wet nurse's bed, until she heard her soft snoring.

Wanting nothing more than to creep into Seguín's bed, she craved his strength and warmth. If he didn't want her for a lifetime, she felt certain he would want her for tonight. She couldn't face leaving México without lying in his arms and feeling the rush of passion he drew from her. She realized she would be sorry tomorrow—their intimacy would only make it more difficult to leave him—but she couldn't help herself. Only tonight was important.

Cautiously, she rose from her bed and moved through the dark room. Sliding the bolt on the door, she let herself into the flagstone corridor.

Seguín's room was only a feet away, across the hallway. Summoning her courage, she knocked and waited. There was no movement, no sound from within. She knocked harder and waited again. Nothing.

A voice inside her head told her she was probably insane, and at the very least, hopelessly wanton for seeking him out. Dismissing the voice, she boldly tugged at the door latch. The door swung open at her touch. The dim light shining from the corridor revealed an empty room.

Disappointed and filled with shame for her uncontrollable yearnings, she stumbled back to her room. She knew it wasn't reasonable, but she felt angry at him for his unexpected absence.

Exhausted as he was from their awful escape through the swamp, Seguín's blood was heated with desire—a consuming desire for Diana. Holding her in his arms had been a kind of torture. Painful yet wonderful, it had raised his need to a feverish pitch. But he hadn't ventured into the night to satisfy his passion at a convenient brothel. No whore would suffice, and he knew it.

Instead, he decided to use his wakefulness to reconnoiter the port town. He roused innkeepers and talked to beggars in the streets. After only an hour or so, he had pieced together a rough estimate of the number of French soldiers in the city.

At the same time, he searched each *posada* for the remainder of his party. The Red Cloud wasn't due to sail for a few more days, but he guessed they would be staying close to the harbor. At the last *posada* along the waterfront, a sleepy innkeeper finally recognized one of the guard's names.

"*Sí,* Julio Gomez is here, *señor.* But the others," the innkeeper shrugged and yawned. "I do not know, *señor.*"

"Julio's room, which one is it?"

"*Cuatro,* but *señor,* he's been abed—"

"*Gracias,*" he said, cutting off the innkeeper's halfhearted protest as he strode down the hallway, looking for room number four.

Hesitating at the door for a moment, he was afraid of what he might find. Shrugging aside his fears, he pounded on the door and called out, "Julio, wake up! It's Seguín Torres. *Por favor,* open the door."

He heard a muffled groan from inside and then shuffling footsteps. Julio cracked the door and peered out sleepily. Seguín thrust his foot inside and pushed the door open. Slipping inside the room, he demanded, "Where are the others?"

Julio gazed owlishly at him, attempting to gather his wits. "They are gone."

"Gone," he echoed. "What do you mean?"

"We thought you lost, *señor.* We knew the French were right behind us. Fearful, we galloped all the way to Veracruz and arrived two nights ago. The *Yanquís* sailed with the next day's evening tide."

His heart sank. The Red Cloud had already set sail. What was to become of Diana and the baby? Not wanting to believe the bald fact, he quizzed Julio. "Why would the ship sail so soon? It wasn't due to leave for days."

"The French, *señor.* The captain of the Red Cloud was afraid to stay any longer. He worried that the French would seize his ship and make him take soldiers to Europe."

"What about the rest of *Señor* York's guard?"

"They left this morning. I requested to remain for several days. I have relatives in a village a few miles away. I go tomorrow to visit them. We didn't expect you . . . we thought . . ."

Dropping his eyes, Seguín cleared his throat to cover the awkward moment. It was obvious Julio and the others had thought they were dead.

"I hope the *señoritas* and *niño* are safe, too," Julio ventured.

"Sí."

"Bueno, bueno. But the French soldiers were everywhere. How did you escape?"

"The swamp."

The guard's eyes widened with fear, and he stepped back. Crossing himself, he muttered, "At least you made it to Veracruz safely. It's better than what happened to Estéban."

Seguín felt hollow inside, knowing he had sent Estéban into the soldiers. He dreaded asking, but realized Julio was grimly waiting. "What happened?"

"Dead." He paused for a moment and continued in a hushed voice, "After the *Yanquís* departed, we went to the cathedral and prayed for his soul and lit candles."

He nodded. They had done all they could. There was nothing more to do. And there was nothing more he could do, nothing more he could say. He hadn't known he was sending Estéban to his death, but that didn't make him feel less guilty.

"I must return to the women and baby. Thank you for

the information, Julio. I'm sorry to have wakened you. *Adios.*"

Retracing his steps, he felt defeated . . . a failure. Despite all his careful plans, he had lost Estéban to the French. And on top of that, he was faced with telling Diana the ship had sailed with her mother and the Yorks.

The next morning, after a sleepless night, Seguín went to the port authority to inquire about another ship for Diana. Once there, he began to understand the urgency which prompted the captain of the Red Cloud to sail early.

The crowds on the dock were thick, composed primarily of French troops being evacuated. He waited in line for hours before he reached the harbor master's desk. Finally, when he was standing before the harbor master, a *Señor* Ramírez, he asked, "Did the Red Cloud sail for Panama two days ago?"

"*Sí.*"

"Didn't she sail early?"

"*Sí, señor.* Her captain feared if he waited, the French would confiscate his ship."

The harbor master's words confirmed what Julio had told him the night before. Guessing he wouldn't like the answer before he even asked the question, he inquired, "When is the next ship scheduled to leave for *Los Estados Unidos?* I need to book passage for two women and a baby," he added, hoping he might appeal to the official's sense of chivalry.

Señor Ramírez spread his pudgy fingers wide and shook his head. "The French have commandeered all ships for the foreseeable future." The harbor master's voice was full of contempt for the European soldiers when he added, "Napoleon's troops are in a hurry to return home. There is no room for civilians, *señor.* Although I sympathize with your plight, Veracruz is no place for women and children."

He glanced pointedly at the shoving and foul-mouthed crowd of French soldiers behind Seguín.

"You are right, *Señor* Ramírez, this is no place for women and children. I appreciate your concern."

Seguín turned to leave, but the harbor master called him back. "Wait! *Señor* . . . ah, you. Come back." He motioned with his fat fingers. "I have a suggestion."

Pushing his way to the front of the line again, Seguín responded, "Did you want me?"

"*Señor*, ah—?

"Torres."

The harbor master gazed at him. There was a curious light in his eyes, as if he was privy to some secret Seguín had no way of knowing. It was disconcerting, that measuring look from the fat man.

Lowering his eyes, *Señor* Ramírez shuffled the papers on his desk before offering, "There is another way to take ship to *Los Estados Unidos.*"

"How?"

"By way of our western port in Acapulco. There has been no fighting in that part of México. Ships leave regularly for California from Acapulco."

Nodding, Seguín turned the information over in his mind. It would entail an overland journey of approximately five hundred kilometers, and even if he could avoid the fighting there were other dangers. But it was an alternative, and it seemed infinitely better than sitting in Veracruz and waiting months for space on a ship.

Bowing to the harbor master, he thanked him, *"Gracias, Señor* Ramírez. I appreciate the suggestion."

Señor Ramírez inclined his head. "Happy to be of service."

Gilberto leaned over the railing of the ship, breathing deeply of the salty air. Being topside was infinitely better than being locked in a cargo hold. His stomach still felt queasy from the gentle roll of the ship, but he was more than happy to withstand any discomfort.

He was on his way to Sarah in San Francisco. His plan had worked like a charm. After purchasing his ticket and some necessities, he still had money left from the sale of the diamond. The jeweler in Lisbon had agreed it was a unique stone.

At least he wouldn't go to Sarah without a *peso* in his pockets.

Seguín entered the dark interior of the public room at their *posada*. The stench of unwashed bodies mingled with the overpowering smell of garlic and onions. The *posada* was poor and shabby, but with the crush of French soldiers in town they had been lucky to obtain two rooms . . . at an exorbitant price.

The midday meal was being served, and he searched for Diana among the crowded tables. Straining his eyes to accustom them to the gloom, he found her, sitting in a corner with Lydia and the baby.

Maneuvering his way through the masses, his eyes traveled over the two women. Even in the dark room, it was easy to see their clothes were ruined. They had obviously tried to clean their garments, but the swamp had taken its toll.

Glancing down at his own clothes, he realized he looked as bad as they did, except that his shirt was clean. After tearing his other shirt to make a papoose for the baby, he had donned the extra shirt he carried in his saddlebag. His pants and boots were ripped and caked with swamp mud. He hadn't taken the time to clean them. One thing was certain—as soon as their plans were made they needed to buy new clothes.

He squeezed in beside Diana on the crude wooden

bench lining the wall and greeted them, *"Buenas tardes, señoritas."*

"Buenas tardes, Señor Torres," Lydia returned his greeting, but Diana didn't respond. She had her eyes fixed firmly on her plate while she toyed with her food.

Ignoring her unusual silence, he asked, "What's for dinner?"

"Menudo," Lydia replied as she soaked up the sauce from her plate with a rolled tortilla.

"My favorite. I hope there's some left."

"Here." Diana shoved her plate at him. "Take mine. Cow tripe doesn't appeal to me."

Grinning, he accepted her plate. *"Gracias."*

While eating the spicy *menudo,* he studied her from the corner of his eye. What was wrong with her? She held her body rigidly, and her face looked as if it was carved from stone. He had expected her to be upset when he told her the news about the ship, but she couldn't know that yet, could she?

Reaching for a tortilla from the stack in the center of the table, he thought of how to broach the painful subject. Before he had time to form the words, she rose abruptly and edged past him.

Placing his hand on her arm, he asked, "Diana, where are you going?"

"Back to my room. I'm not eating, so there's no reason for me to stay."

Frowning, he wondered again at what might be troubling her. "Diana, *por favor,* you must stay. We have a great deal to discuss."

She hesitated before slumping onto the bench and moving to the corner. It was obvious she wanted to get as far away from him as possible. He sighed to himself, puzzled by her behavior.

Lydia pushed her empty plate across the table. *"Con permiso, Señor* Torres, if you don't need me, it's time for the baby's feeding and nap." She rose with the infant in her arms.

Seguín, who had been studying Diana's implacably set features, turned his attention to Lydia. "How is Pepito today?"

"Doing much better, *señor*. The ointment has soothed his insect bites."

"*Bueno*, Lydia." He nodded his head in dismissal. "I hope Pepito has a good nap." The nurse inclined her head and left the room with the baby tucked in her arms.

"Why do you call James that?" Diana snapped.

"What?"

"Pepito."

He shrugged and replied, "It's my pet name for him. Every child in México has their own special nickname."

"What was yours, Seguín?"

He felt as if she had punched him in the gut. Her question reminded him of his mother. It was she who had given him his nickname, and he had done his best to forget it, along with everything else about her.

Narrowing his eyes, he wondered what Diana was trying to get at. She knew his family was a forbidden topic with him. As she did the time in the vault at his mine, she seemed to be purposely prodding him. But why?

That time, he had silenced her with a kiss but when he had wanted to kiss her on the way to Veracruz, she had run from him. He would be damned before he would force himself upon her.

"I don't remember my nickname," he replied.

"How convenient," she noted sarcastically.

He wanted to drag her from the corner and shake her, but instead he asked, "What's wrong, Diana? You've been particularly nasty since I came in."

Cold fury shone in her eyes, turning the hazel a shimmering gold color, rivaling the hue of her hair. "Where were you last night?"

Surprised by the vehemence of her question and curious to know how she knew he had been gone, he countered, "How do you know I wasn't in my room?"

Even in the murky gloom of the public room, he discerned her flush of embarrassment. She hesitated before admitting, "I went to your room."

"Oh?"

Her flush deepened, and she stammered, "I . . . needed to . . . to . . . ask you something."

"Sí?"

She made a dismissive gesture with her hand and averted her eyes. "Never mind. It wasn't important." Gazing steadily in the direction of his chest, she refused to look at his face. "Have you found my mother and the Yorks?"

With half of his mind, he heard her question. She obviously didn't know what had happened, and he dreaded telling her, but his attention wasn't focused on that. He was wondering what had made her go to his room in the middle of the night. He didn't believe she had gone to ask him a simple question; her blush belied such an innocent reason.

And her blush told him a great deal more, too. At the very thought of her seeking him out, the blood rushed through his veins, and his manhood stirred, straining against the placket of his pants. He had an overwhelming desire to gather her into his arms and take her back to his room . . . now . . . this very instant.

Unfortunately, now wasn't the time, with her staring at him like a cornered animal. He had to tell her what had happened to the others. If she went along with his plan to go to Acapulco, they would be together for weeks.

He wanted her so much that he ached with it. Selfishly, he was glad the others were gone. It would give them more time to . . . satisfy his desires? No. He wouldn't think like that. But if she wanted him, too, then . . .

"Seguín, I asked you if you found the others," she prompted.

"That's where I was last night, trying to locate the rest of our party. I didn't want to wait until morning and take the chance of missing them."

Her features softened, and she nodded her head.

"The Red Cloud has already sailed, the day before yesterday. The captain was afraid to stay in port longer. He didn't want the French to commandeer his ship."

"And the Yorks and my mother?"

"They were lucky enough to make ship before it sailed."

Her face fell, and she dropped her head again, avoiding his eyes.

He wished he could take her his arms and soothe the pain away. He knew it must hurt her to realize that she and the baby had been left behind. Unfortunately, the public room at their *posada* wasn't the place to embrace her. And he needed to explain what had happened. Leaning forward, he covered her hands with his.

She snatched her hands away. Leaning back, he felt empty, not knowing what to do for her . . . not knowing what to say.

"I don't know for certain, but my guess would be that Herbert York wanted to get the other women away before the port shut down to civilian travel," he explained. "Julio Gomez—you remember him, he was one of our guard—I found him, and he told me they feared we were—"

"I understand. What else could they do, not knowing?" Pausing, she added, "Poor Sarah, thinking she's lost a second baby. What will it do to her, Seguín?"

"I don't know." He dragged his fingers through his hair, not wanting to think how Sarah might feel. Glancing at Diana, he felt his admiration for her grow. Even though she was the one who had been abandoned, her first thoughts were for her best friend.

"Do you think I can get a letter to the States from here?"

"I don't see why not. Freight ships are still leaving. It's just passenger ships that are the problem."

"Good. I'll write to Sarah. I hope the letter will reach her as soon as she arrives in San Francisco, and—" She stopped abruptly, and raised her gaze to his. "What will I tell her? We're all right for now, but the baby and I can't leave, can we? Is there another ship we can take?"

"That's where I was this morning, trying to find out." Drumming his fingers on the rough-planked table, he said, "All the ships are committed to evacuating French troops. It could be weeks or months before another ship goes to the States with civilian passengers."

She didn't reply, so he rushed ahead. "I have an alternate plan, Diana. The harbor master assured me the western port of Acapulco is open. Ships sail from Acapulco to the States freely. You can travel directly north to California."

"That's perfect." Her voice lifted and her face brightened. "How far is Acapulco?"

"About five hundred kilometers, or three hundred of your miles, although I propose taking a longer route. I want to skirt south to avoid the fighting around the capitol."

"That seems like a good idea."

"You're not afraid? It's a long trip, and a dangerous one. Even if we manage to avoid the civil war there are bandits everywhere, and the mountains are even rougher than the ones we just crossed."

Pinning him with her gaze, her eyes were sharp as agates. "It's the only chance we have. I'll be relying on you to get us there safely."

Seguín spent the following days preparing for the trip. Clothing, supplies, a new mount for Lydia, and a pack animal had to be found. Veracruz had few provisions for sale. The French soldiers had exhausted the town's supplies.

He made trips to outlying villages to obtain the provisions and animals they needed. He also needed men to accompany them as a guard, but there was no one he trusted. Somehow, he had to get a message to Juan at the mines in the north. He wanted Juan and some of his own men to escort them, but getting a message through wouldn't be easy. The messenger must be trustworthy, as well as willing to travel through the heaviest fighting.

Having procured the last available mule in the village of Hermosa, Seguín doffed his hat and wiped his brow. The stable owner had driven a hard bargain, but the mule was the sturdiest one he had seen so far. Glancing at the setting sun, he realized it was time to return to Veracruz. He had all the supplies and animals they needed, but the problem of a trustworthy messenger still remained.

Pulling the mule behind him, he crossed the dusty main street of Hermosa and came face-to-face with Julio Gomez. Seguín stopped and stared at him for a moment, making certain the man's familiar face wasn't a mirage.

Julio appeared as surprised as he was by their chance meeting. Removing his hat, the guard greeted him, *"Hola, Señor* Torres. *Buenas tardes."*

"Buenas tardes, Julio." Slapping him on the shoulder, Seguín exclaimed, "What a wonderful surprise! Is this where your relatives live?"

He bobbed his head. *"Sí, señor,* but my visit is almost over. It is time I returned to México City."

"Would you join me in the *taverna,* Julio? I would like to buy you a drink."

One hour later, Seguín emerged from the *taverna.* Finding Julio had been a stroke of fortune. He had explained the situation and obtained the man's agreement to help. He penned a note to the York's foreman, requesting that Julio be allowed to serve as his messenger.

Then he had written a letter, in their own private code, to Juan. The letter outlined the route they would take, and asked him to join them with an escort as soon as possible. He concluded the arrangements by giving Julio a hefty purse for his services and expenses.

Finding Julio had been lucky, but even under the best of circumstances, it would take him many days to reach Juan. Then it would take more time for Juan and the men to join them.

Seguín had already decided they couldn't afford to wait in Veracruz. It was far too dangerous, one of the few Imperial strongholds left in México. The Juáristas might decide to besiege the town as soon as the remaining French troops thinned.

It was also dangerous to travel alone with two women and a baby. Neither alternative was ideal, but he had weighed his options and decided to press forward to Acapulco.

They headed south, along the coast, away from the civil war. When they reached the fishing village of Boca del Rio, Seguín explained to Diana they would follow the Atoyac river into the Sierra Madre Oriental, the eastern wing of the Sierra Madre mountains.

Diana was glad to be moving again. The long days of waiting in Veracruz, while Seguín found provisions for their journey, had strained her nerves to the breaking point. There had been too much time to think, too much time to worry about Sarah and the others.

And then there was Seguín. When he had proposed the alternate route, her heart had rejoiced, realizing she would spend several more weeks with him. As happy as her heart was, her mind worried. If he didn't love her, why would she want to prolong the torment? Because she still hoped?

Or because, as torturous as it was to be near him, it was far worse to be without him?

Loving someone, she was finding out, didn't always make sense.

She glanced at James, who was riding placidly in his improvised papoose, strapped to Seguín's back. Riding this way, he seldom fussed unless he was hungry or wet.

To her surprise, they all took turns carrying the child. She had assumed after their initial flight to Veracruz that Seguín would relinquish the task of carrying the baby to her and Lydia, but she had been wrong. He insisted upon taking a turn, too. He even appeared to enjoy having the baby near him, and he never complained when James had an accident while he was carrying him.

She knew he possessed a tender side, but she had never expected him to be so solicitous and caring. Unfortunately, this revelation only made her yearnings deepen. She could visualize them raising children, making a new family together. But he didn't want her that way. His attraction to her was transitory, of the flesh.

With a certainty that was almost frightening, she knew she wouldn't want to have a family with anyone else. Seguín, and what they might have had together, would haunt her until the end of her days.

Seventeen

After several days of traveling they reached the foothills and camped near one of the streams serving as a tributary of the Atoyac river. It was Lydia's turn to prepare the evening meal, and Diana's turn to watch the baby. Lydia had already nursed James, so Diana busied herself with giving him a sponge bath and changing him.

Baby James appeared to be in good spirits that evening, cooing and gurgling, waving his chubby arms and legs. Sitting beside him on the blanket, she watched his innocent exuberance with amusement.

A shadow blotted the setting sun behind her, and she glanced up to find Seguín there. He had been gathering wood and caring for the animals. He walked past her and squatted beside the stream to fill their canteens. When finished, he straightened and gazed down at the baby.

"He has the darkest eyes," Seguín observed.

Rising to her feet, she nodded. She had already come to that same conclusion. "As black as yours, Seguín."

The infant did have unusual eyes. Unlike most newborns, whose eyes were light and then darkened later, James had had midnight-black eyes when Diana first saw him at two weeks old.

"Did you have dark eyes when you were born?" she asked.

He stiffened and muttered, "I don't remember."

Too late, she realized her blunder. When she had been angry at him in Veracruz, she had taunted him about his childhood. It had been petty and mean of her, and she wished she hadn't done it. He had never mentioned the incident, or criticized her for it.

As unsettled as her early life had been, she retained pleasant memories of her childhood. Seguín obviously had none, or didn't want to remember. Because he had lost his father when he was young and had been estranged from his mother, it was as if he had systematically eradicated his early life.

She wished she could draw him out. He believed his mother had turned her face from him, but he shouldn't hold any rancor toward his father.

"How young were you when you lost your father?"

His eyes met hers, obviously searching for her motive. She returned his gaze, willing her features to show a calm interest. After a brief hesitation, he answered, "I was four years old."

"Do you remember him?"

He took a deep breath, and his eyes glazed over as if he was looking at something far away, across the horizon. His voice sounded strained, laden with unspoken emotions, "A little. He had stern features and a large mustache, much like Juan's. His hands were very strong, but gentle at the same time."

When he turned away, she realized he was battling for self-control, but he managed. "When I was little he used to lift me over his head and swoop me through the air, telling me to fly like a bird. When I was older, I did the same for Gilberto."

She was sorry she had encouraged him to talk about his father. Obviously, such a discussion was still painful for him. She sighed to herself. It seemed this was her night for blunders. Squatting down, she gathered James into her arms, intent upon ending the conversation.

But, his voice was calmer now and with a note of reflection in it, he continued. "I remember he loved music. He could strum a guitar for hours. His voice was a rich baritone."

Diana rose to her feet with the baby in her arms. She studied Seguín's face. The hurt was gone. His features were composed, and there was a special light in his eyes. It was as if after overcoming his initial reticence, he wanted to talk about his father. She wondered if he had shared his long-buried feelings before. Intuition told her he hadn't.

"Do you remember the songs he used to sing?"

"Some."

"Would you sing one for me and the baby?"

He shot her a startled look, and his lips twitched in obvious amusement. "I, ah, didn't inherit his talent for music."

Although he was clearly embarrassed by her request, she refused to let him off so easily. She wouldn't force him to talk about painful subjects again, but this was different. Only his masculine pride was at stake.

Touching his arm lightly, she said, "Please. I've heard you humming to the baby when you carry him. The melodies are lovely."

Slanting his gaze at her, he quirked one jet-black eyebrow. "This isn't some kind of joke, is it? You're asking me to sing?"

"Your father sang for you. What harm could it do? I promise not to laugh, if that worries you. Please."

He moved closer to her. Their gazes locked, and he raised his hand to lightly stroke her cheek. She shut her eyes, trembling at his touch.

His voice was husky when he negotiated, "What are you willing to offer me in return?"

Her eyes flew open, only to be transfixed by the silent, black pull of his gaze. She felt a warm flush steal across her flesh, and she knew she was blushing. She wanted him so much, but he had the power to burn her heart to ashes. Did she dare answer?

She knew better than to invite intimacies with him, but she couldn't stop herself from bargaining. "A kiss?"

He bent his head, and his lips brushed hers lightly, quickly, like the flutter of moth wings. She was surprised he hadn't demanded more. Gazing into his licorice-colored eyes, she read the pent-up desire there . . . fires banked, but smoldering.

"A delicious bargain," he winked. "But if Pepito starts to cry at the sound of my rough voice, I stop immediately. Agreed?"

"Agreed." She offered James to him, and Seguín took him. He still appeared uncomfortable. He glanced toward the campfire where Lydia was cooking, obviously not wanting her to overhear.

"Sing for Pepito," she urged, purposely using his pet name for the child. "It's time for him to sleep."

He glanced at the infant and cleared his throat.

> " *El dia que tu naciste*
> *Nacieron todos los flores.*
> *En tu pila de bautismo*
> *Cantaron los ruisenores.'* "

Enthralled, she listened to the deep, rich timbre of his voice, the soft inflection of Spanish. When the song was over, she went over the words, translating them into English to fix them in her memory:

> " 'On the day when you were born
> Then were born all of the flowers.
> And at your baptismal fountain
> Meadowlarks sang their sweet carols.' "

"It's not the same in English. Will you teach me the words of Spanish songs so I can remember them?" When she asked him, their heads were bent over the baby, their faces within inches of each other.

"*Sí*, if you wish it." For one brief moment, she thought he might kiss her again. But he didn't. Instead, he transferred the sleeping baby to her arms. "Why is it so important?"

Lowering her eyes, she felt the rush of blood to her face. She had wanted him to kiss her, and when he didn't she felt ashamed of her secret longings. To cover her discomfort, she took the baby's blanket and began swaddling him for the night, going slowly, not wanting to disturb his slumber.

When she finished, she tucked him into the crook of her arm and explained to Seguín, "I don't know what will happen to Gilberto and Sarah. I don't know if they will live here or in the States. Pepito's heritage is Spanish. I want him to grow up knowing that. Sarah would want it, too. I'll memorize the songs and teach them to her."

She didn't tell him the other reason. That she would carefully store away his songs as keepsakes, something living she could pass to James. It would be a piece of Seguín and his heritage she would cherish.

"You sound as if you're uncertain about Gilberto. That you think he might not return to Sarah," he observed.

"Nothing's certain in this world."

"No, I guess not."

"You told me Sarah shouldn't get involved with your half-brother. Since then, you've helped us and even tried to help Gilberto. Why, Seguín?"

He hesitated, dropping his gaze. "I don't know, Diana. It just seemed the thing to do."

"Then you've altered your opinion of your half-brother?"

"Maybe."

Frustrated by his reticence, she spun on her heel, intent upon returning to camp. *"Buenas noches,"* she offered in parting.

He stepped in front of her. His gaze snagged hers, and he stared at her for a long moment. Pulling her into his arms, he kissed the top of her head.

"Gracias, Diana for caring about me . . . and the baby." Leaning down, he kissed the sleeping infant's cheek. "You're a very fine person. Pepito is lucky to have you as his godmother."

When he released her and stepped back, she noticed his eyes glittered with a suspicious brightness, but before she could speak again he turned and disappeared into the deepening shadows.

Don Carlos sat behind the massive mahogany desk in his private study. He read the note Ignacio had brought him before crumpling it into a ball and tossing it into the low-burning fire.

"Is it good news, Don Carlos?" Ignacio asked.

"You mean you didn't read it first?"

"Of course not, *Señor* Don," he sputtered, "I would never "

The don waved his hand, signaling him to be quiet.

"I don't know if it's good news, but it's enlightening."

"Señor Don?"

"I instructed my friend, the harbor master at Veracruz, to watch for Gilberto, should he try to return to México. Instead of my son, he netted another fish . . . my stepson. It seems Seguín tried to book passage to *Los Estados Unidos* for two women and a baby. Now it becomes clear why my son refused to give up the *gringa.* She carried his bastard."

He waggled his head. "So my handsome son finally got caught. But why didn't he tell me? We could have made certain arrangements." Shifting his bulk, he belched. "My son's too noble for his own good."

Ignacio remained silent, knowing Don Carlos didn't expect an answer.

Stroking his chin, he continued. "I would like to see my grandchild, even if it's a half-breed, and a bastard to boot. I wonder if it's a boy." He paused and fingered the expensive, silver filigreed inkwell on his desk. "And I wonder why Seguín is helping his half-brother. I made certain Seguín would hate him—or so I thought." Swinging his gaze to Ignacio, he asked, "What about the formula?"

Surprised by the sudden change of subject, Ignacio gathered his wits to reply. "I was able to bribe one of the workers. It took him several weeks of watching carefully, but he wrote down the procedure, along with the quantities and materials used." Bowing and stepping forward, he handed the don a second sheet of paper.

Don Carlos gave it a cursory glance and grunted. "Looks right. Half the mercury, only eight hours to vaporize. Interesting. We must test it, but not now. You're aware the Juáristas have seized the mines."

"*Sí, señor,* I left before they took control."

"Everything will be a shambles until this damnable war is over. Then, if the peasant army hasn't stripped our mines, we'll try the formula. Seguín can't benefit from it until they return his mines, either."

Ignacio knew better than to voice his doubts, but it was common knowledge that Don Carlos had supported the French, hating the Juáristas. He wondered if they would return the don's mines.

The same thought must have been going through Don Carlos's head because he muttered, "If we allow him to benefit." He glanced at Ignacio. "I'm tired of playing games with my stepson. Now, while the civil war has everyone's attention, is the time to even old scores. You've wanted your revenge for a long time, Ignacio."

He didn't have to say it. Ignacio understood perfectly. The don was finally giving him permission to kill Seguín.

"I want the girl killed, too, but I want my grandchild saved. We must make it look like Seguín murdered the mother, and I saved the child. Then I'll send for Gilberto and earn his undying gratitude. He'll be an obedient son after this."

Ignacio didn't bother to ask how to execute such an elaborate plan. He didn't really care. All he cared about was killing Seguín and satisfying his revenge.

"It sounds like a good plan. How can I be of service, Don Carlos?"

"Gather the men and supplies. We leave for Acapulco at sunrise." He glanced at the mounted trophies on the walls. "I haven't been on a good hunt in a long time."

Before, when they had crossed the mountains to reach Veracruz, Seguín had led them through the valleys between the peaks, avoiding steep climbs because of the cumbersome wagon. But this time he cut straight through the heart of the mountains. Surrounded by tall peaks on all sides, they climbed steadily, following trails meant for goats or mountain sheep.

As they climbed, the air became thinner but cooler and more humid. It was as if they were ascending through the clouds, and as they did so the moisture increased. But the moisture didn't fall like rain. Instead, it shrouded them like a thick blanket, covering them in a constant mist.

Seguín explained that because it was winter, this was the dry season, relatively speaking. If they had been crossing the mountains in the spring or summer, they would have been drowned in daily torrential rains.

Diana was grateful for his foresight in purchasing thick, woolen cloaks with hoods before they set out from Veracruz. The cloaks were a welcome comfort in the cool, moist air.

They climbed past forests of juniper trees and sweet gums, maples, and enormous twisted oaks, and even some stands of evergreen conifers. The higher they climbed into the moisture-laden mountains, the greener and thicker the foliage became. The paths were overgrown with creepers and lazy-leafed banana trees.

The rain forest was deep and lush, filled with the sensory delights of the jungle. Bright orange and green and yellow butterflies drifted through the mist. Parrots cawed noisily from treetops, and *chachalacas*—birds about the size of bantam chickens—cackled like old women. Ruby-throated woodpeckers clung to trees pecking for grubs, and iridescent parakeets streaked through the treetops.

Flowers, even at this time of the year, lifted their bright heads. Strange flowers, exotically shaped like star-bursts or shells or streamers, delighted the eye with their gaudy, multicolored profusion. The only flowers she recognized were the orchids. Atop tall stems, clinging to trees, and nestled among the bony outcrops of limestone, they bloomed everywhere.

The rain forest was wild and beautiful, nature at its most rich offering, but it wasn't devoid of humans. The paths they took led them through villages, and she observed that their inhabitants were different.

There, high in the mountains, the villages were home to the indigenous Indian population who had inhabited México for millennia. Poor and rustic, the isolated villagers kept to their old ways. The only intrusions of European culture were the Catholic priests and their churches.

They had struggled up a steep incline for the better part of a day. At various intervals the trail became so rugged they were forced to dismount and lead the horses on foot. The clouds overhead loomed thick and dark, close enough to touch.

Pulling her gelding behind her, she felt as if her lungs would explode from the combination of climbing and thin air. When she felt she couldn't take another step, Seguín halted at the top of a ridge and called out, "Diana, come see this."

Huffing and puffing, she reached his side. When she stepped beside him, it seemed as if they stood at the apex of the world. Mountain peaks undulated, in stair-step fashion before them, tapering downward. She glimpsed the outline of a huge basin at the foot of the mountains far away.

Pointing to the basin, he told her, "That's the Oaxaca Valley. It's where we're headed. When we reach it, we'll be halfway to our destination."

She nodded, trying to catch her breath. Gazing at the far horizon, she had missed the village sprawled at their feet. Rough, stone houses, thatched with scrub brush, lay less than a mile below them.

He followed her gaze. "That's Santa María. A poor village, but there's a couple who takes in travelers, the Sotos."

Diana started to reply, but a pounding rumble stopped her. Turning toward the sound, she spied a cascading waterfall, perhaps one hundred feet tall. Its white spume was glorious, falling in a long, bridal veil of rushing water to a rock-rimmed pool behind the village.

"Oh, how beautiful!"

"*Sí*, I thought you would like it. In the rainy months, it's a torrent. Some of the houses flood when the rains are unusually heavy, but it's the lifeblood of the village. Even though moisture is all around us, the limestone absorbs it so quickly most streams go underground," he explained.

As he paused, his obsidian eyes slid over her, laden with the promise of sensual delights. "In the summer months it's pleasant to bathe beneath the falls, but now, I fear it's too chilly."

Trembling under his provocative gaze, she knew exactly

what he was thinking of . . . swimming naked, together, in the enchanted pool, with the water cascading over them. She wanted to answer his invitation with unbridled enthusiasm, but something held her back. She had been ready in Veracruz, but now she wasn't so certain. She couldn't bear to think of leaving him when they reached Acapulco.

"The waterfall is beautiful. Thank you for showing me. But it's only mid-day, I'm surprised you're willing to stop."

Shrugging his shoulders, he turned away from her to gaze at the horizon again. She sensed he wasn't pleased with her neutral answer.

"You and Lydia haven't complained about the fast pace and camping out. I've purposely avoided staying in other villages, because I didn't know what danger might befall us. But I know this one. They're all good people." He faced her again, and his voice held a note of teasing. "Surely, you wouldn't object to spending the night on a mattress and taking a bath."

Realizing he had been thinking of her comfort and feeling strangely guilty for her earlier reticence, she whooped with joy and stretched on tiptoe, kissing him full on the mouth.

When she tried to end the impromptu kiss, he pulled her back and lowered his head. Before his lips recaptured hers, Lydia joined them, interrupting with, "What's the celebration about?"

Flushing, Diana retreated from his embrace. "A mattress and bath tonight. That's the celebration!"

Lydia smiled. "Sounds like heaven."

Seguín's midnight-black gaze riveted Diana. Blatant disappointment burned in his eyes. She felt a thrill chase up her spine, knowing how much he wanted to kiss her.

Turning from them, he started down the steep, winding path to the village, calling over his shoulder, "What are you waiting for?"

* * *

Diana splashed happily in the warm water. What a luxury—a real bath. The old tin tub was small but spotlessly clean. The Sotos were friendly and kind. Their house was sparsely furnished, and the mattress Seguín had promised was stuffed with corn shucks and rested on a hard-packed earth floor.

She didn't care. Barren as the house might be, it was neat as a pin. The stew she had eaten for supper had been tasty. A fire crackled on the hearth beside the tub, banishing the chill of the January night.

Sighing, she enjoyed the cozy charm of the place. A slow languor crept through her muscles as the heated water worked its magic. Her eyelids drooped, and she promised herself a few minutes of blissful laziness before she washed her hair.

Baby James's cries shattered her repose. He had been napping in the adjoining room. Wondering what was wrong, she expected Lydia to pick him up. Fully awake, she realized her bath water had cooled. Muttering under her breath, she began washing her hair. Through the washing and rinsing, his wailing continued. He seemed to be working himself into a frenzy, ending each cry on a choked hiccup.

Where was Lydia?

Hurrying, she finished her hair and stepped from the tub. Wrapping her hair in the only available towel, she draped a quilt around her body. Ironically, as soon as she covered herself the baby quieted, just as abruptly as he had started crying. Expecting to find Lydia with him, she pulled back the woolen blanket serving as a door between the two rooms.

It wasn't Lydia who was holding baby James. It was Seguín.

Color and heat flooded her, rising from her damp, na-

ked toes to the top of her turbaned head. She was excru-
ciatingly aware of her near nudity, and his gaze seemed to
strip away her casually draped quilt.

Lightning awareness leapt between them. A sudden impulse, like a magnetic force, overcame her, and she felt an
almost irresistible urge to throw herself into his arms. Man-
aging to control her reaction, she drew the quilt tighter
around her body.

Lowering her eyes from his burning gaze, she murmured, "I heard the baby. I thought Lydia had come."

Shifting James to his shoulder, he patted the baby's back.
Nonchalantly, he commented, "It's gas." As if on cue,
James burped loudly.

At the baby's noisy belch, she lifted her eyes and barely
suppressed a giggle. Studying the two of them from beneath her eyelashes, she smiled at his easy handling of the
infant. She wouldn't have expected him to know how to
burp a baby. He seemed to be surprising her with increasing frequency, constantly revealing new faces of himself.

He returned her smile with a hint of smugness and lowered the baby into the wooden box serving as his crib.
"Lydia isn't here," he explained. "She wanted to join the
celebration. I would have heard Pepito's cries sooner, but
I was outside with *Señor* Soto helping him carry firewood."

"What celebration?"

"Tomorrow is *Los Tres Reyes,* the day of the Epiphany
and the end of the holiday season. There will be feasting
and gifts for the children, and tonight there is dancing in
the village *taverna.*"

"I didn't know."

And in fact, she had lost track of time. Christmas must
have passed while they were journeying. Suddenly, cut off
from her mother and Sarah, she felt very alone. If only
Seguín would love her, she wouldn't feel so alone.

Shaking off her gloomy thoughts, she realized she did
still have the baby. Little James, her father's namesake,

needed her. Moving to the opposite side of the makeshift crib, she gazed down at him. The potent allure of Seguín was still there, but she ignored it, concentrating on the infant.

Checking the baby's napkin, she found it to be dry. Lydia had fed him after supper, so she knew he wasn't hungry, and he appeared content now. He was lying on his stomach with one tiny fist in his mouth, looking all the world like a little dark-haired angel.

She lightly brushed his cheek and then his neck, testing his downy skin for signs of a fever. She remembered their exposure in that horrid swamp, and even though several weeks had passed, she routinely checked him for signs of illness. His skin was cool to the touch.

Seguín's lips formed into a half-smile. "Satisfied?"

"Yes." She tilted her head at him. "Where did you learn to do that?"

"I have eyes. I've watched you and Lydia. It's not so difficult as you women pretend."

Rising to the bait, she retorted, "Don't be so smug. I want to see you change his dirty . . ." Her voice trailed off, her argument forgotten, while she watched his eyes slide over her exposed skin.

His glance was like a caress. Her heart hammered, and her nipples hardened, longing for the touch of his calloused hands. She was glad she had taken the precaution of putting the baby's crib between them. Self-consciously, she clutched the quilt higher and tighter around her throat.

Amusement at her obvious discomfort battled with the frank desire in his eyes. "Get dressed. You don't want to miss the celebration."

"What?"

"The celebration. I want you to come with me. I've even dressed for the occasion."

Preoccupied with her own state of undress and the

baby's well-being, she hadn't noticed his attire until he drew her attention to it. He wore an indigo cotton shirt, accented by a bright red sash tied at his waist. Her gaze dropped lower, and the breath left her body.

His lower body was encased in black leather pants. Oiled and supple, the breeches clung to every swell of muscle and tendon and . . .

Diana's heart pulsed in her throat. Her mouth went dry. The raw masculine power of him in skintight leather breeches caused a rush of desire to sweep over her. Her stomach fluttered, and lower there was a pleasurable, intimate tightening.

"What about the baby?"

"*Señora* Soto has graciously offered to look in on him. We'll only be a few doors away. The village is small. If he awakens, our hostess has promised to fetch us or Lydia." His smoldering gaze swept her again. "No more excuses. Get dressed. I'll wait for you."

When they reached the *taverna,* they were greeted warmly by *Señor* Beñiquez, the unofficial *alcalde* of Santa María. He was a huge man, garrulous and friendly, with a heavily waxed handlebar mustache that defied gravity by protruding at least three-inches from either side of his face.

Seguín was obviously acquainted with the *alcalde,* as well as most of the people present, and they welcomed him as if he were a brother. Diana wondered how he had come to know this place and its people.

The villagers of Santa María, like *Señor* Beñiquez, were easy to like. They were open and outgoing. They entered into the merrymaking with a carefree zest. The villagers chattered and laughed, danced and ate in joyous abandon.

The enthusiasm of the natives was evident in their decorations. The crude *taverna* had been transformed by hun-

dreds of colorful and cleverly wrought paper decorations.
Evergreen boughs hung from every available surface, laced
with brilliant rain forest flowers for color. Waxy tapers,
strewn throughout the room, nestled in gaily painted ce-
ramic holders, bathing the *taverna* in a golden, flickering
glow.

Diana spotted Lydia across the room. The young widow
was surrounded by a bevy of handsome admirers. Diana
was happy for her. Lydia's unswerving loyalty had been a
godsend. She wanted Lydia to enjoy herself.

Her attention was drawn from Lydia to Seguín as he
threaded his way through the boisterous crowd. Hips
thrust forward, he walked with his characteristic cocky
stride. In his glove-tight breeches, he was a sight to behold.
It was all she could do to not stare at him . . . from the
waist down. Dragging her eyes upward, she noticed he held
an earthenware cup in each hand. Stopping before her,
he bowed and offered her one.

"Thank you. What is it?" She took a sip and made a
face.

He chuckled. "It's a fruit punch for the ladies. But most
ladies prefer this." He held the other cup to her lips.

Taking a large gulp, she hoped the second liquid would
erase the tart taste of the first. It hit the back of her throat
like molten fire, burning an eye-watering path to her stomach. Gasping and gagging, she croaked, "What was that?"

Seguín roared with laughter, and his eyes twinkled with
mischief. *"Pulque."*

"You did that on purpose, not warning me."

Arching an eyebrow, he admitted, "Maybe."

Taking her arm in his grasp, he stroked the sensitive
underside of her forearm. The touch of his fingers on her
bare skin evoked trailing tendrils of flame that easily
eclipsed the fiery *pulque* in her stomach. She should pull
away, she knew, but she couldn't. For too long, she had
craved his touch.

"The *pulque* takes the edge off, so you can enjoy the festivities." His fingertips traced beguiling patterns on her flesh. "One warning, though—*sip* it. It's strong stuff."

He took a small sip himself and licked his lips, his gaze on her mouth. She had the uncanny sensation his lesson on drinking *pulque* had something to do with watching her mouth. "You'll find the fruit drink isn't so tart when you sip the *pulque* and follow it with the punch. Try it," he urged.

Diana tried not to tremble. Seguín's touch, combined with his provocative gaze, sent shivers of heated awareness streaking through her. Obediently, she swallowed some of the fiery drink, trying not to choke.

"Bueno," he encouraged. "Now follow it with the fruit punch. Together, they're not so bad."

Swallowing the punch, she tested his theory. The fruit juice diluted the *pulque's* burn, and the *pulque* made the punch almost palatable. The two beverages curled together in her stomach, making the golden glow of the room softer, more inviting.

She smiled and nodded.

Returning her smile, he gave her arm a final squeeze and turned his attention to the dance floor. Her flesh tingled where he had touched her, and she rubbed it surreptitiously, as if to erase the sensual power he held over her.

Standing together, shoulder to shoulder, in the boisterous crush, they watched the dancers. She felt uncommonly happy and relaxed. The villager's friendly reception, combined with Seguín's attentions, warmed her like a roaring fire on a snowy night.

"I like this place," she found herself commenting. "How did you find it? We're a long way from the capitol and your silver mine."

Taking another sip of *pulque,* he offered the cup to her. Shaking her head, she declined. After only two tastes, she could feel the drink's potent effect.

Nodding in tacit agreement, he replied, "I found Santa

María when I was a Juárista. We usually hid in the north of México, but one time Juan and I needed to disappear for several months. We decided to stay away from our old camps."

Wanting to ask but knowing he wouldn't tell her, she wondered why he had to disappear for several months. Was that part of his allure, she wondered? The almost palpable sense of danger he carried with him? She remembered the mountain hideout that was his home and realized that, to Seguín, danger was a part of everyday life.

"Speaking of Juan," he added, almost as an afterthought. "I sent for him to join us, and I'm surprised he's not here. I asked around, but no one in Santa María has seen him."

"Why did you expect to find him here? Because you and he came here before? But it must have been a long time ago, and—"

"Santa María is where Juan was born and raised," he interrupted softly. "It was the safest rendezvous point I could think of."

"Oh. Are his parents still living here?"

"No, his parents are dead. He does have some cousins and nieces and nephews here."

Now she understood why he knew everyone, and had been so warmly welcomed. And she realized why he felt comfortable here, too. Juan's relatives and friends would be his natural allies, eager to protect them.

His next words caught her off-guard. "Would you care to dance?"

She glanced up at his handsome face, trying to read his motive. Was the offer genuine, or was he merely teasing her again? Singing, burping the baby, and now wanting to dance? This wasn't the masculine Seguín she knew.

Unsure of herself, she shifted from one foot to the other. Watching the dancers was entertaining, but when she examined their dance closely she found the steps complicated. It was hard to follow the pattern of their feet, although the basic movements appeared simple enough. Approach, dipping and swaying, touching upraised arms and retreating, circling one's partner.

The native dance reminded her of a stylized mating ritual: approach, touch, retreat. It was strangely beguiling, almost mesmerizing. Concentrating on it, she felt the cadence of the music pound in her veins. She swayed to the rhythm. The golden glow remained with her, making her feel bold.

"Yes, I would like to try the dance," she agreed, amazing herself.

Surprise flitted across his features, followed by a look of admiration. Bowing, he extended his arm and led her onto the dance floor.

"Don't worry. It's easier than it appears. Just follow me."

Watching him execute the complex dance steps, she attempted to copy his movements. The broader movements of the dance were no problem. They flowed together, touched and backed off, only to prepare to repeat the pattern again.

Like our relationship, she thought.

Little by little, she felt more comfortable. Her self-consciousness melted away, and the music's compelling beat flowed over her. Her limbs moved naturally, instinctively following the rhythm.

Seguín encouraged her, effortlessly matching his movements to conform to hers. Swaying and dipping, she let her gaze trail over his lithe hips, clearly outlined in his leather breeches. When he turned and raised his arms above his head, her eyes were drawn to the width of his muscular shoulders and chest.

Arms upraised, they touched briefly. Mesmerized, she watched while he executed the steps of his retreat. Her gaze followed the bunch and coil of his powerful thighs, sliding beneath the second skin of the black leather pants.

He was dancing for her . . . and her alone.

His unspoken invitation made her bolder. Dipping and turning, she met his challenge. The music and his compelling magnetism transfixed her, sweeping her along. The room and the other dancers receded. An invisible force surrounded them, an intimate linking. Their movements radiated provocative promise, punctuating the raw sensuality sizzling between them.

Her eyes devoured him, while her body tempted his. Twisting and swaying, she ached to touch him . . . to slide her fingertips along the muscular power of his shoulders and thighs. To taste the salty perspiration pooled in the hollow of his throat. To run her hands through the crisp, sable hair on his chest. Her nipples hardened painfully at the thought of their naked bodies coming together, entwined in passion.

The music ended abruptly. Heated blood sang through her veins. Dazed, she remained on the dance floor, still moving to the invisible tune playing in her head. Rescuing her, Seguín grasped her elbow and led her away.

Realization dawned, and swift upon its heels embarrassment flooded her senses. Her face grew hot. She knew she was blushing. Lowering her head, she wished she were a hundred miles away, where he couldn't see her shameless desire.

Leaning close, he whispered, "You look hot from the dance. Would you care to step outside in the cool air?"

She didn't know if he understood her shame and chose to ignore it, or if he believed she was flushed from the dance. It didn't matter. He had offered her a respite, and she gratefully took it.

Not trusting her voice, she nodded.

Arm in arm, they slipped through the door. Emerging from the closely packed, smoky *taverna* was a relief. The crisp mountain air washed over her, cooling her skin and restoring a modicum of self-composure. Silence enfolded them, and she searched for something to say—anything to dispel the sensual skein of desire entangling them.

The silence was deafening, but after a few moments she lifted her head. A low, rumbling roar throbbed in the background.

It had to be the waterfall.

From where they stood, surrounded by the villagers' steeply thatched huts, she couldn't see it, but she could hear it. Remembering its beauty and thankful for a diversion, she tugged at his arm. "The waterfall, Seguín—I'd like to get a closer look. Will you show it to me?"

His eyes swept her, twin coals of burning desire. He didn't appear distraught by the smoldering sensuality their dance had unleashed. In fact, he seemed to have welcomed it. Without lifting his gaze from her face, he replied simply, "Come."

They walked to the end of the rough pathway between the row of houses and skirted the stables. Behind the village, the waterfall tumbled, as if from the sky, leaping and gurgling—a silver-white flow of water, incandescent against the dark night.

Awe-struck, she watched the graceful rush of water. The waterfall was a column of pure power and constant movement. At the same time, it appeared to hang suspended, falling in a graceful, gravity defying plunge.

A high-pitched cry rent the air. Diana jumped. The shriek sounded again, a cross between a child's wail and a woman's scream. Turning instinctively to the security of Seguín's embrace, she gasped, "What was that?"

"A jaguar, a jungle cat. I saw its spoor near the trail, but I'm surprised it would venture this close to the village."

Clutching him tightly, she felt her mind tumble. She had read about jaguars, and she knew about mountain lions from living in California. Big cats were dangerous animals, capricious and fearless. She had never been close enough to hear one cry. The waterfall's beauty was suddenly marred by the danger lurking in the heart of the jungle.

Lifting her face to him, she asked, "You mean you saw—?"

Her anxious words were lost when his mouth descended upon hers. His lips seared hers with a kiss that branded her very soul. The jaguar and the jungle, their journey and the dangers all slid away, plunging into oblivion, like the waterfall. All she could feel, the only thing that was real, was his mouth, moving over hers with exquisite care, coaxing and soothing.

She leaned closer, meeting his desire with an equal desire of her own. Their tongues twined in feverish abandon, sliding and rubbing, thrusting and exploring. Heat chased through her body. Each nerve awakened with a tingling, yearning desire. Straining toward him, she melted into his embrace.

When his hand cupped her breast, the core of fiery desire that had built during their dance burst into a white-hot pillar of flame, devouring and consuming her. Moaning in wordless need, she heard the sound ripped from the depths of her throat.

His mouth left hers to wander down her throat, licking and tasting, nipping her sensitized flesh and then laving it with tongue tip. His hands covered both her breasts now, kneading and stroking until they swelled with aching desire.

"*Mi rubia,* I want you," he groaned against her neck. His breath scorched her skin. "Do you want me?"

"Yes and yes, and *sí* and *sí.*"

"Even if I cannot give you forever?"

She heard his words, as if from a distance. They were muffled by the sound of the waterfall, or was it the roaring in her ears? She hesitated. What was he trying to tell her? It was difficult to concentrate with him pressed so close, with desire pounding through her veins. He was cautioning her about the future. She had always known the future was a pale ghost, an elusive dream.

But it didn't matter . . . not now. Maybe it would tomorrow. She couldn't deny him, or herself, any longer. Tightening her grip on his shoulders, she breathed, "I want you . . . *now*. Forever can wait."

Eighteen

Seguín exerted his mastery over her. Unable to control his desires any longer, he swept her up and carried her in his arms, afraid that she might change her mind. Through the hushed, dark house, he moved carefully, vowing to himself to keep her with him all night. Propriety be damned. The Sotos and Lydia would have to look the other way.

Entering his room, he laid her gently on the bed and lit the lamp. Blowing out the match, he found she had curled herself into a ball with her face averted. She was innocent and frightened, he realized, despite her passionate response. His heart squeezed at the thought, and he promised himself to be gentle with her.

Seating himself on the edge of the bed, he coaxed, "Come here, Diana."

She came to him hesitantly and when she was close enough, he pulled her into his arms and cradled her on his lap. Covering her mouth, he molded his lips to hers. The essence of her scent, lilac, swept over him, reminding him of all the times he had kissed and held her.

Slowly, tenderly, he lapped at the seam of her mouth, begging entrance. Lightning flashed between them when their tongues touched, twining together, and he savored the honey-sweet taste of her. Caressing her breast through the cotton of her blouse, he gloried in her responsiveness, the quick awakening of her nipple, hardening beneath his fingertips.

Shifting her gently, he returned her to the bed. Kneeling beside the bed, he undressed her slowly. His fingers and tongue worshipped each part of her alabaster skin until she lay naked before him.

His eyes devoured her loveliness. She was more beautiful than he had imagined. The soft glow of the bedside lamp sparked golden glints from her mane of tangled hair, spread on the pillow. The deep hollow of her throat accented the enticing mounds of her full breasts. Her delicious, coral pink nipples were taut with desire . . . desire for him. And lower, the golden triangle of her femininity beckoned him.

Groaning deeply, he felt a powerful surge, an almost painful need to plunge inside of her. Trembling with the effort of holding himself in check, he undressed quickly.

He knew she watched as he ripped his clothes off. Her changeable hazel eyes darkened to a deep emerald green. She lifted her arms to him in silent welcome.

Lying beside her, he devoured her mouth, hungry with his need, while his hands explored her satiny skin. He stroked her breasts, rolling each nipple between his fingers until they became hard as pebbles. His hand strayed lower, and she moved against his fingers, straining toward him.

His mouth followed the path of his fingertips, and he circled the peaks of her breasts, loving them with tongue tip, savoring the delicate texture of her skin. He captured the rosette of one crest and drew her succulent flesh into his mouth, alternately sucking and licking.

Lacing her fingers in his hair, she loosed the leather thong holding his queue. He felt his hair fall about his face. She buried her hands there and pulled him closer, a soft mew of pleasure escaping her lips. Tentatively, she freed one hand and lifted it to his chest, stroking downward. Hesitantly, she caressed his flat male nipples until they responded and hardened. He groaned again. The pleasure-pain was almost too much to endure.

Controlling the consuming, spiraling ache of his body, he dipped his head lower, chasing lazy arcs with his tongue on her abdomen. His fingers strayed downward, too, gently parting her legs and finding the hot, velvet-soft folds of her.

Stroking her, the dew of her passion spilled forth, and he almost lost control. Teetering on the brink of total abandonment, he forced himself to concentrate on giving her pleasure. His mouth moved lower, straying and licking, over her abdomen and flat belly, pausing at her navel to caress and explore that sweet indentation with his tongue.

He reached his hands upward and cupped her breasts, while his mouth trailed lower and lower still. Nuzzling the blond tangle between her legs, his lips and tongue explored until he found the hard nub of her desire and rolled it between his lips.

Diana thrashed beneath him and grabbed his shoulders. She cried out, "No, no . . . you mustn't!"

Lifting his head, he pleaded, "Let me pleasure you."

She said nothing but lay rigid beneath him. Recognizing her virginal innocence, he silently vowed he would, before they parted, teach her *all* the ways of loving. Sensitive to her feelings, he rediscovered her breasts with his mouth, allowing his fingers to explore her woman's mound.

With his mouth cherishing her breasts and his hand pressing against her, she bucked and twisted beneath him, her innocence forgotten, replaced with a wild need. Stroking and caressing her, he drove her beyond the brink of sanity into the mindless, swirling maelstrom of passion. She was arching against him, her hands tangled in his hair.

Her breath came in ragged pants. "Seguín, Seguín, my love, my love." Then she stiffened and shuddered, spasms heralding her release.

He took her then, entering in one lightning-hot thrust,

pushing through her maidenhead. Her climax closed around him, squeezing his member in a sweet vise. It was all he could do to keep from coming with her. Beads of perspiration dripped from his forehead, and he ground his teeth with the effort, but he forced himself to remain perfectly motionless until she savored the last tremor of her fulfillment.

When her body relaxed beneath his, she lifted her hand and stroked his cheek. Her eyes were a dark forest green, almost black in the flickering lamplight. Her lips curled into a contented smile, and she murmured, "Seguín, that was wonderful . . . it was . . ."

"I didn't hurt you?"

"No, I didn't feel pain, just a twinge of something . . ."

Pleased that he had spared her pain and brought her pleasure, he couldn't wait any longer. Almost insane with his own need, he wanted her to come again, with him. Stroking slowly, in and out of her body, he leaned down and pulled her breast into his mouth, rolling the nipple with his tongue. Insinuating his fingers between their bodies, he caressed the swollen bud of her passion.

His efforts were rewarded by her amazing responsiveness. Her slender legs tightened around his buttocks, and her eyes glazed over with newfound desire.

Moaning softly, she urged him, "Deeper. Oh, Seguín, please, please. I want . . . I want . . ." Her head turned from side to side on the pillow, and she matched his rhythm almost frantically, pushing her hips high, meeting him thrust for thrust.

The blood pounded through his veins as he plunged into the feverish, tight sheath of her. Straining together, they soared higher and higher, caught in a swirling vortex of pure sensation and glorious ecstasy. When her muscles contracted around his turgid manhood she sent him over the brink, and he found himself transported to the heavens.

Clinging to her, he reveled in the tiny aftershocks of pleasure rippling between them. After a few moments, he slid down into the bed and turned to one side, bringing her with him. They were still intimately linked. He pulled her into his arms and nuzzled the sunshine glory of her hair. He felt completely at peace, saturated with joy.

He couldn't remember feeling this way before. They were one, and it felt right. It was as if she had taken a part of him, a piece of his heart . . . to remain forever in her keeping.

It was not the gray January dawn that penetrated Diana's sleep, bringing her awake. Rather, it was the chilly air that had invaded the room overnight. The fire had died long ago, leaving charred embers.

Blushing, she realized they hadn't needed a fire last night to keep them warm. Their long-denied passion had done that. This morning, they lay curled together, spoon fashion, for warmth. Seguín's hard male body radiated heat, but the cold had still roused her.

Or was it the chill of his warning that had penetrated her sleep? The intimacies of the flesh they had shared had been glorious and consuming, but where did that leave her heart? Facing the empty prospect of living her life without him, she shivered inwardly. Logically, she realized it was too late for regrets. She had lost her heart to him months ago, and there was no turning back.

He stirred beside her, and she wondered how she could face Lydia and the Sotos. Her bed, next to Lydia's, was untouched. Their night of intimacy would be common knowledge. She hadn't heard James cry out . . . yet. Maybe there was time to creep to her bed before the others awakened.

When she tried to ease from Seguín's embrace, his arms gripped her tighter. His voice rumbled, thick with sleep,

"Mi rubia, don't go. I want to savor waking with you." And then, with uncanny intuition, he added, "Don't worry about what the others may think, *mi preciosa.* It's not important. They'll understand."

The others will understand we have only a short time together. The thought formed in her mind. She knew what he meant. Suddenly cold again, she shivered. He must have felt her involuntary shudder, because he drew her closer and threw his leg over hers.

"I'll start a fire in a moment, but I'd rather start a fire here . . . in bed." He punctuated his suggestion by nibbling her neck and brushing his hand in lazy circles over her bare breasts.

She stilled, instantly beguiled by his caresses. Leaning back, she arched her chest, pushing her breasts into his hands. Her body responded to the magic of his touch. The familiar hungry ache started to build in the pit of her stomach, and lower, she felt the heated moisture spill from her woman's passage. It was miraculous, how quickly he could arouse her. She was already hot and ready for him . . . wanting nothing more than to feel him inside of her.

A loud, banging noise sounded, and she jerked up. Reality landed like a black raven, and the spell was broken. Baby James wailed, and she pulled away from Seguín. She knew her face must be flaming. Her cheeks felt hot to touch.

The house was awake. She should return to her own room.

Catching her by the wrist, he pulled her back. He sighed and bent to kiss her wrist. "Don't go. I won't . . . we won't . . . not with the others waking up. But *por favor,* wait a minute. I have something I've been saving for you. Let me get it."

Throwing back the covers, he slid from the rumpled bed. His naked body riveted her. She watched him while he padded across the floor. His body was shockingly male,

dusted with fine, black hair. The raw, primitive power of
him was evident in his broad, muscular shoulders and the
tensile strength of his thighs. His buttocks were well-
formed, rounded yet taut with muscle. He moved with an
agile grace that made her think of the jaguar they'd heard.

He found his saddlebags, tossed on an old trunk beneath the window. Rummaging through them, he pulled
out a small parcel, wrapped in creased and grimy tissue
paper. Returning to the bed, he draped himself casually
across the foot, totally nude and seemingly oblivious to the
chilly air. He offered the tissue-covered box to her.

"I've wanted to give you this for weeks. I wasn't certain
if I would have the opportunity to . . . or if you would
want . . ." He ran his hand through his long, tousled hair,
obviously searching for the right words. "Since today is *Los
Tres Reyes,* the time for gifts, it seemed appropriate to give
it to you now."

She accepted the battered package and stared at it.
Turning it over in her hands, she felt a lump rise to her
throat, and she didn't know what to say.

"Open it, *por favor.* I know it doesn't look like much
after all this time in my saddlebags, but I—"

"No, don't apologize," she stopped him. "It's just so
unexpected . . . I have nothing to give you in return."

Lifting his eyes to her half-exposed breasts, he grinned.
"I wouldn't say you have *nothing* to offer me."

Flushing at his inference, she couldn't stop the self-
satisfied smile tugging at her lips. It felt good to be openly
admired and wanted. She tore at the tissue paper, hoping
to hide her conflicted emotions.

It was a bracelet. A silver bracelet, cunningly crafted to
resemble a coiled snake with glittering topaz eyes.

"It's beautiful, Seguín. Thank you." She slipped it onto
her left wrist and turned her arm over and back again.
The snake appeared to writhe on her bare skin. "It's so
unusual. Why—?"

"It's my own design. Made from the purest silver of the mines. Silver refined using your father's process." His eyes twinkled, and she wondered if he was remembering their old enmity over her father's formula. "The topaz eyes match your golden hair. But that's not what you wanted to know, is it? You want to know why I chose a snake for the design?"

It was what she had been wondering, but she didn't want to appear ungrateful. The bracelet was lovely, a work of superb craftsmanship. "Yes. Why *did* you choose a snake?"

"You're always thinking, always analyzing the 'why' of things, aren't you, Diana?"

She wasn't certain if he meant the words to be a compliment, but they touched her. They meant he was attuned to her. He had taken the time to try to understand her. His admission was more important than a thousand silver bracelets.

Bowing her head, she willed the sudden tears to go away.

Grasping her chin, he tilted her head up. He must have seen the sheen of moisture in her eyes, because he lowered his head and kissed her eyelids with a tenderness that took her breath away.

"I chose a snake because it's the emblem of México. The Aztecs, who settled what is now México City, believe they were led to the site by their gods. The legend says they knew the spot when they found an eagle, perched on a cactus with a snake in its mouth."

"But what—?" She interjected.

"Wait, *mi preciosa.*" He stopped her question by brushing his lips with hers. "You didn't let me finish. I chose the emblem of my country to remind you of México and . . . me."

The tears that had threatened before welled up and splashed down her cheeks. It was a farewell gift of sorts . . . to remind her of him and México, she thought bitterly.

He had granted her heaven last night, only to steal it away in the cold morning light.

"I want to thank you again," she couldn't keep the chill from her voice. "It's beautiful."

He drew her into his arms and gently brushed the tears from her cheeks with one calloused thumb. "I know you're moved, *mi rubia,* but don't cry."

Not understanding her tears, he teased, "I had another reason for choosing a serpent. Not since Eve tempted Adam has a woman so sorely tempted a man."

The reflection from the sun on San Francisco Bay almost blinded Sarah. The fog had burned off early. It was gone by the time they'd returned from church. In the distance small, white sails bobbed—Sunday sailors. Sometimes, she felt a twinge of envy for those faceless people who could enjoy themselves.

Seated beneath the bow window in her bedroom, with a book open in her lap, she found herself staring out. It was a habit she had gotten into at Seguín's home, after she lost . . .

Diana's letter had reached her when they arrived in California. Seguín had managed to get Diana, baby James, and Lydia safely to Veracruz. But there were no ships for them. He planned on taking them overland to Acapulco.

That had been weeks ago, and still no word. And nothing from Gilberto.

A knock sounded at the front door, echoing loudly in the hushed Sunday silence. She hoped it wasn't another social caller. She couldn't abide smiling and making small talk when she didn't know what had happened to her husband, or Diana, or the baby.

Lowering her head, she tried to concentrate on the printed words. If she looked occupied, maybe her mother wouldn't require her presence in the parlor.

* * *

Lifting the brass knocker, Gilberto murmured a short prayer to the Blessed Virgin Mary. He didn't know what to expect, but he had escaped his father's henchmen and traveled halfway around the world to find his wife.

A plump maid in a frilly, white cap opened the door. "Good afternoon, sir. This is the York residence. Can I help you, sir?"

"Yes, thank you. Is Sarah Aguir—is Sarah York at home?"

Bobbing her head, the servant replied, "Yes, sir. May I have your name, sir?"

The moment he had dreaded for weeks was upon him. He wouldn't allow them to turn him away. They couldn't keep him from his wife, his Sarah.

"My name is Gilberto Aguirre. Could you announce me, please?"

"Why certainly, sir. If you'll just wait here."

As if on cue, like an actor on the stage, Herbert York appeared behind the maid. "That won't be necessary, Molly. I'll see Mr. Aguirre." The maid sketched a curtsy and disappeared.

Gilberto and Herbert locked gazes. After a long moment Herbert raised his arm and extended his hand, saying, "It's good to see you, Gilberto. We thought you were in Europe."

Stunned by the unexpected reception, he clasped Herbert's hand and shook it. "I'm glad to be here," was all he could think to say . . . for the first few seconds. Then he blurted, "Can I see Sarah?"

Herbert clapped him on the back and smiled. "I understand your impatience. But if I may have a few words with you first, Gilberto. I'm only thinking of Sarah's welfare. I won't stand in the way of you two, but I must talk with you."

"Of course, sir."

"Please call me Herbert. And you don't mind me calling

you Gilberto, do you?" Clasping his elbow, Sarah's father propelled him to a room directly off the foyer. It was a parlor, done in brightly colored chintz fabrics and Empire furniture.

"No, sir, er, Herbert. I would be honored if you would call me by my given name."

"Good. Please, take a seat, Gilberto. Do you care for refreshments?"

"Not now. I'll hear what you have to say. Begging your pardon, but I want to see Sarah as soon as possible."

"I understand," Herbert repeated. "But first, you must listen. I will not stop your marriage. Sarah loves you too much for that. I know it now. Since the day of your marriage and abduction, more has happened than you realize. And it's important you know because Sarah has changed."

Gilberto gripped the carved armrests of the chair. What was Sarah's father trying to tell him? Had something terrible happened to his wife? *Por Dios,* he couldn't stand it if . . .

"Don't glower so, Gilberto," Herbert jerked him back to their conversation. "I believe your coming will rectify everything."

He relaxed a fraction, but what followed was a wild tale he could barely credit. His half-brother, Seguin, had taken Sarah and her friend to his mountain hideout because his wife refused to leave him behind in México. There, she had a miscarriage and adopted an orphaned boy. Diana and the child were still in México, or so Herbert thought. The Yorks had been forced to sail without them.

"I had to get Sarah and her mother to safety, and we didn't know what had happened to them. Unfortunately, we feared the worst. Sarah was exceptionally distraught. It was one loss after another, Gilberto. First you, and then your child. After that . . ." He paused and cleared his throat. "Her mother and I feared for Sarah's sanity."

"What about Seguín and the others?"

"At the Isthmus of Panama, I left Sarah and Mary with a friend. I leased a small ship and returned to Veracruz to try and locate them. The Mexican authorities, because of the escalating hostilities, refused me admittance. I had no choice but to turn back."

"So they're dead?" he found himself asking, feeling empty and despondent and wondering why. Sarah was alive and safe. She might be grieving, but *Señor* York had said he wouldn't stand in the way of their marriage. They had their whole life ahead of them.

Why did he care about the others?

He and Seguín hadn't gotten along since their mother's death. In fact, he thought Seguín despised him. Yet, his brother had tried to help him . . . and his wife, facing dangers and hardships to do so. And although he had only seen Diana three times, he liked her, and knew she was Sarah's oldest and best friend. Then there was the baby. If the orphaned boy helped to assuage his wife's loss over their own child, he would accept the baby as his own.

"No, I don't think they're dead," Herbert reassured him. "After we arrived here, Sarah received a letter from Diana. It was posted from Veracruz. Somehow, Seguín got through, but our ship had already sailed. They planned to travel overland to Acapulco to find another ship."

"After I see Sarah, I must go to Acapulco." The statement, when it left his mouth, surprised him. During the long and torturous journey to California, he had debated with himself whether he would return to México or not. Unable to reach a decision, he had thrust the question from his mind, concentrating on being reunited with his wife.

Now the decision had been made for him. He couldn't cower behind Herbert York's coattails, here in the States, without confronting his father. And he couldn't desert Seguín, Diana, and the baby to their fates. They were too important to his wife.

And important to him.

The thought of being reunited with his half-brother warmed him, especially after what Seguín had done for Sarah.

"I'll go with you," Herbert declared.

"You'll have to take me, too." It was the voice of his dreams. He would have known it anywhere.

Turning, he found Sarah standing in the doorway. She looked thinner and paler than he remembered her, but she was real . . . flesh and blood. Who said dreams didn't come true?

They fell into each other's arms.

Descending from the mountain peaks of the Sierra Madre Oriental, they entered the valley of Oaxaca. The basin, lying below high peaks, stretched across the horizon in a seemingly limitless plateau at an altitude of five thousand feet. The days were mild, but the nights were chilly.

Perfect for cuddling.

The physical barriers between Diana and Seguín had crumbled in Santa María. Diana tried to thrust the painful prospect of their parting from her mind, living only for the moment. Like schoolchildren, they savored their new-found relationship, experiencing the age-old thrill of lovers, stealing heated glances, touching and kissing at every opportunity.

At night, they crept from the campfire and spent the night locked in each other's arms. Lydia knew, without being told, that they were lovers, and she discreetly observed their privacy.

Pepito was thriving. She thought of baby James as Pepito now, adopting Seguín's pet name for him. It fit his cherubic disposition. The baby had become a seasoned traveler, accustomed to his swaying papoose rides. He had grown and gained weight. Diana enjoyed playing with him after supper, when he was wide awake and eager for attention.

They stopped one evening in the foothills surrounding the city of Oaxaca. She took Pepito from Lydia and wandered over to a grassy slope. Spreading a blanket on the ground, she placed him there and sat down.

He crowed and gurgled, waving his pudgy arms and kicking against the restraints of his bundling. She gently unwrapped him. The air wasn't chilly yet, and she knew he liked to be free to move his limbs.

The child was a marvel to her. He had learned to flip himself over, and he could smile on cue. With a little help, he could sit up by himself for a few minutes before falling over. He liked shiny objects, and had learned he could throw them. Each day brought a new development. He was growing fast.

As she played "creepy mouse" on his stomach, Pepito giggled and flailed his arms until Diana stopped. Feeling a rush of pure love, she lifted him in her arms and held him close, inhaling his fresh baby scent. Unfortunately, he didn't want to be cuddled. He wiggled and squirmed in her embrace, obviously wanting to resume their play.

"Pepito, you little wiggle worm, I just wanted to hug you. But that's not exciting enough for you any more, is it?" She laughed and lowered him back to the blanket. "Satisfied?"

Chortling, he reached up to grab her hair, one of his favorite pastimes. He yanked hard, and she chided, "You're too rough, little one." Carefully, she extricated her hair from his chubby fist and pulled a strand of colored glass beads from the pocket of her riding skirt. Dangling the beads in front of his face, she tempted, "Here, grab these, not my hair."

His dark eyes widened at the sight of the gaudy beads. He loved bright objects. Smacking his lips in anticipation, he latched onto the strand as if it were a lifeline and pulled

them from her grasp. Smiling and cooing, he dropped the
beads repeatedly and she retrieved them.

When he sent the beads sailing through the air, they
landed with a soft plop at the edge of the blanket. He
twisted his small body toward them, but to his infant mind,
they must have seemed a million miles away. His face
screwed into a grimace and he loosed a furious scream,
frustration etched in the rigid posture of his arched body.

She retrieved the beads and placed them in his grasping
fingers. "No need to bellow, Pepito. You know I'll get them
for you. You're just so impatient." She laughed softly.
"Sometimes you bear a marked resemblance to Seguín."

With his play pretty returned, he underwent a transfor-
mation. Like the sun emerging from a lowering bank of
thunderclouds, his features cleared and his lips curled
sweetly. Clutching the beads tightly, he had already forgotten his momentary frustration.

"Did I hear my name?" Seguín's voice, accompanied by
the familiar jangle of his spurs, sounded behind Diana.

Twisting on the blanket, she greeted him, *"Buenas noches."*

Squatting beside her and the baby, he kissed her on the
lips and chucked the baby under his chin. *"Buenas noches.*
Why was he crying? Were you threatening him with me?"
He grinned.

"Seguín! Don't be silly. He lost the beads and threw a
fit." Glancing at Seguín, she teased, "It reminded me of
someone else I know, and how impatient he gets. I merely
mentioned to Pepito that you—"

He silenced her by covering her mouth with his. At first,
his kiss was playful, nipping and licking at the corners of
her mouth. But after a few moments, it deepened. His
tongue slipped inside her mouth and stroked her with lan-
guid movements. Feeling her blood warm, she strained
toward him, curling her hands behind his neck.

Pepito screamed, and they broke their embrace. Seguín

raised both his eyebrows in question, and they glanced at the baby. He had flung his beads away again.

"I see what you mean . . . about his impatience." He chuckled and picked up the wailing baby. When he tossed Pepito a few inches in the air, the baby's cries stopped immediately and turned into delighted shrieks.

There was one thing Pepito enjoyed more than bright objects, and that was Seguín's rough play with him. Diana watched them, half of her joining in their merriment, while the other half of her, the maternal half, felt secretly concerned about their rough play. What if Seguín dropped him? Even as the thought crossed her mind, she knew she was being silly. He was always careful with Pepito.

And the baby didn't appear frightened, bouncing in his arms. He was in his element, cooing and laughing so hard he started to hiccup. Seguín stopped the jostling and cradled him close, gently patting his back.

"Enough for one night, old man?"

Drawing nearer, she ran one finger over the baby's soft cheek. "Yes, that's enough for tonight, or Lydia will never get him down—" She broke off abruptly, wrinkling her nose. "I think you got more of a response from him than just a bout of hiccups." She stared pointedly at Pepito's napkin.

Sniffing and grimacing, he thrust the baby at her. "I see . . . er, smell, what you mean. Here, take him. Your turn."

Her mouth quirked, and she raised her hands with palms up. Backing away, she couldn't help but taunt, "Oh, no. This one is all yours."

His midnight gaze snagged hers, and he shook his head. Righteous indignation blanketed his features. "Play is fine, but this is a woman's—"

"Says who?" She cut him off. "I remember how smug you were in Santa María when you burped him. Now it's time to further your education, *Papá.*"

Not giving him the opportunity to argue, she rose to her feet. "Wait here. I'll be back in a minute."

She returned with damp rags and a fresh napkin. Stifling a giggle, she watched as Seguín paced up and down with a scowl on his face while he held the bewildered baby at arm's length.

Taking the infant from him, she laid Pepito on the blanket and executed the necessary task with easy aplomb, instructing Seguín through each step. When she finished, she placed the baby in his arms. "See, it wasn't so bad. Next time it'll be your turn."

Seguín merely grunted.

Seguín ignored the women's pleas to stop, for just one night, in the city of Oaxaca. He sympathized with their need for a civilized bed and bath, but the danger was too great. His traveling alone with two women made them all easy targets. Out in the open countryside, he felt safer. He could rely upon the survival skills he had learned as a Juárista.

He had felt relatively safe until they skirted Oaxaca and encountered the forest to the west of the city. He didn't relish riding through the thick trees; there were too many opportunities for an ambush. But they didn't have a choice. The band of trees stretched in an unbroken line for many kilometers. It would take too long to ride around the forest.

At this particular moment, he almost wished he had taken the time to circle the trees. The forest was unusually quiet: no screaming birds overhead, and even the insects had suspended their monotonous metallic whir. The short hairs on his neck stood on end. He could sense something wasn't right.

Acting on impulse, he rode between the two women, his voice low but commanding, "Stop." Pointing to the right, he said, "See that ravine? Dismount and lead your horses into the bottom. Stay quiet and try to keep Pepito quiet. Don't come out until I come for you."

A frown pleated Diana's brow, and her eyes widened in fear. Whispering urgently, she asked, "Seguín, what is it? Are we in danger?"

"I'm not certain. It's a feeling I have. I want you to stay hidden while I ride ahead."

"But what if you—?"

His eyes held hers.

"Diana, promise me, even if you hear shots and I don't return—don't come out. Stay hidden." He reached out and grasped her shoulder, squeezing for emphasis, "Promise me." He felt the trembling of her body, and her wide hazel eyes seemed to eclipse her face. After a long moment, she nodded.

"Bueno." Releasing her, he gathered his reins. "If I don't come back, wait until nightfall to leave the ravine. Use the North Star as your guide, and go due west. Understand?"

"Yes, I understand."

"I'll wait until you're hidden."

He watched while the women dismounted and carefully picked their way down the steep side of the gully. When he couldn't hear them any longer, the eerie quiet descended again. Pulling on his reins, he turned the black's head.

Moving slowly, he continued west, following the faint trail through the thick trees. He had covered approximately one kilometer when the trail dipped down to cross a shallow stream. He descended to the streambed. Once there, he dismounted and allowed his stallion to drink. While filling his canteen with fresh water, he heard hoofbeats on the ridge above.

Twirling around, he jerked his carbine from its saddleboot. But when he raised the rifle to the ridge, it was already too late. Six carbines were pointed directly at him.

The men on the ridge wore the wide *sombreros* and crossed bandoliers that characterized bandits. Seguín searched their shadowed faces, but he didn't recognize any of them.

A burly man who appeared to be missing his nose broke the tense silence. "Drop the carbine, and your revolver, too."

Seguín said nothing, but his mind worked feverishly, searching for a way out, some way to escape. Nothing presented itself. He knew he was trapped, and hesitating to obey the order would only make things worse. Lowering his carbine carefully to the earth, he would wait to see what they wanted. Maybe they would take his money and let him go. When he reached to unbuckle his holster, the deadly calm erupted with shots.

Believing he was already a dead man, he reacted instinctively and dropped to the ground. From the corner of his eye, he glimpsed a boulder a few meters away. Expecting to feel the searing agony of a bullet hit his flesh at any moment, he rolled as quickly as he could toward the large rock.

Nothing happened. He gained the boulder's protection without harm. Crouching behind its bulk, he drew his revolver and cocked it. He waited, straining his ears for the inevitable sounds of attack from the ridge overhead. But the sounds from the ridge receded. Hoofbeats and shouts echoed distantly from the woods above.

What the hell? he wondered.

The whine and sharp report of bullets faded away. He waited and listened. Silence descended. A sudden thought occurred to him and he spun around, half expecting to find that the bandits had circled behind him.

Not a leaf rustled in the forest. No one was there.

Turning back, he released his breath with a rush. Hugging the rock's rough side, he thought it might be a trap. At the same time, he realized that didn't make sense. There had been six of them, and he was alone. Why would they need to trap him? They could have easily overpowered him.

Carefully, he assessed the situation. His carbine was where he had dropped it, several meters away. The black was gone. Seguín remembered him bolting when the gunfire began, but his horse was well-trained. The stallion wouldn't be far away.

Seguín watched the shadow of the boulder lengthen in the afternoon sun and while he waited, the silence lifted. Bit by bit, the familiar noises of the forest resumed. Birds called, insects buzzed, and forest creatures moved in the underbrush. Finally, when he was certain there was no one around, he stepped in front of the boulder. Glancing at the ridge, he wasn't surprised to find it empty.

Curious about what had happened, he ascended the steep incline. At the top he found churned earth and hoofprints. Moving in a wide arc, he studied the ground, searching for clues.

And he found what he was looking for.

There were two distinct sets of tracks, each approaching the ridge from a different angle. The bandits that had confronted him must have been frightened away by another band of men. He wondered who had rescued him without knowing it. Were they another group of bandits, protecting their territory? Or was the second band of men soldiers, or a posse?

Shaking his head, he realized he would probably never know the answer. But the timing couldn't have been better if he had planned it.

Noticing the lengthening shadows, he realized it was getting late. Diana would be frantic. She would have heard the gunfire and then waited as he had instructed her to do. He glanced at the sun. It was probably over two hours since the shooting had started. Descending the ridge, he splashed across the rocky stream and retrieved his carbine.

He found his stallion, placidly munching grass, in a

small clearing beside the trail. When he swung into the saddle, he offered a short prayer of thanks to the Blessed Virgin Mary for his deliverance. He was happy to be returning to Diana in one piece.

Two things bothered him. It was late, and they would be forced to spend the night in the forest . . . an unappealing prospect. His other worry was Juan.

Where was Juan, and the men he had sent for? Had Julio Gomez failed to get through with his letter? If Juan and his men had been with them, this near miss would never have happened.

Seguín had expected to find Juan waiting for him in Santa María, but he hadn't been there. Besotted by his new relationship with Diana, he had pushed their need for an escort to the back of his mind. If he were completely honest with himself, he would admit that he had enjoyed his privacy with her. With Juan and an escort tagging along, it would have been difficult for them to be together.

He knew he would carry the memories of Diana and their nightly lovemaking with him forever. He would remember Pepito and Lydia . . . and Diana as they had been on this trip, happy and free. They were like his own family . . . the only family he would ever know.

With an effort of will, he pushed aside his poignant thoughts. He had more pressing worries—like reaching Acapulco safely without an escort. Juan wasn't coming. Something must have gone wrong. He was on his own. For the remainder of the journey, he must be doubly careful.

Nineteen

"*Coño!*" Don Carlos swore and dismounted from his heaving, lathered horse. He and his men had found a narrow canyon to hide in.

The don called to Ignacio, "Who were those men?"

"I believe they were Juan Martínez's men."

"So they know we're following Seguín?"

"*Sí*, Don Carlos, they must know."

"*¡Perdición!* I wanted surprise on my side. What's a good hunt without surprise?"

Ignacio knew better than to answer.

"But Seguín didn't see us?"

"No, *Señor* Don. He just saw our men. I doubt he'll know we're following him. He probably thought we're *banditos.*"

"Martínez knows, and he'll tell him."

Shrugging, Ignacio pointed out, "Martínez has never met us. How would he know?"

The don glanced at him sharply and nodded. "You're right. Where were the women and baby?"

"I don't know, Don Carlos."

"I don't like it. Martínez has more men."

"*Sí, Señor* Don. I think we should hold back and wait until Acapulco. In a city, it's not a question of more men. Planning and surprise is important. Martínez will believe we were *banditos,* left behind."

"You'd better be right," Don Carlos warned him.

Ignacio licked his lips. He didn't like being held responsible. All he cared about was killing Seguín.

"The horses are spent," the don observed. "We'll camp
here and pick up the trail later."

His words were casual, but Ignacio knew they couldn't
fail. If they failed, he wouldn't have his revenge. And he
had waited a long time for it.

The last few days and nights were torture for Seguín.
Gone were the sensual nights and carefree days. After his
close escape, he was constantly on guard. He kept them
to the open spaces, skirting groves of trees and maintain-
ing a swift pace.

He spent his nights awake, with his carbine cradled
across his lap. During the days, he snatched a few minutes
of sleep while they traveled. He hadn't touched Diana
since they entered the forest. Although he knew she shared
his concern, he sensed she missed their time together as
much as he did.

They still found time to talk. Diana kept him company,
every night, for several hours. But the lack of sleep was
beginning to show on her face. Her features appeared
more finely drawn, her ivory skin stretched taut over the
bones of her face. There were dark smudges beneath her
expressive eyes. He hated to think how badly he must look.

He couldn't go on this way much longer. He had to rest,
and so did Diana. He knew of a place that was close by, a
scant day's ride. It was a city of pyramids built by the Ancient Ones. There were hundreds of similar places scattered throughout the country.

This particular city was special because of its location.
Reached only by a tunnel through a cliff wall, it was well
hidden. He hoped he could remember where the entrance
was. An old Indian had shown him the tunnel several years
ago when he had searched for silver in these mountains.

When they had entered the Sierra Madre del Sur, another branch of the Sierra Madre mountains, they left the vast plateau of Oaxaca behind. On the other side of the mountains lay Acapulco. They would reach their destination in a few days . . . if he could get some rest.

The following day he pushed forward, slumped in his saddle. The buzzing in his ears had steadily increased in volume. Today, it sounded deafening. Black dots swam before his eyes. It took an effort of will to stay upright, and he didn't know how much longer he could remain conscious. Shaking his head vigorously, he banished the black dots for a moment. When his vision cleared, he spotted an unusual pillar of pinkish-gray stone at the mouth of a canyon.

Exultation swept him. He remembered that peculiar rock. In the canyon beyond, there should be a wall of limestone, honeycombed with caves. And one of those caves led to the mouth of the tunnel.

Urging his mount forward, he passed the rock pillar. To the north of the canyon's mouth stood the limestone cliff, riddled with caves and holes, just as he had remembered it. Diana and Lydia followed him into the canyon.

"I'm going to find a place that's safe for us to rest." He pointed to the limestone wall. "See that cliff with the caves? There's a tunnel in one of the caves that leads to an ancient, hidden city. We must try to find it." He spurred the black forward. Diana and Lydia fell in behind him.

When they reached the limestone cliff, they dismounted. He instructed them, "The cave is on ground level. It has a drawing of a jaguar etched above the entrance. The figure is faded, but if you look closely, you'll see it."

The women nodded and the three of them split up, working their way slowly through the rocks and under-

brush at the foot of the cliff. It was Diana who called out
excitedly, "Seguín, Lydia, I think I've found it! Come
quick."

They hurried to her side. Pulling back an overhanging
mesquite tree, she pointed and there it was, a carving of
a jungle cat, almost obliterated by age.

Smiling, Seguín kissed her and affirmed, "That's it."

She put her head inside the opening, but he pulled her
back, warning, "Wait, Diana, there might be bats or other
animals inside. Let me make a torch and have a look
around first."

Obediently, she moved aside, and the three of them
searched for wood and tinder. Bending to pick up a stout
stick, he felt suddenly dizzy, and he stumbled forward. Diana caught and steadied him.

"What is it, Seguín? Are you ill?"

Passing a hand over his forehead, he straightened slowly,
waiting for the lightheaded feeling to pass.

"Seguín?"

"I'm fine, just exhausted. That's why I wanted to find
this place. I need to rest, but I want us to be safe. Help
me finish the torch. The sooner we're inside, the sooner
I can rest."

Nodding, she bent to the task. He didn't tell her his
other reason for haste. He had had plenty of time to think
these past few days. What if the bandits in the forest
weren't bandits? What if the men were still following them?
If that were the case, they needed to disappear without
leaving a trace and throw the men off their trail.

She found some rough twine in one of the saddlebags,
and they fashioned a thick torch. If he remembered correctly, the tunnel was twisting and dark, but relatively short.
The torch should last until they emerged on the other
side.

He lit the torch and searched the cave, startling some
bats. They squeaked angrily at having their sleep disturbed.

After they were gone, he motioned to the women to lead the horses inside. At the last moment, Lydia balked.

She stood several meters from the cave, shaking her head slowly. Her eyes were wide with fright. Pepito, who happened to be strapped to her back, must have sensed her distress, because he began to cry.

Diana moved behind Lydia and stroked the baby's cheek, murmuring low, soothing words until he quieted. Then she put her arm around Lydia's shoulders and asked, "What's wrong?"

Crossing herself, Lydia lifted the crucifix at her throat and kissed it. "The cities of the Ancient Ones are cursed. I thought I could go in . . . but . . ."

Squeezing her shoulders, Diana talked to her quietly, trying to soothe her, just as she had calmed the baby. "Lydia, *por favor,* surely the Ancient Ones would not refuse us their hospitality. You mustn't believe in curses. You are a Christian, *sí?*"

Lydia nodded.

"Then nothing can harm you." Although she dropped her voice to a whisper, he couldn't help but overhear, "Lydia, Seguín is exhausted. He'll collapse if he doesn't rest. We have no choice."

Tears glistened in Lydia's warm, brown eyes. Lowering her head, she clenched her crucifix tightly and held it in front of her like a talisman to ward off the evil eye. Glancing sheepishly at Diana, she nodded again.

The tunnel was narrow and twisting and pitch black except for the feeble light of their torch. The passageway smelled of decay and earth. The horses seemed to be as frightened as Lydia, stomping their hooves and tossing their heads, the whites of their eyes gleaming eerily in the torchlight.

It was lucky their journey through the bowels of the earth only lasted for a few minutes. Had it been longer, Seguín feared either Lydia or the horses would have bolted. As it was, they breathed a collective sigh of relief when they stepped into the bright sunlight.

The ancient city loomed on the horizon, perfectly centered in the middle of a verdant valley. Diana broke the hushed silence, her voice filled with awe. "It's . . . it's . . . I've never . . ." Her words trailed off, and she shook her head.

Lydia dropped to her knees and crossed herself again, beseeching the protection of the Virgin of Guadalupe, the patron saint of México.

Seguín shaded his eyes and studied the valley. It appeared to be untouched. He didn't see any paths or recent signs of human habitation. The rich grass swayed in the wind, undisturbed, almost reaching to their waists. He remembered there were spring-fed wells within the city. It looked safe, and he hoped he could rest here.

Diana felt as if her eyes would bulge from her head. She had never seen anything like this city of the Ancient Ones.

They rode through the tall grass for half a mile until Seguín led them to a stone-paved avenue. The avenue lay broken by bushes and tufts of grass growing between the cracks in the pavement. Every few feet, on either side of the roadway, almost obscured by grass and vegetation, lay terraces of stone interlaced by low masonry walls.

As they approached the center of the city, the ruins of stone and mason buildings increased, growing thicker, crowded cheek by jowl. Some ruins were built on platforms and others featured pillars, standing haphazardly, supporting empty air.

When they entered the heart of the city, their mounts' hooves clattered discordantly over the vast cobblestone *plaza*. The noise seemed, to Diana's ears, to desecrate the unearthly silence of this long-deserted place, bouncing off the three enclosed sides of the central square.

To the west of the *plaza* hunched a long, colonnaded building. On the opposite side stood an unusual structure resembling an open-air amphitheater with stone rows of shallow bench seats, facing each other across a rectangular field.

To the north a huge pyramid formed the apex of the square, looming over them. She guessed it to be about two hundred feet tall with narrow steps carved into its face. The top of the pyramid was flat, as if truncated, and crowned by an open-sided stone pavilion.

Her gaze wandered over the strange buildings. Awestruck, the ancient city pulled at her, its allure both potent and mysterious. The very air vibrated as if laden with spirits of the past. She felt strangely drawn to its solitary majesty, but at the same time, a frisson of fear snaked down her spine. Craving to explore the ruins, she felt like an interloper. It was both fascinating . . . and disturbing.

Seguín halted at the northern corner of the long, colonnaded building and dismounted. "We'll camp inside." Turning toward the center of the square, he gestured. "There's a well for water. Inside, are hearths for cooking. This building must have been a palace. It has hundreds of rooms and fronts the square."

His memory proved to be correct, and they moved into one of the large, airy rooms, which contained a hearth. Broken bits of pottery and intact vessels lay strewn on the floor. The room was filthy, covered in layers of grime.

While Seguín unloaded their supplies and cared for the animals, Diana and Lydia drew water, found firewood, and used bushes as makeshift brooms to clear away the worst of the dirt. By the time they finished cleaning and started supper, Seguín had succumbed to exhaustion. He lay sprawled on his blankets in a corner of the room.

* * *

Diana spent a restless night. Lydia begged to sleep with her because she still feared the silent, deserted city. Soothed by Diana's proximity, Lydia fell into a deep sleep. Diana wasn't so fortunate. She lay awake half of the night, her mind filled with questions.

There were mosaics on the walls of the room, done in glazed tile, depicting fantastic creatures, half-human and half-beast. Outside, when she had gathered wood and drawn water, she glimpsed stone carvings on the walls of the buildings and pyramid. The carvings danced before her eyes: contorted humans, bizarre animals, mysterious symbols, and geometric designs. The strange and compelling figures wouldn't leave her mind. They invaded her dreams. What did they mean? And why did they disturb her so?

Not knowing what to think, she wanted to ask Seguín, but he was still sleeping. Evening shadows encroached, and he slept on. Lydia started supper, and she played with Pepito.

Finally, Seguín stirred and lurched up, obviously groggy. Stretching and yawning, he drug his fists through sleep-hooded eyes. "How long did I sleep?"

Placing Pepito on a blanket, Diana rose and went to him.

"All night and all day. It's evening again. You must be hungry. There's stew, but our meat supply is running low. Do you think there might be game in the valley?"

"I'm sure there is. I'll hunt tomorrow." He reached out and cupped her chin in his hand, gazing at her with affection. As he studied her, his tender look disappeared and his brow furrowed. "Diana, what's wrong?" Dropping his hand, he glanced at the baby across the room. "Is Pepito ill?"

"Pepito's fine." She shot a quick look over her shoulder, hoping Lydia couldn't hear them. Whispering as a precaution, she admitted, "It's this place. It's so strange . . . and there's something . . . I can't . . . I want to understand it, but it frightens me."

Catching her wrist, he pulled her into his lap and held her close, murmuring into her hair, "Don't worry, *mi preciosa.*" He kissed her temple. "I know how you feel. Later, after supper, we'll talk. But if *you're* feeling strange, how's Lydia holding up?"

"I slept with her last night so she wouldn't be afraid. She seems fine, now, but I don't know how she will feel when darkness falls."

"Don't worry," he repeated. "Let me take care of you."

His words warmed her, and her heart leapt, thrilled by his offer. It wasn't new, him taking care of her. He had been doing that since she first came to México. But he refused to commit to her, even though she knew he cared. He had never mentioned love, not even in the heat of passion, but his actions had proven his feelings . . . over and over.

If only he would accept the love they shared . . . if only he wanted to spend the rest of his life with her, she would follow him to the ends of the earth. No matter what dangers they might face.

Supper passed peacefully. To Diana, Lydia appeared to have calmed and settled into a routine. Seguín must have wanted to reassure himself, because he asked, "Lydia, are you feeling better about this place?"

She looked up from nursing Pepito. Pursing her lips, she said, "I'm no longer afraid, but there's something here . . . I don't know . . ." Shrugging, she added, "I don't think we should stay long. I feel we aren't wanted."

"I agree with you. It's a place of spirits. We'll stay a few days. Just long enough so I can rest and kill some fresh game."

Later that evening, Lydia settled quietly with Pepito at

her side. When she was snoring softly, Seguín turned to
Diana and took her hand, pulling her to her feet. "Come.
There's something I want to show you."

Hand in hand, they climbed the great pyramid together.
Darkness had fallen, but a full moon rode high in the sky.
The moon turned the worn steps of the pyramid into pools
of silver.

The climb proved arduous, but when they reached the
top Diana was enthralled. Catching her breath, she gazed
at the valley. Like the steps of the pyramid, the moon had
filled the valley with silver, and the ancient buildings appeared to glow with their own incandescence.

They stood together for a long time, transfixed by the
play of light and shadow over the city and valley. They
walked around the perimeter of the pyramid. The city was
even larger than she had thought. It stretched to all four
quadrants of the compass: terraced rubble, fallen walls,
smaller pyramids, pillars holding up air and arches that
led to nowhere.

She squeezed Seguín's hand. "It's lovely, like an image
from a fairy tale. New World castles . . . I wish my father
could have seen this."

"He did."

She turned and stared at him, wondering what he
meant.

"Not these ruins. Other ones, closer to the capitol. His
reaction was similar to yours. He was filled with wonder . . .
and questions. Some day, someone will find the answers,
but for now we only have old Indian tales and some written
accounts from the Spaniards who conquered México."

"Even if we understood how or why these cities were
built and what the carvings mean . . . there's something
here that transcends mere knowledge," Diana observed
quietly. "Something that—"

"Evil."

His face had hardened, and his voice was barely a hiss.

Not certain if she had heard him correctly, she opened her mouth. Before she could form the question he pulled her toward the stone pavilion with one sharp word— "Come."

He led her inside. The pavilion housed a thick slab of stone resting on carved pedestals. The middle of the slab was worn into a curved depression. At the front of the slab stood a stone cistern, sculpted to resemble the most hideous monster she had ever seen.

The air inside the pavilion felt thick, even though it was open to the elements on all aides. She gasped for breath; it was as if the place sucked the very air from her lungs. Her chest rose and fell quickly, her breath coming in labored pants.

"You're in the presence of a great evil, Diana. That's what is frightening about this place."

Her gaze flew to his face. "What do you mean?"

"Human sacrifice. Not a few lives, not a hundred, but thousands upon thousands."

Shuddering, she glanced at him but found no comfort there. It was as if he had purposely removed himself from her. His midnight eyes were opaque, unfathomable, and his features appeared to be chiseled from stone, like the carvings on the side of the pyramid. She forced herself to ask, "Why?"

"It was the Ancient Ones' religion. They believed their gods thirsted for blood . . . human blood."

Shivering again, she clasped his hand tighter.

"That slab was their altar. They would cut the living heart from their sacrificial victims with sacred knives and offer the heart to their gods. The victim's blood filled the cistern." His voice sounded weary when he observed, "There cannot be good in the world without its opposing force . . . evil. The two forces are necessary so man can chose, exercise his free will. Why else would an all-powerful God allow Satan to reign in hell?"

Wrenching her hand from his grasp, she ran blindly to the edge of the pyramid. Tortured images chased themselves through her brain. Why was he telling her these awful things? She covered her face with her hands.

Following her, he tore her hands from her face. "Look at me, Diana. Look at me!" Tracing his high cheekbones with strong fingers, he commanded, "Look at my face, at my black eyes. The blood of the Ancient Ones runs in my veins . . . the blood of these mass murderers. Can you say you love me, knowing this? Knowing the terrible secret of México?"

He turned away from her and whispered, "My mother abandoned me . . . she believed I was evil. Maybe she was right." His voice choked off, and he strode away, retreating to the far side of the pavilion.

Before his words had died away in the heavy air, she understood what he was trying to tell her. He knew she loved him, and he was warning her not to. It was not what she wanted to hear, and her heart went out to him.

How many times had she doubted herself, worried that her father thought she was plain, incapable of finding a husband? But what Seguín had confessed was far worse. The burden he bore went beyond anything she could imagine. Did he truly feel he was evil? A man who could gently care for a baby.

Appalled by the depth of his self-loathing, at the same time she responded to his openness. What had it cost him to admit his fears? Yet, he had possessed the courage to do so. He had wanted to explain himself to her . . . even if his explanation was misguided. Her eyes filled with tears, and she felt closer to him, this very instant, than she had ever felt before, even locked in their most passionate embrace.

He was wrong about himself . . . so wrong. He was right about only one thing: she did love him. She didn't care what blood ran in his veins. She loved him the way he was, with all his dark moments and demanding ways. Nothing else mattered . . . and she must convince him.

Rushing to his side, she threw her arms around him and buried her face in the muscled hardness of his back.

"Seguín, you can't carry the burden of what your ancestors did. History is full of killing, killing by all races of man. In the States, we're exterminating the Indians. My father believed that by the end of this century the Indians will all be dead, and it's not because our religion demands it. On the contrary. If we were really Christians, we wouldn't allow it. But we do so because of greed . . . ugly greed for the Indians' land, their game, and their gold. What you said is true—evil *is* in the world as a counter force to good."

Pausing for breath, she could feel her heart thudding in her chest. "We're not responsible for all of mankind. Each one of us must be responsible for our own actions . . . and none of us is without blemish."

He finally turned to face her, his black eyes glittering with some unreadable emotion. "I forgot how educated and intelligent you are, Diana. I shouldn't have entered into a philosophical discussion with you."

"Philosophy be damned, Seguín," she said with heat. "But you were right about one thing. I love you . . . just as you are."

His mouth crashed down upon hers. His kiss wasn't gentle; it was hungry and demanding. His tongue pressed with desperate urgency against her lips, and she opened readily, welcoming its hot thrust. The stroke of his tongue filled her mouth completely, awakening her senses, starting the blood pounding in her veins, and reminding her how long it had been since they made love.

Holding her in a fierce embrace, his hands clasped her buttocks. She pressed closer to him, glorying in the hard, throbbing shaft of his manhood against her abdomen. Groaning, he released her long enough to tear open her blouse. The cool night air touched her heated skin, and she arched her chest, offering her naked breasts to him in wanton abandonment.

He didn't accept her invitation. Instead, he scooped her into his arms and strode to the altar. Draping her across it, he growled, "Do you really love me, Diana? Can you love me when I'm like this? Harsh and raw?" He traced one exposed breast, kneading the taut nipple with his calloused thumb. "Will you allow me to worship you in primitive splendor? The moon is full, and you are Diana, the moon goddess. *Si?*"

His words and touch enflamed her. The ache inside of her spiraled, hot and mindless. The need expanding, begging for release, pleading for surcease.

As she stared up at him, he changed before her eyes. Gone was the Seguín she knew, replaced by a bronzed warrior clothed only in dazzling feathers. It was a dream . . . it was magic. Lifting her arms to him, she saw the silver snake slither down her arm, burning her skin.

Undressing her quickly, he flung his own clothes to the side. She lay naked, crossways on the cold, hard slab with her legs dangling over the side. Her most intimate female self was on display for his hungry eyes and hands. She reveled in the wild, primeval rite of being worshipped as a goddess, offering herself on the altar of their passion.

Kneeling down, he fulfilled his harsh promise, covering every inch of her body slowly, with reverence. His lips, his tongue, and fingertips traced erotic patterns on her heated flesh, seeking her most secret, sensitive places. His touch scorched her, sending molten waves of pleasure-pain racing along her veins.

And when he worshipped at the dewy gates of her womanhood, she heard the first wild strains of music.

It wafted to her on the breeze playing over her body. The haunting notes of a primitive flute, the tinkle of thousand-tongued bells, and the rasping rattle of a gourd, underlain with the pounding throb of a drum. The flute pulled her upward, its spiraling notes carrying her on a whirlwind of desire. The tinkle of the bells vibrated along her nerves, intensifying the sensation of his caresses. The rattle grated against her skin, and she writhed in mindless, forbidden need. The drum echoed the pounding of her heart, the throbbing of her blood.

Was it spirit music, or the music of her own body?

The haunting, pulsing melody rose and fell, mounted and ebbed. But with each swell it built and built . . . until it reached a crescendo, rushing over her . . . crashing in waves and waves of ecstasy.

And then she felt the surging, white-hot hardness of him—the essence of his maleness filling her to bursting. Like a stallion . . . like a supplicant . . . he filled her greedy, empty femaleness. They were complete together . . . two beings made whole.

The music died away, leaving a lingering vibration in the air. She raked her fingers through his long, sable mane and drew him closer. She didn't want the music to leave them. She clung to it fiercely in her mind, her heart, and her soul. But it drifted away . . . swallowed by the vastness of the ancient city.

After a few days, they left the city behind. Seguín had rested and hunted for fresh meat. Diana and he had reveled in their sensuality, giving full rein to their passions. She loved him, and he realized he loved her in return.

Unfortunately, it wasn't enough. He couldn't forget . . . or forgive what his mother had done to him. It was easy to love when there were no challenges, no disappointments. As brutally as possible, he had tried to explain his fears to her. He couldn't face losing her love if he didn't always measure up to her expectations. And he didn't know if he were capable of sustaining the kind of gentle, thoughtful love needed for a marriage.

Now, while their passions were at a feverish pitch, he wanted her beside him. But what would happen when the flame died down? Would she be willing to ignore his inevitable failures and continue to love him?

If his mother couldn't love him, how could anyone else? He had loved and trusted completely once, with the innocence of youth. And when that love had been wrenched from him, it almost destroyed him.

He couldn't survive such a loss again.

When Seguín announced they would reach Acapulco the next day, Diana asked him to find a stream so she and Lydia could bathe and tidy their appearances. Complying with her request, he found a gurgling brook with a deep green pool, curtained by trailing willows.

Diana and Lydia took turns bathing, and Diana wanted to give Pepito a bath, too before the light was completely gone. She had just undressed the baby when Seguín approached them, the ever-present carbine cradled in his arms. Handing a clean napkin to her, he said, "Here. Lydia sent me with this. She said you forgot it."

Glancing at her supplies, she realized Lydia was right. She had forgotten a fresh napkin for the baby. "Thank you. I was just starting his bath. Would you care to watch?"

Propping his carbine against a rock, he surprised her by replying, "No, I'd like to bathe him myself. I welcome any help you can give me."

"That's fine with me, but you should roll up your pants and shirtsleeves. Pepito takes his baths seriously." She smiled, warning, "He loves to splash."

Nodding, he rolled his pants to his knees. Stripping off his shirt, he winked at her. "Can't be too careful."

She handed him the squirming, naked infant and found

a flat stone on the bank where she could sit and watch. Kneeling, he placed Pepito in a shallow pool of water.

With a lump in her throat, she watched the rippling play of his muscles across his chest and flat stomach. The setting sun tinted his skin bronze, skin she had explored and tasted, inch by inch. Her throat went dry, and she felt her heart pound, just thinking of their intimate times together. The wet essence of her desire slicked the insides of her thighs.

Embarrassed by the power he held over her body, she shifted uncomfortably on the hard rock and focused her attention on the baby's antics. Just as she had predicted, Pepito splashed and crowed with delight. Seguín managed to wash his pudgy body without mishap, but when it came time to rinse his soapy hair he turned to her with a bewildered expression on his face.

Laughing at his perplexed expression, she held out her canteen. "Here, use this. Pour it over his head slowly. I warn you, though, he won't like it."

Accepting the canteen, he poured it over the baby's head but as soon as the water touched him, Pepito let out a yell that could have been heard in Acapulco.

"Come on, Pepito, you're a big *hombre*. It's just a little water. Don't cry," he coaxed. The baby's yells pitched higher as Seguín sluiced water over his head.

She stood up and handed him a clean cloth. He lifted Pepito from the water and began drying him. Once Pepito was out of the water, he stopped screaming. Seguín waded to shore with the baby in his arms, muttering something under his breath that sounded suspiciously like, "It would be easier to just dunk him."

Hiding her grin, she offered sweetly, "You should have tried to bathe him when he couldn't sit up. Since we've been traveling, there hasn't been a handy basin."

"Why does he bawl like that? It's just water."

"Because, *Papá*, no baby likes water in his face. Sarah

will have her hands full when she gets him properly christened in the States."

"Diana, about the States . . . I . . . ah . . ."

Her heart leapt to her throat, and an uncontrollable trembling seized her. Was he going to make her dreams come true, and ask her to remain with him? She held her breath, silently urging him to say the long-awaited words.

A loud, rude noise interrupted her thoughts, and Pepito grunted, his face turning red with the effort. A familiar, pungent smell filled the air. Seguín looked down at the baby, chagrin stamped on his handsome features.

Disappointed by the untimely interruption, Diana decided to rescue him. She didn't want the baby's unfortunate accident to distract Seguín. Holding out her arms, she offered, "Give Pepito to me, I'll take care of him."

"No, that's all right." Gazing at the baby, he wagged his head and chided, "Indiscreet choice of time, old man, just after your bath. Now, I've got to clean you up again. But I promise, no water on the head . . . just the other end." Crossing his eyes, he made a face.

Pepito chortled at his antics, and Diana laughed until her sides ached. Gasping for breath, she managed, "Are you certain you don't want me to—?"

"Certainly not. I distinctly remember your saying that the next time it would be my turn. Correct?"

"Correct." She handed the clean napkin to him with a flourish.

Lowering Pepito to the blanket, he made a passable effort at cleaning the baby's bottom. Next he struggled with the napkin, and with some help from Diana he managed to get it in place. Obviously gratified by his accomplishment, he washed his hands in the stream and crowed, "I did it. Nothing to it."

Kissing him on the cheek, she congratulated, "I'm proud of you."

He grinned broadly.

She took a deep breath. Tomorrow, they would reach Acapulco. There was no time left. She had never thought she would be so willing to sacrifice her pride, but her love for him was stronger . . . far stronger than pride. It was now or never. She had waited for him, hoping he would ask her to stay, but he hadn't.

Hesitantly, she began, "Seguín, you were saying earlier . . . about the States?"

Shrugging into his shirt, he buttoned it and rolled down his pants legs. "*Sí*, I was wondering."

"Yes."

Straightening, he clasped her shoulders. "Diana, I'll never forget you or Pepito." He pulled her close and tucked her head beneath his chin. "You'll always remain in México with me . . . in my heart."

His words, caring and heartfelt as they might be, weren't what she wanted to hear. Instead of consoling her, they pierced like daggers, killing her last hope. Anger and hurt battled in her chest, and she pulled free of his embrace. Tears burned at the back of her eyes. He cared about her, but not enough to ask her to stay. She swallowed and willed the tears back.

Glancing down to check on Pepito, she watched with half of her mind as he happily scooted across the blanket into the dirt, getting grimy all over again. Stooping down, she picked him up. Hugging the child tightly, she felt tears start, and this time she couldn't stop them. Like a rainstorm in the desert, they roared and spilled, surprising her with their elemental force.

He reached his hand toward her.

She retreated. "Don't."

Pepito started to whimper, and he beseeched her, "Diana, I—"

"Don't," she repeated. "You don't want me, although I'm yours—body, heart and soul. But that's not enough."

She shook her head sadly, trembling inwardly. "I want us to have our own family."

His eyes touched her, filled with an ugly anguish. "Diana, I can't. I told you in the ancient city, I can't love like you want me to. I'm—"

"Evil," she finished for him.

"I don't know." He dragged his fingers through his hair. "Evil or . . . lacking. My mother loved me, but when I failed . . . or she thought I failed . . . she turned her back on me. What if I disappoint you, Diana? I couldn't bear—"

"I'm not your mother, Seguín."

"No, but—"

"I'm a woman, so I can't be trusted. That's it, isn't it?"

He lowered his eyes and stared at the ground.

There was nothing left to say. She felt as if the very breath in her lungs had been squeezed from her body, making her pant for air. And her heart . . . her heart felt like a raisin inside of her chest . . . shriveled and dry.

He had refused her love.

There was nothing left to say.

Twenty

The following day Diana kept James strapped to her back and avoided Seguín. Putting Lydia between them, she purposely ignored him.

The hours dragged by while they continued to plod through the rugged desert mountains of the Sierra del Sur. The sun was dropping swiftly in the western sky when they struggled up a steep mountain. Pausing on the brink of a precipice, she gazed down and saw the Pacific Ocean spread before her.

Below, was the perfect harbor of Acapulco, shaped like an open mouth and protected on three sides by land. To the north, on a curving peninsula, sprawled the town, clustered around the port's fort, Fuerte de San Diego. The remainder of the town sprawled haphazardly, some buildings hugging the shoreline while others clung, like mountain goats, to the sheer cliffs surrounding the harbor.

An indefinable feeling skittered along her nerves, and she glanced up to find Seguín watching her. "It's beautiful, isn't it?" His words were hushed, almost reverent, as if he spoke only to himself.

Choosing to ignore his observation about the scenery, she countered, "How do we get down to the town?"

"*Vengase.* I will show you."

After a dusty and treacherous descent, they entered the bustling port. It was twilight and growing dark fast, but she

noticed there were a number of tall-masted schooners an-
chored in the harbor. One of the ships would carry her
to California.

They found a *posada* on a quiet side street away from
the clamor of the waterfront. It was a low, rambling white
stucco building with crimson-flowered bougainvillea climbing its unadorned walls. When they dismounted, a stable
lad ran up to take their tired mounts. Seguín inquired,
"Are there rooms available?"

The boy bobbed his head and answered, *"Sí, señor."*

"Bueno. See that our horses are rubbed down and fed
an extra ration of grain." He smiled at the boy and tossed
him a coin.

The boy caught it and returned his smile. *"Muchas gracias, señor."*

"De nada."

Wincing inwardly at the innocent byplay between him
and the boy, Diana knew Seguín would make a good father.
If only he could believe in himself. If only he would realize
he was capable of love. She shook her head. He didn't
believe in himself, and he would probably go to his grave
distrusting women.

When he returned with their rooms, she was surprised
to find she had a room to herself, next door to Lydia and
the baby. He made light of the extra room, saying the
posada had plenty of them, but she guessed the real reason
for her separate room.

He planned to come to her during the night.

And heaven help her, she didn't know if she would have
the strength to turn him away.

Seguín knocked on Diana's door, and she called out,
"Enter."

As he stepped inside, the breath caught in Seguín's
throat. Diana was dressed in a high-necked cotton

nightshift, worn thin by many washings. Her sleek curves were outlined perfectly against the lamp's light. The half-hidden beauty of her form was more provocative than if she had been naked. He remembered vividly every satiny hollow and rounded firmness.

And her hair was loose down her back. He had interrupted her while she was brushing it, with her arm raised as if suspended in time. The lift of her arm pulled the worn fabric tight across one nipple. He watched as her nipple responded to his gaze, hardening and straining against the cloth.

His loins ached in answer.

She dropped her arm and placed the brush on the table beside the bed. Facing him, her hair drifted around her like an angel's dream of spun glory, tendrils of molten gold. *Mi rubia,* he thought. Would he ever be able to erase her from his body and soul?

Forcing himself to look into her eyes, he knew he was lost if he continued to gaze at her beguiling body and the sunshine of her hair. His eyes locked with hers. Her wide hazel eyes. The golden glints echoing the color of her hair. The green depths softened by the shadings of brown.

He would never forget her eyes. He had never seen eyes like hers before, which changed color with each of her moods: soft hazel when she was calm, blue tints dominated when she was happy, golden flecks crackling in anger and deep green when she was aroused. . . .

Por Dios, she was tearing him apart. He couldn't even look at her. Best to say farewell and leave, but first, he had to speak. "Diana, I know I've been low sometimes . . . that you think I don't care. I can't ask you to stay because I . . ." He was struggling to tell her good-bye without hurting her again. It was an impossible task. "You'll meet someone in the States that can give you—"

"No!" The word sounded as if it had been ripped from the depths of her soul. Shaking her head, her breath came in quick pants. "Don't say that to me! I don't want anyone else . . . only *you*." Tears sparkled like crystal on her tawny lashes.

And then she did something that stunned him.

She held her arms out to him.

Covering the space between them in two strides, he clasped her in his arms. He buried his face in the glorious, golden splendor of her hair.

They were both trembling.

Sweeping her into his arms, he carried her to bed and eased her gently against the pillows. He cursed himself silently as he stripped off his clothes. He was a coward. He was a user—to take this gift of hers again, when he knew he would leave her . . .

But he had always known he would leave her . . . hadn't he? And it hadn't stopped him before. Tonight was different. The reckoning was at hand. Could he really leave her?

He didn't know.

His body was on fire for her, with a craving that stopped his heart and stilled the breath in his lungs. It was all consuming, with a life of its own. His only relief was in the sweet surcease of her body.

Naked and with his manhood throbbing, he lowered himself beside her. His mouth covered hers greedily, forcing her lips open. He thrust his tongue inside the warm, honeyed essence of her mouth and rubbed his tongue along hers, swirling and eddying, thrusting and tasting.

And she opened to him, meeting each foray of his tongue with sensuous sweetness. He remembered the first time he had kissed her. She had opened for him then, too, even in the blush of her pristine innocence.

Tonight seemed to be a night for memories—memories he would cherish forever because they were all he would have.

Unfastening the row of tiny buttons at her neck, he slid the gown off her shoulders, exposing her blue-veined, high tilted breasts. So beautiful and responsive, each one filled his hand perfectly, their coral points leaping to attention and pouting for his hands.

That first night that he had loved her, she had been shy and embarrassed. Uncomfortable with her body, she had pulled away from him. But not now . . . now she arched into his touch. Her hands twined in his hair, worrying the cord loose, drawing him closer.

Diana then . . . Diana now. Each image imprinted indelibly on his mind.

His hands smoothed her nightgown down and down, until it was a tangled mass at her ankles. Rearing above her, he drew the velvety-hard tip of her nipple into his mouth. He laved the strutted point with gentle strokes, reveling in the soft pleated surface of its aureola. With a groan, he fastened onto her breast and began a tender sucking, tasting the sweet juices of her body.

She lurched up and grasped his shoulders, shuddering under him and moving her hips in the age-old rhythm. One slender hand drifted down and found his manhood. Her fingers whispered over him, stroking and caressing, drawing shudders from him.

He remembered that primeval night on the heathen altar . . . of intimate, wanton pleasures given and taken. *Por Dios,* could he stop remembering?

Did he want to?

Trailing kisses across one breast, he moved his attention to her other breast, licking and sucking. His fingers splayed over the hollow of her abdomen, circling and soothing. Promising her pleasure.

His mouth followed his hands, worshipping the beautiful, taut lines of her body. Abrading tongue against satiny flesh, he lingered at the deep cleft of her navel, exploring and licking while his hands skimmed the perfect musculature of her calves and stroked the sensitive flesh behind her knees.

When he lowered himself over her, she reached up to toy with the paps of his nipples. Her fingers combed through the hair on his chest. He remembered the first time she had touched him like that, high in the mountains, with the thunder of the waterfall in the distance.

The memories crowded around him—All of them glorious, all of them unforgettable, all of them cherished . . . but not more than tonight. Tonight he would remember each soft sigh, every touch of her skin against his, splendor upon splendor, time seeping away that would never be captured again.

His mouth strayed further, and he spread the petal-like folds of her. Cupping her buttocks in his hands, he lifted her to his mouth, laving her with his tongue until the hard bud of her desire took form, shaped and aroused by the tender adhesion of his mouth.

Pulling the essence of her between his lips, he sucked and played, titillated and licked. Her fingernails scored his shoulders, and her head thrashed from side to side. Gasping, she cried out, "Yes! Oh yes, please . . . Seguín."

With the first shuddering spirals of her release, he rose above her and in one sure stroke entered her. Her white-hot center burned him, and her powerful contractions pushed him over the edge. Like a boy with his first woman, he came with her, within seconds of entering.

It was the first time for him . . . and the last.

His mouth covered hers, skimming her lips, worshipping their rose softness, gentling her, soothing her. She sighed into his mouth, and her eyelids drifted down. Within moments, she nestled her head into his shoulder and fell asleep. She trusted him implicitly, falling asleep in his arms. Why couldn't he return the same trust?

He held her for a long time . . . remembering everything: their fights, their tentative attempts at friendship, their bond of love for Pepito, their passionate lovemaking.

Could he exist for the rest of his life on memories?

When he was near her, he could think of only her. She filled his senses, stealing his reason. Rolling to the side of the bed, he retrieved his pants and pulled them on. Covering her nakedness with the sheet, he retreated from the island of their intimacy.

Lifting a slat-back chair, he placed it by the window. Throwing open the shutter, he leaned out, gulping the salty air. He turned down the lamp and sat in darkness.

His mind went over all the old arguments . . . circles within circles.

The scratch and flare of a match awakened Diana. Reaching out her hand, she touched the bed beside her. It was empty, and she wondered if Seguín had left her. How long had she slept?

Then she saw the bright ember of his cheroot. He was sitting at the window. A faint light illuminated him. It must be almost dawn. The sky silhouetted his profile with the luminous quality of first light, and she heard a cock crow in the distance.

She had never seen him smoke before. She wondered why he had left her to smoke by the window. Her fingertips trailed over the sheets. They were cool to the touch. He must have been gone from her bed for a long time.

Studying him from beneath half-closed eyelids, she noticed that his long, sable hair was loose, spread across his broad shoulders. Smiling to herself, she realized she was the one who had freed it, worrying loose his carefully clubbed hair. She thought it made him look very handsome . . . and half-wild.

Her gaze drifted over the planes of his face. Noticing the worried pleat between his brows, her stomach clenched. She knew and feared that look. She had hoped last night would have convinced him of their mutual love, although she had been careful to not speak of it. Watching him, all of her earlier doubts returned.

He was going to send her away.

Drawing deeply on the cheroot, smoke streamers trailed from his nostrils. Half turning, he flicked the stub out the window. He rose to his feet and appeared to be searching for his shirt. Rage boiled through her. Would he sneak from her bedroom without a farewell? How dare he?

Bolting upright in bed, she clutched the sheet around her naked bosom. Her voice broke the silence. "Light the lamp so you can see to dress."

Lifting his head at the sound of her words, he fumbled for the tinder box but didn't reply. Striking a match, he lit the bedside lamp. Its soft glow mingled with the pearly light from the window.

Her gaze followed him while he found his shirt and pulled on his boots. Watching him, she felt as if a wild bird were trapped inside of her, slowing tearing her apart with steel-edged talons.

When he had finished dressing, he gazed at her. His eyes reminded her of the old Seguín. They were hooded, unfathomable. He reached behind his head and tied his hair with a leather thong.

The silence stretched between them like a thin wire, ready to snap at any moment. She wanted to scream, to beg, to cry, to throw herself at his feet. But she did none of those things.

His words, when they finally came, were stilted. "I'll find a ship for you. Do you want to wire your mother or the Yorks?"

She shrugged. The sheet rustled. "Does it matter?"

"No, I just wondered—"

"Making idle conversation to cover your departure?"

"Diana, I—"

"Please, spare me."

His eyes glittered with unspoken anger at her brittle

words. And something else lived, for a brief second only, in the depths of his gaze. It looked like pain.

As he turned his face away, his voice sounded harsh. "I won't bother you again, except to make the necessary arrangements and see you off."

This was it.

A tremor passed through her. He was walking out of her life without a backward glance. How could he do this to her?

She bit her lip savagely to keep from crying out. The metallic, salty taste of her own blood filled her mouth. Despite her inner resolve, she found herself blurting, "I'll be in San Francisco. You know that." As soon as the words left her mouth, she hated herself for speaking, telling him where she could be found . . . it was a form of begging, of clinging to him.

He wouldn't come for her.

"Thank you for the information. When James is older, I might want to write him. With your permission, of course."

"Sarah's permission, you mean." Her voice sounded strained, even to her own ears.

Why was he acting like a stranger? Did it make the pain less for him? she thought angrily.

She had never believed she could stand such agony, the fierce shredding of every hope and every ounce of love within her heart. Savage anguish screamed along her nerves. It was all she could do to lie quietly. Silently, she willed him to leave, praying the hurt would lessen when he was gone.

One vein throbbed visibly in his forehead. This was as difficult for him as it was for her, she realized. She felt his anguish like her own. How was he able to move her so? When he was ready to walk out of life and she should hate him, how could she feel such tenderness and sorrow for him?

He placed his hand on the latch of the door.

"No!" she shrieked.

Whirling around, he instinctively reached for the gun on his hip.

Jumping from the bed, she wrapped the sheet around her naked body, tucking it, toga fashion, under her arms. His eyes followed her frantic movements, and his brow creased with concern.

They faced each other across the foot of the bed. It was a moment frozen in time. A pause pregnant with possibilities.

Relinquishing every last shred of pride, she held her arms out to him, just as she had done the night before. But this was different. Last night, she had been silently pleading for his love. This time, she was begging for his very soul.

"Please, please, Seguín. I don't want to say anything about your mother, but maybe she was misguided and died before she . . . understood. Can't you forgive her? Must you throw your whole life away, unwilling to trust and love? I know you're not perfect, and I accept you for what you are. I won't fail you, Seguín, even if you disappoint me. Can't you trust me a little?" Her throat closed, and she felt as if she were choking. "Whether you walk out that door now or we live together for a lifetime, I'll never stop loving you. Please, Seguín."

He stood as still as a statue. Lifting his eyes from her face, he stared intently at the space above her head. Confusion suffused his features, and she understood the silent battle he waged within himself.

The door rattled. She glanced at him, wondering if it were Lydia. Was Pepito ill?

Crossing to the door, he pulled it open. Gilberto rushed in, out of breath and gasping, "Seguín, you must get away. There are men outside the *posada*. My father's men.

Stunned by Gilberto's sudden appearance, Diana clutched the sheet tighter and retreated to the bed.

"How did you find us?" Seguín asked.

"I escaped from my father's men and went to Sarah in San Francisco. She had Diana's letter, saying you were coming to Acapulco."

"And you sailed here?"

"*Sí*, I had to return, both for myself as well as for you."

"But we haven't—"

"Been close. I know you were wronged, Seguín. I should have done something sooner, but I feared my father's wrath. I was weak. Loving Sarah has taught me that." Tentatively, he stretched his hand to Seguín, pleading, "Forgive me. I need your forgiveness and love, especially after what you did for my wife."

Accepting his brother's hand, he shook it. "It was nothing. You would have done the same."

"Now, maybe. Before, no." Gilberto's gaze raked Diana. "I see you've found love, too. That's good." He slapped Seguín on the back, offering, "We'll be brothers twice. Sarah and I will be married again in the church. Let's make it a double wedding."

Trembling, she waited for Seguín's answer, all her hopes suddenly revived, but Seguín ignored Gilberto's offer, asking instead, "How did you find us?"

"Herbert York came with me. Since we arrived, we took turns each night, asking for you at the *posadas*. Tonight was my turn."

"Where's Sarah?" Diana couldn't keep from asking. "And my mother and Mary York?"

Gilberto turned to her and smiled. "Sarah is with us. She wouldn't stay behind. *Señoras* York and McFarland remained in California. For now, Sarah is with her father, but I know she wants to see you and the baby." As if the thought had just occurred to him, he asked, "Where is the baby?"

"Next door, with his wet nurse, Lydia," she replied.

"*Bueno*. But we must make haste." His easy demeanor changed in the blink of an eye. She remembered his warning when he burst into the room. They were in danger. "Get Lydia and the baby," he directed, sounding like someone she knew. "Diana, you'll need to get dressed. We'll step into the hallway while—"

The door flew open.

Her worst nightmare stood on the threshold. It was the scar-faced man, the one Seguín had identified as Ignacio Hernández.

Four other men rushed into the room. One of them was missing a nose.

Ignacio barked orders. "Get their weapons and tie their hands." Seguín had his gun halfway out of the holster, but the no-nose man grabbed his arm, and thrust his gun in Seguín's face. They searched Gilberto, but all he carried was a thin stiletto, tucked inside his boot.

Satisfied that they had stripped Seguín and Gilberto of their weapons, Ignacio's men tied their hands. Ignacio called over his shoulder, "Do you have the other woman and baby?"

"*Sí*, Ignacio," a voice responded from the hallway.

Diana's heart felt as if it had stopped. Don Carlos's men were in command. They had Lydia and the baby. Seguín and Gilberto were powerless. How could she send word to Mr. York? It was their only chance, but Gilberto hadn't mentioned where they were staying. Couldn't Gilberto help them? After all, these were his father's men. Wouldn't Don Carlos listen to his only son?

The hairs at the nape of her neck stood on end. Glancing up, she found Ignacio's malevolent gaze trained on her. "Get dressed, *puta*, while we watch. You and the other woman will pleasure us later. You'll be well used." He glanced at Seguín and Gilberto. "It would seem you've already used her."

Seguín snarled, a primitive howl torn from the depths of his throat as he tried to tackle Ignacio. With his hands tied, it was easy for the other men to overwhelm him and throw him to the floor.

Ignacio stared down at him, landing one quick kick to his midsection. Seguín groaned. "I'll deal with you later," Ignacio promised, "after Don Carlos is through with you. You'll pay for what you did to my sister."

Spitting on Seguín for final emphasis, he raised his head and called out to the men in the hallway, "Don Carlos doesn't want the baby harmed."

Turning back to Diana, he ordered, "Get dressed."

Rage, combined with terror, erupted within her. She would rather be dead than submit. Raising her hands, she rushed him, wanting to scratch his eyes out.

Something heavy struck her head. Black dots swarmed before her eyes, closing around her . . . sucking her down.

Twenty-one

Don Carlos looked the same, Seguín thought. Perhaps some extra flesh around his middle and few more lines in his face, he assessed. That was his stepfather's outward appearance. But inside, if anything, he had become harder and more . . . evil.

This is what happens when you let your guard down, Seguín silently cursed himself. If he hadn't been focused on Diana, he wouldn't have allowed it to happen. Now, all their lives, with the possible exception of Gilberto and the child, were in jeopardy. He would need to keep his head, see what Don Carlos wanted. Maybe there was a way to save the women.

Glancing around the room, he realized they had been taken to the private parlor of the *posada*. Along with himself and Gilberto, there was just his stepfather and Ignacio in the room. Some of the men had taken away the women and baby. Others stood guard outside the door.

"So, we meet again, Seguín." His stepfather sketched a mock bow.

"What's the meaning of this, Don Carlos? You have no right to take me prisoner."

"Haven't I? There's the matter of the formula you're using to ruin me."

"You can have the formula. Just let the women and baby go," he offered. He had heard Ignacio's instruction to keep the baby safe, and didn't understand it. Not certain of what it meant, and knowing how much Pepito meant to Sarah and Diana, he was willing to plead for the baby's freedom, too.

The don waved his hand in a dismissive gesture. "Ignacio has already obtained the formula. You can't use it to negotiate. Even your workers aren't above taking bribes if the money is good enough."

"Then what do you want?" Seguín asked.

"My grandson, for one thing." Turning to Gilberto, he commented, "Finally got caught with your pants down, eh, *mi hijo*? Now I know why you were so desperate to marry the *gringa*."

"But the baby's not—" Gilberto started to explain.

Seguín kicked his shin and shot him a pointed glance, hoping his half-brother would take the hint. Let Don Carlos think the child was his grandson if it would keep the baby safe.

Gilberto understood, and he closed his mouth.

"The baby's not what, *mi hijo*?"

"Not old enough to be taken from his wet nurse," Gilberto improvised. Relief flooded Seguín at his quick thinking.

"That's one of the things that bothers me," the don confessed. "When I learned Seguín was helping two women, I thought one of them would be the *gringa* you married. But instead, we find another *Yanquí* whore, and this one belongs to Seguín." His gaze bored into his son. "Where's your so-called wife?"

"In California with her parents. The baby was left behind when they fled the country."

"Not much of a mother," he snorted contemptuously. "Good riddance. I have you and my grandson. The *gringa* would have been a problem. Now you're free to marry María, and you've already started a family. Very fortunate,

indeed," he observed, obviously pleased. But as quickly as
a viper strikes, his demeanor changed.

Pointing a finger at Gilberto, he hissed, "I understand
your noble efforts to return to México to rescue your son.
But you still disobeyed me. You will answer for it. Ignacio,
find Gilberto a seat. I'll deal with him later."

Obeying the order, Ignacio roughly pushed Gilberto
into a chair. "The wet nurse can remain with my grandson
until her usefulness is at an end," he directed. "See to it,
Ignacio."

"*Sí*, Señor Don."

Revolving slowly to face Seguín again, Don Carlos said,
"The other woman is nothing to me. The men will have
sport with her, and she will die or be sold to a brothel. As
for you, dear stepson, I will turn you over to the graces of
Ignacio. He's wanted to kill you for a long time. Not here,
of course. It's too public."

Realizing his stepfather wanted him to grovel and beg
for his life, he refused to give him the satisfaction. But for
Diana's life he was willing to do anything. "If you allow
Ignacio to kill me, what will you gain?"

"Nothing, but I'm tired of your meddling. I know you
tried to help Gilberto's *gringa* wife. I don't know why, but
you interfered where you shouldn't have. And you tried
to ruin me, too. You're nothing to me but a thorn in my
side. Ignacio has been my faithful servant. He deserves his
revenge."

"I'm a very wealthy man, Don Carlos."

"*Sí*. You've the luck of the devil."

"If I die, Juan gets all the money. But if you let the other
woman go, I'll give you a bank draft for whatever you ask.
Think it over."

Although his heart thundered in his chest, he tried to
remain outwardly calm. He couldn't let his stepfather
know how much Diana meant to him. The don was evil
enough to have her raped and slain before his eyes, to

torture him. His only hope was that his stepfather's greed would get the better of him.

Don Carlos narrowed his eyes. "How would you know she was safe?"

"Put her on a ship and let me watch it sail. Then turn me over to Ignacio."

"Father, you can't mean what you're saying," Gilberto interrupted, rising to his feet. "Seguín and Diana have done nothing to you."

Ignacio shoved him back into the chair.

Red-faced, Gilberto struggled to his feet again, hampered by his bound hands. "And you've no reason for revenge against Seguín, either, Ignacio."

"He got my sister, Esmeralda, pregnant. Then he refused to marry her, thinking he was too good for her. She hung herself," he spat. "That's reason enough."

"Oh, but you're wrong, Ignacio. I may have been a child then, but children see and hear a lot of things their elders don't realize." Gilberto's gaze snagged his father's. "For instance, our mother never cut Seguín from her will, did she, Father?" He didn't wait for an answer, plowing relentlessly ahead.

"I didn't understand everything then, but later when I was older, I put two and two together. I remember the shyster lawyer who came to the house after mother died. You had him alter her will, didn't you?"

"For you, my son," Don Carlos thundered, "So you would inherit everything. And this is the way you repay me, whelp!" Striding to Gilberto, he backhanded him viciously across the mouth.

Reeling under the blow, Gilberto turned to his half-brother. "I'm sorry, Seguín. I should have told you my suspicions sooner, but you left and I went to school in Europe. I knew I couldn't prove anything, and I was . . . a coward and greedy. I beg your forgiveness."

"Our mother didn't disinherit me?" He knew his voice

sounded strange. The truth was almost too much to take in. He had lived his life based on a lie. He had been willing to give up Diana because of what his mother had done. Diana—where was she now? He had to save her. He would give anything to save her.

"*Mamá* knew the truth. I don't know how she found out, but she knew the truth in the end. Then she became sick and died." Gilberto raised his head and glowered at his father. "I never wanted to face it before, but you killed her, didn't you? To cover your own evil deeds."

Palms out in supplication, Don Carlos retreated, his voice turning to a whine, "Don't say that *mi hijo,* it's not true. I altered the will, but I loved your mother. I didn't kill her. She miscarried and contracted a fever. You must believe me."

"Maybe you didn't do it purposely, but when she found out the truth it hurt her so much she didn't care to live. She gave up, my dear *Papá,* not wanting to face what you had done. Not wanting to face what you were doing to Seguín to cover your tracks," he accused.

"What truth?" Seguín asked.

Ignoring his brother's question, Gilberto faced Ignacio. "Esmeralda was pregnant with Don Carlos's baby. My father used Seguín as the scapegoat, making Esmeralda lie about who the father was. When she realized her lies hadn't worked, the shame overwhelmed her. If she confronted my father, he would turn you both out. And you, Ignacio, would have been forced to provide for her and the baby. To save you and to hide her shame, she killed herself."

Ignacio's face had turned an alarming shade of purple. "You can prove this?"

"She left a note for you, but you never found it. As a curious boy, I read the note and replaced it. It's in the bottom of her jewelry chest that you've always kept."

Facing Don Carlos, Ignacio grated out, "Is this true?"

"What if it is?" The don shrugged and adopted his most imperious tone. "I'm your *patrón*. I took you and your sister off the streets. You would have starved if it hadn't been for me. She owed me . . . you both owed me. I tried to obtain her a suitable husband, but my stepson refused to cooperate. I would have found her someone else, but she was young and scared. How could I know she would hang herself?"

"All these years, you let me believe . . ." Touching the scar on his face, Ignacio hissed, "I got this doing your dirty work. And all the time, it was you!" Unsheathing his knife, he advanced upon Don Carlos.

"You crazy *bastardo*, put that knife away. You hear me?" Retreating behind a table, he drew his pistol, warning, "Take another step, and I'll shoot."

Ignacio's features contorted, and he lunged forward, the knife held high. The gunshot boomed in the close room. A raw wound opened in Ignacio's chest, but still he advanced. The knife made an ugly whistling noise, sundering the air. A scarlet gash opened in the don's neck, looking like a grinning mouth.

The two men crashed to the tile floor together.

Seguín and Gilberto rushed to them. Their eyes were glazing already. Their chests didn't move. They were dead.

The door burst open.

The agony in Diana's stiff and twisted limbs forced her eyes open. Tied in an unnatural position with her arms and legs bowed and bound behind her, she felt her every nerve and muscle scream its protest. A gag filled her mouth, and her throat felt like a desert. She tried to swallow, but the effort was pitiful. Her head felt as if it were going to split open. The blow to her temple ached like a sore tooth.

She was lying on a plain dirt floor, and someone had

dressed her in a blouse and skirt. It was dark as a tomb in her prison.

Forcing herself to lie still, she concentrated, ignoring her throbbing head. Listening carefully, she tried to get her bearings. At first she heard nothing, only silence. After a few moments, deep voices drifted to her from somewhere outside the blackness. Fear sluiced through her like a cold rain. She shivered. Her captors were close by.

A muffled groan reached her, and she twisted toward the sound. It must be Lydia. Relief warmed her for a moment, keeping the icy chill of terror at bay. She was comforted to know Lydia was beside her, and not dead. Her consolation was short-lived as panic flooded her. She remembered Ignacio had said something about not harming the baby, but where was he?

As if in answer to her silent question, she heard the sound of a small body scooting across the earth in the dark. She strained her ears. It must be Pepito. Then she heard the faintest whimper. It was him! He was alive and with them. Tears of relief poured down her cheeks.

But her relief fled when his whimpers turned to wails. She knew that cry. He was hungry, and there was no way to feed him. Desolation filled her, listening to his pathetic cries. His howling reached a crescendo and then trailed off. He hiccuped a few times and was silent. Then he started screaming hysterically.

Feeling utterly helpless, she was unable to do anything for him. It was pure torture to listen to him cry, worse than her strained limbs and pounding head.

His pitiful wails surrounded her, blotting everything else out. It was unbearable to listen . . . but she had no choice. Needing to do something, she carefully inched forward in the dirt. Straining toward the sound of his crying, she finally bumped into him. With the touch of her body, he stopped shrieking and gurgled in happy anticipation of being fed. When all she could do was lie beside him like a lump, his gurgles became frustrated, and he started shrieking again.

And then she heard loud shouts and curses outside . . . so loud they drowned out Pepito's tormented cries. Gunshots roared, momentarily deafening her. When they stopped, her ears rang.

Running feet pounded nearby . . . the footsteps coming closer.

She froze in fear.

Seguín released his breath in one long rush. "It's about time you got here. Come in."

Juan entered the room.

"I sent for you weeks ago. What happened?"

"Is this a proper greeting, *mí hijo?*"

Seguín relaxed a fraction, but the burden on his mind was too heavy to dismiss. "We must rescue the women and baby."

"It's been done. They're in their rooms, cleaning up."

"Are they all right?" He felt as if a boulder had just been lifted from his shoulders. Diana . . . and Lydia and Pepito were safe.

"They're fine. A few scratches and bruises, but nothing serious. Don Carlos's men had them in the back room of a warehouse by the waterfront. They were more scared than hurt." Juan combed his beard with his fingers, and his eyes twinkled. "The little one has a fine set of pipes. It seems he was hungry."

"I'm not surprised."

"Who's this fine fellow?" Juan asked, indicating Gilberto.

"My half—my brother, Gilberto Aguirre. Gilberto, this is my oldest friend and partner, Juan Martínez."

Juan stepped forward, extending his hand.

Gilberto raised his bound hands and grimaced.

"Let's see what we can do about that." Pulling a knife from his belt, Juan cut through the rope. Then they shook hands and greeted each other.

"Hey, what about me?" Seguín asked indignantly, raising his hands, too.

"Patience, patience, *mi hijo.*" His partner cut through the ropes and hugged him.

"I see we have some casualties here," Juan observed.

"*Sí*. They killed each other." Seguín rubbed his wrists to return the blood flow. "It's a long story. I'll tell you later." Turning to his brother, he noticed for the first time that Gilberto's face was ashen. Realizing that despite everything, his half-brother had loved his father, Seguín asked, "How are you holding up?"

"As well as can be expected, considering what happened," he answered obliquely. "I need to see Sarah, and then I'll be fine."

"Juan, send one of your men to fetch Sarah and her father. Gilberto, where are they staying?"

"*El Gato Negro*. It's a *posada* near the fort."

Nodding, Juan stepped into the hallway. Seguín overheard him giving orders to the men. Two men followed Juan into the room and took the bodies out.

When they had finished, Seguín asked Juan, "How did you find us?"

"I received your letter and started after you. We were caught by a two day downpour in the rain forest. When we reached Santa María, you had just left." He paused and scated himself on a chair. Seguín and Gilberto remained standing. "It was after Santa María that we came across the men following you."

"Don Carlos and his men?"

Juan shifted in the chair, hooking one arm over the slatted back. "Remember old No Nose?"

"How could I forget him? He may be the only man more

evil than—" He stopped himself, out of consideration for Gilberto's feelings.

Then it came to him—the bandits in the forest, the man who had asked him to put his carbine on the ground . . . everything had happened so fast, but he remembered the man had been missing his nose. At the time, he hadn't made the connection. It had been years since he had seen No Nose.

"My father and Ignacio hung back so I wouldn't recognize them?"

"*Sí*. It surprised them to find you alone. They wanted the woman and the baby. Someone saved your skin in that forest. Eh, *mí hijo?*"

"You!" It wasn't a question.

Juan inclined his head. "When I realized Don Carlos was following you, I decided it was better to trail him than join you." He winked. "To keep an eye on them for you."

"Why did my father want the woman and the baby?" Gilberto interjected.

"He believed the woman was your wife, and he wanted to dispose of her. The baby, he thought, was his grandson."

"Where did he get that idea?" Gilberto asked.

"Must have assumed it when his spies told him Seguín was traveling with two women and a baby."

"What did you do when we holed up in the ruins?" Seguín inquired, changing direction.

"Followed Don Carlos while he searched in circles. I knew where you were, or I thought I knew—I remembered you telling me about the city—but you had them confused for days."

"So you went off and saved the women, leaving us to the kind graces of my stepfather?" Seguín shook his head.

"Not so, ye of little faith," his partner quipped. "I split the men. Some of us overpowered the women's guards. The others followed you and took out the remainder of Don Carlos' men. We thought you'd be safe enough in

the parlor of your *posada*. Besides, it was time for a reckoning between the two of you."

"Ignacio bribed someone to get the formula for Don
Carlos," Seguín declared.

"I know. It was José Benito. He needed money for doc-
tors for his wife. I've already fired him." He shrugged.
"No loss. The secret died with Ignacio and the don."

Pulling Juan from his chair, Seguín hugged him again
and murmured, *"Gracias,* old friend." Seeing Gilberto
standing awkwardly to one side, he opened his embrace
to include him, saying, "It's good to have a brother after
all these years."

Seguín felt as if his family had been returned to him
this day. His mother hadn't abandoned him. He had been
reunited with his brother. His heart went out to Gilberto,
because even though Don Carlos was evil, he knew Gilberto loved his father. He wished Sarah would arrive. And
what about Diana? He couldn't wait to see her.

As if in answer to his thoughts, Diana rushed into the
room and flew into his arms. Nothing in his life had ever
felt so good as holding her close. After a few moments, he
drew back and studied her. His fingertips trailed over the
purplish bruise at her temple, and the cuts on her wrists.
Tenderly, he bent and brushed his lips over her wounds.
"I'm sorry you were hurt."

"Don Carlos and Ignacio?" she asked.

"They killed each other. My stepfather got Ignacio's sister pregnant. He tried to use me to cover it up." Pausing,
he gazed deeply into her eyes. "My mother didn't disinherit me. It was Don Carlos's doing. She knew I wasn't
guilty."

He knew what else he wanted to say, but he couldn't
seem to get the words out. Finding out about his mother
had changed everything. Or had it? he asked himself.
Would he have let Diana go if he hadn't discovered the
truth? The answer he had been seeking for weeks finally

came to him. He wouldn't have let her go. He couldn't have let her go. He would have risked everything, even his heart, to keep her with him.

Before he could tell her, Lydia and the baby entered the room, followed by Sarah and her father. Sarah and Gilberto embraced. Gilberto saw Pepito for the first time, and more introductions followed. They all milled around the room, a festive note in the air, hugging and talking loudly.

After a few minutes, Seguín caught Diana's hand and drew her to a corner, away from the others. "I must remain in México. My work is here, my livelihood."

"Maximilian was executed yesterday. All of Juan's men were talking about it," Diana informed him.

"Then the fighting will end soon. Juárez will be president again." Going down on one knee before her, he admitted, "I love you, Diana. I have always loved you. Even before I learned about my mother, I knew I couldn't let you sail away. Will you stay and be my wife?"

Her expressive hazel eyes widened, sparkling blue like the waters of the Pacific. Clasping his shoulders, she pulled him to his feet and gasped, "Yes and yes and *sí* and *sí*. Oh, Seguín, I don't care where we live. I love you so much!"

His mouth found hers in a sizzling kiss, hungry with promise . . . promise of the future. When they came up for air, they found Sarah and Gilberto standing beside them, smiling.

"A double wedding in San Francisco, and then we return to México, *mi hermano?*" Gilberto suggested.

Seguín gazed at Diana, the question in his eyes.

She nodded.

Sí," he said, "a double wedding, *mi hermano.*"

ROMANCE FROM JANELLE TAYLOR

ANYTHING FOR LOVE	(0-8217-4992-7, $5.99)
DESTINY MINE	(0-8217-5185-9, $5.99)
CHASE THE WIND	(0-8217-4740-1, $5.99)
MIDNIGHT SECRETS	(0-8217-5280-4, $5.99)
MOONBEAMS AND MAGIC	(0-8217-0184-4, $5.99)
SWEET SAVAGE HEART	(0-8217-5276-6, $5.99)

Available wherever paperbacks are sold, or order direct from the Publisher. Send cover price plus 50¢ per copy for mailing and handling to Kensington Publishing Corp., Consumer Orders, or call (toll free) 888-345-BOOK, to place your order using Mastercard or Visa. Residents of New York and Tennessee must include sales tax. DO NOT SEND CASH.

ROMANCE FROM FERN MICHAELS

DEAR EMILY   (0-8217-4952-8, $5.99)

WISH LIST   (0-8217-5228-6, $6.99)

AND IN HARDCOVER:

VEGAS RICH   (1-57566-057-1, $25.00)

*Available wherever paperbacks are sold, or order direct from the
Publisher. Send cover price plus 50¢ per copy for mailing and
handling to Kensington Publishing Corp., Consumer Orders,
or call (toll free) 888-345-BOOK, to place your order using
Mastercard or Visa. Residents of New York and Tennessee must
include sales tax. DO NOT SEND CASH.*